"A young Tsarina traveling toward tragedy and an aging Grand Duchess, penniless and betrayed. Twin stories so gripping you will believe history itself can be rewritten. Told with masterful intensity and moments of true human compassion."

—Helen Simonson, *New York Times* bestselling author of *The Summer Before the War*

"Ariel Lawhon is a masterful storyteller; *I Was Anastasia* is a wild ride, extravagant with its vivid sensory experiences and page-turning suspense. Inspired by history and infused with imagination and intrigue, this novel satisfies with every twist and turn. I was both captivated and enchanted; I will carry this story—from its beguiling opening to its catch-my-breath ending—in my heart and imagination for a long, long while."

—Patti Callahan Henry, *New York Times* bestselling author of *Driftwood Summer* and *The Bookshop at Water's End*

"Was Anna Anderson really the only survivor of the Romanovs, or was she a persistent fraud? Somehow, Lawhon, a masterly writer, not only leads her readers to ponder this riddle but to care about it as well. This is a deft and deeply moving saga."

—Jacquelyn Mitchard, *New York Times* bestselling author of *The Deep End of the Ocean*

Ariel Lawhon

I Was Anastasia

Ariel Lawhon is a critically acclaimed author of historical fiction. Her books have been translated into numerous languages and have been selections of LibraryReads, One Book One County, and Book of the Month Club. She is the cofounder of SheReads.org and lives in the rolling hills outside Nashville, Tennessee, with her husband, their four sons, a black Lab, and a deranged cat. She splits her time between the grocery store and the baseball field.

ariellawhon.com

ALSO BY ARIEL LAWHON

The Wife, the Maid, and the Mistress

Flight of Dreams

I Was Anastasia

· A NOVEL ·

Ariel Lawhon

ANCHOR BOOKS

A DIVISION OF PENGUIN RANDOM HOUSE LLC

NEW YORK

FIRST ANCHOR BOOKS EDITION, FEBRUARY 2019

Copyright © 2018 by Ariel Lawhon

The Library of Congress cataloged the Doubleday edition as follows:
Name: Lawhon, Ariel, author.
Title: I was Anastasia : a novel / Ariel Lawhon.
Description: First edition. | New York : Doubleday, 2018
Identifiers: LCCN 2017030326
Subjects: LCSH: Anastasiëiìa Nikolaevna, Grand Duchess, daughter of Nicholas II, Emperor of Russia, 1901–1918—Fiction. | Nicholas II, Emperor of Russia, 1868–1918—Family—Assassination—Fiction. | Romanov, House of—History—20th century—Fiction. | Princesses—Russia—Fiction. | Impersonation—Fiction. | BISAC: FICTION / Historical. | FICTION / Mystery & Detective / Historical. FICTION / Biographical. | GSAFD: Biographical fiction. | Historical fiction. | Suspense fiction. | Mystery fiction.
Classification: LCC PS3601.L447 I22 2018 | DDC 813/.6—dc23
LC record available at https://lccn.loc.gov/2017030326

Book design by Pei Loi Koay

Anchor Books Trade Paperback ISBN: 978-1-101-97331-8
eBook ISBN: 978-0-385-54170-1

www.anchorbooks.com

Printed in the United States of America
10 9 8 7 6 5 4 3 2 1

As always, for my husband, Ashley, because I would be lost without him.

Also, for Marybeth because she gave me the title.

And for Melissa: editor, champion, and friend.

If history were taught in the form of stories,

it would never be forgotten.

— RUDYARD KIPLING, *THE COLLECTED WORKS*

I Was Anastasia

Fair Warning

If I tell you what happened that night in Ekaterinburg I will have to unwind my memory—all the twisted coils—and lay it in your palm. It will be the gift and the curse I bestow upon you. A confession for which you may never forgive me. Are you ready for that? Can you hold this truth in your hand and not crush it like the rest of them? Because I do not think you can. I do not think you are brave enough. But, like so many others through the years, you have asked:

Am I truly Anastasia Romanov? A beloved daughter. A revered icon. A Russian grand duchess.

Or am I an impostor? A fraud. A liar. The thief of another woman's legacy.

That is for you to decide, of course. Countless others have rendered their verdict. Now it is your turn. But if you want the truth, you must pay attention. Do not daydream or drift off. Do not speak or interrupt. You will have your answers. But first you must understand why the years have brought me to this point and why such loss has made the journey necessary. When I am finished, and only then, will you have the right to tell me who I am.

Are you ready? Good.

Let us begin.

PART ONE

The End and the Beginning

Once you eliminate the impossible, whatever remains,

no matter how improbable, must be the truth.

—SIR ARTHUR CONAN DOYLE

Anna

FOLIE À DEUX

1970, 1968

Charlottesville, Virginia
February 17, 1970

Fifty years ago tonight Anna threw herself off a bridge in Berlin. It wasn't her first brush with death, or even the most violent, but it was the only one that came at her hands. Anna's husband does not know this, however. She watches him, watching her, and she knows he sees only a fragile old woman who has waited too long for vindication. He sees the carefully cultivated image she presents to the world: a crown of thinning silver hair and tired blue eyes. Age and confusion and a gentle aura of helplessness. This impression could not be further from the truth. She has been many things through the years, but helpless is not one of them. At the moment, however, Anna is simply impatient. She sits in this living room, two thousand miles from her past, waiting for a verdict.

Jack is like a frightened rabbit, all nerves and tension. He springs from his chair and begins to pace through the cluttered den. "Why haven't they called? They should have called by now."

"I'm sure they read the verdict hours ago," Anna says, leaning her head against the fold of her wingback chair and closing her eyes.

Whatever news awaits them is not good, but Anna does

not have the heart to tell him this. Jack is so hopeful. He has already written a press release and taken a Polaroid so he can bring both to *The Daily Progress* first thing in the morning. Jack spoke with the editor this afternoon, suggesting they reserve a front-page spot for the story. He's hoping for something above the fold. He's hoping for exclamation points.

Even though Jack hasn't admitted it, Anna knows that he is looking forward to reporters showing up again. They haven't had any in months, and she suspects he's gotten lonely with only her and the animals for company. She feels a bit sorry for him, being saddled with her like this. But there was no other way. Gleb insisted on it, and in all the years she knew him, Gleb Botkin remained her truest friend, her staunchest champion. He's been dead two years now. Another loss in an unending string of losses. Jack is kind to her—just as Gleb promised— and beggars can't be choosers anyway. Anna reminds herself of this daily.

The phone rings. Three startling metallic alarms and then Jack snatches it from the cradle.

"Manahan residence." A pause, and then, "Yes, she's here. Hold on a moment." The cord won't stretch across the room, so Jack lays the receiver on the sideboard. He grins. "It's from Germany."

"Who?"

"The Prince." He beams, then clarifies—there have been a number of princes in her life. "Frederick."

Anna feels a wild stab of anger at the name. She hasn't forgotten what Frederick did, hasn't forgotten the burn pile behind her cottage at the edge of the Black Forest. All those charred little bones. If the news had come from anyone else she would take the call. "I don't want to speak with him."

"But—"

"He knows why."

"I really think it's time you—"

Anna holds her hand up, palm out, a firm, final sort of motion. "Take a message."

Jack pouts but doesn't protest. He knows that arguing is futile. Anna does not change her mind. Nor does she forgive. He picks up the receiver again. "I'm sorry. She doesn't want to speak right now. Why don't you give me the news?"

And then she watches Jack's countenance fall by tiny, heartbreaking increments. First his smile. Then his lifted, expectant brows. His right arm drops to his side. He is deflated. "I don't understand," he says, finally, then clears his throat as though he has swallowed a cobweb.

"Write it down," Anna instructs. "Word for word." She doesn't want to interpret the verdict through his anger once he hangs up. Anna wants to know exactly what the appeals court has to say. Jack is too emotional and prone to exaggeration. He needs to transcribe the decision in its entirety or vital bits of information will be lost the moment he hangs up. Gleb wouldn't need this instruction. He would know what to do. He would know what questions to ask. But Gleb is no longer here, and, once again, this reality leaves her feeling adrift.

"Let me write this down," Jack says, like it's his idea. She watches him shuffle through piles of paper on the cluttered sideboard, looking for a notebook with blank pages. Finding none, he grabs an envelope and turns it over. "Go ahead. I'm ready."

A decade ago Anna's lawyer told her this lawsuit was the longest-running case in German history. This appeal has stretched it into something worse, something interminable. And there stands Jack, writing the footnote to her quest on the back of their electric bill in his tidy, ever-legible script. "How do you spell that?" he asks at one point, holding the phone with one hand and recording the verdict with the other. He doesn't rush or scribble but pens each word with painstaking precision, occasionally asking Frederick to repeat himself.

Jack and Anna don't have many friends. They haven't been married long, only two years, and theirs is a relationship based on convenience and necessity, not romance. They are old and eccentric and not fit for polite society in this quaint college town. But a handful of people—mostly former professors at the University of Virginia, like Jack—are due to arrive shortly. Anna doesn't want to know how he convinced them to come. Entertaining would have been awkward if the decision had gone in her favor. It will be excruciating now. Anna decides there won't be a party tonight. She doesn't have the heart to entertain strangers this evening.

But Jack, in all his eagerness, has cooked for a celebration. Their small den is littered with trays of fruit and sandwiches. Deviled eggs and cheese platters. Tiny brined pickles and cocktail sausages skewered with toothpicks. He even bought three bottles of champagne that sit in a bowl of ice, unopened beneath the string of Christmas lights he stapled to the ceiling. Anna stares at the bottles with suspicion. She hasn't touched the stuff in almost four decades. The last time Anna drank champagne she ended up naked on a rooftop in New York City.

The entire setting is tacky and festive—just like her husband. Jack bought a rhinestone tiara from the costume shop near the college campus just for the occasion. It sits on a gaudy red velvet pillow next to the champagne. He's been dying to crown her since they met, and only today, only in the hopes of a positive verdict, has she humored him. But that hope is gone now. Snuffed out in a German courtroom on the other side of the world.

"Thank you," he finally says, and then lower, almost a whisper, "I will. I'm sorry. You know how she can be. I'm sure she'll speak with you next time. Good-bye."

When he turns back to Anna, Jack has the envelope pressed to his chest. He doesn't speak.

"We need to call our guests and tell them the party's canceled," she says.

He looks crushed. "I'm so sorry."

"This isn't your fault. You did what you could." A shrug. A deep breath. "What did Frederick say?"

"Your appeal was rejected. They won't reverse the lower court's ruling."

"I gathered that. Tell me his words *exactly*."

Jack looks to the paper. "They regard your claim as 'non liquet.'"

"Interesting."

"What does that mean?"

"'Not clear' or 'not proven.'"

When Jack frowns, he puckers his mouth until his upper lip nearly touches his nose. It's an odd, childish expression and one he's used with greater frequency the longer he has known her. "Is that German?"

"Latin."

"You know *Latin*?"

"Very little at this point." Anna swats at him. "Go on."

"The judges said that even though your death has never been proven, neither has your escape."

"Ah. Clever." She smiles at this dilemma. It is the ultimate Catch-22. Her escape *can't* be proven without a formal declaration of identity from the court. "Read the rest please."

Jack holds the envelope six inches from his nose and slowly recites the verdict. "'We have *not* decided that the plaintiff is *not* Grand Duchess Anastasia, but only that the Hamburg court made its decision without legal mistakes and without procedural errors.'" He looks up. "So they have decided . . . *nothing*?"

She shakes her head slowly and then with more determination. "Oh, they have decided everything."

"It was that photo, wasn't it? The court must have seen it.

There's no other reason they would rule against you. Damn that Rasputin. *Damn* her!" Jack begins to pace again. "We could make a statement—"

"No. It's over." Anna lifts her chin with all the dignity she can muster and folds her hands in her lap. She is resigned and regal. "They will never formally recognize me as Anastasia Romanov."

TWO YEARS EARLIER

Charlottesville, Virginia
December 23, 1968

Anna does not want to marry Jack Manahan. She would rather marry Gleb. Even after all the trouble he has caused through the years. But theirs is a story of false starts and near misses. Bad timing. Distance. And rash decisions. They were not meant to be. So Gleb has urged her to marry Jack instead. This whole fiasco is his idea—the courthouse, the silly pink dress, the bouquet of roses and pinecones, the white rabbit-fur hat that she's supposed to wear out of the courthouse to greet the photographers (these arranged by Jack because the damnable man cannot help but make a scene everywhere he goes). Gleb insists the hat makes her look the part of a Russian grand duchess. She refuses to wear the thing. Poor rabbit.

When they discussed this ridiculous plan in August, Gleb said his health was to blame. He couldn't marry her himself because she would end up having to take care of him. Anna believes that this is punishment for a long-held resentment. Tit for tat. Wound for wound. He has loved her for decades, and she has never been able to fully reciprocate. Now he stands as witness to her unwilling nuptials. As best man, in fact.

It is snowing outside the courthouse. Not the angry, hard,

blistering shards of snow she is used to in Germany, but fat, lethargic flakes that drift and flutter and take their time getting to the ground. Lazy snow. American snow.

Anna's had only a single tryst since that limpid summer in Bavaria all those years ago, but Gleb moved on. Got married. Had children. They've never talked about the intervening years, and it's not worth bringing up now. Anna is in her seventies—too old to get married at all, much less for the first time. Jack Manahan is twenty years her junior. A former professor enamored with Russian history, and with her—or, at least, the *idea* of her. Regardless, he hasn't put up much of a fight since being presented with the plan. Jack's only show of hesitation was a long, curious look at Gleb. Assessing his attachment and willingness to let Anna go.

It occurred to her, far too late in the process, that she had not considered the issue of sex. Jack is young. *Younger* at least. And she is . . . well . . . she is *not*. The idea of consummation almost caused her to back out of this arrangement entirely. All of those hormones have shriveled up, turned to dust, and blown away. Desire is little more than a fond memory these days.

Gleb has taken care of that issue as well, however, assuring her that sex isn't a necessary part of this bargain. She and Jack will have separate bedrooms. This will be a legal marriage, enough to keep her in the United States once her visa expires in three weeks, but it will be a marriage of convenience only. Gleb swore this, endless times, over their last shared bottle of wine. Jack will not lay a hand on her. Unless she wants him to. Why Gleb added that last part she isn't sure. He wouldn't meet her eyes as he said it, and she did not reply. It was a small cruelty. This is how it is with them, apparently. Little wounds. Paper cuts. Just enough to sting but not really harm. Perhaps it's best that they aren't marrying each other after all.

Gleb slips into the antechamber beside the courtroom and surveys her tiny, slender form. "You look nice."

He seems weary and pale and infirm. He's lost weight recently, and his once broad shoulders have narrowed with illness and age. Anna wants to ask Gleb if his heart has gotten worse. But she's afraid of what his answer might be. So she says, "I look ridiculous."

"All brides look ridiculous. That's why they're so charming."

Anna turns back to the window. It's late afternoon, getting darker by the moment, and the overhead light bounces off the glass, throwing her reflection back at her. She touches a hand to her cheek. Traces one deep wrinkle after another, each of them telling a story she's long since decided to forget.

"I am too old for this," she says.

"I know."

"You admit it then?" She studies his reflection too, hovering over her shoulder. "But no apology, I see."

"It is this or you return to Germany," he says. "We are out of time."

"That always seems to be the case with us, doesn't it?"

"Ships in the night," he whispers and sets a large, warm hand on her shoulder. "Are you ready? Sergeant Pace is waiting. So is Jack."

"*Sergeant?*"

"Judge Morris called in sick this morning."

Anna turns to him and looks, not at his face, but at the knot in his tie. She stares at the red and blue alternating stripes on the fabric, those thin lines circling back on themselves, all twisted and turned around. Anna is knotted up as well, but now, suddenly, it's with mirth.

"I am to be married," she asks, tilting her chin to meet those twinkling green eyes, "not by a priest, or a judge, but by a *police officer?*"

"It gives an entirely new meaning to being read your rights, doesn't it?"

They laugh, then, long and loud. She turns back to the window and they stand in comfortable silence, watching Charlottesville disappear beneath the snow.

Finally Anna leans her head back against Gleb's chest. "How did I get here?" Anna sighs, already knowing the answer. She has gotten here, she has survived, by always doing the thing that needs to be done.

FOUR MONTHS EARLIER

Charlottesville, Virginia
August 20, 1968

Virginia in August feels very much to Anna as though she has taken up residence directly in the white-hot center of Satan's armpit. She has never known such heat. Nor has the word *humidity* meant anything at all prior to her arrival in the United States. And yet here she sits, on Jack Manahan's front patio drinking tea—with *ice*, no less—and melting into her rocking chair as they talk about nothing in particular.

Anna fans her face with an old magazine—something about gardens and guns—wishing the sun would slide down the horizon a little more quickly. "How can you live like this?"

Jack peers at her over the top of a glass that is beaded with sweat. "Like what?"

"Like a potato put in the oven to roast. It's intolerable."

"This is August," he says as though that explains everything. He's wearing trousers, long sleeves, and a gaudy checkered tie cinched up tight to his Adam's apple. He doesn't seem the least bit uncomfortable. "I hardly notice it anymore."

It is a distinctly American thing, Anna thinks, to have an entire conversation about the weather. They have been sitting on this patio for the better part of two hours waiting for Gleb. He's off running some errand in town and has promised to return by dinner. So far they have discussed variations in climate along the Eastern Seaboard of the United States, rain patterns in the Midwest, and a damaging drought in California that is threatening almond growers. The man is absurdly pleased by the sound of his own voice, needing very little encouragement from her. A simple hum or murmur is enough to launch him into another monologue. Anna wonders how much more she can tolerate before crawling out of her skin when a long, sleek, black car enters University Circle and approaches the house. It's the kind of vehicle that smacks of importance and a need to be seen.

"Who is that?" Jack asks as the car pulls into the driveway and parks behind his station wagon.

"I'm not sure." Anna tries not to feel guilty about the lie. She has an unwelcome suspicion about who this visitor might be.

"They look very determined." Jack leans forward, taking in the women who spring from the car and march up the sidewalk toward them.

"Anastasia!" shouts the older of the two as she reaches the bottom of the steps. The look on her face is one of alarming enthusiasm.

This woman is Russian. This woman is dangerous.

She mounts the stairs with an energy and aggression that Anna lost years ago. Following two steps behind her and watching cautiously is the woman's companion. She has coiffed hair, lips painted red, and eyes framed by black designer glasses. In one hand she carries a notepad and in the other a tape recorder. A reporter. Anna stiffens in her seat.

And then the first woman is in front of Anna, chatting and bending at the waist—not quite a bow but an allusion to one. Anna shrinks away as she confirms the familiar face and the deep, throaty voice. The dark hair—dyed now, she thinks; there's not a strand of gray—and sharp eyes. The angular nose. The sly mouth. The large body shaped like a concrete block.

The woman grabs her hand and shakes it with vigor. Anna fears being yanked out of her chair and forced into a hug.

The thing Anna has always hated most about being a small woman is the disadvantage she has in situations like this. People assume they can touch you, pat you, shake your hand without permission. They assume that if your size is little more than that of a child, you must be one. That you can be talked down to or coerced. It is hard for a small person to be intimidating or to be taken seriously. This lack of stature has forced Anna to develop other skills through the years: to sharpen her wit, to treat her tongue like a blade and her mind like a whetstone.

"I am not a rag doll. You needn't shake me like one. Or touch me at all for that matter," she says

"I'm sorry," the other woman says, stepping forward. "We have failed to introduce ourselves. I am Patricia Barham but please, call me Patte—"

"I have no interest in speaking with reporters today."

Patte looks at the objects in her hands and then tucks both behind her back, as though she'd forgotten they were there and is suddenly ashamed of them. "I'm not a reporter, at least not in the traditional sense. I'm a biographer." She tips her head toward her friend. "And of course you remember Maria Rasputin. As she tells it, the two of you have known each other since childhood."

"Rasputin?" The name has Jack's full attention and he sits ramrod straight in his chair. "As in relation to Grigory? The heretic monk?"

"Not a monk," Maria says, "as is evidenced by my existence. The heretic label is, of course, open to interpretation." She has the pinched look of a woman who is tired of defending the indefensible.

Anna has yet to rise from her seat or offer one to their uninvited guests. She is wary of Maria Rasputin and for good reason.

The melodramatic rise and fall of Maria's voice makes it sound as though she's in a stage production. Anna doesn't like the grand, sweeping gestures she makes with her arms or the aggressive way she smiles. Those small white teeth that snap and flash. But it is her eyes that disturb Anna most. They are a bright—almost unnatural—blue. Piercing, but not in a way that compels someone to come closer. Anna finds herself wanting to turn away and hide from that penetrating gaze. She shouldn't be surprised. Grigory Rasputin was known to have those same terrifying, hypnotic eyes. Like father, like daughter.

But Maria's stare is hard to escape, and she moves closer, nearly leaning over Anna's chair.

"Yes," she says, as though finally coming to some long-awaited conclusion. "There's something about her." Again, waving that arm in a grandiose manner. "A certain nobility. It's there in her demeanor. In her voice." Maria nods sharply. "I believe this to be Anastasia Romanov."

"What do you want?" Anna presses her palms against her knees so she won't strike that self-satisfied grin from Maria's face.

"Only to visit with an old friend—"

"We thought, perhaps, that we could take you to dinner," Patte interrupts. She has tucked the notepad and recorder into her purse, and her hands now hang free and nonthreatening at her sides.

Jack perks up at the mention of food. "Dinner with friends could be fun. There's a wonderful Italian restaurant not too far from here."

"You came all the way here—where did you say you came from . . . ?" Anna asks.

"I didn't. But New York, since you're curious."

"All the way from New York just to have dinner?"

"Dinner, yes." And it's here that Maria shows her cards

because she cannot keep the devilish smile at bay. "But I've also got a proposition for you."

———

"I am not going to Hollywood." Anna sets her fork down.

Jack taped a note to the front door when they left with Maria and Patte Barham, telling Gleb that they'd be at Salvio's, but he's yet to join them and Anna looks to the door every few moments. This was a mistake. She and Jack are a captive audience for these women and their ludicrous plan. She regrets consenting to have dinner with them.

"Don't be so hasty," Patte says. "There's a lot of money to be made."

"My story is not for sale."

Patte doesn't say it, but her Cheshire cat smile suggests that she believes everyone's story is for sale. She shrugs. Spears a piece of mushroom. Swallows it without chewing. "People are curious. They want to know what it was like. They want to know how you survived. There's nothing wrong with supporting yourself in the process." She looks at Anna's simple cotton dress, frayed at the collar, faded by too many turns through the wash, and lets her gaze linger just long enough to declare that she knows Anna needs the money. And then, to drive the point home, she adjusts the chain of an expensive gold necklace draped around her own neck.

Anna pushes her plate away. "I would like to go home."

"And where, exactly, is home?" Maria Rasputin asks.

"I am staying with Jack."

Maria smiles privately and takes a slow, careful bite of her manicotti. The change in tactics comes without warning. "How long did you say you would be in the States?"

"Six months."

"And you've been here for, what, two? Three?"

Anna knows she's being baited but she can't see the hook. "Two."

"What type of visa did you get?"

"Tourist."

"A pity. International travel is so expensive."

Anna does the thing she's been doing for decades. She tilts her head up and to the side. She gives this woman the ghost of a smile, a condescending smirk that suggests she won't acknowledge the insinuation or admit that yes, she's running out of money and has few options left.

Maria is undaunted. She takes another bite. Dips her bread in the thick, nutty olive oil. Sips her wine. "And what will you do when your visa runs out? Will you go back to Germany? To your friends in Unterlengenhardt? Your pets?"

And there it is. The barb settles deep. It takes everything in her not to gasp in outrage. Maria clearly knows Anna doesn't have a home to return to, that nothing remains but a mass grave behind the cottage she once called home. Maria's involvement in those events hangs unspoken and heavy between them.

Rasputin's daughter grins, victorious. "I suppose Prince Frederick would welcome you back. He's always been so fond of you." She chews a bite. Swallows. "Such a loyal man."

Jack is oblivious, the fool. He ate a bowl of chicken Alfredo as big as his head, along with half a loaf of bread, and now he's pushed back from the table to listen and pat his belly. To him this is simply a conversation between two women discussing old friends. To her it is blackmail.

Anna shrugs, noncommittal. "When you've lived as long as I have you take each day at a time. I've not settled on any firm plan."

"Which means you don't have one, correct?"

Jack and Patte look at each other, confused.

"What are they saying?" Jack asks.

"I don't know," Patte says.

It's only then that Anna realizes that she and Maria have shifted into German. The transition was so smooth, so subtle that she didn't even realize it. Had Maria turned the conversation to Russian, Anna would have noticed immediately. She would have refused to participate. Even though Anna speaks fluent English—she has lived in the United States before—German is her preferred language. Her security blanket.

"I thought as much." Maria reaches across the table and pats Anna's hand. It looks like a tender gesture, easily mistaken for something kinder than it actually is. "Don't be ashamed. It's hard. I know. Why do you think I've let Patte trail after me like a puppy for so long? We all have to make a living. There's no shame in that."

Anna withdraws her hand but doesn't break eye contact.

"I want to make this perfectly clear. You will not use me as a *meal ticket*." She selects this descriptor purposefully, saying it slowly, enjoying the look of recognition on Maria's face. It's the same phrase Maria used when she showed up unannounced in Unterlengenhardt and conspired to burn Anna's world to the ground.

Maria laughs as though Anna has said something funny. She settles back into her chair, but now there's an angry, dangerous glint in her eyes.

"I will not go to California with you. Or anywhere else for that matter. I will not sell my story." Anna looks first to Patte and then to Jack as she repeats her earlier request in English. "I would like to go home."

"Well, I would like dessert," Maria says.

The table is already littered with plates and bread baskets and empty bottles of wine. Anna doesn't think there's room for another dish, but Maria waves the waiter over and orders panettone and coffee. Anna curses herself once again for not insisting that Jack drive. They are at the mercy of these interlopers. So she waits patiently as Maria finishes yet another course.

This Rasputin is nothing more than an old woman acting like a petulant child, punishing Anna for refusing to play along.

"How did you find me?" Anna asks. This is the second time Maria Rasputin has hunted her down. It remains to be seen whether the results will be as catastrophic as the first time.

"It wasn't hard." She tips her head toward Jack. "This man you've taken up with is fond of the newspapers. You've been written up quite a bit since arriving in the United States."

"I haven't taken up with him."

"Yet. I'd wager it's only a matter of time. You do love your . . . *benefactors*."

Jack and Patte have given up trying to follow their conversation and are chatting quietly about writing and research on the other side of the table. It's almost nine o'clock before the waiter brings the check. Hours have been spent listening to first Patte, then Maria try to convince her to sign over the rights to her life story so they can make a film. They throw words around and name-drop. They suggest a variety of famous actresses who might play the role of Anastasia. She doesn't bother to remind them that Ingrid Bergman has already done so and that the part won her an Academy Award in 1957. But neither of them is all that interested in Anna's opinion. They are only concerned with what they see as a hefty payday.

Maria takes the check and Anna stands, relieved to be done with this dinner and on her way home again. But then she slides the bill across the table and sets it right in front of Anna. There is no charm or humor in her smile, only vindictiveness.

"It was wonderful to see you again . . . *Anastasia*," she says. "Thank you for dinner."

———

"What else would you expect from a Rasputin?" Gleb's voice inches toward a scream as he paces through Jack's living room. "Lying, thieving con artists, the lot of them!"

Jack flinches, defensive. "I didn't know she stuck us with the bill. I wasn't paying attention."

"She didn't stick *you* with the bill. *You* can afford it. She stuck Anna. And I'm sure that was her plan all along."

"No," Anna says. "If I'd agreed to her scheme, she would have paid. She was just trying to punish me."

"You've been punished enough."

Jack is embarrassed now. Flustered. "What was I supposed to do?"

"You could have started by not speaking with her at all."

"It was just dinner."

"It wasn't just dinner; it was public association. A Rasputin gives our case a bad name. Every connection to that family is dangerous. Nothing good will come of it." Gleb stops shifting from foot to foot and looks at Anna. "Do not mention to anyone, not a single person, that you spent the evening with that woman. Can you promise me that?"

Her silence says everything.

Gleb groans. "*What?*"

"She asked that biographer of hers to take a picture of us together before dinner."

———

The photo is published several days later. It doesn't make as many front pages as Maria Rasputin likely hoped for, but it does appear in the society columns of several newspapers, and it's also picked up by the Associated Press. Before the week is out, half of America and much of the world knows that Maria Rasputin has declared Anna to be Grand Duchess Anastasia Romanov. Maria is interviewed at length, gushing about her long-lost friend, brought to tears even as she recalls their childhood memories. Anna burns the papers in disgust.

"We need those!" Jack yells in horror as the last of them goes up in flames.

Anna ignores him. She looks at Gleb. "I'm so sorry. I didn't know she would do something like this."

"You couldn't have."

That's not entirely true, Anna thinks, but she doesn't admit this to Gleb yet. Instead she asks, "How badly will this hurt the appeal?"

"No telling. The Rasputins are hated abroad. And for good reason. It depends who reads those articles. And how they're perceived."

"Surely the court won't think that I'm behind this? That I'm fabricating evidence?"

"We'll have to wait and see."

Anna takes a deep breath before saying, "Maria mentioned one thing we should discuss."

"What's that?"

"What I'm going to do when my visa runs out."

First sadness and then resignation settle into the fine lines around his eyes. "Don't worry," Gleb says. "I have a plan."

Anna knows instantly what he has in mind. "No." She cringes. His plans rarely turn out well.

"It's the only way."

"I won't do it." She lowers her voice to a whisper and casts a dismayed look at Jack Manahan. He sits across the room sorting through a pile of old newspapers.

Gleb matches her whisper for whisper. "You have to. I can't do it. Look at me. The doctor says I have a year. Maybe. If I'm lucky. Jack can take good care of you."

Anna drops her face into her hands. Here she is, cast once again onto a stranger. Beggared because her only friend has congestive heart failure. But it is her heart that aches at the moment. "If I marry him, I prove that Maria Rasputin was right all along."

"What do you mean?"

"She said it was only a matter of time before I took up with him. She implied that I look to benefactors, that I use people."

Gleb growls out a curse. "That woman is a scourge. We won't let her near you again."

"She can't harm me any more than she already has."

Gleb pulls away, confused, and Anna answers the unspoken question in his gaze. "Have I never told you about that? I suppose not. It happened right before I accepted your invitation to come here."

"*What* happened?"

"The last time that woman showed up at my door unannounced, I ended up in the hospital for three days."

Anastasia

REVOLUTION

1917

Alexander Palace, Tsarskoe Selo, Russia
February 28

The first shots ring out before dawn. I count fifteen—each of them splitting the air with a sound like cracking glaciers—before I go to the window and throw it open. Soldiers, drunk and mutinous, stumble through the park and onto the palace lawn. They shake their fists and fire wantonly at the sky as fear—hard, cold, and tangible—lodges in my throat. But still I watch, oblivious to the fact that any one of them could turn and aim a rifle at me. That any one of them could pull the trigger and pick me off as though I were a sparrow on a branch. I am frozen. Mesmerized by the chaos. Because even here, behind the palace walls and amid the muffling drifts of snow, I can hear rioting in the city and I know that fate has turned against us.

There is a whimper and rustling behind me, followed by a trembling voice. "Do not to worry, Tsarevitch, the gunfire only sounds so loud and so close because of the frost."

I shut the window and yank the curtains tight. I find our lady's maid bent over my brother, her mouth close to his ear, her fingers pushing hair away from his eyes. "What are you doing?" I ask.

"He's afraid," Dova says, as though this excuses the lie.

The gunfire *is* loud and close. But the frost has nothing to do with it. Dova, however, fears upsetting my sickly brother—and therefore my mother—above all else.

"Are they going to kill us?" Alexey asks. His eyes are large with concern and he lies curled around his little brown spaniel. Joy pokes her curly head from beneath the blanket and sniffs at his chin. A smile twitches at the corner of his mouth as she licks him.

"No." I perch on the edge of his cot and run my hand along Joy's soft, floppy ears. "The Imperial Guard surrounds the palace. They will protect us."

"Are you sure?"

"Of course. Would you like to see?"

Dova takes a step forward. "I don't think—"

"He will be fine. But you should get some rest. You look exhausted."

Dova doesn't argue, but her mouth snaps open and then closed. She straightens her shoulders and, after a brief hesitation, offers a stiff curtsy and goes to bed.

I wait until she slips from the room before helping Alexey to his feet and taking him to the window. The arm Alexey hangs around my shoulders is thin as a willow switch, and I can feel his ribs press against my side. Born a hemophiliac, he's been small and infirm his entire life, but since falling ill with the measles a week earlier, he has diminished to little more than shadow and bone. I want to take from my own soft form—all those places that my sisters poke and tease mercilessly—and pad the sharp points of his body. Ribs. Shoulder blades. Hips. I want to make him well again. To put color in his cheeks and laughter in his voice.

To his credit, my brother does not flinch when I show him the bright orange bursts of gunfire and the thin ribbon of flame at the horizon. We watch the chaos from a gap in the curtain, mindful not to push it open wide. I am careful with *his* life at least.

"What is that burning?" he asks.

"Tsarskoe Selo."

"The entire city?"

"No. Just the parts closest to us."

"Who lit the fires?"

"The people, most likely."

"They must stop," he says with an imperious sniff. "I do not approve."

Alexey has known from birth that he will be tsar. Not just king or ruler, but emperor; sovereign of a dynasty that has ruled for more than three hundred years; leader of an empire that grows by fifty-five square miles every day; commander of a military that protects one-sixth of the earth's surface. He is the recipient of a terrible, divine inheritance and I do not know how to explain that he cannot command this trouble away.

So I try to phrase it in a way he will understand. "I'm afraid they don't care about your approval. Or Father's. They do not want to be ruled any longer."

"They don't get to make that decision," he says, unconcerned in the way only a child born of utter privilege can be. "They will be sorry for this when Father returns."

If he returns. I think this but do not say it aloud. We have not heard from Father in days, nor do we know his current location. His last missive simply ordered us not to evacuate without him. And so we wait as the fires burn ever closer.

After locating the Imperial Guard in the courtyard, Alexey returns to his cot, wraps himself around Joy once more, and promptly falls asleep. At twelve, my brother hovers somewhere between foolish child and future monarch. He is spoiled and naïve, but I love him completely and irrationally.

When Alexey succumbed to measles, I offered the bedroom I share with Maria as an infirmary. It was only days later that Olga, and then Tatiana, joined him in the sick room. I convinced Mother and our beloved Dr. Botkin to let me play nurse and have tended them ever since. Now the three of them lie in their cots, picking at painful, itching rashes as they sleep, while I scrub my hands with harsh lye soap to keep the illness at bay.

I can see Olga's pale face in the dark room, her eyes open now, a line of frustration carved between her brows. So she has only been pretending to sleep. Her clavicles protrude with alarming definition as she pushes onto her elbows. "You are a terribly good liar, Schwibsik."

I grace my sister with a smile befitting my nickname. Little Imp. "I do not know what you're talking about."

Olga rolls her eyes and places her long, elegant fingers on the blanket beside her. Piano-playing fingers, Mother calls them. "You told Alexey we are safe."

"No. I told him that the Guard would protect us."

"Semantics."

"You can say it, but can you spell it?" I ask. "Or is Master Gilliard right about your hopeless academic prospects?"

Olga smiles. "Gilliard adores me. You're the one who should be worried. He'll force you to study Latin for another year if your attitude in the schoolroom doesn't improve."

"That man is a pestilence, an oozing sore upon my brain." Pierre Gilliard and I have had an ongoing feud since he began tutoring us several years ago, though we are currently at a stalemate concerning my lessons. But he is the least of my concerns tonight. I set a hand on Olga's forehead only to find that it is still hot. "Besides," I say, "we are safe. For now."

"Liar," she says, again, but with a smile this time. "We are under siege."

"What would you know of it? Your eyes are swollen shut."

"Only the left one. Besides, my ears are in perfect working order."

"Your ears," I counter, "are tuned only to hear flattery."

She laughs at this, and I feel as though I have won a small victory. Laughter in the face of fear is no small accomplishment. But Olga's rally is short-lived. Her smile dissolves and she flops back onto her pillow, depleted. She is asleep in seconds and I mop her damp forehead with a cloth, feeling hollow and exhausted myself. I make one final pass through the room, tucking the covers around Alexey's shoulders and reapplying cold compresses to the flushed foreheads of my sisters.

My own dog, Jimmy, is curled beside the fire with Tatiana's French bulldog, Ortimo. Jimmy watches me cross the room, his ears up and alert, while Ortimo snores like an ugly, drunken sailor, splayed on his back, legs spread and tongue lolling to the side.

"Come," I say, and Jimmy immediately lurches to his feet. I am always amazed at how he can move that huge body so quickly. The small black puppy Father gave me years ago has turned into a great lumbering beast half my height and weight. We knew Siberian huskies grew large; we simply didn't expect him to be *this* large. "Let us go learn the truth of this siege."

Four short taps on Mother's bedroom door let her know which of her children waits outside. I know she will be awake just as I know my sister Maria will be sprawled in her bed, snoring and oblivious, her soft curly hair spread out on the pillow, and her dark lashes fanned across her high cheekbones. Since Olga and Tatiana fell ill, and with Father gone, Maria and I relish our more frequent turns sleeping in Mother's great canopied bed, and we fight over it in the small, petty ways that only sisters can.

"Come in, Schwibsik," Mother says.

So she is feeling sentimental. A good sign. I take a deep breath and push the door open, with Jimmy trotting at my heels. Mother stands before the window watching revolution spill onto the palace grounds. She is of practical British stock, after all, and it is her people who pioneered a form of battle so orderly that men stand in rows and shoot at one another by turns. Yet upon closer inspection I see that it is disdain, not courage, that is etched into the tight corners of her mouth.

"Mother?"

"You should be asleep," she says, beckoning me to her side.

"Everyone keeps saying that."

"Everyone is right."

"I can't sleep through this." Out across the grounds, where the manicured lawn rolls down toward the edge of the park, the muzzle flashes are dimmer now against the growing light. "I don't understand what is happening."

"Revolution, it would seem." She snaps the curtain closed and moves toward a long, padded bench at the foot of her bed. Mother pats the seat and I curl up next to her, my eyes suddenly heavy and dry. "They've been threatening it for years," she says.

I think of my father and how, when we were little and naughty, he would threaten and threaten until he finally snapped and bent one of us over his knee. Perhaps, like Father, the people have grown tired of threatening.

"What do we do now?" I ask, my voice tremulous with exhaustion and growing fear. Jimmy, ever sensitive to my moods, presses his cold, wet nose against the back of my hand.

Mother clutches the amulet at her throat. It was given to her by Grigory Rasputin shortly before his murder last year and is identical to the ones she requires each of us to wear at all times. "We pray," she says.

―――――

Most of the servants flee that first night. They slip quietly from the palace in groups of three and four. Some go out to smoke their hand-rolled cigarettes with trembling fingers and don't return, not for their friends and not for their coats. Others finish their work and walk boldly through the servants' entrance and into the night, toward Tsarskoe Selo and the burning horizon. Some take silverware and candlesticks, knowing they will never receive their final wages. A few cry, but most never look back as they tromp through the snow with their heads down and their collars turned up against the wind.

Cook tells me this in the morning when I wander into the kitchen, bleary-eyed, in search of the chambermaid and our missing breakfast.

"I watched them go. Every damn one," he says. "Sat right here and they didn't so much as lift an arm in farewell. That maid of yours was the last to sneak away. She left the door open in her haste."

He stands in front of a great, sweltering woodstove, boiling eggs and coffee. I drift closer, drawn by the warmth and smell of breakfast, until I am dwarfed by his bulk. Cook is a giant of a man. Arms like posts and legs like pillars. Voice like the boom of a cannon. His jaw is as square and strong as a granite cornerstone. It is his back that commands attention, however. It is twice the width of a normal man and corded with muscle. I've heard the maids whisper that normal men can't grow a back like that unless they're under duress. I've heard them say he must have been sentenced to man the oars in a prison ship. Or hew stone in a gulag. All ridiculous, unfounded rumors that Cook never bothers to dispel. He likes the mystery, I think. Likes it when the servants scurry from his path. But to me he is simply Cook. Baker of bread. Maker of coffee. Teacher of profanity. Not that I would ever admit this last part to my parents. I like the man too much to see him dismissed.

"I can't let you carry that yourself." Cook scowls at a silver platter now holding a steaming carafe and a plate of warm French rolls fresh from the oven. "Where is Dova?"

"Sleeping."

He grunts, as though this is a moral failure.

"I can take it upstairs. I'm strong enough."

"That's not the point. Your mother would have my head."
He looks around the kitchen, as though to grab the first person
who passes, but we are quite alone. Everyone else has fled.

There are few men who can make cursing sound like poetry,
but Cook is one of them. I don't blush and he doesn't apologize
when the diatribe is complete. Instead he carefully lifts the tray
and stomps from the kitchen with me in tow.

Dova meets us upstairs on the landing looking somewhat
abashed but eager to see breakfast. She murmurs thanks, and
Cook gently relinquishes the tray into her waiting hands before
he retreats to safer, more familiar territory downstairs. As Dova
leads me back to my chambers I tell her what I've learned about
our missing chambermaid and the other servants.

"Cowards," she hisses, and pours me a cup of coffee. It is
warm between my hands, comforting, and we settle beside the
fire, listening to the popping, hissing sounds as we sip the dark,
fragrant brew. Coffee is an art form to Cook and we are his
devoted patrons.

It doesn't take long for Mother to join us, still wearing her
dressing gown. Maria, I assume, is still asleep. Undeterred
by the missing chambermaid, she waves Dova aside and goes
straight to the coffee and fills a cup, then drowns it in cream and
sugar. I have never seen Mother pour her own coffee before,
and I marvel that she is familiar with such a small domestic
task. It is so unlike an empress. She drinks the entire thing with
her eyes closed before imparting her news.

"The telephone lines have been cut," she says. "The electricity has been turned off. So has the water. You know about the
servants, of course. Most of them are gone. They left because
they are afraid. I don't blame them, I suppose, but I would be
lying if I said I don't hate them a little for it." Her voice is
steady but her hand trembles as she lifts her cup to her lips.

"What about the guards?" I ask.

"They're still here. For now."

"And Father?"

"God only knows."

By midafternoon, the palace is flooded with reports of brawls and bombings, of shootings in Tsarskoe Selo and men lying dead in the streets. Things are, according to Cook, apparently no better in Petrograd, thirty kilometers away. Here at the palace all that remains between us and mutiny is the Imperial Guard and the protective circle they maintain. It is a feeble shield—no thicker than an eggshell—and even they keep a wary eye turned toward the billowing line of smoke at the horizon.

———

It is nearing sunset when Viktor Zborovsky, captain of the Imperial Guard, kneels before Mother and kisses her hand. He is a great, tall man with kind brown eyes and a beard so white that I believed him to be Ded Moroz—or Grandfather Frost—for an entire decade.

"I am so sorry, Tsarina. Alexander Kerensky has ordered the Imperial Guard to stand down. If we refuse, we will all be shot for treason."

Kerensky. This name is familiar, but I have little reason to place it. Alexander Kerensky is in the government, and Father runs the government, and that's all I have ever cared to learn about political structure. Now every name and rank and title suddenly matters, and I find myself struggling to keep them all straight beyond the general categories of "for us" and "against us." Kerensky, I suspect, falls in the latter.

Mother gives Viktor a gracious nod. "Do not fight. There is no point."

"You are kinder to us than we deserve." He rises from her feet and sits across from her at the fireplace. "The entire combined regiment will be sent back to Petrograd tonight. We're being replaced with three hundred troops of the First Rifles, all of them under Kerensky's command."

"And what of us? What do they intend?"

"I am told that once the tsar arrives you will all be sent to Murmansk where a British cruiser will carry you to England."

"I'd hoped for Crimea," Mother whispers.

"I think that is more than anyone can hope for, under the circumstances." Viktor takes a deep breath and releases it slowly. He fiddles with the brass buttons on his jacket for a moment, then says, "It pains me to leave you unprotected. I don't like the whispers coming from Petrograd."

"Nicholas will be here soon. Everything will be fine once we're all together again. Please. Don't create trouble for yourself or your men. I don't want anyone's son sent before a firing squad on our account."

"The Guard asked me to pass along their sentiments. They remain loyal in their hearts. Please do not judge them for leaving."

"I judge no one other than those cadets from Stavka you brought in to play with Alexey last month. One of them infected him with the measles, and now Olga and Tatiana are ill as well." The words are harsh but she says them with a smile.

Viktor Zborovsky looks to Mother for absolution and she grants it in her own way, rising from her chair beside the fire and crossing to a small sideboard where she chooses a hand-painted icon of Saint Anna of Kashin—holy protector of women—and places it in his hands. "Take this as a sign of my gratitude," she says, and then whispers so low that I almost don't hear, "You know what to do with it."

Viktor wraps the icon in his kerchief and tucks it inside his coat. "They let me in through the main entrance. Everything else, apart from a side door in the kitchen, has been locked and sealed. Guards are stationed at all the doors, and the first-floor windows are nailed shut. Anyone in your court who wishes to leave will have to go through the main entrance and they will be required to give their names and their relationship to your household. All the information given will be recorded. I'm sorry for that. There is nothing I can do."

"You have done enough. Take your men to safety."

Mother and I stand at the window once again, more aware than ever of how completely we have been separated from everything on the other side of the wall. We watch as Viktor gathers the men of the Imperial Guard and marches them from the palace in orderly ranks. We watch as our beloved soldiers and friends are replaced by three hundred strangers who are loyal to a regime that hates us.

"What did you put in that icon, Mother?"

She smiles. "Oh, you are a clever girl."

"It wasn't just a gift, was it?"

"No. It was a message."

"What sort?"

"The sort I hope we do not need."

A disconcerting silence falls between us again as the soldiers of the First Rifles are being ordered about in the courtyard.

After a moment I say, "At least one good thing came of this."

"Is that so?"

"We are going to England."

"Are we?"

"You don't believe him?"

Mother motions to the cobblestone courtyard below where an artillery gun is being wheeled across the stones and aimed toward the house. And there behind it stand one hundred men and their wall of bayonets.

"I suspect that part was a lie," she says.

Anna

DEPARTURE

1968

Neuenbürg, Germany
August

Anna wakes in the hospital. She knows immediately that she has been drugged because she has to pull herself up and out of the fog, to work at keeping her eyes open and her mind clear. This is an old, unpleasant, and unwelcome sensation. The difference this time is that she comes to, not in an asylum but in a hospital. There is no screaming. No crying. It smells of antiseptic instead of urine. And she is in a room by herself instead of in an open ward. It is as though she's surfacing headfirst from the bottom of a deep, dark pool. Anna can think before she can move her limbs; the result is a brief, suffocating panic in which she fears she is paralyzed. But within moments the rest of her body begins to cooperate and she is once again able to wiggle fingers and toes.

Anna feels the IV in the back of her left hand. The site is stiff and sore; she peels off the tape and pulls the needle from her skin. There is a brief, cool, bizarre feeling as it slips out of her vein, like someone has drawn a sliver of ice from beneath her skin.

Two bags hang from the stand beside her bed, one large and filled with glucose, and the other small and empty. Anna guesses the latter to be a sedative.

Her clothes are folded in neat little rectangles on the chair beside the bed, her shoes perched on top. The hospital gown she wears is clean and white and buttons up the back. They've removed her undergarments as well, which means they've seen the worst of her scars. This violation of her privacy never gets easier. It is bad enough that the eyes of strangers are always drawn to the thin, silvery lines at her temple and collarbones. But those are small and curious compared to the jagged, puckered scars on her torso and thighs. Her visible scars suggest there might be an interesting story involved. But the ones hidden beneath her clothes tell the grisly truth of what happened to her all those years ago. It is why she does not willingly allow others to see her naked. There is simply no way to explain. And she cannot tolerate the pity that comes with their discovery.

Anna swings her feet lightly over the side of the bed and places them on the cold floor. She tests her balance. And when she's certain that the drugs have faded from her system, she stands. She is clothed in moments, each article jerked onto her thin frame with little attention paid to tags and buttons or concern for neatness. She cares only about having her armor in place once again. So when a nurse enters several minutes later, she finds Anna standing at the window, arms crossed, as though prepared for battle.

"You're awake!" The nurse is young and plain but absurdly cheerful.

"Where am I?" Anna demands.

"The district hospital at Neuenbürg."

"Why?"

"They found you unconscious and brought you here."

"They?"

"The paramedics. You were on the floor, unresponsive."

"No," Anna says, "they drugged me."

The nurse hesitates. Then smiles. It's meant to be a reassuring gesture. "Only because you resisted."

"Who wouldn't resist being drugged?"

"You resisted coming *here*." Now a tight-lipped smirk.

"How could I do such a thing if I was unconscious?"

Anna knows what she looks like, a somewhat senile and helpless old woman in her early seventies. But this young nurse has just realized the incongruence between her appearance and her intellect and is adjusting accordingly. This time the smile she offers Anna is one of concession.

"Would you like me to fetch the doctor? I'm sure you have questions."

"Yes."

If Anna had a franc for every doctor she has seen over the years, for every unwanted examination, and every question evaded, she would be a very wealthy woman. In the early years, the exams sent her into a feral panic—*episodes*, the doctors called them—but it has been decades since that happened. She is no longer afraid of doctors. They are all the same to her at this point. Anna doesn't even bother asking the name of this one; she glares at him when he enters the small, sterile room.

"I would like to be taken home."

"I'm afraid that's not possible." He sits on the chair recently occupied by her clothing. "You need rest and care."

"And?"

"And what?"

"The real reason you're keeping me here. What is it?"

"There is no other reason. You've been ill."

She glances out the window. Looks at the sky. "How long have I been here?"

A long pause. "Three days."

There is an immediate uptick in her pulse. A rage begins to settle in her core. "You've kept me drugged for three days?"

He opens his mouth. Closes it. He is wise, in the end, not to answer her question at all.

Anna does not argue or interrogate him. She stands very

quiet and straight and still. This unexpected silence does exactly what she intends. The doctor begins to fidget.

"Your heart—"

"Is perfectly healthy."

"We were concerned—"

"Needlessly. Why am I here?"

Seeing no way around it, he admits the truth. "Your dacha is being cleaned."

It is interesting that he uses the word *dacha*, the Russian word for "cottage." Perhaps this is some attempt at sympathy? A way to ingratiate himself or to acknowledge her identity? It doesn't matter. She would have preferred a diagnosis of cancer to this. Anything, really. While she has been sedated in this hospital, strangers have been rummaging through her things. Looking at years' worth of papers and documents and legal filings. They can see anything. They can take anything.

Sometimes rage is hot and explosive. But other times it is cool and sharp and vicious, and she directs the pointed end of it directly at this idiot doctor. "You will release me from this facility," she says. "You will arrange immediate transportation for my return to Unterlengenhardt. And you will *not*, under any circumstances, release details of my condition or my stay to anyone."

"This is a mistake. You really should—"

"I am not here under psychiatric observation, correct?" Noting the slight shake of his head, she continues, "Nor do I have any pressing health issues. This is my decision. You are obligated by law to release me."

He offers bristling acknowledgment that she is, in fact, right.

"You know who I am?"

"Yes, Fräulein Anderson."

Anderson. It's not her real name, of course, merely one she had to assume in order to leave Germany forty years ago. And yet it sticks, as do the recriminations that come along with it.

"Then you know that I have excellent attorneys?"

He nods.

"Good. Prepare my release papers immediately."

———

Unterlengenhardt has been Anna's home for decades, and even though she doesn't love it the way she loves Wasserburg or Paris, it is familiar and comfortable. A soft landing place. And while she has never claimed to be a good housekeeper—or shown interest in being one for that matter—she does realize that others find her clutter alarming. They call it hoarding and chaos. Sometimes they use other, more offensive words. But what they do not understand is that it gives her the ability to remain invisible and to hide what she does not want seen. The boxes and piles and stacks distract the relentless stream of visitors from noticing things she would rather keep hidden. A photo album filled with pictures of the imperial family. An ivory chess set. A pen knife with a golden crest. And the small hand-painted icon of Saint Anna of Kashin.

Mainly, though, people take issue with the cats. There are so many—half of them identical, long-haired, and bright orange, as though they've sprung right out of a malfunctioning copy machine. They breed faster than Anna can control. There are always more kittens than she can find homes for. And, yes, there is a certain . . . *odor*, inherent to such a collection. But it's not as though she lives in an apartment in Manhattan—at least not anymore. And when she did, all she had were the birds. She's not a fool, for God's sake. Anna lives in a small cottage outside a remote village on the edge of the Black Forest. Who cares if her animals run rampant?

The neighbors, apparently. And the town council. She has been thumbing her nose at them for years, insisting that they have no say in how she keeps her house or cares for her pets. Now she can see they've had their vengeance at last. Anna can tolerate the fact that Prince Frederick has had her home cleared of rubbish (he left a note apologizing for the necessity), but she cannot forgive him for allowing the town to gas and cremate her animals. Sixty-two cats—she knew each and every one of their names—and four dogs. Murdered. Gone. Euthanized and turned to ashes.

At first, when Anna saw the burn pile behind the house she assumed that was where they discarded the trash. But she only realized its true purpose when she found the charred collar.

Anna raised Baby from a puppy, and now all that is left of him is a bit of burnt leather and a crumpled metal tag with his name. Frederick could have saved Baby. He could have made this one exception. But he didn't, and Anna will never forgive him for it.

———

Anna says good-bye to no one. Certainly not Frederick. She simply makes a phone call.

"I am ready. Come get me." This has always been part of the plan, but what has happened here over the last several days has forced her to move more quickly. When there is a long pause on the other end, Anna realizes that she has not bothered with pleasantries or given her name. After a moment she adds, "This is Anna."

"Yes. I gathered that." The man clears his throat. "It was my impression that you didn't want to leave for a few more months, that you had other plans."

"They have ransacked my house and killed my animals."

A curse and then, "Bastards."

"That is a far too gentle word." She clenches her fist, then releases it, flexing the fingers wide. "When can I expect you?"

"An hour. Maybe less."

"I'll be waiting at the road."

Anna grabs a pile of rumpled clothing, giving little thought to what she stuffs in the leather valise. Apart from that she takes only the chess set, her pen knife, the photo album, and the icon. Inside the hollow statue is a set of carefully rolled documents—some legal, some forged. For all the accusations that she is slovenly, Anna can find exactly what she needs when she needs it. She tucks the items neatly inside her bag, then turns her back on the cottage that has been her home for twenty-two years.

The driveway is long and winding, and she staggers under the weight of her valise. She is a small woman, grown weak with age, but her anger pushes her forward, one indignant step at a time. Anna is out of breath and red-faced by the time she shuffles to a stop beside the mailbox and plops down on a stump, exhausted. She doesn't have to wait long. Faster than promised, he soon slows to a stop beside her in a government-issue vehicle. The man who steps out is tall and dark and wears an official-looking suit. He opens the door for her, then takes her valise and sets it in the trunk of the car.

"Thank you, Tartar."

He slides behind the wheel and looks at her in the rearview mirror. "Why do you call me that? I've always meant to ask."

Anna thinks for a moment, then laughs. Her first real laugh since waking up in the hospital at Neuenbürg. "You know, I can't remember."

It's a lie, of course. Anna does not forget. Her memory is as sound and as solid as a gun safe. And just as impenetrable. But she can't very well tell this man that she gave him the nick-name because she once watched him eat a steak so rare that a puddle of blood collected on his plate. It reminded her of beef tartare. *Tartare* became Tartar, and that has been his name ever since. Nor does Anna tell him that she has labeled people for as long as she can remember, given them monikers as both a way to remember all these names and faces that have been forced upon her through the decades, and a means of reminding herself of their true nature in case she's tempted to lower her defenses. And it has worked. The Heiress and the Duck and the Private Investigator are proof of this. Tartar is just one in a long list of bynames. He might be loyal, but she does not want to forget that he is a man with a taste for blood.

"Are you hungry?" he asks after they've driven a few miles. "It will take us several hours to drive to Frankfurt. We can stop and eat on the way."

"I'm fine for now. Just drive. I want to leave this place."

"Trust me, Tsarevna, you'll be in America before they even know you've left."

———

Tartar hands her the visa and plane ticket only once they've reached the airport. "You will fly from Frankfurt to Dulles," he says. "You will have a two-hour layover in Washington, but you mustn't leave the airport. You have no time to sightsee. None whatsoever. I know how you are with gardens and monuments, but you'll have to resist this time. You can come back later. Just go directly to your gate and wait for your flight to Charlottesville. Gleb will meet you at the gate."

Gleb Botkin.

So it has come to this. She hasn't seen him in many years, and they have both grown old in the meantime. He married and had children and became a widower. Anna feels guilty that she is grateful for this, but she couldn't go to him if his wife were still living. It would be too strange, with their history. Anna regrets the way she kept Gleb at arm's length, unable to surrender to his affections. But his mistake in Wasserburg was the beginning of everything going wrong. Had it not been for the Private Investigator, she would have proved her case before the courts long ago and she wouldn't have spent decades living in a ramshackle cottage waiting for the verdict of her appeal. She would have a title and an estate and the dispersed fortune of Tsar Nicholas II of Russia.

ONE MONTH EARLIER

Unterlengenhardt, Germany
July 1968

Baby lays his head on the hard knob of Anna's knee. This is a thing he has done since he was a puppy. Whenever he finds her sitting for more than ten seconds at a time, he plops down on his haunches, drops his chin to her knee, and sighs like an arthritic old man. When Anna first found him on the side of the road with his siblings, he was sick and skinny with the mange, one eye swollen shut. The runt of the litter. She didn't know that he was mostly Irish wolfhound and would grow so large that he would nearly reach her shoulder. In hindsight, she should have guessed. His paws were almost the size of her hand even then. But the rest of him was so scrawny and emaciated she didn't pay attention. Now, eleven years later, he is a shaggy, bearded, gentle giant. He's a shadow with eyes the color of a copper penny and a huge pink, wagging tongue. He is a beautiful dog despite the fact that he hasn't been groomed in years and has grown quite matted around the edges. He is ridiculous, but she loves him entirely. At this point in Anna's life, Baby is the closest thing she has to a real friend. Everyone else objects to the cats.

This train of thought has put Anna into a gloomy frame of mind and she wants a change of scenery. "Come, Baby, let's check the mail."

She wraps her hand around his collar and he pulls back on his hind legs, giving her a little tug, the smallest boost to get her out of the chair. She is moving more slowly these days, fighting a constant series of aches and pains.

Anna and Baby meander down the drive. The dog walks in large, lazy circles around her, sniffing at plants and trees, lifting his leg at any large rock in his path. Anna takes her time, allowing herself the simple luxury of stretching tight muscles and letting the sun warm her face.

There are two letters in the mailbox. One from Gleb Botkin and the other from Maria Rasputin.

Anna scowls when she sees the overly elegant, feminine handwriting on the latter. All that looping, swirling calligraphy. The telltale marks of a woman who is trying too hard. She understands this to a degree. The years cannot have been any kinder to Grigory Rasputin's daughter than they have been to her.

"That woman needs to stop writing me," Anna says. Baby looks up as though she has addressed him directly.

Baby nudges her in the hip with his cold, wet nose. It leaves a damp mark on her cotton skirt. He's telling her it's time to go back to the house. The dog herds her as though she is a child. Anna turns obediently and they begin the slow ascent back up the drive.

Not only has Anna never responded to Maria's letters; she hasn't read any of them. They are on the bookshelf, tucked between two cumbersome German law tomes that she found at a yard sale in the village. It was a rash purchase, a half-hearted attempt to navigate the legal system and her endless series of court cases and appeals.

Once they get back to the cottage, Anna retrieves the other letters from the shelf, evicts an orange, pregnant cat from her chair, and settles in to finally see what devilry the woman is up to.

Maria Rasputin is long-winded, prone to flattery, and impressed with her own vocabulary. She also has a frenzied need to insert herself into Anna's life. She wants to visit and, though she hasn't stated it directly, is now insinuating an unnecessary concern for Anna. She's wondering why Anna hasn't responded to her other missives, and she has floated the idea that she might "pop in" one day soon to check on her. Anna finds it quite interesting that even though Maria has gone to some trouble to dig up her address (it is not publicly listed), she has not been forthcoming with her own. The return address on each of the three letters shows only a post office box in Straubing. Whether or not she actually lives there, Maria Rasputin is sending her letters from the hinterlands of Germany.

There are no circumstances under which Anna will willingly entertain the woman. And since an answer to this quandary does not immediately present itself, she moves on to Gleb's letter.

His handwriting is as familiar as her own. A gentle, nonpretentious scrawl that loses steam at the end of each line and squiggles into nothing. As if he can't remember what he meant to say next. Not unlike the man himself.

Gleb's letter is short. He wants her to come visit him in the United States. He has made a friend, some professor by the name of Dr. Jack Manahan, who has just retired from the University of Virginia, and they've come up with a plan to have her declared, finally, as Anastasia Romanov. What Anna finds interesting is that inside Gleb's letter is another short note from Jack Manahan himself, offering to be her host. He never comes out and directly mentions her financial woes, but he says that she won't need to be concerned about a place to live if she chooses to accept the invitation. His home is available to her. And knowing she might question his motives, he lays them out plainly. Jack is an academic who specializes in genealogy and family history. On a broader level he wants to set the record straight about her identity, and on a personal level, doing so would be the crowning accomplishment of his career. He's honest enough to admit that outright.

She carefully folds the letters up the way they came and tucks them back in the envelopes. Anna grins at the thought of this new opportunity. She is more than willing to let them fight on her behalf.

———

Three days later Anna posts a letter accepting Gleb's invitation. By her calculations, it won't reach him for at least a month, what with the glacial pace of international mail. His letter took a similar length of time to arrive, and she feels the wait will be good for him. Let him fret and pace for a change.

Once back at the cottage, Anna makes a phone call. "Hello," she says once the man on the other end answers. "I'm going to need a visa."

The conversation is short and to the point. She has known Tartar for years but has never heard him speak more than three sentences at a time.

"Thank you," she says when he assures her the request will be processed immediately.

"Anything for you, Tsarevna."

Anna imagines him sitting behind that large, bureaucratic desk, bowing at the neck. The thought makes her laugh. The lightness of her mood is interrupted by a car speeding up the driveway. It comes to an abrupt stop before her door, slinging gravel against the window where she sits. Anna can see a hairline fracture spread out at the corner of one pane, not five inches from her face. All is still and silent for one long breath, then two car doors creak open and slam shut simultaneously.

Anna's hips ache constantly these days, as does a single vertebra in the small of her back. But neither of these maladies stops her from sliding out of the chair like a lizard, then crawling toward the front door. She pushes the lock into place seconds before the pounding begins.

"Anna! I know you're in there. Are you okay?" A woman's voice, disingenuous, and in Russian.

Not concerned enough to call first. Or to alert the authorities. Or to send a doctor. Not even troubled enough to summon anyone to check on her. No, this is an ambush and Anna won't play along.

Across the room Baby lifts his head from the rug and begins to growl, low and deep. It reverberates through the floorboards and into Anna's palms. She raises a calming hand to him and whispers, "I'm okay," but he strains forward anyway, suspicious. After a short, silent pause, he heaves to his feet and pads to the door, his long nails clacking against the wood. He sniffs twice, listens for a moment to the shuffling on the other side, and releases a series of thunderous barks.

"Did you receive my letters?" The woman is now shouting to be heard.

Of course it would be a Rasputin at the door.

Anna sets a hand on Baby's head. He drops back onto his haunches, tail wagging.

Another woman speaks, but in English, and not to Anna. "Look at this place," she says. "I've not seen anything like it outside of a Third World country."

Maria Rasputin answers in English and they begin the thoughtless, self-righteous sort of conversation usually inflicted on the feebleminded and the impoverished. If they intend to be secretive, they have failed. Anna lived in the United States for many years and speaks fluent English.

"I hear she's always been fond of cats," Maria Rasputin says.

"The smell is . . . *impressive*."

"We're dealing with an eccentric. Keep that in mind. We must coddle her. In this case, flattery will get you everywhere. When she opens the door make a point to bow and call her tsarevna. Use her full name, Anastasia, as often as possible."

"I'm not convinced she's home."

"Oh, she is; the trouble is getting her to let us in."

Finally, after they have knocked and pleaded and called to her, one of them leans against the door—Anna can hear it groan under her weight. "She's not answering. What do we do now?"

There is a ruthless note to Maria Rasputin's voice when she answers. "We have to flush her out."

"And how, pray tell, are we going to do that?"

"It's a pity anyone is forced to live under these conditions," Maria says loudly, in German, and with a note of obscene pleasure. "I think a call to the town council is in order. Don't you? Surely this has to be a health hazard."

"You devious old harpy."

"Takes one to know one. But you should be nice to me, Patte. I'm your meal ticket."

"I thought you said *she* was *our* meal ticket?"

"Well, you don't get to *her* without *me*, now do you?"

Anna listens as the two of them bicker, now in English, and walk back toward the car. The last thing she hears before the doors shut is this strange woman—Patte, Maria called her—say, "I'm beginning to doubt whether anyone can get to her."

Baby growls again as the car roars to life, and he sends them off with another earsplitting round of barks.

"Enough," Anna says, swatting at him. "I'll go deaf if you keep that up."

It takes her a moment to get off the floor, and by the time she makes it to the window her visitors have already disappeared down the drive.

———

Within the week, Anna gets three surprise visits from the health department. Each time they knock on the door she stays hidden within the house, only to rip the citation up and throw it away once they've left. She has been ordered to clean up the property. They are concerned about the cats and the garbage and the piles of books and boxes they can see in the windows. They are concerned about her health. There's been a report she's ill—*damn that Rasputin*—and they want to check on her. Anna doesn't know much German law, but she does know they can't actually enter her home without a warrant or a doctor's order—unless they can see that she is incapacitated.

The following week, people begin to arrive in one fretting group after another. They come in twos and threes and peek in the windows and bang on the door. They slip notes under the door and beg her to come out. They don't bother lowering their voices as they talk about her health and the condition of the cottage. They malign the animals, as though any of this is their fault, and they disparage Anna herself. At first she doesn't open the door to them because she is suspicious. Now she keeps it closed because she's angry.

It is easy enough to barricade herself inside the cottage, to let her world shrink to a pinprick. The cats come and go at their leisure through a small pet door at the back. Anna lets Baby out twice a day to do his business. Mostly her days are filled with reading—letters and old newspapers and tedious volumes of German law—things she's been meaning to get to for years. She eats what is in the house, giving little thought to preparation or taste or expiration date.

At first she doesn't mind the stomachache. It's easy enough to pass off as indigestion. Only when the aching turns to cramping and the sweat turns to chills a day later does Anna begin to consider the possibility of food poisoning. But in this new, feverish state, the only word that makes any sense to her at all is *poison*, and she begins to fear, and then believe, that she has actually *been* poisoned. Anna spends one long tortured night walking a path between the bedroom and the bathroom, making a mental list of all the people who want her dead. If she were not afraid of actually dying, she might laugh. The list is obscenely long.

———————

Baby presses his nose against Anna's cheek, trying to rouse her. It isn't cold and wet the way a dog's nose should be, but dry and warm and rough, and even in her condition Anna knows that he is dehydrated. Anna also knows that she is very ill. She vacillates wildly between hot and cold. She's thirsty but not hungry. Anna is very tired and wants to stay exactly where she is, in her slender bed in her crowded bedroom beneath the window, curled up in a glorious patch of sunlight. It feels good on her old, thin skin. She feels as though the sun is coming directly through, warming her blood. If she opened her mouth she could taste the warmth itself. Drink it in—it would be like citrus, sour and explosive. It would make her mouth pucker and her entire body would shudder a bit with the sensation. The hairs on her arms would stand to attention. The sun is a lemon hanging in the sky. Floating fruit. Flaming fruit. Hotter now, on her cheek, uncomfortably so. The lemon is burning her. She should roll over to her other side but her left arm has gone numb beneath the weight of her body and she can't quite get her limbs to cooperate and shift her around. Oh well. The sun-lemon will fall lower in the sky eventually. It will drop from its celestial tree and her cheek will stop hurting then.

Baby barks, loud in her ear. He nudges her. A groan is all she can muster in reply. Anna assumes he wants to be let out and she feels guilty that she can't get up and open the door for him. If he messes the floor, she'll just clean it up later.

He pads away and barks again, louder this time. Incessantly. Now she's angry. *Be quiet*, she thinks, *I can't take care of you right now. I can't even take care of myself.*

That's what mothers are for. To take care of you. Anna wants her mother suddenly. Badly. She has reverted full circle to a child curled on her bed crying for her mother. Wanting to be soothed and have the pain taken away. There is a pain somewhere in her abdomen, and it begins to bloom brighter and bigger now that she's aware of it.

"Mother," she moans and Baby goes berserk.

He throws himself against the front door.

And then there are the sounds of splintering wood and breaking glass. Voices. Footsteps. Rough hands that shake and poke her. Anna screams. She thrashes. There is an acute, needle-like pain at her left wrist. And then all is devoured by darkness.

4

Anastasia

Alexander Palace, Tsarskoe Selo, Russia
March 9

When my father finally returns home, none of us go out to greet him. We've been trained to wait for the trumpets, for the choreographed footfalls of a hundred officers in full regalia. That's the point at which we're allowed to throw wide the front doors and line up in our finery. When our father makes an entrance, we are to be accessories—ornamental figures meant to enhance his glory. But no one has ever bothered to tell us what role to play should he come home disgraced and despondent. So when Nikolai Alexandrovich Romanov the Second, tsar of all Russia, is brought back to the Alexander Palace unshaven, in a common carriage, under armed guard, we are nowhere to be seen.

He finds us in the parlor, staring at the fire, our spirits waning. I look up and there he is, standing in the door, the toe of one muddy boot resting on the Persian rug. For just a moment he looks like a god, tall and strong and surrounded by light. This is my father and he has come home and I could burst with joy at the sight of him. I am too stunned, too relieved to speak. But then he steps forward and I realize that he is not at all the man I have known. Or perhaps he is simply a man and not the emperor I remember him to be. I was tricked by the light and by my own hope, for he is weary and haggard, looking every bit the mortal. It's all there in the lines around his eyes and the stubble along his cheekbones. The impressive mustache that he always takes such pains to wax and curl hangs limp at the corners of his mouth.

"Nicky!" Mother sees him next but she does not rise from her chair or throw herself into his arms. It's as though she's a puppet and whatever strings keep her up are snipped by invisible scissors. Mother collapses in upon herself and goes quietly to pieces right there on the couch.

Father can barely get her name out without choking on a sob of his own. "Alix," he says, eyes full of a rare softness and longing.

Alexey flies at him, all elbows and knees. Large eyes. Pale skin. Bright freckles. He is twelve, but he looks like he's two, the way he wraps himself around Father and buries his face in his chest.

My sisters rush him, and Father can't scoop them up quickly enough. I am the last to approach, and he does not see me for several long moments because his eyes are squeezed tight. But when he does, he utters a single sentence and some shattered thing inside me is pieced back together.

"Schwibsik," he whispers, "come here."

I throw myself into his arms, unable to stop a sudden, frightful wave of tears.

The caterwauling and celebrating is extraordinary, and the remaining servants come running from all directions in panic. I can't blame them. It does sound as though someone is being slaughtered right there on the floor. But then Father slowly extricates himself from the pile of children and they see him. I've never realized before how clearly men need leaders. How adrift we are without them and how the mere sight of one can breathe courage into a room.

The servants' cheers are different, elated and filled with

expectation. Whooping and hollering and whistling. All will be well now that their sovereign has returned. They believe this. I can hear it in every jubilant shout, and for one perfect moment I forget that we are under siege.

But then a sharp, official rap sounds on the parlor door and we lift tearstained faces to find a soldier standing in the doorway. Behind him are three more, all of them uncomfortable and stoic. One of them looks to be about my age.

"Alexander Kerensky is waiting for you in the formal reception room downstairs," the soldier says.

Father straightens his collar. He gives us a reassuring smile. "I'll be back shortly. I want to hear everything that's happened while I was gone."

"Kerensky has requested that your family come as well. He wishes to speak with all of you at once."

Father studies us for a moment. We are wilted and exhausted, wrung out from fear and waiting. Olga and Tatiana, though recovered from their bout with measles, are blanched and painfully thin. Alexey has a gray tint to his skin and his hair hasn't been brushed in days. Maria, though pretty as always, is disheveled, and Mother's hair has slipped from her pins, giving her a harried, schoolmarmish appearance. God only knows how frightful I look. Father, clearly, is not impressed by what he sees.

"Kerensky can wait a few moments," he says. "We'll be down shortly." Father closes the parlor door and says to us, "Come along and freshen up. We have an appearance to make."

This, at least, is familiar. We are handed off to Dova to make ourselves as presentable as possible while Father slips away to shave. Mother situates herself in front of a gilded mirror and wrestles her wayward hair under control. It doesn't take long, in the end, to have our hair combed and our faces scrubbed. Dova yanks dresses from the wardrobe at random and pulls them over our heads while we shove our feet into tight pointy-toed shoes. Alexey is given the sailor suit he wore last year. But he's lost so much weight from his illness that it fits him again.

We assemble again fifteen minutes later, and while not entirely dignified, at least we no longer look ragged. Father pulls open the parlor door, glares at the soldiers standing guard, and walks toward the grand staircase with all the dignity he can muster. Mother rises graciously from her seat and follows him down the great, wide steps. We go after them. First Olga, tall and beautiful. I can feel the soldiers watching her. I can almost feel them smile. Tatiana goes next, the air stirred by her perfume and the muttered words of appreciation from Kerensky's men. Maria is only a step behind, statuesque and aloof, her chin held high, certain of her place as the prettiest of us, certain they will look at her the longest. I bring up the rear with Alexey at my side, just as we've been taught. He the little heir and me the guardian. I wrap an arm around his thin shoulders and slow my steps to match his. I do not glance at the soldiers, and I'm certain that none of them bothers to take much note of my presence other than to complete a head count.

Seven Romanovs.

Seven captives.

The formal reception room is the sunniest in the entire palace and therefore my favorite. It is where we have our art lessons and, in the absence of visitors, where we sprawl about reading in the summertime. The room sits in the bottom right corner of the palace, near our parents' suite, and has seven enormous ornate windows that overlook the park. The walls are covered, floor to ceiling, in white artificial marble and topped by ornate entablature that Father once told me cost a king's ransom to install. I dared not ask then, much less now, what it cost to ransom a king.

The rear wall of the reception room showcases two of the most valuable paintings on the entire grounds: Detaille's *Cos-*

sacks, an enormous canvas spanning almost ten feet that details the famed march during Napoleon's Russian campaign, and Vigée Le Brun's infamous *Marie Antoinette and Her Children*— my family always has bordered on being Francophiles, I'm afraid. We've spent so many hours with our tutor, Pierre Gilliard, discussing the differences between neoclassical and academic painting styles that I can recite the differences on command and in French no less. Impressive, I suppose, unless you consider that I am fifteen years old and cannot lace my own boots without assistance from Dova.

The paintings have been hung so they will be seen immediately upon entering the room. Most visitors are speechless at the sight of them, but the man who sits at a small round table beneath the chandelier seems impervious to their spell. He does not rise or bow as we approach, but rather waits, one arm draped over the back of his chair. He wears a high-collared suit instead of the military uniform I expect. Kerensky is a lean, pale man with short dark hair that forms a widow's peak in the middle of his forehead. His dark eyes are nearly obscured by thick brows, and the combination gives him a distinctly hostile appearance.

Alexey squeezes my hand and I can feel the bird-like pulse at his wrist—that tiny, strumming thread of fear. He looks paler than usual and is trembling because he has just noticed the bayonets. Mother passes two armed guards, chin held high in disdain, then my sisters in their gowns and ridiculous shoes follow behind her. Alexey and I bring up the rear, eyes wide. Both guards hold a rifle, their bayonets affixed and polished to a malicious shine. Now that I've seen them I cannot look away. I stare at them as we pass, noting the unholy sheen at each pointed end.

"You are scaring my family," Father growls the moment he comes to a stop before the seated man.

It is his angered voice that grounds me.

"Perhaps they could do with some fear," Kerensky says, his voice rich and confident. There is no hint of triumph or pride there, simply a calm assurance that we will do as we are told. "Your family has long since forgotten their place."

I can hear the snap of Father's jaw from fifteen feet away, the way he forces his teeth together to stop an imperious retort. Instead he introduces this stranger. "This is Alexander Kerensky, minister of justice. There's no need to stand before him, children. Please take a seat."

Father moves to the window and looks over the snow-covered gardens while Mother takes her place in a chair beside him. The rest of us find our usual seats around the room—my sisters, each on their favorite chaise, and Alexey and I in the red and gold brocade armchair beside the fireplace. My feet do not touch the floor and I hate that this cruel man notes it immediately, his gaze going straight to the toes of my beaded slippers as they dangle three inches from the rug. I hate him from that moment on. I hate him for making me feel small and vulnerable and so different from my elegant sisters.

"Nicholas," he says, finally, with a curt nod toward my father.

Not *Tsar*.

Not *Your Majesty*.

Not even *Nikolai*. But Nicholas, the barbaric English version of his name. Nicholas the citizen. Nicholas the prisoner.

Father makes a show of sitting now and folding his hands theatrically in his lap. "I see you've made yourself comfortable."

Kerensky's face betrays no emotion. "Let us be frank. Alexander Palace is no longer under your control, and I do not need your permission to enter, much less sit."

"I see that mutiny has added nothing to your manners," Father says.

"You find yourself in a revolution and complain there are no manners?"

"I find myself in my home with company I did not invite and do not welcome."

"You are in a palace that belongs to the Russian people. As of today you and your family are prisoners. You may not leave and you may not speak to anyone from the outside."

From the corner of my eye I see Mother reach for Father's sleeve with a trembling hand. This should not come as a surprise—we've had no contact with the outside world for nine days—but still, to hear the truth from Kerensky is unnerving. Yet I am not afraid. Perhaps I should be—my siblings certainly are—but the only thing I feel at this pronouncement is anger. I am like my father in that way, I fear. Anger first, reason second.

Kerensky gives us a moment to let this sink in, then continues. "The stubborn loyalty of your household is regrettable, but those who desire to leave have forty-eight hours. Any who stay longer will be under house arrest with you and your family. They will share whatever fate awaits you."

"No." Father shakes his head. "Our servants have nothing to do with this. They should be left alone."

"You have been arrested. You have no say and nothing with which to negotiate. You have abdicated the throne, not only for yourself, but for your son as well. You are no longer emperor. Anything granted to you is by my good grace alone."

Father maintains his composure at this disclosure, but Mother draws in a sharp breath and digs her fingernails into the fine wool of Father's sleeve.

"Oh. I see. You haven't told them yet. Let me make it clear then." Kerensky turns a cruel, thin-lipped smile to each of us in turn. He pauses to make sure we're paying attention. I want to glance at my sisters, to read their expressions, but force myself to remain still. When Kerensky looks at me, I sit up defiantly, my spine stretched to its full length, trying to be braver than I really am, trying to radiate defiance. "As of three days ago, you are no longer the royal family of Russia. Your only title is that of *prisoner*."

If Mother looked pale and weak before, she is stricken now, stunned into silence.

"You are citizens now," Kerensky says. "Each and every one of you. And it is only out of respect for the past that you will not be sent to a citizens' prison. Instead you will stay here in the Alexander Palace under house arrest until other arrangements can be made. Your rooms will be limited, as will your activities. Your servants will be few, and you will be supervised at all times. I will personally oversee your schedule, and you will adhere to it without question or complaint. The sooner you accept this, the easier it will be for all of you."

"How long"—Mother's voice is thin and reedy, so she clears her throat and tries again—"how long will this last?"

Kerensky studies her. She has grown thinner since Father left, but not in a healthy way. Her cheeks look like paste. Her hair is dull. The skin at the back of her hands lies wrinkled and loose against her bones. If I knew Kerensky better, I would say that the look on his face is one of pity, but I do not yet know what sort of man he is, so I cannot place the expression.

He takes a step forward and bends over Mother's chair, speaking as though she is an imbecile child and not Alexandra Feodorovna, granddaughter of Queen Victoria and empress consort of Russia. "Have you not realized it yet? This is *never* going to end."

———

"Three days ago my train was stopped at Malaya Vishera," Father says. Now that Kerensky has returned to his soldiers, Father gathers us around the fire to explain his abdication. "Revolutionaries crowded the line and forced the train to stop. The routes to Petrograd and Tsarskoe Selo were closed and we were diverted to Pskov. I was met there by Alexander Kerensky and a delegation from the Duma. They brought a declaration of abdication with them. There was little conversation about me signing. It was expected that I do so without argument."

"You fought them. Please. Tell me you fought them at least," Mother says, her voice strangled.

"For what? My honor? The country? The military? Would you have me face a firing squad right there on the tracks to preserve those things?"

"I would have you do it for Alexey!" Mother snaps, her composure thin and brittle.

He looks at my brother with lips pressed firmly together. Whatever he might say to Mother in private will not be uttered out loud in front of their son. This is their ongoing argument, the fissure that hisses and spits between them. Mother believes, without qualification, the word of Grigory Rasputin, that Alexey has been healed, and she will not be convinced otherwise. She has repeated this assurance to my brother; therefore it is a fact and will not be denied in her hearing. The price Mother paid for this promise is too great; it is unspeakable. It has cost her reputation and, many whisper, her honor as well. We are forbidden to speak of Alexey's condition—neither in his hearing nor at any other time. The only time my mother ever struck me was when I dared to question Rasputin's claims while Alexey suffered from a three-day nosebleed. She split my lip with the emerald ring on the back of her hand. And while Mother never apologized for the blow, she did stop wearing the large princess-cut emerald. I like to think that means she's sorry.

Father, however, is a man of logic and he believes the physicians; his son might live for many years, but the hemophilia will never be cured and Alexey will never father children of his own. In the end he answers Mother but does not look at her.

"Fighting was a risk I could not take. Alexey's life is too important."

"So is his birthright!"

"Had I fought them, we would all be dead right now! None of you would have lived through that night. Can you understand this? I did the best I could."

My mother was born to the name Alix Victoria Helena Louise Beatrice of Hesse and by Rhine. Only upon her reception into the Russian Orthodox Church and subsequent marriage to my father was she given the name Alexandra Feodorovna. She is a dual German and British duchess, and she is more proud of her beautiful children than any other thing in her life, including her own title. Beauty is power and power is all she knows. To have four fair daughters gives her an advantage over every other royal family in Europe. The fact that she has rounded out her brood with Alexey, a male heir for the Romanov dynasty, gives her a satisfaction and sense of superiority unrivaled among her peers. To have all of this stripped from her in an afternoon is unthinkable. Mother, finally, is at a loss for words.

The consequences of Father's abdication are finally occurring to my brother, however. He springs from the chair beside me. "Don't I have a say?" he demands.

"No."

"But I'm the tsarevich!"

"You are a child."

"I am not. I'm a man. All the officers say so." He stamps his foot in rage. "You should have asked me."

Father sighs. "The officers coddle you. And besides, the decision was not yours to make. It was mine and it is done."

"But what about my soldiers? And my regiments?" Alexey demands. "Won't I see them again?" He stands in the middle of the large room, bewildered, his voice echoing off the polished floor and high ceilings. He is worked up now, frantic. "And the

Shtandart? What about all my friends on board? Will we go yachting anymore?"

"No," Father says. There is a finality in his tone that silences my brother. "We will never see the *Shtandart* again. It doesn't belong to us now."

Alexey slumps back into the chair, crestfallen. "But who is going to be tsar now?"

"No one."

"But if there isn't a tsar, who will govern Russia?"

Father grimaces. "You just met him."

Anna

AT THE MOVIES, IN PARIS

1968, 1958, 1955

Paris, France
July 27, 1968

Anna can feel the entire city of Paris inhale as she stands on the Pont Alexandre III, at the highest point of its arch, overlooking the Seine. The air is perfect—neither hot nor cold, but balmy and pleasant, a gift at the midpoint of this long summer. She can smell the river—fragrant like wet rocks and green grass. The scent of freshly baked bread wafts up from the cafés that line the streets on either side. It is not yet seven o'clock but the sun is up, and she can feel its warmth on the back of her neck. Anna closes her eyes and drinks it in. Her chaperone will find her before long and then she will be forced to deal with today's task. Prince Frederick is no doubt frantically searching the suite at this very moment, chiding himself for giving her a key and a room of her own. But she doesn't care. She is in her early seventies, not a child in need of babysitting. Anna wants a moment to herself, a bit of silence and tranquility. He is the one who insisted she come. If she has to be in Paris she will enjoy it on her own terms, and in the ways that have always brought her pleasure.

Anna saw this bridge from the balcony of her hotel room at La Maison Champs Elysées last night and made up her mind to visit. It is broad and ornate, boasting pillars topped with gilded, winged horses. Four lanes of traffic consume the middle, but on either side are well-lit sidewalks that allow breathtaking views of the Eiffel Tower. It is nothing like that drab bridge she remembers in Berlin, and she has no plans to pitch herself over the side today.

Frederick does not know this, of course. But he's been worried about her since the court in Hamburg decided her case earlier in the year. She hears the panic in his voice now as he calls her name, "Anna!"

She turns to find him ten feet away, his hand out, dismay written across his face. Frederick looks every inch the aristocrat. Tall and lean, perfectly groomed, and with the sort of cheekbones that could cut glass. His eyes are gray, his hair, once black, is now sprinkled with silver, and his chin is strong. He's the sort of man who walks in a room and demands attention just by his presence. Even those who pass him on the bridge look twice, curious about him.

"What are you doing here?"

"I've come to collect you. It's time to get ready for your appointment."

He has pulled the car over and parked it a good twenty feet away. He stands there, scowling.

"My appointment isn't until ten o'clock. Can't a woman take a walk and get breakfast in peace?"

"You didn't leave a note. I was worried."

"You needn't be."

Frederick gives her a tight-lipped smile of reassurance. And then he tries to distract her. "Dominique bought you a new dress. She sent me to find you. She wants to make sure it fits."

"Is she a seamstress now too? In addition to being a journalist?" Anna hates it when they coddle her. She is old, not senile, but she relents and follows him back to the waiting car.

Moments later Frederick helps her out of the vehicle and

shuffles her up to the room where Dominique waits with a smart-looking knee-length print dress. It is cream with small black roses and shiny black buttons up the front.

"I couldn't help myself!" Dominique says, holding up a pair of pumps and a small hat with a tiny black veil as well.

Dominique Aucléres was assigned to cover Anna's first trial for *Figaro*, one of Paris's most prominent newspapers, in 1958. "The hardest part," she'd said later, "was writing the facts and not my opinion. I was convinced you were Anastasia from the start."

Convinced, loyal, and, for a Frenchwoman, surprisingly easy to make friends with. Ten years later, Dominique is still one of Anna's closest confidantes and insisted on seeing Anna the moment she learned they were coming to Paris. Then, when she heard the reason for their visit, she insisted on tagging along for the appointment as well.

"You didn't have to buy me a dress."

"I didn't, in fact. It belonged to my mother. You're about the same size. I thought it would look lovely on you. And I hate the idea of it sitting in her closet getting eaten by moths."

"I didn't realize she'd passed on. I'm sorry."

"Don't be. She's very much alive. Mother has run off with some Bohemian to Switzerland. They're living in a nudist colony near a hot spring, and she's left me to deal with her belongings. Again." Dominique offers a weary sigh and blows a piece of hair away from her face. "It is so difficult to raise our parents, no?"

"I'm the wrong person to ask."

"Ah . . . of course. I forgot. Now it's my turn to apologize." She kisses both of Anna's cheeks, then tugs at the sleeve of her worn and ragged dress. "Truth be told, I probably would have bought you one anyway. How long have you had this?"

"A long time."

"Well, we certainly can't let you go meet with a film producer in this tatty old rag, can we? Appearances are everything."

Anna has known many women through the years who spouted this mantra, Dominique chief among them. But, perhaps because she is French and cannot help it, Anna isn't put off when her friend recites it in her throaty, rich voice. Dominique is the classic Frenchwoman. Slender and beautiful and cultured. She is brunette with striking, large brown eyes and a wide smile. She moves with grace and purpose and is one of those women who wears off-the-shoulder sweaters in the dead of winter and who inevitably finds herself in extraordinary circumstances without even trying. At the age of nineteen, she marched into the apartment of famed Austrian novelist Arthur Schnitzler and asked if she could translate all his works into French. The poor man was so taken aback by the request— and, Anna suspects, staggered by her beauty—that he agreed. It is unlikely that Dominique even needs her job at the newspaper because she has held the copyright to Schnitzler's work in France ever since. Her profile soared after that, with her coverage of Anna's case for *Figaro* over the last decade comprising only a small portion of her career.

And so Anna wears the dress and allows Dominique to curl and set her hair. She rejects the use of makeup outright but does submit to wearing a necklace and bracelet. Frederick is impressed, smiling and complimenting her appearance as he leads her to the lobby. She waits a moment while he pulls the car around and she takes one long glance at herself in a mirror hung between two light sconces. Anna has forgotten what it feels like to be pretty, to have the attention of men. And she knows that she isn't exactly *pretty* now. Not in the traditional sense. Time and scars and trials have all taken their toll. But she does look nice. Put together, even. And this gives her a bit of needed courage.

Gilbert Prouteau greets them at the door to his studio.

"Come in!" the tall Frenchman bellows, sweeping his arm wide. He has the look of a man who was recently handsome but doesn't know what to do with himself now that's he's turned the corner of bald and portly. He clasps Anna's small hands in his larger ones and grins, kissing each of her cheeks in that carefree, elegant French way. "I am so glad to finally meet you. And"—he pauses to give her a look of solidarity—"for what it's worth, I think the Hamburg verdict was a grave miscarriage of justice. That's why I want to make the film. To set things right in the public eye."

Chances are she will never see this man again, so she doesn't bother trying to learn his name. Anna decides he will simply be the Producer. She shakes the one hand that remains around hers. "Thank you. But I must say, I'm surprised you invited me. None of the others asked my permission first."

The Producer has the good grace to flush a little at this. He clears his throat. "Let's refer to it as your *blessing*. It is my hope that the film will be in production soon."

Of course he has gone ahead anyway. Filmmakers can't seem to help themselves. "On the phone you referred to it as a documentary."

"It is. But large parts will be reenactments." He takes a step back into the large, elegant room. The spacious studio takes up the entire top floor of an office building facing the Avenue des Champs-Élysées in Paris's 8th Arrondissement. At this height she can see swaths of the entire tree-lined avenue and the imposing Arc de Triomphe at its western end. One entire wall is floor-to-ceiling windows that let in copious amounts of natural light. The floors are wide-planked wood and the walls a bone-colored plaster. "But where are my manners? Please, come in. Look around. We plan to film all the court scenes here."

Frederick and Dominique follow them into the room and remain quiet as the Producer gives a lengthy tour of the studio and introduces them to a few key staff who work out of the space. After showing them a series of possible set designs the Producer says, "I simply cannot believe they ruled against you."

"We have already filed an appeal," Prince Frederick says and casts a sideways glance in Anna's direction. Her friends keep discussion of this subject to a minimum for fear she will become depressive again. She reached a low point after the court in Hamburg offered its verdict several months earlier. "There is still hope."

"Good news! The film should be ready by then." He pats a large stack of papers. "Here is the script. The structure is quite ingenious, I think. We've created a fictional premise in which two attorneys argue your case before the World Court at the Hague." He slaps the pile in excitement. "Vittorio De Sica and Paul Meurisse have already signed on for the roles. Isn't that fantastic?"

"Yes. This is . . . *bonnes nouvelles,*" Dominique says, her voice dripping with suspicion.

The Producer is too wrapped up in his vision to note her tone. "We aim to dramatize your story while keeping a faithful record of the actual witness testimony. When the world sees it they will know how poorly you were treated. They will demand justice. The Mayer testimony in particular is a known perjury."

Anna stiffens at the mention of the charming Austrian who gleefully upturned her case. "I appreciate your support," Anna says. It's her standard, noncommittal answer, the thing she says when she doesn't know how to receive a kindness.

"Now"—the Producer claps his hands together with a loud

crack and the sound echoes off the high ceiling—"I have a surprise for you. Please, come with me to the screening room."

Frederick and Dominique exchange a concerned look but
do not question him. They all follow him to the back of the
studio and into a room with thick carpet and eight stuffed,
velvet-covered chairs. A large canvas screen covers one wall
and a projector sits opposite.

"Have a seat," the Producer says.

Anna lowers herself slowly into the chair nearest the door.
"You said production has not yet begun on the film."

"It hasn't. This is something else, my gift to you. Something
I found in the archives while doing research. I plan to include
it in our film."

Ours, as though she has any say in the matter.

The Producer's assistant comes in while everyone else
chooses a seat. He fiddles with the projector and soon there
is a whirring and clicking behind her and faint images fly onto
the screen. It's only when he turns out the light that Anna sees
the grainy black-and-white images that flicker and then come
to life. On the screen, Tsar Nicholas II walks into view with
Empress Alexandra on his arm. They are laughing soundlessly
at someone behind them and moving in that quick, jerky fashion that is common in old newsreel footage. Then Tsarevitch
Alexey skips into the frame, a mere toddler, and Anna gasps
loudly, her hand going to her heart. She can see Dominique
out of the corner of her eye, rising as though she will come to
assist Anna. But Frederick puts a hand to her arm and she settles into her chair again. One by one the three oldest Romanov
girls enter the frame, and even after all this time, on splotchy
film, in black and white, they are breathtaking in their court
dresses and wide-brimmed bonnets. They are in their mid-
teens, slender and youthful. Each of them is escorted down the
tree-lined avenue by a handsome cavalier. The girls are smil-

ing, bright and vivacious, and Anna leans forward as though she could touch them, as though she could step through the frame herself and disappear into the past.

It takes her a moment to state the obvious. "Where am I?" Anna says. "I know I was there."

No sooner are the words out of her mouth than a little girl runs up behind her sisters, frantic, hair wild, hat blown off and attached only by a ribbon knotted beneath her chin. There appears to be a smudge of dirt on her chin and bruises on her knees. Soundlessly her father laughs, then scoops her up, planting a sloppy kiss on her cheek. The look on little Anastasia Romanov's face is one of peace and delight. It is the look of a child who is loved and secure and completely free of pain and fear.

When Anna speaks, her voice is clear and calm, without a tremor. "This was the tercentenary of the Romanovs in Moscow." She pauses for a moment. "I remember everything about that day."

It is cruel, really, how the Producer set her up. Because seconds later the shot changes to a clip of soldiers storming the Winter Palace. One moment the family laughs together and the next there is revolution.

There is a commotion at the front of the room as Frederick and Dominique chastise the Producer. They are indignant that he would show her this clip without warning or permission. They demand he offer an apology while he insists no wrongdoing. Anna hears all of this but pays it little mind. Because when she stands to leave the room she finds that the Producer's assistant has been filming her reaction to the footage. This visit was a setup. They lured her here to get a tawdry clip they could add to their ridiculous film. They are charlatans, like all the others.

When her hands stop shaking Anna faces the Producer. "You do not have my permission to use the footage you just shot. Do you understand? Not in your film. Not ever."

"I think you have misconstrued—"

"I will sign no papers. I will take no part in this. Not today. Not at any point. And if I find out you have violated my wishes you will be contacted directly by my attorneys."

"Please, I beg you to reconsider—"

Dominique is cursing beneath her breath—an eye-raising amount of profanity from such a pretty mouth—and Frederick looks as though he has eaten something rotten. The two of them are angry and appalled. Ashamed. As though this were their fault somehow. And perhaps it is, Anna thinks; they should have known better. They should not have insisted she come.

"I am *tired* of being exploited," Anna says and then walks from the studio.

TEN YEARS EARLIER

The High Court of Hamburg, Germany
March 30, 1958

"I don't know what else they want!" Anna screams. "Haven't I given them everything they've asked for?"

She feels like a toddler throwing a fit. Still, she cannot help herself. Overcome with exhaustion and fury, Anna grabs the closest thing she can find and throws it at Prince Frederick. He ducks as the small leather-bound journal goes sailing past his head. It hits the wall with a wet clapping sound, then drops to the floor, its pages fluttering open to some diary entry that Anna has abandoned after half a page. Her handwriting is jittery and so is her voice. They're standing in a sparse conference room in the Twenty-fourth Chamber for Civil Cases in the High Court of Hamburg and Frederick has just told her that the court has asked for more evidence.

She is well over fifty years old, yet he insists on treating her like a child. His voice has the pained, gentle tone of a frustrated parent. "They need more photographs of you as a young child—"

"How, pray tell, am I supposed to get those? They're in *Russia*, for God's sake. With the rest of my family's things. Assuming they haven't been burned or stolen or pillaged like everything else."

She does not tell him about the photo album hidden in her dacha. There is only one other person who knows about its contents, and neither of them can present it as evidence to the courts without jeopardizing her case at large. Judges tend to frown upon withheld evidence.

"They want handwriting specimens," Frederick continues calmly. "And nearer proof of your relationship to the witnesses. They want every document we have that might give bearing on the case."

"We gave it all to them. Years and years ago. I wrote pages for them. Even went to all that trouble to have my ear photographed. My *ear* of all things!" Anna runs out of steam and drops to the nearest chair.

Frederick squats down in front of her. She is so small that they are nearly eye to eye. "You know it was all lost during the war when your lawyer's office was bombed in Berlin."

"No. No," she protests. "There was more. He had more stored at another building."

"That too was lost."

"How is that possible?"

"The Central District Court was in the Soviet sector of the city afterward. Whatever evidence that could have supported your case has long since been destroyed. All of the original exhibits are gone. We have to do this over again. We have no choice. Not if you want this to be over. Not if you want to move on with your life. You do want that, right? *Please* tell me you want that. Please tell me this isn't a game to you. We're all too damn old for games."

Anna isn't ready to give up yet. She doesn't want to go through this whole routine again. "Annette Fallows has everything. All of Edward's files. He kept meticulous copies. Maybe we can—"

"Stop. Annette hates you. You know this. She hasn't gotten over what happened."

"Edward's death was not my fault! Am I to be blamed for *everything*?"

"She doesn't hate you for her father's death. She hates you because Edward Fallows gave everything he owned—his entire estate—to advance your case and she was left to pay his debts. Annette is only now piecing her life back together."

It's been years since Anna allowed herself to feel guilty for the overwhelming sacrifice of her first attorney. She never asked him to spend his fortune in her defense and condemn his wife and daughter to poverty. "Perhaps if I speak with her myself—"

"No. We cannot go to her again. We have to do this the hard way." Frederick pinches the narrow stretch of bone between his eyes again. He's been doing this all morning; the bridge of his nose will be bruised if he keeps at it much longer.

Anna snorts. "I didn't realize there was a way other than hard."

It is raining in Hamburg, a blistering, angry deluge that lashes the courthouse and makes the wind scream in outrage as it swirls below the eaves. Anna knew she shouldn't have come. She knew better than to let Frederick talk her into this.

"I want to go home," she finally says.

"I'll take you home. But please, come to the courtroom first. At least listen to Pierre Gilliard's testimony."

"Why? So I can be tormented by yet another traitor?"

"He's not a traitor, Anna. He's old. And he's confused. He suffered too."

"I am not Christ. I cannot bear my own suffering, much less his."

"Then come and learn. His testimony will give us an idea of how this case will go. We'll know what tactic to try next."

———

"Who is that woman in the front row?" Anna whispers, pointing at a gorgeous brunette seated right behind the prosecution. She's wearing a black cashmere sweater, a pencil skirt, and lipstick the color of crushed raspberries. There's a notepad on her lap and a devious grin on her face. Even from this distance she looks both formidable and provocative. *Ah, to be French*, Anna thinks.

They are sitting in the far corner of the upper balcony, partially hidden behind a large granite column. There are only a handful of people on the second level, and none of them pay attention to the small, fine-boned woman and her well-tailored companion. Instead, they're watching the clamor below. The courtroom is filled with press and busybodies. Scandalmongers and tabloid photographers. European royalty and a pack of distant Romanov relatives led by Dmitri Leuchtenberg. He sits in the second row, looking smug. All of these spectators want to be as close to the action as possible and are crammed into the seats below, shoulder to shoulder. Frederick telegrammed the court a week earlier, letting them know that Anna would not be in attendance. So no one is watching for her. No one notices her at all. It is the only way she can relax enough to focus on the proceedings. Anna hates photographers. She hates cameras pointed at her and the bright, startling snap of a flashbulb. But most of all she hates giving statements to the press. They always want to know how she *feels*, and she always wants to poke them in the eye with a freshly sharpened pencil.

"That," Prince Frederick says, in answer to her question, his voice dripping with appreciation, "is Dominique Aucléres. She's a reporter with *Figaro*. I hear she's very good. Very . . . thorough."

Anna snorts. Thorough. *Is that what they're calling it these days?*

"Is it common to have three judges presiding over a case?" she asks, nodding toward the bench where an alarmingly young blonde woman in jurist's robes sits between two older scowling gentlemen.

Frederick gives her the side-eye. "This is a *tribunal*, Anna. Judge and jury all at once."

"That one in the middle looks like a pinup girl. She doesn't seem old enough to have finished university, much less sit a bench."

"That is Judge Reisse. And she is far older than she looks. Far more frightening as well. She's considered to have one of the best legal minds in Germany," he says, then adds, "Whatever you do, don't piss her off. That woman is your best hope of a favorable verdict. But she also loves a good courtroom tussle and is known to change her opinions without warning."

"And the others?"

"Equally dangerous. More conventional. But less testy. Age has mellowed them a bit." He points to each of the men. "Werkmeister and Backen."

Now that Anna has resigned herself to watch the proceedings, her sense of humor has returned. "Do you know what the press is calling this? The 'Trial of Doubt and Coincidence' and the 'Lawsuit of Ghosts.'"

"Ignore them."

"Difficult, given that they use the front pages of their newspapers to scream at me." She points to the man sitting at the defendant's table. "And of course there's Gilliard, more than willing to give them fodder."

"They only called him because he wrote that damnable book. Remember, Gilliard does not represent the imperial family. He speaks for himself. Don't be too hard on him, Anna. Few of us wouldn't do the same if a gun were placed to our heads."

Anna's eyes have grown lighter with age but they are still a crisp and penetrating blue. "Must we speak of guns today?"

The session is called to order and the crowd whispers now instead of shouting across the room. All eyes are turned toward the front where Judge Werkmeister, president of the Hamburg tribunal, calls Pierre Gilliard forward to give his testimony. The famed Romanov tutor is showing his age. Seventy-eight years old, with silver hair and bad joints, he moves slowly to the bar, wearing a dark suit and obvious disdain. In his hands is a copy of his book, *The False Anastasia*, and he grips it like a life preserver. Anna studies her fingernails while the judges go through the preliminary questions. She knows all these answers, has heard them for years. Pierre Gilliard was tutor to the imperial family. He served them for over a decade, and he went into exile with them after the revolution. Gilliard accompanied the family, right up to the train station in Ekaterinburg, and was one of the last people to see them all alive. He has denounced Anna's claim to the rights and title of Anastasia Romanov since he met with her in Berlin in 1925. That encounter is documented in great detail in his book. But no one knows about their second meeting in 1954. He has chosen not to publish *those* details.

Anna returns her attention to the bench when she hears Gilliard speaking, and she realizes she has missed a question from the judges.

"The intimates of the Russian court have been categorical on this subject," Gilliard says. "None of them could find the slightest resemblance between that woman and Anastasia Romanov. Not a single one of them."

Judge Werkmeister drops his chin and raises his eyebrows,

looking like a dubious turkey. "How do you know that?" he asks.

"They have told me a hundred times."

"A *hundred* times?" the judge asks. "This is not a classroom. And we have not invited you here to give lessons on hyperbole. I remind you, Herr Gilliard, that you must be ready to swear to what you say."

Anna has always found it odd that in German courtrooms the witness is only sworn in after giving testimony and usually only if the testimony is considered highly relevant or if the justices are trying to catch a witness perjuring himself.

Gilliard clears his throat and straightens his spine. "If I said a hundred times, I meant many times. As for Anastasia's own aunt, she issued a peremptory declaration to the Danish newspapers. That can be easily verified as it is part of the official record."

"Again, I remind you that, as a witness, we have called you here to tell us only what you yourself have seen and experienced."

The old tutor sighs, and Anna cannot help but smile. She has always found that teachers are the least teachable of all people. Pierre Gilliard has to restrain himself from lecturing the judges as they continue with a relentless series of questions. Judge Reisse is the hardest on him. She wants to know specifics of his meeting with Anna in 1925. Where they met. What time of day it was. How long they spoke. Anna decides she likes Reisse immensely when she asks Gilliard if he can remember what Anna wore that day.

He looks dumbfounded at the question. "What she wore? I don't have the slightest idea. Why is that important?"

"Because," Judge Reisse smiles sweetly, "you say in your book that you performed a 'thorough investigation.'"

"I did."

"Then you should remember all of those details. They were enough to convince you that the plaintiff is not Grand Duchess Anastasia."

"But her clothing has nothing to do with that." Pierre Gilliard nearly growls through his clenched jaw when he speaks again. "I wrote my book so that I would not have to remember the details. I cannot recall them anymore."

Judge Backen has been content to listen until this point, but he speaks now, dryly. "Ordinarily a witness who knows that he is going to be heard finds a way to freshen his memory."

Gilliard lifts his book and shakes it before the judges. *"Monsieur le Président,"* he says, voice trembling, "I wrote this thirty-five years ago, and I can swear that everything in it is true."

"A book is not evidence, Herr Gilliard," Judge Backen says. He doesn't blink or show the slightest bit of emotion. Anna cannot, for the life of her, decipher what he's thinking.

Judge Reisse adjusts her robe, pulling the collar away from her neck so it doesn't chafe. "Your account of those events is of little interest to the court. We would, however, love to see your original documentation. You cite it thoroughly in your book. Of particular interest are a series of letters you say your wife, Shura Tegleva, received from the empress's sister. You place great weight on them given that she was a governess in the Romanov household."

"Not just a governess," he says. "Anastasia's governess."

Frederick leans toward Anna and whispers in her ear. "Shura died three years ago. Pierre hasn't been the same since."

Judge Reisse continues. "It was these letters that first convinced you to meet with Anastasia in Berlin, yes?"

"Yes. But I met with Anna Anderson, *not* Anastasia," he stresses.

"I want to see your correspondence with the duke of Leuchtenberg. And also the entirety of your written exchanges with Harriet von Rathlef, one of the plaintiff's first supporters.

You state in your book it was these conversations that led you with certainty to believe that she is not Anastasia Romanov." The judge points to the book in Gilliard's hands. He is now grasping it to his chest and stroking as though about to swear on the Bible. "In your book, *The False Anastasia*, you published photographs and handwriting samples. But the court has not been granted access to any of the original documents. Will you make them available?"

"No," Pierre Gilliard says resolutely. There is a good ten seconds of stunned silence in the courtroom before he explains himself. "I do not have them anymore."

"Why not?"

"I destroyed the entire dossier after the last court ruled against her. I thought the case was closed. I didn't think I needed to keep my research any longer."

Judge Reisse's voice is a low, dangerous purr. "What did you do with those documents?"

"I burned them."

"A historian who burns his archives," she says, bending over the bench and getting as close to the withered old tutor as possible, "is like a corpse that stinks."

"I can look!" he says, desperate. "Perhaps there is still something left in my safe-deposit box."

"This witness is dismissed," Judge Werkmeister says in disgust.

Frederick is helping Anna to her feet when a lawyer for the defense rises quickly from his seat and says, "We would like to call another witness."

The tribunal looks none too pleased at this surprise but they confer among themselves for a moment. "Who?" Werkmeister asks.

"His name is Hans-Johann Mayer. In 1918 he was a prisoner of war being held in Ekaterinburg in the basement of the Ipatiev House. He was an eyewitness to the slaughter of the entire Romanov family and can prove, definitively, that Anastasia Romanov is dead."

————

"No. No. No. It can't be. I have never seen that man before," Anna says, gripping the rail and leaning forward. She no longer cares if anyone in the courtroom discovers her presence. But, again, no one is looking at her. All eyes are on the tall bald man with perfect posture. He must be several years older than Anna, but he has aged very well and moves like a man in his forties. As he takes his place at the bar a spectral quiet settles over the courtroom.

"Please state your name for the court," Judge Reisse says. She has the pinched look of a woman who has just been given vinegar when she thought she was getting wine.

"Hans-Johann Mayer."

"And you are German?"

"Austrian."

"How did an Austrian come to be a prisoner of war in Siberia in 1918?"

"The same way Russians, Germans, Ukrainians, and a handful of Mongolians ended up there as well. The Bolsheviks were no respecters of persons, I'm afraid. They hated everyone equally." He smiles at the judges and then turns to the courtroom to let everyone see the grin. "Have an opinion, rot in jail. If that wasn't their official mantra it was certainly close to it. As for me personally, I had the great misfortune of being in Petrograd the previous October when the Bolsheviks wrested control away from the provisional government. Wrong place. Wrong time. Long train ride to exile."

"And why were you in Petrograd to begin with?" Judge Reisse asks.

Mayer sighs and there is a wistful note to his voice. "A woman."

And, just like that, he has everyone in the palm of his hand. The Austrian is handsome, funny, and well spoken. Anna feels a pit begin to open in her stomach. "Where did they find this man?" she whispers to Prince Frederick. "I don't like him."

"I don't know," he says, looking rather dispirited. Everything that Anna feels is being played out on her friend's face. "But this isn't good."

For his part, Hans-Johann Mayer is a master storyteller. And the tale he spins before the court is not only compelling, but is immensely probable and peppered with enough details to be damnably believable as well. He makes no attempt to hide the fact that he has recently serialized his story in a tabloid called 7-*Tage*. He makes no apologies for this but simply explains that he is only now appearing before the court because he has finally made his story public.

"I was, as you can imagine, traumatized for many years."

Anna's voice is dry as dust when she says, "It must have been horrible for him."

"He's very good," Prince Frederick growls.

"What's worse, he's charming. Just look at Judge Reisse."

The beautiful blonde jurist is listening raptly, her lips pursed in thought, her full concentration bent on this witness.

Mayer goes on to explain that once imprisoned in the Ipatiev House in Ekaterinburg he was put to work doing menial labor. He was kept in a small room in the cellar, and it was there, he says, that the imperial family was brought on the night of July 17, 1918. His account of what happened next is detailed and shocking; it leaves many of the journalists looking ill, dabbing at their eyes, and covering their mouths. Mayer describes the slow thump of footsteps descending the cellar stairs. The questions of confused children. A tired family yanked from their beds. And then silence in the cellar as their captors leave and go into an adjacent room and drink enough vodka to finish the task. Mayer describes in detail, and with shaking voice, what gunshots sound like in an enclosed space and how the smell of gunpowder can drift beneath a closed door. He tells of screaming and crying and the dull thud of gunmetal hitting human flesh. The worst sound, he explains, was the silence afterward and the knowledge of what it meant. None of that could compare to what the Bolsheviks asked him to do next, however. Hans-Johann Mayer was taken into the cellar and told to help load the bodies onto a wagon. He tells the court how those bloodied, battered bodies lay still and mangled in death. He tells them of the iron-laced stench of blood mixed with the scent of bodily waste voided upon death. How he wretched until his throat was raw and bloodied. He tells them with tears in his eyes how those sights and sounds have haunted him every day since. Mayer explains to Judges Reisse, Werkmeister, and Backen how desperate he was to believe that a Romanov, any Romanov, had survived the slaughter and how he followed those soldiers into the woods. Mayer waited until the soldiers left to fetch supplies so they could destroy the evidence of their grisly deeds. Only then did he creep forward. His voice is hollow when he explains that, in the middle of a warm summer night he stood in the clearing known as Pig's Meadow and counted the bodies of seven Romanovs and four servants and wept because he had been unable to save any of them.

"You have to understand," Mayer says, turning toward his audience. "There is no one who wanted that young woman to live more than I did. That's why I went there at risk to my own life. If she had been alive I would have helped her. But none of them survived that night. I speak the truth in this. Anastasia Romanov is gone."

The gavel is a distinctly American symbol, and Anna has watched her fair share of Hollywood films in which a judge bangs his gavel to bring order or closure to the court. The gavel is not a tool used in German courts, and there certainly is not one in the room today, but she can hear the pounding in her mind anyway. She knows with certainty how the judges will decide, and she is confirmed in this belief when Mayer produces a single piece of evidence to support his claim: an official Bolshevik announcement of the imperial family's execution, which he claims to have received from the Ural Regional Soviet in Ekaterinburg and smuggled out of Russia on his release a short time after the massacre.

Anna's lawyers fly into action, insisting the judges give them time to refute Mayer's account. They question his credibility and recent appearance, given that the case is decades old. They beg for more time. They demand that he be officially sworn in. The fact that her attorneys are so stunned by this new development seems to work against them.

After a brief huddle, Werkmeister announces that "the objections raised by the petitioner against the credibility of the witness Mayer are not valid. We will hear no other witnesses in this matter."

The verdict comes, not days or weeks later as Anna and Frederick expect, but that very afternoon. By the time Mayer steps away from the bar, it has grown late and dark and a cold wind howls through the streets of Hamburg, whipping the rain into little cyclones in the gutter. Frederick and Anna decide to stay the night and drive to the Black Forest the following day. They are called back to the courtroom before they've had time to collect all of their belongings from the small conference room where the day began.

It is Judge Werkmeister who delivers the verdict while Judges Reisse and Backen nod in agreement.

"It is the belief of this court," Werkmeister says, "that Mayer's knowledge of these details can only have come from things he witnessed firsthand. We do not believe they were gleaned from other writings, stories, or rumors circulating at the time of these events. It is the belief of this court that his account is true, that the entire Romanov family was murdered in 1918, and therefore we deny the petitioner's suit to be legally recognized as Anastasia Romanov."

Anna sits back, bewildered, as the judges rise from their bench and begin to adjust their robes. Bedlam overtakes the courtroom as flashbulbs go off and a din of voices erupts. Dmitri Leuchtenberg looks as though he's just been declared the king of England.

"I don't understand—" Anna says.

"We can appeal. I refuse to let it end like this," Prince Frederick says. There is metal in his voice, and his hands are wrapped around the railing like shackles.

Neither of them notices the stunning brunette who settles into the chair beside Frederick until she speaks. "I think an appeal is a brilliant idea," she says.

They look at her in astonishment.

"Forgive me," the brunette says. "I saw you up here in the balcony when they called for a verdict. If I'd known you were here today I would have sat with you all along." She smiles, bright and cheerful—as though this were not in fact a terrible day—and sticks out her lovely, long-fingered hand in greeting. "My name is Dominique Aucléres and I would like to help with your case."

THREE YEARS EARLIER

Paris, France
August 1955

Ingrid Bergman is nothing like Anna thought she would be. Lovely, yes. Thin enough to make Anna cringe with envy. Glamorous. Statuesque. Exotic in that cool, disinterested Swedish way. All of these things, of course. But what strikes

Anna most is simply how *kind* the woman is. They sit in her dressing room, on the set of her Twentieth Century Fox film, *Anastasia*, drinking tea and eating thin, frosted cookies that taste like pure sugar. Anna isn't going to complain, however. She still isn't sure this is actually happening; to criticize the food might spoil the illusion.

"Thank you for accepting my invitation. I didn't think you would," Bergman says.

"I didn't think it was real."

The Actress laughs—Anna has to give her this moniker. To admit that she is sitting in a room with one of the world's most beloved actresses is too much to wrap her mind around. "What convinced you, then? Apparently not the stationery."

"No. I get letters all the time. That's easy enough to fake. It was the offer of an all-expenses-paid trip to Paris. I decided to call your bluff."

The Actress's smile is wide, nearly blinding. "I assure you, this is no bluff."

"So I see." If Anna had actually believed this was real she would have worn something nicer. It's probably a good thing that she assumed it was just another cruel joke—right up until the limousine pulled to a stop at her hotel—because she came as herself, and it immediately disarmed the Actress. "What I don't understand is why you wanted me to come in the first place."

The Actress thinks for a moment, trying to figure out how to answer. When she speaks, there's a slight accent to her voice, mellow now that she's no longer trying to sound American; the Swedish is coming through.

"People think this is an easy job. They assume you just pop in front of a camera and look pretty, that you dance or laugh or cry on command. But what most people don't realize is that you have to *find* the character first." She reaches out and braves a single pat of Anna's hand. "This is the first time in my career that my character can actually, literally be found, you see. You're all over the weekly papers. You have been for years. They call you the 'Empress of Unterlengenhardt' and the 'Hermit of the Black Forest.'"

"I am a milch cow for the journalists," Anna says.

The Actress sounds like carbonated joy when she laughs. "You are funny."

"Most people don't think so. Most people call me a liar and a fraud."

"Would you like to know what they call me?" Again that bewitching smile. "Adultress. Whore. The 'star who fell from heaven.' I was denounced on the floor of the American Senate as being a 'powerful influence for evil.' If I had the choice I would prefer to be called a liar any day. I am an actress after all. That's what I do for a living. I lie all day long in front of the camera and no one cares a whit. The difference, I suppose, is that I get paid for it while you get punished."

"Do you think I'm lying?" Anna asks. The Actress's answer to this question will determine whether she stays for the remainder of this meeting.

"I don't care."

Anna blinks at her a few times. She expected a hard answer on either side. Anything but ambivalence.

"I realize that sounds harsh. And I apologize. But the issue of lying is irrelevant. What I want to know can't be verified by anyone but you."

"And what exactly do you want to know?"

"What drove you off the Bendler Bridge."

Anna sets her teacup down carefully on the saucer, then places it on the small table beside her. The dressing room is spacious and bright. Soft pink walls and floor-to-ceiling windows covered in gauzy curtains. There are costumes and shoes scattered about. An entire apothecary's selection of perfumes and makeup. Lamps covered with scarves to mute the light.

Bottles and boxes and powders of all sorts. It is the lair of a star, and there is Ingrid Bergman herself, wearing gray slacks and a white cashmere sweater. Her feet are bare, and there's not a stitch of makeup on her face. Her hair is pulled back and tied with a ribbon at the nape of her neck. She looks serene and comfortable in her own skin. And the only thing she wants to know is why Anna tried to kill herself. The irony of this is impossible to escape. One of the worst moments of Anna's life has become one of the most interesting things about her.

Anna can't explain what makes her tell the truth. The word simply comes unbidden from her. "Despair."

The Actress is neither triumphant nor pitying. She simply nods as though she expected as much. "I know what that feels like. To be disgraced. To be hated and driven to extremes. But I don't know what drove *you* to feel those things. And I can't make this film until I do." She smiles briefly. "As you know, this is my return to the American screen. This is my chance at redemption, at finding my way back to who I used to be. And I realize that I have to use you to accomplish it. There are only slivers of resemblance between this fiction and your life. But it begins with you, in Berlin, on that bridge. You are the seed of inspiration. My character shares your name. That's why I invited you here. I need your help."

Anna can feel herself leaning forward, hypnotized by that smooth voice, eager to comply. No wonder this woman holds the world in the palm of her hand. Still, she isn't ready to acquiesce just yet. "I fear you are wrong in assuming that I know anything about your movie. What news I receive in the Black Forest is rarely accurate or on time."

The Actress is genuinely surprised at this. "Oh," she says. "Forgive me. I often assume the entire world knows my business before I do. The story revolves around a clever young woman who has lost her memory. It is a melodrama inspired by a play written by Marcelle Maurette." Here she stops and blushes. "Mademoiselle Maurette was horribly embarrassed to learn, only after her play was published, that you were still alive. She assures me that she would have consulted you otherwise."

"A convenient platitude now that she has made her fortune," Anna says. "But it does explain the current legal situation the producers of your film are facing, I suppose. Twentieth Century Fox is having to pay for her omission."

If the Actress is bothered by this jab she doesn't let on. The legalities are not hers to worry about. Instead she chooses to offer Anna specifics about the film, much the way she would if giving an interview. "The story begins with a young woman on the Bendler Bridge in Berlin, ready to take her own life. She is rescued and later persuaded by three power-hungry Russian émigrés to impersonate Grand Duchess Anastasia for the purposes of swindling the dowager empress, the late tsar's mother. As you know, I play Anna. But you may not have heard that Yul Brynner is playing her lover, and Helen Hayes is playing the dowager empress. The cast is impressive. So is the script. And I am delighted to be a part. Principal photography is taking place in Paris, Copenhagen, and London." It is here that Ingrid Bergman looks like a small girl, delighted by her surroundings. "I cannot wait to film at the Eiffel Tower and the Tivoli Gardens. You can't imagine how lovely they are."

But she can imagine. Anna went to see the Eiffel Tower at sunset last night and stayed until the sky looked like black ink littered with silver confetti.

Anna pulls a large envelope from her purse and slides out a single sheet of paper. It is filled with legal jargon and disclaimers. "I have yet to be convinced why I should sign this waiver your studio sent."

"You have read it then?"

"Many times," Anna says.

"And you have objections?"

"I object to being bought."

"Most people do. But I'm told that signing will earn you thirty thousand U.S. dollars. That's a great deal of money."

Anna looks pointedly at the Actress, a woman known for her lavish lifestyle. "Is it?"

Ingrid Bergman gives a hearty, genuine laugh. "They warned me you were sharp. And no, I suppose it's not a great deal of money to someone like me—"

"But someone like me should be grateful?"

"No. That's not what I was going to say at all."

"Then what?"

"Simply that I care not a whit about money, regardless of the amount."

"Spoken like a true film star."

"Meaning a lie?"

Anna studies the dressing room and notes the trappings of Ingrid Bergman's wealth. "Meaning well acted but totally disingenuous."

The Actress shrugs. It's a simple gesture, as though she's shaking off the insult, and that one small movement makes Anna feel a flicker of shame.

"Believe what you want," the Actress says, "but I have learned the old adage well. Money cannot buy happiness."

"Perhaps not. But it makes a nice down payment."

Another hearty laugh and the Actress gazes at Anna with genuine fondness. "How much is enough, then, if not the amount offered?"

"It doesn't matter. My lawyers will take the lion's share regardless. You can't imagine the legal fees I've accrued through the years."

"Ah, I see."

"Don't feel sorry for me. I despise pity," Anna says.

"As do I. And I wouldn't insult you with it."

Anna believes her. And it is only for this reason that she takes a pen from the dressing table and scrawls her name on the line at the bottom of the waiver. She hands it to the Actress matter-of-factly. "Please do not portray me as a fool. I am tired of being the punch line."

When the Actress takes Anna's hand this time it is with great tenderness. "You have my promise. But please, I need to know your story. Tell me. I must know why you were in Berlin that night, on that bridge. I need to know what you felt."

So Anna tells her. The story is long, and heart-wrenching, and there is silence in the dressing room afterward. She leaves Ingrid Bergman curled up in her chair like a stunned child, her eyes red, her perfect porcelain cheeks wet with tears, and a signed waiver in her hands.

Anastasia

HOUSE ARREST

1917

Alexander Palace, Tsarskoe Selo, Russia
April 9

As soon as we enter the sitting garden Alexey sees the indecent figures scrawled on the garden wall. The walled enclosure filled with willow trees, stone benches, and a large, clear reflecting pool is my favorite spot on the palace grounds. And now the guards have ruined it.

They are so full of disdain for my family that they have taken to studying us, watching for the things that give us pleasure and then systematically ruining them. I must have smiled on one of our previous visits. Or made a passing comment about its beauty. A sigh would have been enough, really, to betray my feelings. The guards are several paces behind, no doubt waiting for us to discover the graffiti, positioning themselves to witness our horror.

"Is that . . . ?" Alexey asks, and I follow the long, thin line of his finger to the crude phallic symbol.

Dr. Botkin clamps a protective hand over his son's eyes. Gleb has joined us in the garden today, mostly to keep Alexey company, but also because he is his father's shadow and cannot stay away for more than a day or two. The square line of Botkin's jaw goes tight, teeth clenched together as he studies what Alexey has found. "Look away, children."

But it is too late. We've all seen the picture of Rasputin sodomizing our mother. It is scrawled in red paint, the caricatures clearly meant to portray the two of them enjoying the vile act. I look at the ground, at the dirty toe of my slipper as it pokes out from the hem of my skirt. Shame. Embarrassment. Anger. I shake with that anger, clenching my fists, fighting the sudden urge to hit something. No, someone, the junior lieutenant they call Semyon, to be exact. He follows us on our walks, always skulking nearby. Leering and laughing. He stares at my sisters' bosoms as they pass, and Kerensky does nothing to stop him. He has thrown so many rocks at Tatiana's little dog, Ortimo, that the poor thing refuses to walk with us anymore.

The sight of that drawing makes me want to strike Semyon. But tsarevnas do not hit. It is a phrase Mother has repeated to me—never to my sisters; they don't need the reminder—a thousand times. Tsarevnas do not hit. So I decide to hurl a rock instead. Semyon has thrown his fair share in the last month. Why shouldn't it be my turn? The guards are not far away and I have wicked aim, so I bend to pick up a gray stone the size of a small egg, certain I can hit Semyon if he comes close enough. I nestle it in my palm, waiting, hoping for an opportunity.

"Not such a lovely garden anymore, is it?" Semyon, with his oily voice and the narrow gap between his front teeth. I can see him press his tongue against the gap, can see that little bulge of pink between the white. He has crept up behind us and laughs as we blush. "Would you like me to draw one of you? I'd be happy to pose with you. Or maybe you'd like a turn with the heretic as well?" His voice is drawling, scurrilous. "Perhaps you've already been with Rasputin? I know your mother has."

I've always considered the garden to be mine, and I fear my love of the place has inspired them to ruin it. So at first I think he's talking to me. But he's looking over my shoulder at Olga. Tall, pretty, slender Olga. Oldest, privileged daughter. His favorite target. She shrinks from him as he reaches out a hand to stroke her face.

Dr. Botkin steps between them. Tall and broad and filled with righteous indignation. He is the imperial physician, chaperoning today's excursion so he can keep watch over us. "How dare you? You have no right to touch her!"

"She is a prisoner," Semyon says. "Prisoners have no rights."

"She is a tsarevna."

"Not anymore."

There, he's given me permission. Tsarevnas do not hit. But I'm not one anymore. I pull my arm back, ready to loose the stone in my hand, but Botkin grabs my wrist with his free hand—the other is still covering Gleb's face—and drags me against his side. He disguises the movement as an act of comfort, but he is protecting me. The barest shake of his noble head makes his intent clear. No. He will not let me provoke the soldiers into further aggression.

What little hair Botkin has left is trimmed close to his head, making him look almost entirely bald, but he has a full, black goatee and bright green eyes that flash when he's angry. I've always thought that he looks very Balkan. Very fierce. Semyon has the good sense to walk away from him.

Botkin turns Gleb away from the wall and releases him. The physical similarities between father and son are so startling it appears as though Botkin spit the boy directly out of his mouth. Eyes, large and a bright sort of green, that radiate extreme kindness. Full smiles that tilt a bit higher on the left side than the right. Strong, straight noses. Small ears that sit close to their heads. And dark hair that would be wavy if it were not religiously cropped.

"I apologize, Anastasia," Gleb says with a pained expression that mirrors his father's. "It is crass of him to treat you this way."

"It's what he does. Don't apologize for him."

Gleb is four years my junior but already two inches taller. I suspect he harbors something of a crush on me as well. "Someone must apologize. I'm happy for it to be me."

Satisfied with our reaction, the guards wander away to inspect Semyon's handiwork. They slap one another on the back. Point at my mother's naked figure. They have accomplished their goal and we are no longer needed for their entertainment. But the damage is done. My sisters are shaken, Botkin is enraged, and Alexey has gone pale and quiet. Unlike the rest of us, he didn't turn from the graffiti during Semyon's little tirade, and his young gaze is filled with the sight. I can see a clouding in his eyes, the loss of innocence, and I squeeze the stone in my palm so tightly that the skin across my knuckles stretches white.

"Come along, Alexey," Botkin urges.

But he stays fixed to the path, staring at the garden wall. "Rasputin," he says.

"*Our friend* Rasputin," Olga corrects automatically, as we've been trained to say whenever speaking of the mystic. Mother insists on it still, even though he has been dead several months and, until recently, was buried in the park.

The first thing Kerensky's soldiers did upon taking control of the palace was to exhume and dismember the body of Grigory Rasputin. We watched from the second-story window as the coffin was dropped in the courtyard and the lid thrown off. Mother immediately fled to her room in horror. But no one protected the rest of us from the grisly sight. We stood aghast as Semyon pried a brick loose from the ground and used it to measure the length of Rasputin's decaying penis. My sisters wept and hid themselves in the couch pillows. Only Alexey and I saw him cut it off and display it as a trophy on the end of a bayonet. Semyon had it propped up for weeks afterward in the courtyard, but we kept the curtains drawn on that side of the house until it disappeared one morning. Where it went after Semyon had his fun, no one could say. The rest of Rasputin's body, however, was put on display in Tsarskoe Selo a few miles away.

"*Our friend* Rasputin," Alexey mutters, his soft blue eyes transfixed by the vulgar proportions of the drawn bodies.

Friend or not, I won't repeat the words. My devotion to the mystic waned considerably after suffering that blow on his behalf. Mother might not wear the ring any longer, but I wear a tiny scar above my lip as a result.

"Enough of this," I say and gently pull my brother away. I turn to Botkin. "Is there nothing we can do?"

He looks at my clenched fist and shakes his head. "We can leave. We've complied with Kerensky's orders. We have taken our daily walk."

"But the garden—"

"It will be best if we take a different path tomorrow." Botkin's implication is clear: we won't return to the sitting garden. As we leave I throw my stone into the reflecting pool. It shatters the calm surface of the water, and the disturbance pleases me immensely. It is only a small act of defiance, unseen by the guards, but I am learning those can be the most satisfying.

———

We find Kerensky waiting for us when we return to the palace. He travels from Petrograd only when there is unwelcome news to deliver. He sits in the formal reception room with my parents, and none of them speak as we enter, flustered and hot from our walk. Father stands at the bookcase, his hand on a bound collection of maps, but his eyes are unfocused. Mother knits what appears to be a scarf from delicate pink cashmere. But she is unable to concentrate whenever Kerensky is near, so she has dropped half her stitches. The result is some shapeless thing that she will no doubt pull apart the moment he leaves.

I groan and drop gracelessly into the nearest chair. "What now?" I ask.

"Schwibsik," Mother hisses. "He has come to give us news."

I already regret leaving my rock in the garden. "Bad news, no doubt."

My parents blink at me, startled by my boldness.

"I would watch that daughter of yours, Nicholas. She has a viper's tongue."

Dr. Botkin steps forward then, Gleb no longer in tow. "You will have to pardon her anger, Chairman Kerensky. Anastasia, her sisters, along with Alexey and my son, have just been subjected to vulgar treatment from your soldiers. She has cause for venom."

Mother casts a protective glance at each of us, and Father moves from his place at the shelf, swiveling in the middle of the room, unsure who to comfort first. But Botkin raises a hand, palm out, to reassure them that we are fine.

Kerensky ignores the accusation altogether. "It is good we are all together," he says. "We won't have to do this twice."

Father grinds his teeth. "Do what?"

"Let me show you." And with that Kerensky spins on his heel and leaves the room. We follow him with reluctance out the door and through the grand foyer. He stops at the broad mahogany front doors, waiting for effect. Such theatrics. This is all a game to him. A ridiculous, elaborate game of chess. And we are the pawns he offers up as sacrifice.

Kerensky motions for the guards to open the doors. The guards are young, my age or a little older perhaps, and one of them is in possession of a matching pair of dimples. As we pass through the door he nods at me, ever so slightly. Not enough for Kerensky to notice but enough that I do.

There is a crowd far down the drive, outside the palace gates, nearly two hundred people, and when they see us they begin to scream, to shake their fists and rattle the wrought-iron bars. I have never witnessed a mob before, never seen such raw anger and hatred.

"You did this," Father says.

"No." Kerensky shakes his head. "They came of their own accord. But it is a valuable lesson."

Father's words are hard and tight. "What could it possibly teach us?"

When Kerensky smiles it makes the widow's peak at his forehead more severe. "That you ought to be grateful for the protection I provide within these walls." He lifts an arm to indicate the crowd, and they roar even louder. "Most of these people want you in prison, Nicholas. They want you sent to the Fortress of Saint Peter and Paul. The rest want you dead."

"I have done nothing—"

"This is true. You did *nothing* after a thousand people were trampled to death at your coronation. You did nothing to protect your soldiers during the war, and you left the rest of your countrymen to starve. It must have been then, when you were tired of doing nothing, that you ordered your Imperial Guard to fire on a crowd of unarmed demonstrators who had the *utter gall* to request safe working conditions and fair pay. You don't get to deny your role in this. They call you Nicholas the Bloody for a reason. You have done *plenty*."

Father spits on the polished marble at Kerensky's feet.

Kerensky looks at the spittle dispassionately, then rubs it away with the toe of his shoe. "I think it is time we make some changes, *Citizen Romanov*." He looks around the lavish entrance, from the gilded mirrors to the crystal chandelier, then to us. He takes in our fine clothes and delicate shoes. Kerensky smiles. "I think it is time you learn how to work."

———

We are each given a bucket, a spade, and bags of seeds. Mother remains inside with Alexey. Kerensky has some sense at least.

My brother, barely recovered from his bout with the measles, is too weak for hard labor. Dr. Botkin and Gleb, however, are happy to take their place. Kerensky leads us to the garden himself. He has allowed us to change into the clothes we wear when helping tend wounded soldiers at the hospital. They are the only work clothes we own—simple skirts with white shirtwaists, stiff canvas aprons, and brown leather boots.

"Practical," Maria says with a sniff as she smooths a crease from her apron, "but decidedly unattractive."

Kerensky thrusts a bucket toward her. "And yet half the women in Petrograd do not possess such finery."

Maria takes the bucket without complaint, but a miserable scowl settles over her countenance.

Joy and Jimmy bound in circles at our feet, barking at the wind and the birds. Ortimo, as usual, refused to join us outside, preferring to stay curled up at Alexey's feet, safe from Semyon and his boots. The others are grateful for the fresh air and the chance to run.

The garden, dormant since last fall, is covered by a layer of leaves and mulch. It is enormous, two acres at least, but private—much larger than the kitchen garden, and surrounded by a short stone wall and tall, thin juniper trees. We can hear the protestors at the gate, some distance away, but we cannot see them.

Kerensky kicks a pile of rotting leaves. "Sixty beds should get us started."

Father seems oddly delighted. He loves being outdoors and relishes physical labor. "Where are the plows?" he asks.

"They are called hands and are attached to the end of your arms."

Even Father balks at this. "You can't be serious. It will take us weeks just to prepare the soil. And several more to make the beds."

"Luckily, your social calendar has been cleared. I don't

believe you have any pressing engagements." Kerensky plucks the seed packets from Father's basket and holds them up one by one. "Carrots. Radishes. Onions. Lettuce. And cabbage. I think it is time you learn what every other Russian citizen understands from the time they can walk. If you want to eat, you must coax food from the ground yourself."

7

Anna

VISITORS TO THE BLACK FOREST

1954, 1946

Unterlengenhardt, Germany
July 1954

Anna's garden is filled with the sweet-smelling rot of fallen peaches. She has been ill again—she cannot seem to escape this lingering respiratory malady—and she has missed the harvest. What few peaches remain hang heavy and overripe on their branches. Every brown spot is an indictment of her poor gardening skills. But mostly Anna is furious with herself that she has lost an entire year's worth of jam. It will be dry toast for her until next summer. Anna curses the tree, but that does no good, so she decides to take her ill temper out on the unfortunate man who has chosen this day to visit.

Anna spins, facing him for the second time in five minutes. "Why are you still here?" she demands, purposefully, in German. "I told you to leave."

The Frenchman looks like a mustachioed pencil wearing glasses—painfully slender, expertly groomed, carefully spectacled, and wearing a prim brown bowler hat that matches his nondescript tan suit. "I am attempting to have a civil conversation with you."

"There is nothing civil about an ambush," she says again in German.

"Or about yourself apparently."

"I did not invite you here."

"Nor did you respond to the countless letters I sent."

"Go in the cottage and find them if you can. I get more mail than I can read. There are piles and piles of it inside. But if you can locate your missives among the marriage proposals, accusations, death threats, and opportunistic schemes, I will be happy to respond to them with every curse word that I know. And, just for fun, I'll repeat them in multiple languages so you get the point."

"For a woman who claims to be multilingual, and the Grand Duchess Anastasia, you display an alarming lack of Russian."

"Just because I have not spoken it does not mean I can't," she says.

"I would kindly ask the lady to prove it."

Anna shifts smoothly into Italian. "The lady is not fond of bullies or threats and is disinclined to cooperate."

"Then I have no other option but to conclude that you are a fraud. Neither a Russian speaker nor the woman you claim to be."

Anna grins, broad and malicious. "Do not insult me by suggesting that you have only now come to this conclusion. Your visit here today is an effort to reinforce a long-held position." Now in French.

"That is ridiculous!"

She wipes her hand on her apron, takes three confident steps toward her visitor, and speaks slowly and clearly, in Polish. "I am no fool, Mr. Gilliard. I know who you are and what you're trying to do." Here she switches to perfectly enunciated Russian. "And I know that you have long since made up your mind about me."

This proof of her ability to speak Russian leaves him flustered. "I don't know what you're talking about—"

"You are clearly ignorant, but please don't make yourself a liar as well. Your libelous book, *The False Anastasia*, is lying on top of today's paper in the bag at your feet."

He looks down as though stunned to learn this.

Anna continues, "This interview was futile from the start. You came here under false pretenses and then you accuse me of being uncivil."

He twitches and splutters before her. "That is the most preposterous thing I have ever heard!"

"Oh, go on, make yourself a fool as well. Why not add that to your list of character faults?"

Pierre Gilliard picks up his book bag and slings it over his shoulder with all the animus he can muster. "You look nothing like the Anastasia I have known! I am quite satisfied that you are the most despicable sort of impostor, and I will swear to this every time I am asked, from now until the day I die. The real grand duchess would no more treat a visitor rudely than she would curse a tree for bearing rotten fruit."

"I will not perform as a dancing monkey to convince you of my personage. Your Anastasia, the gentle girl you knew, no longer exists."

He nods once abruptly. "At least we can agree on that. Anastasia is dead."

EIGHT YEARS EARLIER

French Occupation Zone, Near the Border of France and Germany
December 18, 1946

"In all my forty-plus years," Anna says, tucking one pant leg into her boot, "I have never once been *smuggled* before."

It is raining and cold, and the banks of the Weser River have risen up, muddy and brown in protest. For his part, Prince

Frederick pretends not to hear her. His head is bent low in whisper to a rather suspicious-looking man who stands at the end of a shaky dock keeping guard over a small rowboat. Their heads bob in animated conversation, and then, upon reaching an agreement, they shake hands. Anna cannot see the exchange of payment, but she is certain it happens.

"Come quickly," Frederick says. "We don't have much time."

They drove half the night down country roads that resembled little more than footpaths, with the headlights off and very few words between them. She cannot bring herself to tell him about the soldier in Winterstein and how his mind was bent on rape, much less the knife in her hand or how she tried to protect herself. How can a woman tell such a story without going to pieces? It is easier to stuff it down and bury it and never utter a word. And so she spent the entire night, tight-lipped, gripping the handle of her suitcase. After the bombing in Hannover destroyed her home and nearly everything she owned, Anna has only this one small suitcase to her name. Inside are two changes of clothing and a handful of items she keeps from Frederick's curious gaze. The suitcase dangles from her left hand now as she follows him down the dock. For his part, he has a single, oiled-leather satchel slung over one shoulder. His needs are fewer, and his ability to replace provisions is greater.

Their raincoats do not do much to keep out the persistent drizzle, and she can feel an oblong patch of dampness growing along her neck and moving down her spine. Frederick warned her that this would be a miserable journey, but Anna is only now beginning to take in the extent of his meaning.

"What about the car?" she asks. It is parked, empty and forlorn, beneath a giant pine.

He motions toward the Boatman. "Our new friend here will drive it back to town once he has dropped us on the other side of the river."

The man seems neither trustworthy nor capable of carrying

out either task, but she does not mention this to Frederick. He has gone to great trouble and expense to get her to this point, and she is determined not to punish him for it. Truth is, they have no other options.

"Okay, then," Anna says, eyeing the rowboat with trepidation. "Let's go."

It rocks on the choppy water, bow pulling downstream with the current. There are three small bench seats and two sets of oars inside. No one states it explicitly, but it is clear that her job is to be quiet and stay out of the way. She sees nothing on the other, distant bank that would suggest a dock or a safe place to come ashore.

Frederick sees her peering through the gloom and says, "We have to go downstream three miles until we see a campsite on the banks run by the American Red Cross. We will disembark there and be given further instructions."

"Downstream?"

Frederick frowns at the look of concern on her face. "Can't you swim?"

"Yes. Of course," she says. "I'm just not fond of boats, that's all."

"No choice, I'm afraid. Hop in."

The Boatman says nothing during this exchange, or when they load her into the rickety boat, or when they take up the oars. He simply makes quick work of untying the rope and tossing its waterlogged length back onto the dock. And then they push off into the river with such alarming speed that her stomach lurches. Anna grips the seat and closes her eyes tight.

The longer she has known Frederick, the more he amazes her. His list of talents has always staggered her: historian, archeologist, genealogist, philologist, and linguist. But more than that, he has been her friend, her protector, and her defender. He is impetuous, energetic, unrelenting, and utterly devoted.

Now, she learns, he also happens to be one hell of an oarsman. Even the Boatman surveys his strong, sweeping strokes with approval.

They speed on for some time with efficiency, and she grows sicker by the moment as the little boat rises and falls, slapping against the water. It's not until they pull away from the middle of the river and angle toward the opposite bank that things begin to go wrong. The lip of the dinghy dips and suddenly, before they can adjust, water floods the boat, rising to their ankles. Anna realizes only then what great skill and concentration Frederick and the Boatman have expended keeping them upright so far, because both men curse and wobble, their oars flailing, as they try to correct the mistake. The boat tips dangerously to one side and she is certain it will flip entirely. Anna grips the edge of her seat with one hand and the handle of her suitcase with the other. The nausea presses against her throat and her eyes begin to water.

The Boatman speaks for the first time, yelling to be heard above the wind. "We're too heavy! We can't keep taking on water like this or we'll sink."

"Throw out your suitcase!" Frederick screams.

She grips it tighter. "No!"

"Yes!" he bellows, yanking it cleanly from her grip. "This goes or we all do." And then he lobs it into the current.

Anna watches as it spins in the air and lands on top of the water with a fantastic splash. "Have you lost your mind? I need that!"

Frederick glares at her and takes to his oars again. But Anna isn't willing to give up that easily. The case bobs to the surface and when it drifts close enough to the boat she hooks one foot under her seat, leans out, and grabs the handle. Anna is tempted to clock Frederick over the head with it, but she sets it at her feet.

"I have nothing left but what is in this case!" Anna screams, making him the subject of her undiluted rage. "Never do that again. Never!"

And then she leans over the edge and vomits.

Frederick does not offer an apology, but neither does he argue. He looks at her with a stunned sort of pity and then pours every last scrap of energy into forcing the rowboat toward shore. There is a large clearing several hundred yards downstream and Frederick and the Boatman aim for this, heads bent, backs bowed, and arms strained to the point of quivering. As they row she carefully sets the suitcase on her lap, unlocks it, and lifts the lid. Inside, tossed among her clothing, is a photo album given to her by Gleb's sister, Tanya, filled with private pictures of the imperial family, an ivory chess set carved from the tusk of a butchered elephant, a paper knife, and an icon of Saint Anna of Kashin. Relieved to know that they are safe and dry, she clutches the case to her chest and holds on for dear life.

———

In the end, it takes several more days to reach their destination. One of those is spent at the Red Cross camp near the riverbank, drying out, eating, and sleeping. Frederick, ever the worrier, refuses to continue the journey until he is certain she has not come down with some respiratory calamity. Her history with tuberculosis keeps him in a constant state of concern. But after a day goes by and she has no fever, they depart in the company of an American soldier. She never thinks to ask Frederick about the Boatman or how he got back up river.

Their new escort is far more talkative than their first. He is tall, black, and so frightfully handsome that Anna cannot help but stare. He tells them stories of his childhood growing up on a pecan farm along the Brazos River in Texas. He recounts how he joined the military the day after the bombing of Pearl

Harbor, and how he has spent much of his time stationed in France assisting the Red Cross as a medic. He talks about his desire to become a physician when the war is over. The man is a human steamroller, impervious to any obstacle in his way. As he drives them around the closed border of the Soviet zone, and into the Black Forest, Anna begins to believe, for the first time in years, that her quest is possible after all. If this man can defy the odds, so can she.

"Here," he says, handing her a slip of paper when they pull to the side of the road to eat their meager lunch and stretch their legs. "You'll need this pass if you get stopped later."

Anna unfolds the paper and reads the hastily typed form.

PASS NUMBER: 018 774
NAME: Anderson, Anna
NATIONALITY: Not cleared up
PROFESSION: No profession
REASON FOR TRAVELING: To return home

They stop eventually in the town of Bad Liebenzell. It's the first time in years that Anna has felt compelled to ask anyone's name, but she parts without it, happy to think of this man simply as the Soldier. A hero and a friend. From there, Frederick hires a car to take them to Unterlengenhardt, a small village atop a rocky outcrop nearby. Anna decides immediately upon seeing the place that the title "village" is grossly generous. There can't be fifty people who live here year-round. A single road runs down the middle, and on it sits a small general store, one restaurant, a post office, and an inn. It is here that they stay the night. The next morning, after a long sleep, a warm bath, and a hearty breakfast, Frederick walks her down the road.

"This used to be an army barracks," he tells her, motioning toward a clapboard building at the end of a weed-ridden lane.

"But we are having it converted into a cottage for you. You will finally have a place of your own. No more shuffling from house to house, from friend to friend."

He is so happy, so completely proud of himself, that Anna cannot help but return his smile.

"Welcome home, Anastasia!" Prince Frederick shouts, his voice echoing through the empty woods. "I so hope you will be happy here."

8

Anastasia

ONWARD, INTO PERIL

1917

Alexander Palace, Tsarskoe Selo, Russia
June 18

Today is my sixteenth birthday, and I have spent the afternoon making our tutor, Pierre Gilliard, curse in Latin. Or at least I think he's cursing. Latin is the one language I cannot stomach. However, we are put out of our misery when Dova summons me to the imperial bedroom. I hear the words "your mother" and "birthday present" and rush off without thanking Gilliard for his time.

Of all the things I might expect, it is not to find Mother sitting on the floor of her bedroom surrounded by her entire collection of jewels. And not just hers, but Father's as well, along with a number of infamous family heirlooms. I can barely see the carpet for shiny, glittering items. There are ropes of pearls and strings of diamonds. All three of Mother's diadems. Every size and shape broach you can imagine. Rings and bracelets and necklaces. Opals. Emeralds. Sapphires. Rubies. Diamonds. Pearls. Teardrop earrings. Hoop earrings. Chandelier earrings. Diamond, pearl, and gemstone studs. Everywhere I look something sparkles, and each item is more magnificent than the last. Here, a feather fan with a rock crystal handle inset with diamonds and there, a gold and emerald pin in the shape of a bow. Seven Fabergé eggs. A crown, known as the "splendid diadem," that Mother wore to the opening of the Duma. At least four dozen solid silver flowers, set with diamonds and pearls, that can be sewn onto any item of clothing for a special occasion. A stunning broach with a Siberian aquamarine placed in an open lattice with a diamond-set trellis, which Father gave to Mother upon their engagement.

It is a dizzying display, and I stand gaping at it for a full two minutes without uttering a word. I've seen many of these jewels through the years, but they have always been attached to people. And I've never been allowed to play with them.

"What are you doing?" I finally ask.

"Taking an inventory."

"Why?"

"The Americans would call it an insurance policy," she says. There is a blanket across Mother's knees and a corset in her lap. It looks like one of Olga's—the waist is too small to be mine. She holds a seam ripper in her hand and is methodically plucking at a row of stitches, loosening them for some reason I can't fathom. "But that has nothing to do with why I called you here. I want you to pick a pair of earrings. Something small. A pair of studs."

I brighten immediately. "Is this my birthday present?"

"Of course, silly girl. Dr. Botkin is going to pierce your ears. But you have to choose something little or your ears won't heal correctly. It will be months before you can wear anything heavier."

I look at the sea of jewels, overwhelmed.

"Pick something. Quickly. Botkin needs to get back to Alexey. He's fallen off the garden wall again."

I look up sharply. "Is he—"

"No. Just a bruise. But it needs more ice. His shin is swollen."

It might be just a bruise, but that doesn't mean Alexey isn't bleeding. It's simply on the inside. But Mother doesn't want to discuss the realities of anatomy. This latest injury is just another proof of Rasputin's lie. She gives me a smile filled with false assurance and motions to the pile of baubles at her feet.

If I consider everything I'll be here all day. There's too much. In the end I choose a small pair of diamond studs—each roughly one carat—that lie near a magnificent *collier russe*. Compared to the two-foot spray of Indian and Brazilian diamonds, my earrings seem plain and boring.

Once I've made my selection, Botkin orders me to sit on a small stool. I watch with growing dismay as he holds a sewing needle over a candle flame for several minutes. I watch as the thin sliver of metal turns black. He lets it cool on a porcelain saucer while he pinches my right earlobe between two small cubes of ice. One minute. Two. Three. Four. It tickles at first. And then the cold begins to bite and hurt, but I'm determined not to protest. I abhor whining. So I take long breaths through my nose. I squeeze my eyes closed and force myself not to wiggle my feet. Finally, I feel nothing.

"Keep your eyes closed," Botkin says.

But I can't help opening my right eye just a crack and observing with horror how he lifts that needle from that saucer and drives it through my earlobe without the slightest hesitation. There's a hard, prolonged pinch and then he wipes blood from my ear with his handkerchief. I don't feel him put the earring in at all. It's a bit worse the second time but only because I know what to expect.

"Schwibsik," Mother says.

"Yes?"

There is sadness around her eyes when she smiles. "It would be best if you wore your hair down for a while. Especially when you're outside or anywhere near the guards. Do you understand?"

"Yes, Mother."

"Good. Now come here so I can see how they look."

Mother examines me from all sides and clucks with appreciation. Then she gives me a gentle kiss on the cheek, wishes me a happy birthday, and sends me back to whatever remains of my lessons.

ONE MONTH LATER

Alexander Palace, Tsarskoe Selo, Russia
July 10

"You will be leaving Alexander Palace on July 31," Kerensky announces. This time, Kerensky has summoned us to Father's study to deliver his bad news. We've been in the garden all morning, hard at work planting a late crop of cabbages for winter. Our skirts are dingy, our boots caked with mud, and dirt clings beneath our fingernails.

Kerensky sits behind the enormous oak desk, his face inscrutable. His hands rest casually behind his head. Father stops short in the doorway, startled by this audacious intrusion into his personal space.

"What are you doing at my desk?" Father asks.

"It's not your desk. Not anymore. Sit down. We have things to discuss."

I love Father's study. It's smaller and cozier than the formal reception room and always smells of pipe smoke and old books—ink and leather and cracking paper. I settle onto the couch beside Tatiana and kick off my dirty boots. My entire body aches from hours spent picking rocks from hard soil, so I drape myself over the arm of the settee. On the table beside me is a small paper knife with a mother-of-pearl handle. I pick it up and run my finger along its hard, flat edge, then carefully tap the point with the pad of my finger. With any pressure at all it will slice through not just paper but skin as well.

The day that Father returned to the Alexander Palace, his

study was searched and all of his weapons seized. Kerensky took his revolver, a Mauser pistol, a long rifle, six knives, two ceremonial swords, and a variety of other blades, handguns, and weapons. Kerensky insisted that the protection provided us by his soldiers was more than sufficient and that as prisoners we no longer had a right to bear arms. With such obvious weapons at hand Kerensky must have overlooked the paper knife. Yet it has an edge and a point that might come in handy. So I lower my hand slowly and drop it into my boot while no one is looking.

"What do you mean we're leaving?" Mother demands. "For how long?"

I suspect that Kerensky has long since lost patience with my mother, but he still tolerates her inane questions with relative good grace. "Permanently," he says.

Father takes a step toward the occupied territory of his desk. "Unacceptable. This is our home. You cannot force us out."

Kerensky gives him a humorless smile. "As we've discussed before, this residence is owned by the people of Russia. And they want you removed."

"I am not willing to concede the fate of my family to the mob, Chairman."

"Your other option is less appealing, I'm afraid."

"What option is that?"

"The same fate that your beloved Sammi suffered."

A small, keening sound escapes Alexey's throat as he drops into the chair beside Maria. "What did you do to him?" my brother asks.

"I put a bullet in his skull two days after your father came home."

We haven't been allowed to visit Sammi, the African bull elephant we keep as a pet, since we were put under house arrest. But there are a hundred things we haven't been able to do and, honestly, we have given the elephant little thought. We assumed he, like all the other animals in Alexander Park, has been cared for by the gamekeepers.

Alexey feels that Sammi is his. This isn't far from the truth. For the last one hundred years an elephant has lived on the palace grounds and is a required part of the education of all future tsars. Father and Alexey have regularly visited the elephant enclosure for years. They feed Sammi and watch him swim. He is gentle and enormous and, odd as it might seem, Sammi was an integral part of our childhood. Now, four months after the fact, we learn that he has been dispatched as though he were a lame horse or a rabid dog.

My sisters are pale. Appalled. Mouths open, eyes wide and rimmed with tears. I cannot see Mother's expression because she has turned her face to the floor, but I expect she is simmering with that helpless fury that has consumed her these past weeks.

Kerensky notes our long silence, then asks, "Do you know how difficult it is to kill an elephant?" When no one answers, he proceeds to give us the ghastly details. "There are rifles so large they are, in fact, called elephant guns. The Americans and British specialize in making them. They do love their safaris. The best I could do on short notice, however, was a Fedorov Avtomat. It is an automatic rifle that barely did the job given the thickness of an elephant's skull. But thankfully it took only one shot. Your beast never felt a thing."

Father screams, "Stop! It's bad enough you've committed the act. Must you torture them with the details?"

"Sanctimonious words from a hunter such as yourself." There is an earnestness to Kerensky's face when he says, "And yes, I must. You and your family live in a world disconnected from all reality. Your children in particular need to understand what is happening on the other side of the palace wall so they will understand the choices I make going forward."

Tears run down my brother's face. "Why!" he sobs. "Why did you have to kill him?"

"Because it costs the Russian government eighteen thousand rubles every year just to feed him. Did you know that, boy?"

Alexey wipes snot on the back of his sleeve, then shakes his head.

"And do you know how much the average family earns per year in this country?"

Again my brother shakes his head.

"Approximately four thousand rubles. Your pet is an offense to every family in Russia that eats one meal a day. The people are tired of paying for your luxuries and your frivolities. The sooner you understand that, the better off you'll be."

"Where is he?" Alexey demands. "I want to visit his grave."

"There is no grave," Kerensky says.

"But what—"

"Would you *really* like to know?"

"No," Father interrupts. "Enough."

Kerensky squats down in front of my brother. He balances on the balls of his feet and rests his forearms on his knees. "All that is left of your elephant are the tusks. I sawed them off myself. At the moment they are hanging on my office wall, but once they've cured, I plan to have them carved into a chess set."

Alexey collapses into a sobbing heap while Kerensky stands to look at each of us in turn. "You might think me a monster," he says. "But believe me when I say that killing your pet was a mercy. He would have starved to death otherwise. It would have been long and painful and excruciating to watch. You would have heard his screams echoing through the park. And, without my protection, this is exactly the sort of treatment you will receive from the people who want you handed over to them."

Father snorts. "You're sending us away because you think we'll be starved or shot?"

"Or worse." Kerensky studies my sisters with concern. "I know you find this hard to believe, but I am not your enemy."

"You're certainly not a *friend*," Mother says.

Kerensky's mouth settles into a grim line. "I'm not here to make friends."

Mother clamps her mouth shut and retreats once again into her anger.

"Alexandra," Kerensky says.

"Yes?" The word is small and tight and ends with a slight hiss.

"I have other news that might be of interest to you."

"Little beyond this room is of interest to me."

"It concerns Grigory Rasputin."

Her eyes narrow. "What of him?"

"On my orders five soldiers of the First Rifles went into Tsarskoe Selo before dawn and removed his body from display." His face is impassive as he relates the next details. "I had them burn his remains with gasoline and rebury them in the woods."

Mother swallows a sob and gives Kerensky a single nod. It looks like gratitude.

I cannot get beyond the grisly image, but she clearly considers this a mercy. The body of her friend will no longer be abused or mocked.

"Where will you send us?" Father demands, deftly changing the subject. He disdains all talk of Rasputin. "To Crimea?"

"I'm afraid I cannot divulge that information," Kerensky says. "You will go where I deem it safe. In the meantime I suggest you begin gathering your possessions. Take only what can be easily transported by train. Take only what is meaningful to you."

Then, with a flick of his wrist, we are dismissed. But none

of us moves. We sit in Father's study, in the piles of dirt we've tracked in from the garden, staring at him and then at one another in confusion. Alexey crawls into Mother's lap, his narrow, bird-like shoulders still shaking as he sobs. She pats him as she would a baby and whispers soothing, nonsensical things into his ear. Finally, she gathers her wits enough to speak. "Come, children. To your rooms. It would appear we have packing to do."

"No," Kerensky says. He looks at the clock for confirmation. "Back to the garden. You still have work to do."

———

It is not uncommon for Dr. Botkin to join us in the garden. Like Father, he is a firm believer in the benefits of physical labor. He is also quite handy with a spade. And wherever Botkin goes, Gleb follows. He finds me the moment we enter the garden. And I might be flattered by this if I didn't find it insulting that, compared to my sisters, I cannot attract the attentions of a man. Each of them has been proposed to at least four times while tending soldiers in the infirmary. But I am left to evade the sappy gestures of a boy, a puppy who follows me up and down my garden row, constantly asking if he can carry my spade or my seed sack. Offering to fetch me water or jumping up to give me what little shade is produced by the Krazulya pear tree at midday.

I go in search of that sparse green canopy every day at the end of our work session, watching the fruit, waiting for it to ripen. It won't be ready for another few weeks, but already parts of the glossy green skin are beginning to turn pink. Unlike most pears, the Krazulya is round and has slick skin, giving it the appearance of an apple. The boughs are heavy with fruit but, according to Kerensky, we won't be here to eat it. The Krazulya pear has a uniquely short harvest season—a single, decadent week—but I look forward to it every year. The flesh of this particular pear is soft and sweet and infused with a certain spiciness that lends itself to jams and pies. If eaten too early the fruit puckers your mouth and gives you a bellyache. If eaten too late it's mealy and riddled with worms. The Krazulya season comes and goes all at once the second week of August, but we will already be in some other, unknown location when the pears ripen and hang warm and heavy on their branches.

I plop down beneath the tree to watch Joy and Jimmy chasing each other through the garden like puppies. They are covered in leaves and clumps of dirt, and we'll have to brush them before letting them back in the palace, but it's worth the trouble considering how it makes me smile. The dogs are rowdy today and they bolt toward the garden gate. The young dimpled guard is stationed there, and I see him lunge for Jimmy and catch him by the collar so he doesn't run off through the grounds. The guard kneels down and rubs Jimmy's ears, and then I see him sneak a bit of bread from his pocket and feed it to my dog. The little traitor wags his tail as though they're *friends*.

"Just because you like him doesn't mean I have to," I mutter, picking at a leaf until it's shredded in my palm.

I turn my gaze upward, looking into the branches at one pear that show signs of early ripening. I think of Sammi and wish I could go comfort my brother. Mother took him away and put him to bed the moment we left Father's study. It will likely take him days to recover.

"Would you like me to fetch that pear for you, Tsarevna?" Gleb asks. He follows my gaze to the low-hanging fruit, ready to scramble up the trunk and across the branch.

I shake my head. "No. Let it be. And don't call me that. I'm not a tsarevna anymore. Haven't you heard?"

"I have heard nothing that will convince me otherwise." And with that he offers one of his obnoxious bows.

Gleb is going to be a very handsome man one day and, I suspect, dangerously charming as well. But encouraging him at this age will only make him incorrigible, so I shake my head and roll my eyes and then I look for Jimmy, who is still at the gate seeking affection from the guard. I smile at the sight of Jimmy's tongue-wagging joy, but when I turn back to Gleb he's frowning at both the dog and the soldier.

Dr. Botkin sits down beside me, polishing the edge of his spade with an oiled cloth. "This stops it from rusting," he explains, apropos of nothing.

I don't bother to tell him that I've chucked my spade into the ditch beside the garden and won't retrieve it until we come back tomorrow. Nor do I tell him that I don't care one whit if it rusts.

"Gleb," he says without looking up. His short, capable fingers continue rubbing oil onto the steel in small circular motions.

"Yes, Father?"

"The household staff was told about Kerensky's decision a short time ago. Most of them are leaving before I send you back to your mother at week's end. You'll take the train with any who are left."

Gleb splutters in disgust, then shakes his fist with righteous indignation. "How can they leave?" His eyebrows clench together in fury, and I think he's trying, desperately, to think of an impressive insult. After a few seconds he says, "What an orgy of cowardice and stupidity!"

I can't tell whether Botkin is going to laugh or choke. Mostly I try not to say anything that will get me in trouble later.

"Do you even know what an orgy is?" he asks.

"No," Gleb says.

Botkin clears his throat and, in the driest, most wooden voice I've ever heard, says, "It is a wild gathering in which many people have sex together, often while drunk or under the influence of an opiate."

"Oh." Gleb is so instantly red that it looks at if his head might burst into flames.

"Not the definition you expected?"

I didn't think it possible, but the boy's face grows even hotter. He staunchly refuses to look at me. "No."

"Then perhaps think of another way to phrase your outrage."

Gleb wrinkles his nose in thought and after a moment says, "That is a sickening display of shabby, contemptible disloyalty."

"Much better. I see that you've been minding your vocabulary, though I daresay your assessment is wildly unfair to the staff. Kerensky has ordered them to go."

"It is cowardly of them to obey."

"An unfortunate sentiment, considering you'll be among them." Botkin sets his spade down and turns to his astonished son.

A firm shake of his head and one quick glance in my direction. "I won't," Gleb says.

"You don't have a choice. It's no longer safe for you here. You will return to your mother and sister in Petrograd."

"No. I won't allow it. You can't force me."

Botkin laughs and ruffles his son's hair. "I can, in fact, if it comes to that. But I appreciate your loyalty, and I'm certain you'd rather have me send you home than Kerensky. He'd be far less gentle about it. Nor would he care for your feelings."

Gleb's height suggests that manhood is fast approaching, but he still wrestles with the emotions of a child. He's only twelve after all. Gleb stomps one foot, hard. "My duty is here."

"And my duty is to protect you." Botkin leans over his son and cups the boy's cheek in his palm. "I would not have you end up like the elephant."

THREE WEEKS LATER

Alexandrovsky Train Station, Petrograd, Russia
August 1

Kerensky stomps into the formal reception room before dawn and says, "Your train has arrived."

But he doesn't lead us out to the courtyard as we expect. Instead we are lined up, single file, and walked through the kitchen and out the side door where four motorcars idle quietly with headlights off. The trucks holding our belongings are nowhere to be seen, having long since been spirited away to the train station. We are hustled into the vehicles, in sets of two Romanovs and two staff, along with various frightened pets. I ride with Maria and Dova in the backseat. Botkin sits up front with the young dimpled guard while my sister grasps my hand and cries when we turn, not toward the palace gates, but onto the lawn and around the house. With the headlights off, I doubt the guard can see much of where he's going. We creep as inauspiciously as possible through Alexander Park to avoid the crowd at the gates. Word spread during the night that there was more activity than usual at the palace, so three rows of soldiers were sent to fortify the palace gates and hold back the crowd.

"Why are we taking this route?" Botkin asks.

"Kerensky says we'd have to shoot the protestors just to get through," the guard says. "I'd rather not do that if it's all the same to you."

"Nor would I." Botkin tilts his chin and looks at the boy curiously. "What is your name?"

"Tomas Popov."

We bounce our way around the park and exit through a service entrance and onto the main road only to find that it is lined on both sides, from the palace to the train station, by hundreds of guards. Only now does Tomas flip on the headlights and I turn away from the window, unable to meet the hostile glares of those soldiers, or the sight of their rifles. If we can simply get through this journey, I tell myself, then we will never have to see them again. Jimmy sits on the floor at my feet, his chin on my knee, eyes round and ears peaked, alert. I find his presence, the great shaggy bulk of him, comforting. Once I look up to find Tomas staring at me in the rearview mirror. He is looking at me, not Maria, and this surprises me so much that I return his glance longer than is appropriate. He turns away first.

When we reach Alexandrovsky Station we find that the train is parked, not at the entrance, but farther down the tracks, near an open field. A small but vocal crowd is gathered on the platform, held back by only a handful of guards. I can hear them shouting and cursing as we pull up beside the train and scramble out of the cars.

I stand beside my brother and wrap my arms around his thin shoulders. He is exhausted and confused, and I brush the hair away from his ears to soothe him. "Don't worry," I whisper. "We'll be able to rest soon."

"*Do svidaniya, Nikolashka-durachok!*" The crowd begins to chant from the platform.

Good-bye, Little Nicholas the Fool. It echoes down the tracks, and Father's face turns to granite.

He is staring, not at the imperial train but at a long, ramshackle set of cars marked RED CROSS MISSION.

"What is this?" he demands. "Where is my train?"

Kerensky shrugs. "You no longer have a train. Or a yacht. Or a home. You have only the mercy I choose to extend you. So collect your family, board this train, and be grateful that I did not send you off in your normal transport. Because you can be sure it would've been stopped five miles down the tracks, boarded by your disenfranchised people, and all of you would be shot dead on the spot."

I should be frightened by these words, having been yanked from bed and shuffled to the train station in the middle of the night. But I, like my father, am simply angry that I am here in the first place.

"Don't be ridiculous," Father says.

"He's telling the truth." A man steps forward to join Kerensky, and I can feel Alexey shrink away at the sight of him. Unnaturally tall. Daunting. His skin is smooth and ageless. But his hair and beard are black and bushy, like one of the Chechen highlanders. He has strange slanted eyes that look as though they belong to an animal. A lit cigar rests in the corner of his mouth, and a red handkerchief hangs limp and macabre from the pocket of his military uniform. He puffs on his cigar and blows the smoke in Father's face. "I saw the crowds beside the tracks, waiting, as we traveled from Petrograd."

"This is Evgeny Koblinsky," Kerensky says, motioning to the bizarre newcomer. "He will accompany you on this trip. His word is law in my absence."

"We are to be passed off again?"

"You should thank me, Nicholas. There are worse people I could pass you off to."

Poor Alexey, drained and overwhelmed. I can feel the sob building in his chest. So I hush him, rub his back, and say in a low voice, "Don't be afraid. Look at him. Who does he remind you of?"

He braves a peek from beneath my arm. "A monster."

I laugh. He's gotten the answer right whether he knows it or not. "Yes. But which monster? Think."

"I don't know." Alexey stares at our new escort. His long, gangly arms wave in disagreement, as he argues with Father.

"Do you remember the legends about a peculiar man who travels the forest provoking pilgrims?"

Realization clicks and Alexey looks up at me. "The Leshy?"

I grin. "And what does the Leshy look like?"

Alexey creases his forehead, trying to remember the old folktales our governess read to us. "He's always smoking or stealing tobacco." His eyes drift to that cigar and the trailing line of smoke. "His hair is wild and his eyes strange."

"What's the last thing? How do you know you've found a Leshy in the woods and not just an old man? What does he *always* wear?"

He smiles weakly. "Something red. Like that kerchief in his pocket."

"Smart boy. So let's not worry, okay? He's just a Leshy. Harmless really. Some people even believe they're guardians sent to protect the unlucky traveler. Do you remember how to drive one away when you're tired of it?"

"By praying."

"Or?"

Alexey giggles and pulls away from me. "Cursing."

"We can practice cursing on the train, yes? I'll tell you all of the words that Cook has taught me."

There are dark circles beneath my brother's eyes and he looks as though he could be blown over by the slightest wind, but the fear is gone, so I consider the lesson a success. "We'll call him Leshy. Just the two of us. It will be our joke. Yes?"

Alexey nods, then gathers Joy in his arms. Mollified, he wanders off to join Father beside the tracks.

"You are a very clever girl, Anastasia." Botkin's voice, low near my ear. "And a damn good sister."

I shrug off the compliment. "I don't like to see him afraid."

"He's lucky to have you. They all are."

"You might be the only one who believes that."

"They know it whether they admit it or not." Botkin tugs the end of my braid affectionately. "But let's keep the cursing to a minimum, yes? At least if your parents are within earshot."

The whistle blows, loud and urgent. Kerensky looks to the platform in the distance and the growing crowd. He motions us toward the train, urging us to board.

It is my brother who notices the obvious. Alexey scans the compartments and the legion of curious faces peering back at us. "Father," he asks, "where are we going?"

"They say we are headed to England."

"Then why are there so many soldiers on this train?"

PART TWO

Friends and Enemies

And, after all, what is a lie? 'Tis but the truth

in masquerade.

— LORD BYRON, *DON JUAN*

9

Anna

HANNOVER

1946, 1943

Winterstein, Germany
November 1946

Anna has every intention of cutting the soldier's throat. He has only to take one step closer and she will lunge. The serrated knife in her hand is meant to be used for slicing bread, but she thinks it will handle the soft skin of a man's neck easily enough. He is a Bolshevik, an officer in the Red Army, and he has come, like so many others in recent months, to raid the castle. The war has made the soldiers bold and they pass through daily on their way to Berlin taking what they want and leaving chaos behind them. Occasionally it's food or clothing they seek, but usually their hungers are of a more carnal nature. By the way he stares at the swell of her breasts, Anna doubts this soldier has crept into the kitchen for breakfast. Anna never once thought she would still be facing the threat of rape at this age. Nor did she imagine that she would still be running and hiding.

There are other, safer places where she could have sought refuge, but Anna had so little time when leaving Hannover, what with the bombs falling and the city burning and the earth shaking beneath her feet. She took only what she could carry and showed up here, on the doorstep of a sympathetic acquaintance. A practical choice, though risky and ultimately flawed. She was able to make the journey from Hannover to Winterstein on foot in less than a day, but here she is, staring danger in the face once again.

"Frau," the soldier says, motioning her with his fingers. His voice is sticky with lust. "Come here."

There is not the slightest tremble in Anna's voice when she responds. She speaks clearly and confidently, but in German. Russian is too great a risk with the Red Army forcibly repatriating nationals to the newly formed Soviet Union. Anna has heard the rumors of how Romanov friends and sympathizers were systematically hunted down and assassinated after the revolution. She does not care to think what they would do with a woman who claims to be Grand Duchess Anastasia.

"If I come to you it will be to disembowel you on the threshold," she says, raising the knife and holding it up so he can see the wicked points of the blade. "Or you can come to me and I will do it here, on the kitchen floor."

She is stunned to see that her hand does not shake. Not even the slightest tremble.

This man wants her to fear him. He wants her to run and scream and cry, to beg for mercy. When she does none of this, his posture changes. He looks from her face to the blade, back and forth, measuring her resolve, her distance, his chances. The soldier straightens from his subtle, predatory crouch, his face awash with uncertainty. He does not look like a man who wants to bleed out on a cold November morning. Anna can see him decide that she is not worth the trouble. It's there, on his forehead, as the lines of concentration smooth away, in his hands, as they go from clenched to relaxed.

His shoulders drop.

He takes one step backward.

Then another.

And in five seconds he is gone, retreating out the kitchen door and onto the lawn, a dark, hunched form against the silver blanket of frost.

Her hands shake, now, and the knife clatters to the floor. Anna raises her trembling fingers to the door and slides the bolt into place, then watches the soldier disappear into the tree line.

Damn those nightmares that haunt her dreams since Hannover. They are loud with the whistle of falling bombs and they shatter inside her head, keeping sleep at bay almost every night. She curses herself for rising early and making her way downstairs in search of coffee. For crossing the kitchen yard to collect a jug of cream at the springhouse. For leaving the door unlocked behind her. She didn't consider that the light would draw anything other than moths.

She blows out the lantern on the counter. It was foolish, really, to fight the dreams and leave her bed at all. To come here in the first place. Anna is certain, now more than ever, that she cannot stay in Winterstein. Not with the lingering Soviet occupation and the constant threat of discovery and repatriation. It is time to go.

Anna slips from the kitchen in search of the one working phone in this castle. It is time to send word to Prince Frederick. He's been in Altenburg for several years, waiting out the war like everyone else. He has done so much to help, and she hates to disturb him again, but Anna must find a place where she can disappear forever.

THREE YEARS EARLIER

Hannover, Germany
October 8, 1943

Anna is in bed when the bombs begin to fall. Her apartment is on the third floor of an old building near the Marstall Gate along the bank of the river Leine. The one-bedroom flat has high ceilings, wood floors, and exposed brick walls. Ample windows. Sparse, gently used furniture. There is wallpaper in the bathroom and rusty plumbing throughout. The place smells of lemon oil, mothballs, dust, and cedar. Somehow this combination means home to her, now that she has been here for almost five years. This is the first time since the boardinghouse in Berlin that she has lived entirely by herself, and even though it was a strange adjustment at first, she has grown to love the independence and the solitude. Anna loves the quiet.

No, not quiet. Not now. It is nearly one in the morning and the air is filled with thunder and chaos. Earsplitting bedlam.

As Anna stumbles out of bed the room is lit with a blinding white light. Like a spotlight. Like a vision. The way she imagines it will be when she passes into eternity. And that is her first thought, that she has died, and it is only the raging sound of explosions that convinces her she is still alive.

For now.

Anna blinks furiously and finally sees something out the window. It hangs from a streetlight at the corner, right outside her building, glowing a phosphorescent white. A Christmas tree. But not the kind of tree cut and decorated during the holidays. This is the sort dropped from the warplanes flown by the Allied forces. A nickname given to the parachute flares that mark a designated target on the ground. And there, several blocks farther down the street, is another. They always come in fours, tidily boxing in their targets. Anna does not wait to see where the others will land.

Muscle memory is an odd thing. Linked to music and athletics and survival. Anna does not even have to tell her limbs to move, to run. They do it on their own. She's across the room, yanking open the top drawer of her dresser before she has time to register a single coherent thought.

Anna's thin cotton nightgown falls to her ankles. She wears nothing beneath it, but she does not have time to dress, so she yanks a pile of clothing from her closet and throws it into a suitcase. Then she dumps the contents of the dresser drawer into it as well. A photo album. An icon. A chess set. A paper knife. Keepsakes from a former life that she will not leave behind, cards she might yet need to play.

Boots. She pulls them over her feet but does not lace them. No socks. No stockings. Her toes are cold.

A long, heavy coat hangs on a hook by the door. She yanks it over her shoulders and down her arms. It is not belted or buttoned. There is no time. She tears through the apartment and out her front door.

Anna crosses the landing and plunges down three flights of stairs, holding her suitcase in one hand and the stair rail in the other. She flies down, her feet barely touching the worn wooden steps. Heart banging in her chest. Breath catching in her throat every time the roof rattles and the walls shake. Another blinding flash of cruel white light. The third Christmas tree.

Run for the cellar. It is the single thought she is able to form as she goes down, down, down those steps. And then the lobby with its chipped tile and heavy door. A hard left and she darts down the hallway. Other people are there, but she does not stop and greet them. She runs. They all run. A child cries. A woman cries. A man curses.

Another door.

Another set of stairs descending into darkness, and Anna is only two-thirds of the way down before she is knocked off her feet and sent tumbling down the remaining five steps to land on her knees on the hard concrete floor. The impact sends a jolt of pain through her entire body. She can feel it in her teeth, at the back of her skull. Someone trips over her. Curses. She crawls toward the wall and curls into a ball, suitcase between her knees, hands over her ears, eyes squeezed shut.

The air around her vibrates, filled with the screaming of people and the screaming of bombs, and then one eerie moment of total silence as that sickening white light from the fourth flare spills into the cellar. The single lightbulb hanging from the ceiling explodes, illuminating for one morbid second the terrified faces around her.

And then the air is ripped apart.

———

In the morning there is nothing left but scattered bricks and splintered timber. No building. No apartment. The residents who made it into the cellar step out into the grim reality of Armageddon. The Allied forces had not been targeting their building after all, but something farther down the street. She knows this only because of the ten-foot crater in the ground a block away. The shock of the explosion flattened her building, but those structures that were beside the crater were decimated, turned to ash. In the other direction the buildings are still standing, but their windows and doors are gone, like missing teeth in blackened skulls. Anna cannot bear to look at the people who wander, stricken, through the rubble. The air is filled with soot and ash, with the wailing of women and the blare of distant sirens.

What remains of Hannover is on fire. Smoke billows upward, in every direction, and it takes Anna several minutes to find the sun, to orient herself. Two blocks, picking her way through the rubble—bricks and posts and bits of furniture, bits of people— and she sees the Marstall Gate. It stands unscathed, its white stone arch is eerily pristine, without so much as a crack or a smudge of soot. Anna passes through and finds the footpaths along the river to be mercifully clear of debris.

She stops long enough to wash her face and hands, to tie her boots and belt her coat. Then she walks south, toward Winterstein.

10

Anastasia

EXILE

1917

Cherepovets, Russia
August 1

"From Gleb," Dr. Botkin says, setting a small, round bundle in my hand. I fold back the edges of his crisp white monogrammed handkerchief to find a pear. "It should be ripe in a day or two."

"How—"

"He made me promise I'd deliver it to you. And he was very specific. This pear, not any of the others. And only once we'd left." Botkin sits down beside me and rests his heavy, warm hand on my shoulder. "He said they're your favorite."

"They are." Emotion, heavy and scratching, lodges at the back of my throat. I have to clear it before I can speak. "Thank you."

It is the Krazulya pear Gleb saw me admiring that day in the garden. I didn't let him climb the tree and fetch it for me, but he found a way to make sure I got it anyway. Stupid, stubborn, sweet boy. A ridiculous gesture. Totally unnecessary. I blink hard, pushing back tears.

"Keep the handkerchief," Botkin says, then leaves the compartment and slides the door shut behind him.

I press Botkin's handkerchief to my face and stifle a sob. My mother is a weeper. My sisters as well. But I want to be a different sort of woman. A woman like my great-grandmother, Queen Victoria of England. A woman so calm and collected and sure of herself that she is called a brass-plated bitch behind closed doors. I doubt very much that such a simple gift, an unexpected act of kindness, would make *her* go to pieces. Yet here I am, wiping snot on Dr. Botkin's linen kerchief.

Jimmy presses his cold, wet nose into my hand and I glance up to see those great pale eyes looking at me curiously, his ears turned forward and pitched like a tent. I refuse to believe that animals are incapable of emotion, that they cannot communicate. Jimmy has always possessed a preternatural ability to sense what I am feeling and to comfort me when necessary.

"I'm okay," I whisper and scratch him on the hard knob between his ears. Satisfied that all is well, he flops at my feet again, huffs in contentment, and begins to snore. By the time Alexey enters the compartment several minutes later and sits across from me I am dry eyed and composed once again. At least on the outside. Inside, however, I feel strangely untethered.

Once, when I was very little, I climbed the willow tree in our sitting garden and settled into the crook of a branch to eat a stolen sweet—a jam tart I'd pinched from the kitchen—but I didn't notice the oozing sap that dripped down the trunk. I leaned against it, and by the time I had licked the crumbs from my fingers, a heavy strand of hair was stuck to the bark. Too proud to call for help, I yanked myself free and lost a patch of hair in the process. That's how I feel as the train travels eastward, my thumb brushing the thick, firm skin of the pear. *Ripped away*.

———

We travel east all day, only stopping at sidings in small towns and sparse villages, but we are never allowed off the train. With every mile Father grows more and more grim. Every hour we travel east, into the sun rather than away from it, means our chances of going to England diminish. Father paces up and down the narrow hallway of our car, peering out the small square windows on either end. Three hundred and fifty soldiers travel with us. Farm boys and villagers mostly. Men conscripted into service at the beginning of the war. Neither political nor dangerous, simply following orders and biding their time until they can go home. They are crammed into the other train cars, practically spilling out the windows. Our car remains mercifully private except for Leshy, Semyon, and the boy called Tomas, all of whom watch us carefully anytime the train slows.

When Father isn't pacing the hallway, he sits with Mother in their compartment, methodically tracking each train station we pass, trying to decipher our destination as though it's some puzzle he must solve. I hear them once, discussing our route.

"Tikhvin. Cherepovets. Shavra." Father taps the map with his pencil. "We're still going east."

"I don't even remember these places," Mother says.

"That's because we've never been to them."

"Is that the point, then? Drag us around the whole of Russia and humiliate us?"

"No, Alix," he whispers. "I think they have something else in mind."

I do not stay to hear what he thinks that something else might be, but seek out Botkin for a game of dominoes instead. Only a small retinue of servants has been allowed to travel with us. Dr. Botkin. Dova. Cook. And Alexey Trupp, father's valet, who we simply call Trupp because Mother insists there are already too many Alexeys in our household. Everyone else has been sent away, back to their homes, to relative safety. These four refuse to abandon us, and my affection for them increases daily as a result. Our tutor, Pierre Gilliard, will join us once we reach our final destination.

I spend the afternoon distracting myself with endless games of dominoes and whist. Botkin, ever the gentleman, lets me win four times.

Dinner comes and goes, served to us in our compartment by an Armenian chef hired by the railway line. Cook has been forbidden to leave our train car or help in the galley, so he takes his meal with a sour face and a poor attitude, complaining all the while that the meat is dry. But the simple meal of roasted chicken and vegetables tastes fine to me. It comes with hot bread and is wonderfully seasoned. I don't even realize how hungry I am until I find my plate empty. I want more but am unsure whether that's allowed, so I let my dish be cleared away without speaking a word.

The sun is setting when Leshy finally orders the train to stop so we can stretch our legs. He unwinds his long, rangy body from where he sits beside the door, and leads us outside. There is no station, no railway siding to be seen. Only rolling green fields, dotted with trees and bushes, stretching out in either direction.

Joy, Jimmy, and Ortimo, so eager to relieve themselves, are out, darting between our legs, before any of us can get down the stairs. My parents drift off to speak in low whispers while Alexey and my sisters pick bilberries in a low, scrubby hedge.

"You have fifteen minutes," Semyon announces. Ortimo scuttles away at the harsh sound of his voice, and I see Tomas's brows draw tight beneath the brim of his cap. He says nothing but simply wanders off a short distance and watches us patiently. Semyon, however, slides the bolt on his rifle and rests it against his shoulder, ready, I presume, in the event that any of us decides to run. "Stay near the train!" he shouts.

I press my heels against the tracks and take Gleb's pear from my pocket. The setting sun washes the clouds with a gentle pink that matches the skin of the Krazulya, and I take it for a sign as I bite deeply into the flesh. For once Botkin is wrong. The pear is perfectly, deliciously ripe, and I eat the whole thing, seeds, stem, and core, as the sun disappears below the horizon.

When the whistle blows we all file back toward the train. Semyon stands by the door to our car, waiting, I think, to kick Ortimo as he passes. But Tatiana scoops the little dog into her arms and steps up into the train with her nose in the air. Jimmy stays by my side, attentive and protective as I fall back to walk beside Father. I lean my head against his arm. "Where do you think they're taking us?"

He pulls me closer and kisses the top of my head. His voice tightens when he says, "To Siberia."

FIVE DAYS LATER

Tyumen, Russia
August 6

The penal colonies were established in the early 1800s as a means of punishing criminals, dissidents, and anyone else who ruffled the sensitive feathers of my forefathers. I know this, of *course* I know this. Pierre Gilliard has covered this, along with all of the other grand, sweeping moments of Russian history. But to the best of my knowledge—which I can now admit is grossly insufficient—we are the first royals in history to be condemned to this legendary exile.

We continue rolling east through Katen, Chaikovsky, Perm, Kamyshevo, Poklevskaya, and Ekaterinburg. I am stiff and sore and tired. Every mile in that rattling, old train multiplies into an eternity. I cannot get comfortable. I cannot focus on my thoughts or the book laid open in my lap. The thunder of the tracks pounds in my ears constantly, setting my nerves on edge.

The dogs whine. None of us have bathed, and we've barely slept since leaving Tsarskoe Selo. So it's understandable that, when the train finally pulls to a stop in Tyumen near midnight, we stupidly think our journey is at an end. That is until Leshy orders that our belongings be loaded onto a steamer whose engine is chugging like a tubercular old man beside the dock.

Father, exhausted and belligerent, marches toward him with fists balled. "What is the meaning of this? Why must we leave the train?"

Leshy plucks the cigar from his mouth and blows a cloud of smoke in Father's face. "The tracks stop here." As Father coughs he adds, "Count yourself lucky. Boats can make the passage only a few months each summer. If this were winter you'd be traveling by horse and cart."

It takes hours to load our belongings onto the ship, with those weary, bitter soldiers trudging back and forth, single file, from the train to the ship carrying boxes and trunks and furniture. It is not until dawn that the great, lumbering steamer, *Rus*, pulls away from the dock and into the muddy current.

Brown water. Brown riverbanks. Brown fields. Brown huts. The occasional brown-clad peasant. That's all we see until the next day when we merge first into the Tobol River and then, later, into the Irtysh and the marshes of eastern Siberia.

We have no rooms on board the *Rus*, only hard berths and scratchy blankets in the great, cavernous hold. There is no privacy, no separation from the soldiers, and very little in the way of facilities. The hold smells of bad plumbing and unwashed males, so I stay on deck with Father until forced to bed that second night. We keep to our designated corner, in bunks stacked three high, while Botkin, Trupp, and Cook take turns keeping watch. They do not like the way Semyon leers at us in the darkness, the way he stares shamelessly. Twice I wake to Jimmy's low warning growl as Semyon passes near Olga's bunk. I can feel the rumble against my legs, and I see the points of

Jimmy's sharp, white teeth flashing in the dark. I sleep, finally, but in fits and starts, while Jimmy lies curled beside me, head resting on his paws, his pale blue eyes gleaming in the dark.

I am up before dawn to join Father on the deck. As always, Jimmy follows close behind. The breeze is minimal but the air is clean, and Father smokes his pipe at the rail, telling me stories of his childhood and his travels. I pay no attention to the details, but rather listen to the cadence of his voice, taking comfort when he sets his hand atop my head, when he drapes an arm around my shoulders, in the sweet, rich smell of his pipe.

When breakfast comes I have no appetite whatsoever, so I feed the cold eggs and boiled potatoes to Jimmy. Father takes his portion without complaint and eats it quickly. I marvel at his ability to chew and swallow without tasting or grimacing. He is notoriously picky with Cook at home, yet suddenly his palate seems to have lost all discernment.

"That is the home of Grigory Rasputin," Father says an hour later, pointing toward a white stone house, high on the bank after we pass through Pokrovskoe. He doesn't exactly spit the words, but there is no fondness in his tone.

"Should I get Mother?"

"No. It will only trouble her."

We stand in silence, watching the house fade into the distance. Rasputin came from the borderlands of Russia, only to rise in Mother's favor, and then in power. He embedded himself in our lives. His daughter, Maria, was even my friend for a time. We played together as young children. And then it was all over. Rasputin's end was grisly, and here we are, passing his beginnings. Fate does twist her knife in the most unexpected ways.

Mercifully, our journey comes to a close late that afternoon. We are greeted in Tobolsk, at the far reaches of Siberia, by two memorable things as the *Rus* chugs into position against the dock: church bells pealing loud across the city and mosquitoes the size of bumblebees. A ringing in one ear and a buzzing in the other.

"We have been delivered to hell," Father says, swatting at his neck, then wiping a bloody smudge on his pant leg. "And they are celebrating."

11

Anna

THE SCHANZKOWSKA AFFAIR

1938, 1932, 1931

Hannover, Germany
July 9, 1938

"I see you've gotten married," Anna says, looking at the gold band on the ring finger of Gleb Botkin's left hand. Such an American thing to do. Russians wear their wedding rings on the right. Sellout. This fact disappoints her almost as much as the marriage itself.

"I was going to tell you." Gleb sticks his hand in his pocket defensively. "She's a nice girl. Lovely."

"I didn't say otherwise."

"Listen, I haven't seen you in years. *Seven* years."

"You don't owe me an explanation."

"She's American."

"I assumed as much."

"That means I can *stay* in America. You know how important that is. To your cause." He says it like this is some compromise on his part, as if he has sacrificed something on her behalf.

Anna is exhausted, and Gleb's stammering makes her even more so. It's not like they had any sort of understanding. She hasn't seen him since New York. Since that last fiasco he got her into. Hell, he didn't even know they'd locked her away in that asylum for a year until *after* she'd been shipped back to

Germany. Anna has no claim on him. Yet this still hurts. It's an embarrassing realization to come to in her forties.

Gleb looks so eager to explain, to apologize, that Anna almost asks the name of this strange new wife he has acquired. Almost. But Edward Fallows steps through the door before she has time to give in to sympathy.

Her lawyer has aged considerably in the years since she last saw him. They communicate regularly by letter and telephone but have not been in the same room since New York. His hair has gone gray at the temples. His back has grown rounded. And he wears spectacles, thick and very English-looking. Edward Fallows was not a man blessed with good lips to begin with, and they are tight and thin now, like dried orange peels.

"Are you ready?" he asks.

"No. But I don't have a choice, do I?"

She's only answering this summons because Gleb is present. Anna didn't really think he'd make the trip all the way from America. But now that he has come she can't very well avoid it any longer. The interrogation has been ordered by Adolf Hitler. His interest in Anna's case has only grown in the months since he accosted her in Berlin.

"Let's go then," Gleb says, offering her a hand.

If it hadn't been his left hand, she might have accepted it. But she stares at that gold band for a moment and rises from the couch on her own.

———

The Hannover police headquarters is located seven kilometers from Anna's new apartment. They drive in silence. There is no point in discussing strategy. One does not refuse the Führer. Not if one enjoys breathing. Anna has brushed up against death often enough to know that she is not ready to permanently inhabit its cold, clammy grasp.

Police headquarters are housed inside an ornate building

that was once a library. Libraries these days are frowned upon, but the structure retains its charm, and she hopes that the ghosts of those stories still haunt the corridors. She hopes they torment the Nazis at night.

They are met at the top of five wide steps by an SS officer proudly wearing his red arm patch and a scowl. "This way," he says, snapping his heels together and leading them through the double doors and deep into the building.

Hallways. Corners. Stairs. Anna doesn't keep track of their route. She has little reason to believe she will be led out the same way. It is her assumption that this soldier, or one just like him, will take her out the back in handcuffs.

Anna is wearing her best wool suit for the occasion. Pale gray, soft as a lamb's ear. A matching cloche. Silk stockings. New black leather pumps, satin gloves, and a string of pearls. If she is going to be hauled off to prison, she might as well look sharp. Whatever the outcome of this meeting, it's time to put the Schanzkowska affair to rest.

The officer leads Anna, Gleb, and Fallows into a large inter-rogation room. Inside are four people seated on one side of a long wooden table. There is an enormous, rectangular mirror on the wall behind them. Double-sided no doubt. She guesses that whoever is on the other side will remain anonymous. If the Führer has made the trip from Berlin to witness this meeting firsthand, he hasn't condescended to show himself.

In any case, Anna finds the visible occupants of the room troubling enough: all four Schanzkowska siblings. Valerian, Felix, Gertrude, and Maria-Juliana. Stair-stepped in age, they are very attractive in an earthy, rural sort of way. They are clearly impoverished—both women wear simple homemade dresses of drab black, and neither man has a tie or pair of sus-penders between them, but they have the strong, sinewy look of people who work hard for a living. Clear-eyed and brown from the sun, they have scrubbed up the best they can, but

Anna can still see the residue of manual labor beneath their fingernails. Ordered to attend this meeting, and pulled from their fields and their factories, they are anxious and wary. Not that she can blame them.

Anna takes a seat with Gleb and Fallows on either side of her. The Officer sits at one end of the table while Anna stares at the older woman, Gertrude, knowing immediately what every person around this table sees: a startling resemblance between them. Anna has known Gleb Botkin long enough to perceive when he is nervous. And the telltale tapping of his shoes gives him away now. Gertrude Schanzkowska has Anna's same high cheekbones, dark hair, and startling blue eyes. Their noses and mouths are similar, as is their height and build. The lines around Gertrude's eyes are deeper, and there is more silver in her hair, but even a casual observer can see they could be sisters.

The Officer scribbles in his file.

"Can we please get this over with?" Anna asks in German.

The siblings confer, in Polish, looking at her and then away. They take in her fine clothing and her meticulous grooming. The careful distance she keeps across the table. They size her up against the memory of the woman she is accused of being. Their long-lost sister. A mentally unstable woman who disappeared in early 1920. A charge brought against Anna a decade earlier by relatives of the imperial family. The dates line up, as do appearances, and it's easy to understand why she hasn't been able to shake this accusation since that ambush in Wasserburg.

She knows Gleb is thinking of it now, as he gazes unblinking on these four Polish witnesses. If only he hadn't taken her to the inn that day. If only they hadn't fallen into the trap so neatly laid by that Private Investigator.

Anna shakes her head. Clears her thoughts. Focuses on the present.

The Officer slides a paper across the table and places it

before Valerian Schanzkowska. "This is an affidavit stating that this woman is your sister, Franziska. If you identify her as such today, you will all be required to sign it before leaving."

What the Officer does not mention is that if they sign the affidavit, Anna will be charged with fraud and, at the very least, imprisoned. Whether the Schanzkowska siblings know this is unclear.

Valerian looks at Anna. His eyes are brown, soft and round, like an American penny. He takes in her pearls—the necklace, the earrings, the ring on her right forefinger—and shakes his head slowly. "This lady looks too different. Too elegant. My sister was a simple woman."

"See, I'm not the woman you're looking for," Anna says to the Officer.

But then Valerian speaks to her directly. "Do you have children?" he asks.

"Of course she doesn't have children. What kind of question is that?" Gleb demands.

"Let the woman answer for herself," the Officer says.

Anna can feel a vein throbbing in her throat, right where her neck and chin meet in a gentle curve. There is only the briefest hesitation before she answers, "No," and then, after she has had a second to think, she asks, "Why?"

"Because the last time I saw Franziska she was pregnant."

"Oh, please do record that in your files," Edward Fallows tells the Officer.

He doesn't even glance up, unperturbed at this bit of new information. "And how many years since you last saw your sister?" the Officer asks.

"Nineteen."

"That's a long time. Long enough for anyone to age. To change fortunes." He glances at Anna. "To change appearances."

Valerian stares at her steadily. She meets the gaze. Eyes narrowed. Back stiff. Mouth drawn in tight. She is defiant. Desperate.

Don't do this. *Please*. If she could scream the words at him she would.

"No one changes that much. This woman is not my sister," he says, finally, and slides the affidavit to his brother, seated beside him.

Felix looks at the paper. He has blue eyes. Like Gertrude. Like her. He reads the affidavit slowly, quietly.

The Officer notes Valerian's statement dispassionately in his messy scrawl. "And what of the rest of you? Do you concur?"

Anna has seen Felix Schanzkowska twice in the last two decades. Once in Wasserburg, and once, years earlier, in a meeting that, as far as she knows, remains undocumented to this day. It cannot be brought up now or used against her. But that doesn't ease the tremor of fear that beats against her rib cage. Of all the siblings, his face is the most inscrutable. No hint of his thoughts or what his reaction will be.

"This woman does not look a thing like Franziska," Felix says after staring at Anna for some time. "She doesn't even look like the same woman I saw at Wasserburg eleven years ago. Can we go home now?"

Maria-Juliana agrees. She is the youngest of them, and it is clear she worships her brothers. She will not contradict them. She doesn't want to be here. The woman practically withers beneath the scrutiny. She doesn't even bother to read the affidavit before pushing it farther down the table to her sister Gertrude. Each of Maria-Juliana's fingernails is bitten down to the quick, but that doesn't stop her from picking at them with her teeth. "I've never seen this woman before in my life," she says.

The Officer seems uncomfortable. Three denials. Not the outcome he expected.

Anna is poised in her chair, ready to leave this dank room

behind when Gertrude leaps to her feet. "What is wrong with you?" she screams—actually *screams*—at her siblings. "This woman is our sister!"

Gleb and Fallows push back against their chairs, startled.

Gertrude turns to Anna. "I know you are Franziska. You must recognize me. Please! Look at us! How can anyone deny it?"

The Officer turns his attention to her, triumphant, as though he has caught Anna in the middle of a great fraud. "Well," he asks. "What have you got to say?"

One heartbeat. Four. Nine. Anna counts them slowly, letting her pulse settle, forcing any potential tremor from her voice. "What am I supposed to say?" Another long beat to drive home her point. "She is *lying*."

Gertrude begins to sob.

The Officer regards Anna with a vulture's stare. "How many brothers and sisters do you have?"

"Four," Anna answers, honestly.

"And here we are," Gertrude insists, wiping her nose with the back of her hand, "four—"

"Their names are Olga, Tatiana, Maria, and Alexey," Anna says. "My siblings are all dead."

Gertrude leans across the table now, desperate. "This is insane. *She* is insane. Tell them the truth!"

The Officer watches Anna closely. There is no more scribbling of notes or casual observation. "Where were you born?"

"Russia." Anna spits the word out and folds her arms over her chest, hiding her trembling hands.

Felix's voice is quiet, almost inaudible as he reaches down the table and places his hand on Gertrude's. "Don't you see? It isn't her. Frankie was born in Poland. Like us."

"Admit it!" Gertrude yanks her hand away and glares at Anna. "Admit it!"

"Are any of you willing to sign that?" the Officer asks, nodding toward the affidavit. He looks at each of the siblings in turn.

"No," Valerian, Felix, and Maria-Juliana say in unison.

Gertrude hesitates, lips parted, her arm lifted several inches from her side.

Anna jumps at the opportunity. "Enough of this. I am done here." She rises smoothly from the table and stares at the two-way mirror. Her reflection shows the face of a calm, confident woman. A woman sure of who she is. Then she turns to the door and passes through without another word. Gleb and Fallows come after her a moment later.

Once they are deposited outside on the sidewalk, they rush Anna toward the waiting car.

"Gertrude wouldn't sign it. Too afraid of her siblings, I guess," Gleb says triumphantly. "The German government will take no further action in this case."

Anna is too exhausted, too relieved, to celebrate. She simply wilts into the backseat, pulling the cloche from her head and wiping one hand across her sweaty brow. Perhaps wearing wool in July wasn't such a great idea after all.

"That was close. Far too close," she says.

Edward Fallows grins at her in the rearview mirror. "It doesn't matter now. It's over. And besides, I have other news."

Anna has learned to dread these words from him. "What news?"

"As you know, the Romanovs tried to declare all of the tsar's surviving relatives so his estate could be settled and dispersed among them. But I filed a motion to contest this, stating that you are his only surviving heir. And I've just received news that the court has agreed to see our evidence. Frederick has it in Berlin. Witness testimony. Photographs. Everything he could find." He is elated, almost jubilant. "It's only a matter of time and we'll have you recognized, legally, as Anastasia Romanov."

FOUR MONTHS EARLIER

Berlin, Germany
April 1938

Adolf Hitler is not as tall as Anna imagined. The papers make him out to be a giant, some otherworldly creature that exists on a dais, towering over his subjects, when in reality he is not much taller than she is. Anna only has to lift her chin to meet his curious gaze. The outstretched hand is harder to accept, but what else is there to do? It is an effort not to wipe her hand on her skirt afterward.

Anna is only in Berlin for the day, to give one of Edward Fallows's endless depositions. Twenty minutes ago she stepped out of her hotel and onto the street to go in search of an early lunch when a large black limousine pulled to the curb and two armed SS officers stepped into her path.

"You must come with us, Fräulein," they said. "Your presence is required by the Führer." The sort of words one hears in their nightmares. But slumber is the only place you can resist such a command without consequences.

The officers explained nothing else on the short drive to the Kaiserhof building and now here she stands, in a room with the leader of the Nazi Party, with the man turning the world on its ear.

"Please," he says, "have a seat."

Anna lowers herself to the edge of the wooden chair across from his desk. She is careful not to get too comfortable. "You must forgive me," Anna says, "but I do not understand why I am here. I only came to Berlin on business and I will be leaving first thing in the morning. I have caused no trouble."

The Führer sits on the corner of his desk, a large block

of wood that looks as though it has been cut from the heart of some ancient tree. He has blue eyes, brown hair, and that famous mustache shaved to a mere inch and a half. Anna cannot help but stare at the thing as it sits there on his lip like the dislocated bristles of a toothbrush.

"Do not be alarmed," he says. "I only wished to tell you that I've had my intelligence officers perform a thorough investigation into your claims."

Her voice is more of a squeak than she would like. "My claims?"

"That you are Grand Duchess Anastasia."

She clears her throat. Grips the handle of her purse. "Why?"

"Because it matters." The expression on his face is one of assurance, friendliness, even, yet there is nothing in his eyes. Nothing whatsoever. They are a blank sheet of glass, and Anna has the disturbing sense that his true feelings on the subject will not reach the surface. "As you know, the world is precarious at the moment, and your claims, if true, could alter the course of history."

"If . . . *true*? Am I to assume that you do not believe me?"

A smile, filled with teeth, but it too sits on top of his face, not reaching his eyes. The expression is so out of place, so unnatural, it's as though she's found it on the floor, or hanging on the wall.

"On the contrary," he says. "We have come to the indisputable conclusion that you are, in fact, Anastasia."

This is a good thing. This *should be* a good thing. Yet a holy terror begins to rise in her chest, to fill her with dread. "I am glad you believe me. So few people do."

"I don't just believe you. I support you. And it is my sincere desire that you will support me as well."

So he's getting to the point, finally. "In what way?"

The Führer leaves his perch on the edge of his desk and goes to sit behind it. "My agents have concluded that your family was betrayed by the British government during the revolution of 1917. Disloyalty sickens me. England will pay for what they did to you."

Only the two of them sit in this office, but it does not stop that frenzied, hypnotic tone to his voice, as though he's speaking to a crowd. She hears it often enough on the radio. It is spun up with electricity now, and Anna has to force herself to sit still and listen instead of cringing and turning away. The air almost crackles with his zeal, and she fears any movement on her part will bring a static charge.

He continues, "And when I am finished with Britain, I will move to the Soviet Union. I will annihilate the men who murdered your family."

There are no words. She has no words. So Anna gapes at him stupidly instead.

"That is where you come in," he says.

"Me?"

"Of course. You are the rightful heir to the Russian crown. Your support of my regime is imperative."

"I . . . see."

Whatever the Führer has hidden behind the impenetrable wall of his eyes flashes through now, and Anna sees, for the first time, a glimpse of shrewdness when he adds, "Of course, should I find that your claims are false, should my intelligence be wrong, then imprisonment will be only the beginning of your troubles. In fact, death would be a fate too kind for such a fraud. Don't you agree?"

SIX YEARS EARLIER

Kuranstalt Ilten Psychiatric Home, Hannover, Germany
January 1932

"Hello," the man says, sticking out his hand, "I am Ernest Frederick, Duke of Saxe-Altenburg."

"*Duke?*"

"Well, prince, really, but that sounds awfully pretentious, doesn't it? Please, call me Frederick."

He stands there, awkwardly, until Anna realizes she has not invited him to take a seat. These royals and their manners. It's so easy to forget. "Forgive me," Anna says. "Sit. I did not expect a visit today."

Her little cottage is hidden at the back of the Ilten grounds, tucked into a small copse of silver fir trees. It is bright and open and surprisingly comfortable. Yet it is impossible to forget that it lies within the boundaries of a walled mental institution. If Prince Frederick is uncomfortable with this he doesn't let on.

"Can I get you some tea?" Anna asks.

"No, thank you. I'm quite content."

It is always awkward, this small talk, but Anna lets him plunge ahead. She doesn't even know where to begin.

"Do you know why I'm here?" he asks, finally. He folds his hands in his lap and peers at her with a mixture of hope and wariness.

"I'm afraid I don't read minds. You'll have to inform me the old-fashioned way."

"My sister, Charlotte, married your cousin Sigismund, Irene's son. I am here on his behalf."

"Ah, I see. My cousin sent you." Of course he would be

another Romanov detractor in disguise. Anna stifles her sigh and crosses her feet at the ankles. She sits up straighter. "How can I assist you?"

"You last met with my brother-in-law before the Great War, is that correct?"

Anna narrows her eyes. "It's possible. Though the date escapes me."

"The date doesn't matter. Only the details."

"Details?"

"Of that meeting. He has devised a list of eighteen questions, you see. And the answers to these questions are known only to Anastasia Romanov. He has sent me to ask them in the hopes that you can help put this matter to rest." Frederick leans forward and rests his forearms on his knees. "It's a test, I realize, and I apologize for that because I am certain you are sick to death of being tested. But if you pass, you will have Sigismund's full support. And mine."

"And what of his mother, Princess Irene?"

"Hers too, I believe."

Anna has good reason to doubt this. The last time she sought help from the Empress Alexandra's older sister she ended up at the bottom of the Landwehr Canal in Berlin.

"You realize this is ludicrous?" she says.

This takes Frederick aback. "I am sorry, Tsarevna, I did not mean to insult you. I simply do not know of any other way to deliver Sigismund the proof he needs."

"Not the test, you ridiculous man. The circumstances."

"I . . . I'm sorry . . . ridiculous? I'm afraid I don't catch your meaning."

"We are seated on the grounds of a psychiatric hospital. No matter what I say in response to those questions, Irene will pass it off as insanity."

Frederick pulls a fountain pen from his coat pocket and taps the end of it against his nose. "Oh. I see your concern. And I can assure you that I am familiar with your situation."

"My situation? Meaning that I am an inmate?"

"Meaning that this"—he waves his arm around to indicate the cottage—"is a rather unfortunate misunderstanding. I know that your former host, Miss Jennings, dispatched you rather abruptly. I know that the physician she employed in New York had you committed without any sort of psychiatric evaluation. And I know that you were declared perfectly sane upon your arrival back in Germany. By three different doctors in fact."

Anna wants to clarify a few points but he continues.

"I also know that, given you had nowhere else to turn, Miss Jennings paid for a six-month stay at this facility, not in the ward itself but in this cottage, on the grounds, since they refused to admit you as a patient. It's not exactly a holiday, but no one can accuse you of having been committed to this mental institution."

This man is becoming far more interesting by the moment. "I see you have done your homework."

"I am nothing if not thorough." He smiles and in the process sheds a layer of formality. "Am I also right in believing that your six-month stay at Ilten expires next week?"

"Yes."

"And do you have anywhere to go after that?"

"I always figure something out, Prince—"

"Frederick. Please, I asked you to call me Frederick." He pulls a single piece of paper, folded lengthwise, from the pocket inside his finely woven navy suit coat. "I believe that if you will be so kind as to humor my brother-in-law with answers to his questions, that I can be of great assistance with your next move."

"Is that so?"

"Indeed. I have good friends who have offered to place you in an apartment here in Hannover, near the Marstall Gate—it's a lovely part of the city. A home of your own, for as long as you need it."

"And all I have to do is answer a few questions?"

Prince Ernest Frederick of Saxe-Altenburg hands her the paper, along with his pen. "It is truly as simple as that."

12

Anastasia

THE GOVERNOR'S HOUSE

1917

Tobolsk, Russia
August 7

We arrive at our new home to find it uninhabitable. We decide, in the end, that Kerensky chose the old Governor's House because it was the single dwelling in all of Tobolsk that could be accessed by a wooden walkway from the dock. A small mercy given the channels of mud that serve as streets and alleys in this godforsaken Siberian outpost. From the dock we march under military escort along a narrow boardwalk, passing astonished locals until we reach the two-story clapboard building.

"I don't understand," Mother says, staring, aghast, at the boarded windows and littered porch. "What is this place?"

Leshy pulls the red kerchief from his pocket and wipes the sweat from his brow. He nods toward the abandoned building. "The Governor's House. Your new home."

"Kerensky said we'd be in a mansion."

"I suspect you hear what you want to hear, Alexandra. There are no mansions in Tobolsk."

The Governor's House is large, but it is not elegant. Nor is it clean, hygienic, or livable. Not after being used for several years as an army barracks. We stand there, gaping at the open front door and the dank rooms beyond. After several minutes a stray cat wanders out, takes one look at Jimmy—in crouched position with hackles raised—and bolts up the nearest tree with a furious screech. I lunge for Jimmy and grab him by the collar to stop him from chasing after it, stumbling forward several steps with his momentum.

The interior of the house looks no better than the exterior. Mud—an inescapable reality in Tobolsk—has been tracked over every inch of the floor. I am certain that my hem and shoes will never be the same. There is not a single curtain on the windows, but the panes are intact. They are so filthy that I can scrape off a layer of grime with my fingernail.

"You cannot expect us to live here," Mother says, holding a scented kerchief over her nose. "It is foul."

Leshy stands just inside the door, arms behind his back. "It is your new home. Make of it what you will."

We continue our tour through the squalid rooms, stunned and demoralized. The air is heavy and damp and smells of cat urine and bad plumbing. I turn the tap inside the first-floor bathroom and a weak stream of brown water spurts against the chipped enamel sink.

Behind us, the soldiers trudge in never-ending lines with our trunks and cases, dropping them to the floor without any sort of order.

"What do we do?" Mother groans, turning in a small circle as she takes in the crumbling plaster walls and endless cobwebs.

As a ladies' maid, Dova has never once picked up a broom or a dusting cloth in all the years she was at Alexander Palace. But that does not stop her from taking one shaky breath and assuming control. "We clean it," she says simply, then begins making order out of chaos. Dr. Botkin and Cook are dispatched to the city for cleaning supplies while Dova strong-arms the closest group of soldiers to help with the windows.

"Open them," she orders, sticking a plump finger in each of their faces. "Get the air moving again."

The boys are young—barely older than I am—pink cheeked

and too intimidated to argue. The windows, swollen with humidity, are forced upward with brittle whines, and then the boards are pried from where they've been nailed to the outside of the house. Once the light gets in we can see exactly what needs to be done.

Dova, God bless her, doesn't allow us to crumble beneath the weight of this realization. "One room," she says, fists clenched and voice peppered with flint. "We get one room clean enough to sleep in tonight. This one will do, in fact."

We look around us at what was likely a study and nod feebly. Dova grabs Tomas as he passes. He has just set down a trunk against the wall and is on his way out to pull another off one of the many carts lined up outside the house. "You," she says. "What is your name?"

"Tomas."

"How old are you?"

"Seventeen."

So young, so very young to pick up a rifle and be a soldier.

Dova is one of those people who decides instantly and irrevocably whether she likes someone. Something about the boy must appeal to her because she says, "It is now your job to help me find everything we need. Do you understand?"

Tomas shocks us all by smiling. In addition to those dimples, he's also in possession of high cheekbones and pretty teeth. I can't tell the color of his eyes beneath the brim of his cap, but I find myself suddenly curious about them.

"I'd be happy to," he says.

"Then I suppose you'll be happy to help us scrub the house as well?"

"I have seven brothers," Tomas says. "I've scrubbed worse."

———

We sleep on our camp beds that night. The windows are open and the mosquitoes are relentless, but at least the fresh air helps ease the scent of men and cats and things we are afraid to name. But we sleep. And when morning comes we're better able to face the task of making the house, this prison, into a home.

We get to work immediately. Since my family is forbidden to leave the grounds, Dova and Botkin go in shifts, led by Tomas, to purchase everything from washstands to curtains to candles. The most appreciated acquisition, however, is a laundress. By the time we've scrubbed all the floors, walls, and windows on the first floor our hands are bleeding and chapped, our clothing filthy. The thought of plunging my hands into one more bucket of water—even to wash my underclothes—is enough to make me abandon all hope.

Despite the grimness of our situation, we discover that Tobolsk does have a certain beauty. The Irtysh River is wide and muddy, but at sunset it looks like a winding, golden ribbon trimmed with bright, marshy fringe. We sit on the second-floor balcony after dinner, listening to Father read aloud. The air is balmy and crickets serenade us from the grass. While Father regales us with the adventures of Sherlock Holmes, I stare at the white stone kremlin high on the hill and the cathedral in the middle of town. Such beautiful, elaborate buildings in such a distant, drab outpost.

Apart from these two impressive monuments, the only other point of interest in Tobolsk is a museum that, Tomas says, is used to display various torture devices.

"It's grotesque," he explained that afternoon while discreetly feeding a bit of crust to Jimmy in the yard. My traitorous dog has developed an alarming attachment to the boy, and it is all I can do to keep him from padding after Tomas constantly. "They've got branding irons and shackles, and this *thing* . . . I don't know what it's called . . . that pulls the bone in your nose right out of the skull."

"You've been here before?"

"This is where I was born."

He laughed at my stunned expression and says, "Everyone comes from somewhere, Anastasia." Tomas pointed toward the museum. "My oldest brother dragged me there as punishment for telling our mother that I'd seen him kissing a girl on the boardwalk. The lesson, I believe, was that I learn to keep a secret."

"And did it work?"

"I was so frightened I had nightmares for a month."

"I mean did you learn to keep secrets?"

"I'd sooner have my own nose bone removed than reveal one ever again," he told me with a grin, and I saw, then, that his eyes were a bright and pretty blue.

SEVEN WEEKS LATER

Tobolsk, Russia
September 27

We are summoned to Father's study the first night it snows in Tobolsk. The air was pleasant earlier in the day, but a sudden, brutal wind rushed in from the north after breakfast. It was raining by lunch, and a thin dusting of snow covered the ground by dinner.

We find our parents sitting beside the fireplace with Alexey, who is already asleep on a couch. The lamps are lit, the curtains drawn tight, and a large wooden chest lies in the middle of the floor.

"Come in," Father says. "Let's read." He puts a bit of straw into the fire and uses it to light his pipe. After taking two quick puffs he motions for us to lock the door. Once Olga slides the bolt, Father licks the pad of his thumb, turns a page, and begins reading from "The Musgrave Ritual" a bit louder than necessary.

"'An anomaly which often struck me in the character of my friend Sherlock Holmes was that, although in his methods of thought he was the neatest and most methodical of mankind, and although also he affected a certain quiet primness of dress, he was nonetheless in his personal habits one of the most untidy men that ever drove a fellow-lodger to distraction.'"

There is a difference between *acting* a story and *reading* a story, and though the difference is subtle, Father has mastered it beautifully. There is a richness of voice and command of language that a good reader employs. A cadence that is hard to teach. There is rhythm and flow and a certain clip to the hard consonants, matched by softness with the short vowels. It's all in the vocal tone, and a bad reader will put you to sleep in moments while a good reader will keep you rapt and desperate for more even if you haven't seen a warm bed in a fortnight. I am so immediately transfixed by the sound of his voice that I don't realize they have called us in here for a different reason altogether.

Mother sets a finger to her lips and motions for us to sit on the rug. We obey and watch in confusion as she places a sewing kit in each of our laps.

"Watch me," she whispers, "and do as I do."

Beside her chair is the basket of corsets I noticed weeks ago at the palace, and she hands them out to us without explanation. Mother opens the trunk in the middle of the room, folds back a piece of blue velvet, and reveals a small portion of the jewels I saw on my birthday. Instinctively my hands drift to my earlobes and feel for the studs I chose as my present.

Mother lifts a diamond bracelet from the trunk and returns to her seat. She lays the corset flat across her lap and places the bracelet into one of the seams she has so painstakingly ripped open. Mother looks at us in turn, silently, threads her needle, and places the point against the seam. With slow, deliberate movements she begins to sew the bracelet inside the corset with tiny, precise stitches.

"I am so glad," she says, "that you have mastered your needlework, girls. We have so much mending to do."

Her meaning is clear so we pick up our needles and get to work. Anyone listening at the door would simply hear Father reading and Mother commending our sewing. They would never guess the truth—that we sit before a warm fire sewing jewels into our corsets as the snow begins to come down in earnest beyond the walls of our little prison.

13

Anna

THE COPENHAGEN STATEMENT

1931, 1930

Four Winds Sanatorium, Westchester County, New York
July 1931

Decades later, when Anna thinks about the year and a half she spent living in the Manhattan penthouse of Annie Burr Jennings, she will feel as if she's looking at her own life from a great height, like an eagle circling above, peering with intensity at objects that are hundreds of feet away. Each of these objects—the loss of one parrot and the death of another, a night at the Metropolitan Opera, skinny-dipping on Siasconset Beach, a bottle of champagne tumbling then shattering on the sidewalk, lunch at the Ritz-Carlton, and Edward Fallows's ridiculous idea for the Grandanor Corporation—are viewed as separate from the whole, moments clipped out and set against a larger swath of time, like silver foil against black velvet.

Those memories, however, are currently eclipsed by the way her stay is coming to an end. She sits in the admissions office of the Four Winds Sanatorium being discharged one long year after being admitted.

The thing about being an inconvenience, Anna thinks, is that you're easy to lock away. And if they call you *insane* or *mentally unstable* or, God forbid, *crazy*, they can toss away the key without feeling a shred of guilt. Annie Burr Jennings did so with alarming ease last July, and Anna suspects that she would not find herself being released from the sanatorium even now if this new doctor—she has not even bothered to acquire his name—had not taken over the institution earlier this month and ordered evaluations on every patient housed here. She owes her emancipation to him.

"This woman is no more insane than I am," the doctor says, laying his clipboard down on his desk. "She is clearly upset and undeniably paranoid, but she does not belong in an asylum for the mentally insane. You need to make other arrangements for her." The doctor looks, not at Anna, but at her former host, Annie Burr Jennings, or, as Anna has thought of her since their acquaintance, the Heiress.

"This *woman* has a long history of psychotic behavior. I should know; she lived with me for eighteen months and frequently blacked out, threw things, and locked herself in her room. And if that is not enough, she even concocted a fraudulent scheme with the intent of embezzling money from my friends. At least three of them fell for it before I caught wind of what was happening," the Heiress says, also avoiding eye contact with Anna. "Arrangements have been made. Miss Anderson will return to Germany aboard the *Deutschland* in two days' time. Her ticket has already been purchased."

So it has come to this, Anna thinks. *Miss Anderson*. A demotion. It wasn't so long ago that the Heiress was calling her *Anastasia*, or in one of her more generous moments, *Your Majesty*.

"I do not want to return to Germany," Anna says. "I want to speak with Gleb Botkin."

At this pronouncement the Heiress finally turns to address her. Anna is startled to see that the once-friendly gaze is now harder, almost cruel. "Haven't you spoken with him during your stay?"

"No. He has neither called nor visited, and, as I'm sure you know, I have not been allowed to initiate contact."

"Hhmmm. A pity. I think it's safe to assume that if Mr. Botkin has not reached out to you it is because he does not want to." She turns back to the doctor. "I am disappointed to hear that you do not agree with the diagnosis of my family physician. He believes this woman to be quite insane."

"And I find it concerning that there is no record of his exam—either physical or psychological—in her file."

"I believe that exam was performed in his private office. You would have to contact him for those documents."

The doctor leans back in his chair and shifts his gaze between the two women. "I see. Well, by the time Miss Anderson reached us she was quite sedate. And she has remained so during her stay."

"A stay I have paid for," the Heiress says, "at quite significant financial cost."

"We are not a cheap institution. We are not run by the government. I assume that is why you chose our facility for your friend."

"I chose it for your reputation and your *discretion*." This last word is stressed in such a way that Anna begins to fear there are strings attached to her release. The Heiress's voice is calm and measured—almost pleasant—as she continues. "As you will see from your records, I have paid over twenty-five thousand dollars for Miss Anderson's care. At my request she was placed in your best room—a four-room suite, in fact—and given a personal attendant. I have spared no expense for her care and treatment. Wouldn't you agree?"

His eyes narrow. "Yes."

"And would you also agree that such an investment in the mental health of a woman, someone who is not my blood relation, during the extreme financial crisis our country is currently experiencing is an act of extraordinary grace and kindness on my part?"

"You are quite benevolent," he says, dryly.

"And so humble," Anna adds, but neither of them acknowledges the interruption.

The Heiress leans a bit closer and holds out her withered, jewel-laden hand, palm up. "Then you will understand that I require all of her medical records to be turned over to me immediately."

"I'm sorry, madam, I cannot—"

"This will of course include every detail of her treatment, a list of any visitors, and, most important, all notes and files acquired from my personal physician."

"What you are asking is against the law."

Her hand does not waver. "I'd be happy to bring the law into this if that's what you want. But before we take such drastic measures, you may want to have your accountant look at your books. I think you will find that I paid more to this institution than any other account this year," she says, as though the issue of mental health were a simple business transaction. The Heiress lets this settle in before she makes her final, most potent threat. "And you may also want to check the plaque beside the front door of your institution. You will see my father's name engraved at the top. He was on your board of directors, and he was the largest beneficiary Four Winds has ever had. The trust he set up before his death still keeps the lights on here."

The doctor looks at Anna and then at the inch-thick file on his desk. "What will happen to this young woman when she is returned to Germany?"

"That is not your concern, Doctor." She reaches her hand forward again. "The file, please."

And just like that, any proof Anna might have, anything she might be able to use in her defense later, is surrendered, no doubt to be destroyed by Annie Burr Jennings.

ONE YEAR EARLIER

Private Medical Office, Manhattan
July 25, 1930

Madness is as madness does. And though some would consider it pure insanity to cradle a dead parrot, to Anna this act makes perfect sense. How else will she remember her pair of Januses? She lost the first parrot some time ago, and the second has been crippled ever since. Unable to fly. Destined to spend the rest of its life hopping about the furniture and scooting around the floor. It's no wonder she stepped on it. When the poor thing got caught in the folds of her heavy robe, Anna never saw it, never felt it until her bare foot snapped its fragile little neck.

A tiny crunch, no more than the breaking of a twig. A final, outraged squawk, and then silence. Anna picked up the bird but its head lolled sideways at a grotesque angle.

"No. No. No." She shook the bird, but it nodded feebly, insisting that it was, in fact, dead.

This was many hours ago and she has been moaning pitifully ever since. Refusing food and company, ignoring the urgent pounding on her bedroom door. In the quiet, rational part of her mind, Anna knows that she must pull herself together. She knows Janus was only a bird—or, to be exact, a *pair* of birds. She knows the last few years have taken their toll, and she admits—to herself at least—that she has looked to the bottle far too often to soothe her nerves and her sorrow.

But this death, this small death, is one too many. And that creeping darkness that she has fought for over a decade begins to smother her again. It comes, as it always does, with a blurring at the edge of her vision. A tightness in her chest. Shallow breaths, heavy limbs, and violent, unwanted memories that assault her mind, that fly at her unbidden and unexpected. Tingling in her extremities. Dizziness. And then a sense of panic and fear so deep she begins to scream and pull at her hair.

There is chaos in the penthouse, and then a splintering of her bedroom door. It takes a moment to make sense of the loud, destructive chopping of a pair of fire axes. The heavy North American walnut is no match for the orderlies and their thick trunk-like arms, their single-minded tenacity. Eight whacks, maybe ten—it's hard to count with the thunder in her ears—and the door rips apart. Anna howls again and scoots backward against the floor until she is pressed against the footboard of her bed, Janus in the crook of her arm.

The men make soothing noises as they ease toward her, and the last thing Anna remembers before sliding into total darkness is a white jacket dangling from one large, knuckled hand. It has comically long sleeves and an alarming number of belts and buckles.

———

"Where am I?" Anna asks when she wakes sometime later. Her voice is heavy and inarticulate. Her tongue feels thick, like a piece of saddle leather, and she can't form the proper syllables. She sounds drunk. No, she sounds *medicated*. Even in this semiconscious state she remembers what this feels like. Anna bends her will to the simple act of forming three clear words. "Where. Am. I?"

Somewhere above her a calm male voice answers, "Westchester."

Anna clears her throat. Tries to force her eyes open, but there is only a murky purple sort of light. Several minutes of confusion and looming panic pass before she realizes there is a mask over her face, thirty seconds more before she feels the restraints. She is pinned to a padded, reclined chair at several points along her body. Ankles. Knees. Waist. Forearms. Chest.

Shoulders. Chin. And forehead. Anna can move nothing but her fingers.

As the sedation slowly drains from her bloodstream, she fights the desire to give way to hysteria. Instead she breathes slowly through her nose, in and out, until she is certain she can ask the next question without crying.

"Where am I *exactly*?"

Again that cool, disinterested voice. This time there is the scratching of pen against paper as well. "My office."

"Why?"

"You have been given over to my care. After I collect a bit of data I will have you transferred to the Four Winds Sanatorium."

She wants to ask this brisk, invisible man why she's being committed, what the medical grounds are for this decision. But none of these words or their tricky syllables make themselves available to the lethargic lump of muscle that is her tongue. All she can manage, again, is "Why?"

"It has been determined that you have disordered nerves."

Anna cannot remember seeing a doctor or being examined by one, and she tries to tell this man as much, but her argument is garbled and nonsensical even to her when it tumbles slurred and ungainly from her mouth.

"Calm down, Miss Anderson." A warm hand on her cheek. "We're going to give you a treatment to calm your nerves. It is experimental, you understand, but we expect it to become the leading cure for depressive disorders such as yours in the coming decade."

Anna groans and tries to shake her head. She wants water and a bed and a cool, dark room, not whatever cure this man has concocted.

He ignores her protest. "Because this treatment is new, and under study, we will need your permission to administer it."

"No." This word comes out perfectly clear, forced between her clenched teeth.

The restraint that binds her forearms is loosened slightly and a pen is set between the thumb and forefinger of her right hand. It is held by this man's hand, and he guides the pen across a piece of paper she cannot see. She can only hear the scratch, scratch, scratch as he forges her signature.

"There," he says, with the first hint of inflection in his voice. "Now we can continue. I appreciate your cooperation and can assure you it is not misplaced. Let me explain the procedure I am about to perform."

Anna tries to lash out with her arms, but the strap is yanked tight again and she gasps as the leather digs into the bare skin of her forearms.

"You are sitting in a device known as a Bergonic chair," he says. "As you are aware, you are strapped down, but this is for your own safety. We have found that some patients do not respond well to the electric current and they twitch, especially as the voltage is increased."

Whatever resolve Anna has previously maintained to keep the panic at bay quickly melts at this pronouncement. It is hard to scream and the restraints make it impossible for her to thrash about, so she begins to moan instead.

There is an almost gleeful note to his voice as he continues, "I have found in my research with soldiers during the Great War that electric treatment for psychological disorders is quite effective. I believe you will have a greatly improved disposition going forward."

"No."

"Oh, don't be so negative. I think you—and Miss Jennings—will be quite happy with the results."

There is a slight tugging at each of her restraints as he checks to make sure they are tight. Then he bends low, near her ear, and says, "Now, this shouldn't hurt very much. At least not at first. We will begin with a low voltage."

Like so many of the things doctors have told Anna through the years, it is a lie.

SIX MONTHS EARLIER

Manhattan
January 14, 1930

For us, the nearest relatives of the Tsar's family, it is very
difficult and painful to reconcile ourselves to the fact
that not a single member of that family is still alive. How
gladly we would like to believe that one of them, at least,
had survived the murderous destruction of 1918. We
would shower our love on the survivor. But in the case
of the lady in question, our sense of duty compels us to
state that the story is only a fairy tale. The memory of
our dear departed would be tarnished if we allowed this
fantastic story to spread and gain credence.

The statement was written almost two years ago, less than
twenty-four hours after the death of the Dowager Empress,
but it is reprinted in the *Evening Post* that day, along with a less-
than-flattering article about Anna and her claims. The paper
is brought to her on a silver tray, along with her lunch, by the
Heiress's butler. In time the declaration will come to be known
as the Copenhagen Statement, but that day it simply feels like
another slap in the face. By that evening, after Anna has drunk
an entire bottle of champagne, it feels like a declaration of war.

Anna refuses to leave her room all afternoon despite
repeated summonses by the Heiress. Preparations are under

way for an intimate cocktail party to be held in the penthouse that evening, and Anna's opinion on the flower arrangements is desired. Or so they've said every time they've pounded on her bedroom door.

Anna knows that, in reality, they are simply trying to draw her out of this lingering melancholy. Trying to coax her into forgetting that infuriating statement. Anna didn't take the news any better when Gleb showed it to her the first time, and she has no intention of being docile about it now either. Instead of letting them in, she turns up the volume on her phonograph and opens the window. There is a ferocious bite to the mid-January air, but she's wearing an ankle-length fur coat—albeit with nothing underneath—and the champagne gives her an illusion of warmth. The tip of her nose is soon cold and her cheeks are red, but still she stands there, persisting in the stubborn act of sending puffs of frozen breath out the window.

Behind her the birds squawk in their cage, beating their bright green wings against the thin metal bars. Anna sets the empty champagne bottle on the window ledge and turns to face them.

"I'm sorry, pets, have I not fed you today? I can't remember."

The parrots usually eat a seed blend she buys at the exotic pet store down the street, but they also love fruit—apples in particular. At the moment, however, she has nothing in the room but the dried end of a toasted baguette that came with her lunch, and it will have to do for now.

Why she opens the cage before she has closed the window Anna cannot explain. Perhaps the champagne has clouded her senses. Or maybe it's seeing the Romanov betrayal again. Regardless, the deed is done, and before she has time to react, both parrots launch from their confines and shoot like arrows toward the open window.

"No!" Anna screams. She hears something large drop and then shatter in the other room.

Cursing.

The frantic beat of wings as both parrots fly, perpendicular, toward the window. They are separated by a mere six inches, one above the other.

Someone pounds on her bedroom door. One parrot crashes into the windowpane. The other glides smoothly out the window and into the frigid Manhattan skyline. Anna, only a breath behind the birds, lunges toward the open window, arm outstretched to grab the parrot, and knocks the empty champagne bottle from the ledge.

It falls, forever and ever, only to disintegrate on the sidewalk below, twenty feet from the nearest pedestrian, in a cloud of powdered glass. When she lifts her eyes again, the first bird—her Janus—is little more than a green smudge against the horizon, while the second is lying stunned at her feet, one wing bent at an awkward angle.

———

It is freezing on the rooftop. Anna has no idea how she's lost her coat and really, she doesn't care. Janus is out there in the cold somewhere, winging her way across the skyline in the dark, cold dead of night, so why should Anna be warm? Why should she be so lucky?

She screams the bird's name over and over as she leans across the ledge, her bare skin pressed against the brick and her voice growing hoarser by the moment. An echoing chorus of Januses bounces off the buildings. The bird does not return, but the neighbors scream at her to shut-the-ever-loving-hell-up. Anna does not comply. Compliance is not in her nature.

Another bottle of champagne—the last from her room—sits half empty beside her, and she takes a pull from its long slender neck. The bubbles do nothing to warm her, but they help her forget she's cold.

She is babbling and incoherent now. Beside herself.

The only reason Anna knows someone has come to collect her is because the coat is dropped over her shoulders, cutting off the wind.

Arms around her like a vise.

The scrape of concrete on her heels as she's dragged across the roof and toward the door.

Cursing and muttering in her ear.

The Heiress's enraged shriek somewhere off to the side.

Anna reaches for her bottle but her arm weighs a thousand pounds and will not cooperate.

A stairwell.

The thump of limbs against steps as she's guided down.

Warmth.

The penthouse.

Her bed.

A horrendous banging as someone nails the window shut.

The slamming of her bedroom door.

Darkness.

14

Anastasia

Tobolsk, Russia
October 10

The glare makes me wince. But I cannot protest or move seats because Pierre Gilliard is in one of his *moods*. I can see it written there on his furrowed brow, in his clouded eyes. His long limbs snap with quick, jerky movements. His fingers drum incessantly on his desk and then on the chalkboard. Our tutor has grown increasingly anxious since his arrival in Tobolsk, and though Gilliard is only in his late thirties, he frets like an old man.

Tatiana insists that he is only cranky because he's frightened for us, and this strict, unrelenting dictatorship in the classroom gives him a sense of control over our deteriorating circumstances. Olga believes he is simply humorless and doesn't know how to be anything but a curmudgeon. Both of them are proud of their observations and have taken to discussing them as we lie in bed at night. How worldly they consider themselves to be. How wise and studied in the nature of men. For the most part I think they just like the sound of their own voices, and I wish they would be quiet and go to sleep.

"Sit still," Maria says, driving her elbow into my ribs, "or you'll get us all in trouble."

Maria cannot see Gleb Botkin sitting on the stone wall at

the edge of the yard. Nor can she see the shard of mirror in his hand or the way he uses it to reflect the sunlight into my eyes. *And they call me Schwibsik! He's the imp. Blasted little troublemaker.*

Gleb and his sister, Tanya, arrived in Tobolsk in mid-September after being summoned by their father. The turmoil in Petrograd has made him uneasy and he wants them close at hand. So they stay with Dr. Botkin in his rented rooms several blocks away. Although they are not allowed to visit us, they often come to the Governor's House and eat their lunch on the wall and wait to catch a glimpse of our family. Sometimes they wave or dance to get our attention when they see us in the yard. Often I see Gleb searching the windows, looking for me, I think, in that innocent puppyish way of his. Normally the distraction is welcome, appreciated even. I can't fault his loyalty or enthusiasm. But Gleb has chosen a poor method of getting my attention today. I would throw open the window and scold him if I wasn't worried that I would get my knuckles rapped by Gilliard.

Gleb has been at it for half an hour and my eyes are sore. So I close them. But even with my eyes squeezed tight I can feel the bright little flashes of light, as though someone is turning an electric torch on and off, again and again, an inch from my face. What I do not see, however, is the look of exasperation on Pierre Gilliard's face, so it is a shock when he crosses the room and brings his ruler down firmly on the knuckles of my right hand.

I yelp and jerk my hand away. "Why did you do that?"

"No sleeping in class, Anastasia." His lips press into a tight, thin line.

"I wasn't sleeping!"

"Do not lie, child. I saw you myself."

"I was trying to rest my eyes!" I hate the way my voice pitches higher when I'm angry, how hysterical I sound.

Gilliard laughs, but there is nothing kind or amused in the sound. "Resting your eyes from what, precisely?" he asks.

"Him." I point to where Gleb ought to be, where he was only minutes earlier. "Gleb was reflecting sunlight at me with a mirror."

The wall, of course, is empty, and that little green-eyed troll is nowhere to be seen. I'll throttle the boy with my bare hands the next time I see him.

Pierre Gilliard clasps his hands behind his back and leans over the table. "It is unbecoming of a tsarevna to make up stories just to get out of Latin."

I clench my teeth. "I am not lying."

"There was no one on the wall, Anastasia. There was no one distracting you. You were napping in class. You were being lazy."

"I'm not lying! And I'm not lazy." It's unfair of him to accuse me of this. I think he knows it too because he winces a little.

The problem with having a temper is that my body often moves faster than my mind. It's far too easy to react with action instead of intellect. I don't realize that I've slammed my fist down on the table in fury until pain radiates from the bottom of my pinky up through the heel of my hand. I cannot keep my stupid, traitorous tears at bay so I press my hand to my chest and scowl at Gilliard.

Maria sits to my left and I can feel her stiffen as he looms over me. "Stop," she hisses. "You're only making it worse."

Gilliard's voice is calm and quiet, and I should be more frightened than I am. He reaches into his pocket, draws out a piece of chalk, and places it carefully on the table in front of me.

"To the chalk board," he says. "The ablative case is characterized by three broad uses. You will write an example of each use, in your best handwriting, along with their definitions and parts of speech. Prove to me that you were not napping, Anastasia."

I push back my chair, stand slowly, and pick up the chalk with two fingers. The schoolroom is silent as Alexey and my sisters stare at me in dismay. I snap the chalk in half and throw it against the wall.

"I. Hate. Latin!"

Gilliard, even calmer now, draws another piece of chalk from his pocket and sets it before me. "Then your hate is misplaced, Tsarevna. I am not your enemy. And if you will not learn temperance under my tutelage, I fear you will learn it in other, harsher ways. But your punishment stands. The three uses of the ablative case. On the board. Now."

"Or what?" I hiss. "What will you do if I refuse?"

———

"You should have just done what Gilliard asked," Maria says, setting the bucket on the ground with one hand while she covers her nose with the other. She stands inside the kitchen door, unwilling to cross the threshold into the frozen yard. "You got us both in trouble."

"Don't blame me. I didn't force you to interfere." I step aside as Jimmy bolts through the door and into the yard. The chickens run, squawking in terror, but I don't call him off. Jimmy won't hurt the stupid little birds, and they deserve a good fright.

"Ugh." Maria stomps her foot. "You can be such an ungrateful pest. Be glad Father didn't agree to Gilliard's original suggestion or you'd be cleaning the soldiers' bathroom upstairs."

"Gilliard should be the one getting punished. He rapped my knuckles for no reason!" I lift the bucket with a grunt and watch as the ghastly contents send white ribbons of steam into the air. "He may as well work for the provisional government."

"Sshh. Don't say that," Maria hisses. "He's here, isn't he?

And he's terribly loyal to Father. That alone puts him at risk. He's just trying to do his job. You weren't making it very easy for him, telling stories and all."

"It wasn't a story!" I set the bucket of kitchen slops at my feet. It's heavier than it looks, and the handle cuts into my sore hand. I have no idea how I'll carry the thing all the way to the refuse pit at the far end of the yard. "Gleb was out there, being a little scourge. This is all his fault."

Maria steps backward into the kitchen and shakes her head. "You have to stop looking for trouble, Schwibsik. We have enough as it is."

She kicks the door shut with her foot, leaving me to finish the nauseous chore by myself. I can't look at the contents of the bucket without gagging, so I lift it in both hands and begin shuffling across the yard to where the chickens scratch and peck at the contents of the refuse pit.

It wasn't long after our arrival in Tobolsk that I realized chickens are, in fact, the most odious animals ever created. They are loud and mean. Not to mention horribly stupid and yet ridiculously proud—squawking like Harpies every time they lay an egg. They molt. They defecate everywhere, and the stuff is like tar, impossible to scrape from your shoes or your skin, and the smell is enough to make your eyes water. Their mating is so horrific and loud and violent I am stunned the species has survived. I had the great misfortune of witnessing the act one afternoon when I drew the short straw (none of us would volunteer) and went to collect the eggs for Cook. The rooster had that poor hen pinned to the ground, her wings flailing helplessly, as he ripped feathers from her head and pounded her until she couldn't walk. I asked Father later, with burning cheeks, whether the hen had been raped. He assured me that no, it was just the way chickens went about their business. I, for one, thought it very unfair to the hen, and I had named the rooster *D'Yavol*. Devil. The hens aren't his only victims, however. That evil little red-feathered monster launches himself at us whenever we gather eggs, and we live in fear of his vicious spurs.

So I give the chicken coop a wide berth as I struggle with the bucket, muttering about my punishment. I have to stop every few minutes to move my skirt out of the way lest I trip over my own hem and end up covered in refuse.

"Do you need help with that?"

Tomas stands behind me, hands stuffed deep in his coat pockets, trying not to laugh. His hair is too long and his military cap too big, but he still looks charming, cute even. I can feel an unfamiliar heat rising in my cheeks, so I set the bucket down and look away from him.

"Yes, please. It's very heavy."

Tomas peers into the bucket and curls his lip in distaste. "Entrails?"

"Disgusting, isn't it?"

He leans in a bit closer. "And feathers. So—"

"Cook is roasting chickens for dinner tonight. These are the extra parts. I'm pretty sure that gray blobby thing is a gizzard." I shudder. "Pity he didn't pull D'Yavol from the coop. I wouldn't mind seeing his gizzard in a bucket."

"*D'Yavol?*"

"The rooster."

The corner of Tomas's mouth turns up in a grin. "That bad?"

"He's the spawn of Satan. And"—I hold up one finger as Tomas lifts the bucket, and we begin walking toward the far corner of the yard—"he's a cannibal as well. Just watch when we dump this out. He'll come running. Little monster loves nothing more than gobbling up his friends."

"All chickens are cannibals," Tomas says. "They'll eat anything. They're worse than pigs."

The back portion of the yard slopes downhill slightly, and we walk in silence as Tomas balances the bucket carefully in one hand, trying to make sure the revolting contents don't slosh over the edge and onto his boots.

"How did you end up with this chore?" he asks when we reach our destination.

"Haven't you heard? I am belligerent, quarrelsome, and incorrigible."

"Then I am glad to have made your acquaintance. That's the only sort of person I associate with," Tomas says. "You might want to look away for this part."

For once I don't argue. I wander off a few feet and keep my back to Tomas as he tips the bucket over and sends the contents sliding into the pit. I can hear the wet, splattering sound, and I gag despite my determination not to.

I squeeze my eyes tight and draw in several long breaths of frigid air through my nose to regain control of my roiling stomach. A short temper and an easy gag reflex. My list of flaws grows by the day.

Jimmy has abandoned the chickens in favor of something at the wall. He's digging furiously at a small mound of frozen dirt. His tail lashes back and forth, and he grunts, desperate to reach whatever quarry lies hidden in the soil. A mole no doubt. Or some other small rodent.

"So who did you upset?" Tomas asks. He holds the empty bucket in his other hand, the one farthest from me, and leads the way back to the house.

"Gilliard."

"Your tutor?"

I nod. "He called me a liar. I didn't take it very well."

Tomas casts a sideways glance at me, and I think he smiles. "I can't imagine you would."

I offer him a curtsy and a wry smile. "My reputation precedes me, I see."

"Not at all."

I question him with a glance.

"Observation," he says. "You are different from your sisters. More spirited."

"A polite word for 'poorly behaved.'"

"I like to think it means 'interesting.'"

"A good answer." I flash him a bright smile and am rewarded with one from him. "But that doesn't mean I believe you."

I call and Jimmy comes running, but not to me. He goes directly to Tomas and receives a scratch between the ears as a reward. I glare at Tomas, but he laughs and we tromp back toward the house. It is very strange to befriend a boy whose job it is to keep you under lock and key. Yet Tomas doesn't feel like a captor. He's not an officer. He has never ordered us around like Semyon or Leshy. He is simply there, constantly in the background. Patrolling the yard or playing cards with the others upstairs. He often helps Cook in the kitchen—he isn't stupid; Cook frequently hands out samples—or walks Joy when Alexey is too weak to go outside. The boredom that afflicts us torments the guards as well, and as time goes on the lines between us have begun to blur. These days we barely notice the uniforms.

Maria apparently doesn't notice the uniforms at all, because when I pull open the kitchen door, Tomas on my heels, I find her in the hallway between the kitchen and the pantry, partially hidden in shadow, whispering with a guard.

In the seconds before the cold blast of wind hits her cheeks and she notices our presence, I see the way she looks at him. Not just flirtatious, but adoring. He leans close, one forearm resting on the wall above her head, their faces inches apart. They pull away quickly, fluidly, and if I hadn't seen the way her lips were parted and how round her eyes were I might have believed her when she says, "No, I can manage quite well on my own, thank you."

Maria turns and saunters away, chin up, shoulders stiff, as though she is offended rather than tempted. The guard too is gone, up the stairs before I can say anything to him. Tomas stands behind me, bucket still in hand, and I know by his expression that I'm not mistaken. The look on his nicely angled face is one of revelation, as though he didn't know such a thing was possible. A soldier and a tsarevna.

"What is his name?" I ask. There are so many guards and I know so few of their names.

"Ivan Skorokhodov," he says.

"Do I need to worry about my sister?"

Tomas lifts a hand slowly and then, after drawing a deep breath as though to summon a bit of courage, brushes one finger along my chin. "No more than you need to worry about yourself."

TWO WEEKS LATER

Tobolsk, Russia
October 25

"Don't you think it's ironic that we live on Freedom Street yet we're under house arrest?" Maria asks.

We stand at the corner of the yard peering up at the battered street sign. "*Freedom* is a word I no longer know," I say.

"Don't let Gilliard hear you say that! He'll have you writing vocabulary cards in Latin all morning."

"*Gilliard*," I groan. "He hates me."

"He does not hate you," Maria argues. "He is trying to civilize you."

"He told me to shut up in class this morning."

"To be fair, you talk too much. And you were being rather dreadful."

"Well, you would be dreadful too if he'd written those notes on your paper." We continue walking slowly through the yard.

The wind bites our noses and earlobes, but we take our time. Once back inside we will resume Gilliard's mind-numbing history lesson on the Samoyedic people of western Siberia. "He said that I am lazy in my lessons and that I am ill-mannered."

"But you are." Maria grins, showing there is no malice in the jab.

"No. I'm *bored*."

"We're all bored, Schwibsik. It's no excuse to be a pest in the classroom."

The boredom is something we all deal with in different ways. There are endless games of dominoes and bezique and whist. We read all the books we brought with us from Tsarskoe Selo and then we read them again. I've just gone through *Ivanhoe* for the third time, and I think I might lose my mind if I have to spend one more day in medieval England. We write in our journals. We write letters. We write terrible poems and short stories. Last week Alexey declared he was going to write a novel but never got more than a page or two into his swashbuckling pirate adventure before stopping to illustrate one of the pages. Then he gave up altogether.

Meanwhile, Olga and Tatiana retreat into their books and needlework. Mother knits and unravels and knits again. Or she works on the corsets. Father, unable to curb his need for physical exercise in any other way, has taken to spending hours each day chopping wood in the yard. He is so obsessed with the activity, in fact, that Leshy sent in great piles of birch trunks from a local saw mill for him to chop. Maria has found a more troublesome way of diverting her boredom. She flirts.

We finish our final lap and turn back toward the house when I catch her smiling at Ivan Skorokhodov.

"Is that why you offered to keep me company during this forced exercise? I thought you were just being nice."

"I don't know what you're talking about."

"Yes you do. I see the way you look at him. What's his name anyway? And don't pretend like you don't know." I want her to admit it. I want to hear her say it out loud.

"Oh, you're one to talk. I see the way you flirt with Tomas."

"I do not *flirt* with Tomas. He is only a friend."

"So you can make friends with the guards but I can't?"

I'm cold now, well and truly cold, and I rub my hands together as we hurry up the front steps and into the house. "Don't be ridiculous," I whisper. "We are all friends with the guards." The fact that I have a strong preference for Tomas is not something I admit, however.

We pull off our hats and gloves and shrug out of our long coats and return to the schoolroom, where we expect to spend several excruciating hours at our lessons. Pierre Gilliard is there, along with the rest of our family and all the staff.

"Oh no," I groan. "Am I to be punished publically? I've already apologized to Gilliard. And I've taken a walk. I really didn't—"

"Schwibsik," Father says. "Sit down. We've had news from Petrograd."

Maria grabs my hand as we drop into our seats. "What news?" I ask.

"The Bolsheviks have taken control of the government."

"What does that mean?"

"It is a second revolution," Mother says.

"I still don't understand what it *means*."

"To begin with it means that Alexander Kerensky is no longer there to protect us," Father says.

If he had said that Satan was our benefactor and hell our actual home he would not have received a louder outburst. The litany of Kerensky's sins against us begins. Father patiently endures this for a moment before raising his hand.

"The man is no friend of mine," he says. "But we might all

be dead if not for him." The fact that Father has mellowed in his opinion of Kerensky only makes me angrier.

Alexey will never forgive Kerensky for what he did to the elephant, much less consider him a hero. "He killed Sammi," he protests.

"Yes." Father kneels before Alexey and takes his small, frail hands in his large calloused ones. "Sometimes mercy is severe."

"Do not defend that monster," Mother says.

"I do not defend him. I am only trying to explain that I understand now what he has done. Why he has sent us here."

I hated Alexander Kerensky from the moment I saw him. Hated how he treated us. How he took every precious thing from us. How he took such delight in demoralizing us. To hear Father justify any of his actions feels like a betrayal.

"And is this a mercy too?" I demand. "This muddy hell that we've been forced into?"

"Do not curse, Schwibsik. It is unbecoming of you."

"I'm not cursing. Hell is a location. A noun," I say, looking at Gilliard, and I am gratified to see that he is struggling not to grin.

Father chooses not to fight that particular battle. "Do not forget, child, that there is a great deal of difference between mercy and kindness. Gilliard can school you on the differences later—and yes, I heard about your lesson this morning. I will not argue that Alexander Kerensky showed us no kindness. But it was a *mercy* that he did not throw us out the palace gates and into the hands of the mob that very first day. It was a *mercy* that he forced us to work in the garden for months—"

"How—"

"Because there are horrible food shortages in Petrograd right now. He made us grow that food so we would not starve. And yes, in a way, sending us to this swamp at the edge of the world was also his way of showing mercy. Back in July he knew those Bolshevik buzzards were circling, and he realized that if he did not evacuate us they would be more than happy to render their own bloody form of justice. So here we are, in a town that is closed off from the rest of the world for eight months of the year. The river is freezing and the mud is turning to blocks of ice beneath our feet. We are removed from all civilization and also from harm. At least for the time being. In his own harsh way Kerensky helped us in the only way he could."

"He could have sent us to England," I say.

Father smiles, sadly. "But would we have gotten there alive, Schwibsik?"

It doesn't matter. None of this matters to me. "I won't forgive him. And neither should you."

Father still kneels before my brother so he cannot rise quickly enough to stop me from running from the room. "Schwibsik!"

"Let her go," Mother says. "She has a right to be upset."

Upset isn't the right word for what I feel as I stomp through our quarters and up the stairs, where the soldiers are housed, and out onto the balcony. I am overwhelmed. Upended. To hear father assert that Kerensky had been our *protector* is insanity. To hear that we no longer have a protector at all is terrifying.

It is one of those dismal, overcast days that feels dreary and lethargic. I should have grabbed my coat. I'm still cold from my walk. Or maybe I shouldn't have come at all, but I refuse to go back inside until all evidence of my tears is gone. If I am going to become a weeper then I am determined to do it in private.

"Anastasia?"

Tomas. Of course.

"What?" I wipe my sleeve across my face before I can look at him.

"I was in there playing cards when you ripped through the room—"

"I did not *rip*—"

"You did. Girls always rip when they're mad. I thought I'd see if you're okay."

"Afraid I might jump from the roof?"

He takes one step forward, then another. And when he's confident I mean no harm to myself or to him, he sits down beside me. "I don't know. Maybe."

"You think I'm really that stupid?"

"I think you're sad. I don't think anyone else sees it because you try so hard to be brave for them. But it must be really hard to be a prisoner. I'd likely want to pitch myself off a roof too."

"I don't want to kill myself, Tomas."

"Oh good!" He throws his arm across his forehead in mock relief. "Because they'd likely make me clean up the mess and I'm no good with blood."

I don't laugh so much as snort. "But entrails are acceptable?"

He shrugs. "I draw the line at blood and vomit."

Maria needled me about my friendship with Tomas, but he is easy to talk to and he makes me laugh. I never feel stupid or ugly or invisible when I'm around him. Tomas *sees* me. And Jimmy likes him more and more every day. I have always believed dogs to be wonderful judges of character.

Tomas stretches his legs out in front of him. "What are you doing, then? Since you're not up here to go tumbling over the rail?"

I don't know what makes me tell him the truth. Maybe I'm wrung out emotionally. Maybe I am desperate. Maybe I like him. Liking a boy can do strange things to the mind. "Thinking," I whisper.

"About?"

"Escape."

No sooner is the word out of my mouth than I realize what a terrible mistake I've made. Tomas isn't my friend. He can't ever really be my friend. His job is to make sure we don't escape.

He must recognize the look of terror on my face because he is quick to ask, "Is that a secret?"

I nod like an imbecile.

He pulls at the long, straight bone in the bridge of his nose. "Good thing you know how I feel about keeping secrets."

15

Anna

THE GRANDANOR CORPORATION

1929, 1928

Metropolitan Opera House, New York City
November 1929

The playbill announces that tonight's performance is *Tosca*, the famed Italian opera by Giacomo Puccini. They sit in the Heiress's private box, to the right of the stage, and the seats below are filling up quickly with theatergoers in their evening finest. Below them is a sea of bow ties and feather boas, fur coats, cuff links, and lit cigars. The buzz of human chatter contrasts starkly with the occasional outburst of tuning from the orchestra. A handful of patrons have noticed their presence in the box and they gawk, pointing and lifting their chins in an effort to share the sighting with their companions.

Anna keeps her gaze fixed on the empty stage. She is cold but doesn't dare drape her wrap around her shoulders again. The Heiress objected to her wearing it in the first place, so impressed was she with the Madeleine Vionnet gown Anna has chosen for tonight. The dress is a masterpiece. It is a beaded, cream silk—a slight departure from her standard white. It boasts thin straps and an open back, and gooseflesh has risen all along her arms from the chill. Cut on the bias, the dress has the magical properties of making Anna look exceedingly more glamorous and six inches taller than she really is—a thing she greatly appreciates now that she's in her thirties and is starting to notice the effects of time.

"I am glad to see," the Heiress whispers in her ear, "that the recent financial debacle has not thinned the crowd. It would be such a shame on opening night."

For two weeks the Heiress has been obsessed with the stock market crash and all the news surrounding it. They call it Black Tuesday, and every morning the papers report some new tragedy: lives lost, institutions ruined, families bankrupted. Her host follows it with religious zeal, in much the same way she scours the society pages for news and insists on reporting the salacious details over breakfast. Anna stayed in her room this morning to avoid it altogether, excusing herself by claiming exhaustion when in reality she no longer had the stomach for every tawdry detail. Loss is loss and death is death, and everyone in this city is so surprised to learn of the existence of either.

The Heiress, however, has missed her daily dispensing of gossip and won't be so easily thwarted. "Do you remember John Hammond?" she asks.

Anna knows better than to answer but it would be rude not to. She chooses a lie instead of the rather complicated truth. "I don't believe so, no."

"He was that handsome young banker who joined us on the yacht this summer."

"Oh. Yes," Anna says. "A charming man." She drops her gaze to her lap and this movement does not go unnoticed by the Heiress.

"I've been told he jumped out of the twelfth-floor window of the Bank of the United States on Black Tuesday. Lost everything, they say. Was ruined by a particularly bad investment. Such a shame. He was a lovely young man. Had a bright future ahead of him." Anna looks straight ahead now, unmoving, unwilling to betray her emotions or return the meaningful glance the Heiress directs her way. John Hammond took his life because of a bad investment. She refuses to cry or give way to the explosive sense of guilt that rattles around the back of her skull when the Heiress adds, "I rather thought he took a shine to you."

The lights dim and the cacophony in the orchestra pit grows more urgent and intentional. The buzz of human voices lessens to a murmur as the crimson swath of velvet curtain rustles with some movement backstage. Quiet laughter in the box next to them. The crackle of paper as the Heiress inspects her playbill for the names of familiar singers. *Oh, God, please don't let her drag me backstage afterward*, Anna thinks. *I cannot be put on display tonight, not now.* Anna can hear the blood rushing through her ears with each beat of her heart. Her hands remain where she left them, folded in her lap. Her eyes blink furiously, pushing away the unwanted emotions.

It is only at intermission that Anna finally relaxes enough to clap with the rest of the crowd, but she does not retreat to the lobby with the Heiress, insisting that women's troubles have left her feeling poorly this evening. Not even Annie Burr Jennings—decades removed from her childbearing years—can argue with that. The moment she's alone, Anna pulls the wrap around her shoulders and draws into herself, eyes closed, desperate to become master of her own emotions again. She tries to assure herself that John Hammond's death is not her fault.

And then the Heiress returns and the curtains are pulled back once more and the stage fills with opera singers performing Puccini's classic saga of torment and murder and suicide, all wrapped in the reverberating sound of his legendary, melodic arias.

Suicide.

Suicide.

Suicide.

A theme, it seems, she cannot escape, in life or theater. Anna survived her own attempt, but it seems not everyone is as fortunate as she. A memory surfaces. John Hammond, naked, in the starlight.

There is a darkness that creeps into Anna's peripheral vision, the harbinger of her old nemesis, that creeping, desperate panic whose grip has been loosened only in recent years. But now that it has arrived, there is no keeping it at bay. Her only choice is whether or not to surrender in the company of others.

"If you will excuse me," Anna says, rising to her feet and drawing the wrap tighter around her shoulders, "I think I'm going to be ill."

FOUR MONTHS EARLIER

Siasconset Beach, Nantucket Island
July 1929

It is midnight and the sky is clear, but the only light that reaches the sleek, spacious yacht comes from the stars, for the moon has waned to a mere sliver. The Heiress has gone to bed in her cabin below, as have a small handful of guests, and the boat lies still and placid in the water, anchored several hundred yards from shore.

Anna is alone on deck with a gentleman, some banker from Manhattan, and she's had enough champagne to have forgotten his last name. John something or other. Not enough to fall down drunk, but certainly enough to lose her typical buttoned-up demeanor. And speaking of buttons, several of hers seem to be missing. No, not missing. Undone. Funny, she has no idea how it happened.

"Oh, don't get shy on me now," the Banker says when she

moves to slip the little mother-of-pearl buttons back through their holes. "It's just a bit of fun. No harm intended. The water's warm. We should go for a swim."

His shoes are off, as are his socks, and at this pronouncement, the Banker takes a swig of champagne right from the bottle and unbuttons his own shirt. The man has reason to be confident, and Anna struggles not to stare.

"Your turn," he says, handing her the bottle with an aggressively charming smile. "Double-dog dare you."

"I don't think—"

"I promise I don't bite," he says, flashing those lovely white teeth, "unless you want me to."

Anna cannot remember the last time she felt heat like this in her belly, the last time a man looked at her like that, not as a threat, or a claim, but as a challenge. An invitation. It feels good, and Anna lifts the bottle to her lips. She lets the fizzy liquid settle on her tongue and then swallows a mouthful of courage. And then another. Anna has found her drug of choice, and it comes corked, in a bottle, with a thousand tiny bubbles that tickle her nose. Champagne. Nectar of the gods. She swigs again, deeply. The wonderful thing, she decides, tipping the last of it into her mouth, is that you never feel it coming. She has never been a heavy drinker and abhors most hard liquor—can't stand the harsh, burning fire in her throat, the feel of a million suns on her tongue. But this is different. Special. Sweet. Even better than pear cider. And it ever so easily lifts her mood and strips her inhibitions away. Before she knows it, her white silk blouse comes off, revealing a thin chemise with no bra underneath—the Heiress assured her this was the fashion, and she stands there, uncertain what to do next.

The Banker whoops in approval and drops his trousers to the deck. The ridiculous man knows he's worth looking at because he does not break eye contact while he loses the one remaining garment on his body. Then he steps to the deck rail, all long and silver in the starlight, and swan dives over the edge. She's at the rail quickly enough to catch part of the splash on her face. The boat rocks gently with their movements and her stomach roils in response. When the Heiress suggested they go boating earlier in the evening Anna was terrified she'd spend the entire trip belowdecks holding a bucket in her lap. Thankfully, her host's idea of "boating" was simply to drop anchor several hundred yards off shore and throw a party on the deck. That's easy enough to live with if she doesn't think about it too hard.

"Jump in!" the Banker shouts as he sends a spray of water onto the deck. This stranger, this man she has known for less than twelve hours, beckons her with that muscled arm. Anna considers her scars, what he will think if he sees them. But it is dark, the champagne is going to her head, and for once she doesn't care.

"Don't leave me hanging, pretty lady," he shouts off the starboard side.

Surely he's far enough away. Surely in the dim light he won't be able to see the wreckage of her body.

"Look away!" Anna orders.

"I think you're missing the point of this little exercise, madam." He laughs, long and seductive, and Anna lifts the hem of her chemise without even realizing. "But if you insist, I'll turn around."

The rest of her clothing joins his in a pile on the deck. She's unsure if this is an act of bravery or stupidity, but she goes over the rail anyway, feet first, with a graceless splash. Anna isn't sure how he defines warm water, but to her this doesn't qualify. It's cool enough to shock her into full sobriety, and she treads water a little faster than necessary to stay warm.

The Banker is at her side in moments and they stare at each other, their bare shoulders bobbing above the water.

"That wasn't so bad, was it?" he asks.

"I think I'll survive."

And then she feels a warm hand on the cool skin of her waist as he pulls her closer. The press of full, confident lips against her own. His voice, only a murmur: "Life is too short, madam, for that kind of attitude. Who wants to just survive. Wouldn't you rather *live*?"

Some of us don't have the luxury of that choice, Anna thinks, but then she is lost in the other, urgent questions the Banker is asking with his hands.

SIX MONTHS EARLIER

Law Office of Edward Fallows, Long Island, New York
January 1929

"You want me to do what?" Anna says, utterly baffled when Edward Fallows slides the papers across his desk for her to sign.

"Form a corporation," he answers, as though it's nothing more complicated than baking a loaf of bread.

"Why?"

"To raise money for your cause, of course. We suspect the Romanov family will soon take their argument to the courts and you will need funds to defend yourself." Edward Fallows fiddles with the pen on his desk. "As you know, I continue to work without retainer, but there are other costs to consider. Research. Travel. Appeals. All of these things require funds, and the Grandanor Corporation allows us to raise these funds on your behalf."

"Grandanor?"

"Gleb and I came up with the name. It's an acronym for Grand Duchess Anastasia Nikolaevna of Russia. You will be happy to know that we sent letters to all of Miss Jennings's friends inviting them to invest."

It is a staggering act of hubris, and a quiver of rage creeps into her voice. "How could you do that without even consulting me first?"

Fallows and Gleb exchange a look, and Gleb holds out a hand to him in warning. *Let me handle this*, the gesture says. He turns to Anna. "My dear, that's what a power of attorney does. It allows him to act on your behalf in legal situations. You signed it months ago, remember?"

"Of course I remember! I'm not an idiot!"

"Then help me understand why you're so angry."

"Because I wasn't even asked! You just went and did this without so much as a word."

"And how else did you expect us to acquire the means of support for you?"

"Miss Jennings is my sponsor now. She has assured me that everything will be taken care of."

Gleb smiles the way he would at a child who believes the sun can be hers if she only asks nicely enough. "Yes. She is graciously covering all your living expenses and then some." Gleb hazards a glance at the lavish gold watch that circles her left wrist. "But your legal fees remain your own."

"Don't do that," Anna says.

"Do what?"

"Treat me like an infant. I'm not stupid, you know. I can follow along. But you always run off and do these things. You come up with these plans, and half the time they only make things worse."

"I am trying to *help* you! That's all I've ever done."

"Then help me by explaining what this Grandanor Corporation is. And then allow me the right to have an opinion even if you don't like it."

Gleb takes a deep breath, and she can see him wrestle his anger down a notch. It is true that he has worked tirelessly on

her behalf. But it is also true that his eagerness has complicated matters on more than one occasion. "Of course," he says,
finally. "Mr. Fallows will explain the plan. And I think you'll
find it rather ingenious."

The concept is ambitious, if legally questionable, and Anna
cannot help but admire the simplicity of it. A select group of
"investors," carefully culled from Annie Burr Jennings's social
circle, were invited to "subscribe" to the Grandanor Corporation. In exchange for their investment, they will receive five
times their original amount when Anastasia's inheritance is
awarded. Mr. Fallows, of course, will receive one quarter of the
total monies, and the rest will go to Anastasia. Gleb has asked
for nothing.

"This will never work," Anna groans. "You've made a fool
of me."

Fallows shakes his head. "But it is working. Quite well in
fact. Three of Miss Jennings's friends have already subscribed.
Their checks have been deposited and are earning interest in
an account at the Bank of the United States as we speak. This
opportunity appeals to the younger set in particular. They
appreciate a good opportunity, especially with the financial
markets being so uneasy right now. Your first subscriber was a
young man in his twenties, John Hammond, a banker on Wall
Street." Fallows inches the papers closer to her and sets a pen
on top of them. "All you have to do in order to make it official
is sign."

And so, against her better judgment, she does.

ONE MONTH EARLIER

The Ritz-Carlton, Manhattan
December 1928

"You, my dear, are a social find of the highest order." The Heiress lays one cool hand on top of Anna's. It is loaded with rings and soft with expensive lotion.

Annie Burr Jennings is older, at the latter end of seventy, perhaps, though she doesn't look a day over sixty, and is happily unmarried. A spinster, they would call her, if she lived anywhere other than the glittering center of Manhattan, where wealth and excess are worshiped above a woman's fertility and marital status. They are seated in the center of the Ritz-Carlton dining room, at a table that once belonged to Miss Jennings's father, a director of the original Standard Oil Trust. She is his sole heir. The smile she turns on Anna is feline and hungry. Anna pulls her hand away the moment she thinks it's safe to do so without causing offense.

The restaurant is on the fifteenth floor, with stunning views of the city in every direction. The room is banked by windows, but an occasional stretch of richly paneled wall is visible, giving the space both an airy and an opulent feel. It is decorated for Christmas, and the bows of greenery and swags of red ribbon contrast nicely with the crisp white tablecloths, the polished silver, and gleaming crystal. Waiters in tuxedos with ironed napkins hanging over their forearms. And here they are, seated right in the middle, Anna in her simple white dress and the Heiress in her finery.

Anna cannot shrink far enough from the woman's ravenous gaze, so she drops both hands into her lap and laces her fingers together lest they be clutched again. "I'm sorry," she says, finally, "I don't understand what you mean."

"Goodness, I've frightened you!" The Heiress is amazed, as

though such a thing never occurred to her. "I don't bite, dear girl. You needn't be worried. I only mean to help. You seemed a little puzzled about why I would offer my home to a total stranger. I was simply explaining that you, a genuine Russian princess, are the equivalent to a social goldmine."

"So you've invited me into your home to . . . show me off? Like some exhibit at the zoo? Do you plan on charging admission as well?"

The Heiress frowns and clears her throat as though trying to erase the insult. "Do you know who I am?" she asks.

"Probably as much as you know who *I* am."

"There! I knew we spoke the same language. Let's just say we're both a kind of royalty. And one does not leave one's friend—may I use that word? I do hope we will become friends—out in the cold. So when I heard that you had broken company with Xenia Leeds I thought it only right to extend an invitation of my own. My home is your home for as long as you wish to stay."

Anna has heard offers like this far too often, and she has learned not to trust them. She has grown wiser than her thirty-two years would suggest. "In exchange for what?"

"Your company. Nothing else. I wish you to be my companion."

"Oh. I see. I'm afraid you are under a misapprehension," Anna says. "Whatever you have heard about me is wrong. I do not go in for . . . I mean that I am not interested in . . ." There are no polite words to express her meaning, so she lets her words trail off altogether, blushing furiously, unable to make the necessary, awkward clarification.

Annie Burr Jennings, heiress of legendary proportions, laughs so loudly that the entire dining room turns to look at the two of them. It is a mercy when she whispers her reply.

"I do not go in for the Sapphic arts, if that is what you fear.

Truth be told I'm too aged for *arts* of any kind. Yes, I know, I do not look my years, but that is only because I have good genes and expensive night cream at my disposal. I've also been known to bathe in the blood of virgins occasionally to keep the skin supple."

She laughs again at Anna's look of horror. "That is an Elizabeth Báthory reference by the way. Oh, never mind, I see you don't take my meaning. Let me be clear. I am not interested in your . . ." she waves a hand in Anna's general direction, ". . . *person*. I only wish for you to accompany me around town so that I can liven things up a bit. New York has gone dreadfully dull in the last few years."

"That is all?"

"I'm afraid so. I have no children, an empty penthouse, and more money than I can spend on this side of eternity. Half of the people in this city would be falling all over themselves to accept such a deal."

"I fear that I don't have much in common with either half of this city."

"And that is exactly why I extended the offer to you. Look around, my dear, you've already drawn attention." She leans back in her seat and lifts her tea to her lips. She takes a demure sip. "And it feels *good*, doesn't it?"

Anna's smile draws looks from across the room. Yet she is still hesitant. "But isn't it gauche to trade on my name?"

Again that delighted laugh. "Don't be naïve, my dear. Every woman trades on something. Beauty is easy enough to come by. So is charm. On my block wealthy women are a dime a dozen. Talent won't set you apart. Neither will intelligence or tenacity or ruthless ambition. Not in this city. But royalty? Now that's something special. So you need to ask yourself one question: If none of those other women are ashamed to trade on what they've been given, why should you be?"

TWO MONTHS EARLIER

Garden City, New York
October 1928

"How is it possible," Gleb asks, his left eyebrow crimped into an expression of complete bafflement, "that a picture of your great-great-great-grandmother hangs above your head and you do not even recognize it?"

Anna lobs a small pillow at him in aggravation. Ridiculous man, always fussing about insignificant details. Ridiculous, yes, but also loyal and sweet beyond reason. He has not changed in that regard at all. Yet she has more important things to worry about at the moment than Gleb's finer qualities, not the least of which is the fact that she is homeless once again. Her situation is not helped by the fact that the Romanov family has now publicly accused her of being a fraud. The scathing statement was printed in every major newspaper around the globe and, as a result, her pool of supporters has gone dry. Gleb read the statement to her over dinner last week, and she still hates the fact that a group of scattered royalty on the other side of the Atlantic could make her cry in public.

Anna now sits at a small desk beside the window in her room, gazing at the uninspiring view. The busy two-lane road and supermarket across the street do little to improve her mood. If it were not for the birds chirping in their cage in the corner she might despair entirely. The fact that Xenia Leeds allowed her to keep them after Anna's hasty departure was unexpected but not unappreciated.

"Oh, good grief," she finally says. "Would you recognize a painting of your great-great-great-grandmother if you saw it hanging on the wall in a random hotel room?"

"My grandmother is not Queen Louise of Prussia."

Anna is tempted to throw something else at him but decides to sort through a pile of mail instead. Since leaving Kenwood everything has been forwarded to this second-rate motel. "Consider yourself lucky. I hear she was a proper bitch."

Gleb winces at the profanity. He objects to her use of such language categorically, but today decides to pick on her oversight instead. "You should have recognized her. It's the sort of mistake your detractors will use against you," he says. "They are looking for any small detail to delegitimize your claim."

"And you think a painting will do me in?"

"I think you need to be careful."

Anna lifts the paper knife in her hand. The blade is silver and comes to a fine point. The handle is mother-of-pearl and bears the crest of Empress Alexandra. It has been in Anna's possession for many years, and it's one of the few things she brings with her every time she moves. "Have you ever seen this paper knife before?" she asks, holding it up by the blade.

He looks at it as though she has thrust a hairpin into his face or a pair of chopsticks or some other irrelevant thing. "No."

"What?" Anna gasps in mock outrage. "If you were truly Gleb Botkin you would know this paper knife was once in the possession of your sister. But clearly you are a fraud. I shall send you to Pierre Gilliard for interrogation."

"You're being ridiculous."

"And you are being a jackass."

"Such language! And you call yourself a princess."

"I call myself exhausted and overwhelmed and homeless for the third time in a year. I think I'm entitled to a bit of profanity under the circumstances. Or do you think princesses don't learn to curse like the rest of humanity?"

"I think they have the good sense not to do so. Especially when the eyes of the world are upon them." He drops into the chair by the bed in a huff. "Besides, you aren't homeless. You have a room in this lovely hotel for several weeks. And Rachmaninoff to thank for it."

"So the Composer has taken a turn at the till, has he?" Anna met Sergei Rachmaninoff a number of times during her stay with Xenia Leeds but never really knew why he wanted to help.

"He's a loyalist. Feels it's the least he can do."

"And when his generosity runs out? What then?"

"Rachmaninoff is arranging a meeting with some heiress in New York. She's in Paris at the moment, but he expects her to return before Christmas."

"It is impossible to live like this. Bounced around constantly. It feels as though I'm losing my mind. Like I am dislocated, shifting constantly from one place to the next. Why can't I just live with you?" Anna regrets the words the moment they're out. This is a subject they staunchly avoid.

Gleb turns red, then stares at his hands. "If I thought for a moment you actually wanted that I might consider it." He glances up and offers a half smile. "It's better this way. We just need a little bit more time. Edward Fallows has come up with an idea, and I think it could work. We just need . . ."

"What?"

He clears his throat and does his best to keep a straight face when he answers. "For you to sign power of attorney over to Edward Fallows."

"Oh! Is that all?"

"No," he says. "We also need money."

16

Anastasia

CHRISTMAS IN SIBERIA

1917, 1918

Tobolsk, Russia
December 24, 1917

For most of my life I pictured Siberia in winter as a bleak, barren landscape of ashen sky and blanched earth with the occasional spindly, leafless tree breaking up the monotony. The reality, however, is rather different. Although ferociously cold the first few weeks in December, the snowfall is light and is quickly blown away by the relentless wind or packed by foot traffic in the streets.

Our days take on a pattern of frost, thaw, sunshine, and darkness. They are painfully short, often over before we have the chance to enjoy them, and we never really get warm despite our layers of clothes and the fires that burn constantly in every hearth of the Governor's House. It is not uncommon for the sun to set at four o'clock in the afternoon, and we spend much of our lives in darkness, blinking at one another in the dim light of sputtering lanterns. Father continues reading to us at night, but when his voice grows hoarse he pulls out his maps and studies train routes with Pierre Gilliard. The rest of us continue our needlework. Every corset, coat, camisole, belt, and hat, anything with a seam, is ripped open and lined with jewels from the cache in Mother's trunks. Our underclothes, once light and soft, take on an uncomfortable weight and stiffness. And through it all, I begin to wonder, to *hope*, that some plan of escape is being formed. I daydream about rescue, building fantasies in my mind that rival the plot of *Ivanhoe*. They are foolish, romantic, impossible fantasies, and I share them with no one, not even Tomas. This, I admit only to myself, is because he's in many of them.

We've grown so used to containment, to being locked within the walls and yard of the Governor's House, that none of us really knows what to say when they finally let us out on Christmas Eve. We stare at Leshy, wondering if it is a trick, some cruel bit of entertainment on his part. Those strange animal eyes of his show no signs of deception.

"We can leave?" Father asks, his voice pitched a note higher in disbelief.

"No," Leshy shakes his head, "you may go to the candle-light service at the Blagoveshchensky Church in town. You will be under armed guard, and you will return here immediately afterward. I am allowing an excursion, not an exodus."

Father, now suspicious, asks, "Why?"

Leshy shrugs, but I see a softening in his face, some bit of humanity he tries so hard to keep hidden. "Because it is Christmas."

So we change into what little finery we brought with us. White kidskin boots, petticoats, and dresses of rough silk with straight, simple lines in various shades of gray and taupe. Only a year ago we might have worn them to walk in the woods or tend the garden. We would have thought them plain and ugly. Day dresses. But now, as I run calloused fingers along the elegant fabric, they seem elaborate, an embarrassment of riches. We braid our hair, pinch our cheeks for color, and dig through our drawers until we find the bottle of perfume that Maria smuggled into her trunk. We dab drops of the decadent scent behind our ears and, after primping the best we can, present ourselves in the study. We must, finally, look the part of royalty because the guards—Tomas and Ivan in particular—smile stupidly as we pass.

There is a fine dusting of snow on the boardwalk when we leave the house bundled in our furs. We are joined by the staff, along with Gleb and Tanya Botkin, and surrounded by guards—Semyon and Leshy in front and five others behind. I listen as Tomas and Ivan whisper about the change in weather. I can sense no difference in the cold, pewter sky and frozen air, but these men know that winter has turned a corner and is about to become more sinister. By the time we reach the broad stone steps of the church it is snowing heavily, the ground littered with large, thick flakes.

I've been dragged to church by Mother all of my life. The haunting sound of a choir, the smooth wood of a pew, and the worn fabric of a prayer bench are as familiar to me as the feel of my own sheets. Communion. Prayer. Liturgy. All of these things a second language I speak fluently. Yet I love none of it the way I love a Christmas Eve service. The candles and the incense, the greenery and hymns.

It is different, somehow, holy.

We file into the church behind the officers and look for empty seats. The sanctuary is almost full, and the moment that gust of cold air sweeps into the room, flickering the candles and ruffling the pages of hymnals, the entire congregation turns to note the interruption.

And they *know*.

If the plan was to avoid detection, we fail miserably. So we quietly slide into several empty pews near the back and turn our eyes to the hymnals. But, according to custom, we do not sit. This service, along with most others in the Russian Orthodox church, is performed standing.

The whispering begins as a rustle and grows until it nearly drowns out the choir. Leshy and Semyon go rigid before us. From the corner of my eye I can see Tomas brave a worried glance in my direction. We pull into the shadows, eyes downcast, hands gripping our hymnals. We make no eye contact. We acknowledge no one. Eventually the congregants turn their attention back toward the front. But I can see their rigid backs, their chins angled slightly to the side as though they might catch a glimpse of us if they turn their heads just so.

The service is filled with haunting melodies, incense, Scripture readings, candlelight, and reverent liturgy. After the priest says, "Let us complete our prayers to the Lord," he lifts his face toward the back of the chapel where we stand. Leshy draws in a sharp breath and Semyon curses when the priest begins reciting the *mnogoletie*—a prayer of long life for the imperial family. With each word his voice rises, echoing off the stone walls and the arched wooden ceiling. The prayer is eloquent and lovely and the most dangerous thing he could possibly utter. Because that priest, that devout, foolish, idiotic man, recites, in painful, excruciating detail, each of our imperial titles as he prays.

Tsar Nicholas the Second, emperor of all Russia.
Alexandra Feodorovna, empress of all Russia.
Grand Duchess Olga Nikolaevna.
Grand Duchess Tatiana Nikolaevna.
Grand Duchess Maria Nikolaevna.
Grand Duchess Anastasia Nikolaevna.
Alexey Nikolaevich, tsarevitch of all Russia.

Each word lands like the blow of a hammer in that deathly quiet sanctuary. Each title sounds more preposterous and arrogant than the next. The congregation stares at us brazenly now, half of them with open hostility and the other half with an alarming sort of reverence. The priest himself stands with eyes closed and arms lifted, as though in worship. To us.

It doesn't take long for Leshy and Semyon to hustle us from

the church. I can still hear the last words of the prayer echoing through the room as the doors slam closed behind us.

"I had nothing to do with that," Father says when Leshy turns on him with a look of rage.

"It doesn't matter. That fool declared you to be his sovereign before the entire congregation. Home. Now," Leshy says, turning the collar of his coat up to block the wind. The big, fat snowflakes from earlier have become tiny projectiles that bite our cheeks and sting our noses. "I should have known better than to take you out in public. It will never happen again."

"It shouldn't have happened to start with," Semyon growls. "You've made them objects of worship."

"No," Leshy says. "I have made them targets."

"You are being ridiculous," Father says.

Leshy steps forward, grabs the front of Father's coat, and shakes him so hard his jaw clenches. "Don't you understand, you stupid man? You assinine, entitled fool. The Bolshevik cancer creeps closer every day. Just this morning I got a telegram that the workers' soviet in Tomsk is demanding that your entire family be handed over and put in prison. Not in a palace, not in a comfortable Governor's House, but in a *prison*. A rotting, filthy, piss-covered prison. And that should frighten you." He shakes Father again, harder this time. I take an involuntary step backward at the guttural sound of Leshy's voice and bump into Tomas. I feel his hand at my waist, steadying me, and then he pulls it away, but not before Gleb—lips pinched together in disapproval—notices the glancing touch. I ease away from Tomas.

"You may hate it here. You may hate *me*," Leshy continues. "But the mercy I extend in this frozen outpost is the only thing standing between you and a misery you cannot imagine. Kerensky knew this. And now he's running for his life." Breathless and enraged, Leshy finally lets go of Father and steps back.

He motions for the guards to lead us toward the Governor's House, and we march home in the growing snowstorm without speaking a word. Semyon brings up the rear, and when I look at him there is murder in his eyes. I should be afraid. I should scamper away. But mostly I want to cram the toe of my boot directly into that gap between his teeth.

We stomp through the front door half an hour later, cold, miserable, and subdued after wishing Botkin and his children farewell and a Merry Christmas. The guards disperse to the second floor, and my family retreats to Father's study.

"Is it true? What Leshy said?" I ask.

I watch as Father builds a fire in the hearth and Olga lights the candles on the Christmas tree that Tomas and Ivan cut in the hills behind the house last week. I wait for his answer.

Finally he says, "Yes, the Bolsheviks have wrested power from Alexander Kerensky, but we are secure in this distant exile. At least until the spring thaw. Tobolsk is separated from the rest of the world for half the year. A river made of ice renders travel impossible. And we will find a way out of here long before then." Father kisses the top of my head. "It is late. Let us have dinner and then go to bed."

But I am unwilling to let Christmas slip away just yet.

I pull Alexey aside. He looks at me with those pleading, wide blue eyes—his face pale—and I know he is desperate for some measure of hope and cheer as well.

I lean closer and make him an offer no young boy can refuse. "How would you like to play with fire?" I ask.

The upstairs Christmas tree, when lit, is spectacular. Tomas and Ivan dragged the fat-bottomed balsamic firs into the house a week ago. We set one in Father's study and the other upstairs in the soldiers' quarters. They smell of cloves and oranges and pungent sap and are decorated with a measly assortment of ribbons, pinecones, candles, and beads. They are beautiful.

One by one our guards gather upstairs and their expressions

turn from gloom to wonder. Scowls became smiles. Hunched shoulders relax and furrowed brows smooth into joy. I can see memories dancing in their eyes. Bits and pieces of their own beloved Christmases past, reflected in the candlelight. I see Tomas on the other side of the tree staring at me and I cannot help but smile. The only other person who looks at me like that is Gleb Botkin, and I suddenly feel guilty for reasons I can't explain. He would be furious to see me smile at Tomas like this.

"Merry Christmas!" Alexey shouts, and the guards cheer. Tomas steps around the tree and hoists my brother onto his shoulders. He runs in circles around the tree, singing "O Tannenbaum" loudly and off-key but with great enthusiasm.

And then my parents and sisters come upstairs, their arms full of packages filled with bookmarks, knitted caps, stockings, scarves—our small handmade gifts for these men. All the while the dogs run in circles around us, barking happily and licking the hands of anyone who stoops to pet them.

My gift to Tomas is a card with a hand-painted rooster. He takes it and laughs. I think that if we weren't surrounded by so many others, he might hug me as well. Perhaps he might do something more.

"Thank you," Tomas whispers, and I go completely still as his thumb brushes the back of my hand.

"What is this?" Semyon's hard, angry voice demands from the doorway behind us. Tomas and I spring apart like we've been shocked.

Semyon's eyes are on the tree, however, and the bits of wrapping paper strewn across the floor.

"It is Christmas," Father says.

"Get out. All of you. Prisoners are not allowed on the second floor."

SEVEN WEEKS LATER

Tobolsk, Russia
February 14, 1918

Winter meets us finally, with a savage drop in temperature that confirms everything we've heard about this distant, frozen tundra. This new cold is nothing less than a crucifixion of the soul, and the snow that began on Christmas Eve still remains at Valentine's Day, covered by two additional feet. Father, restless and angry, has shoveled paths through the yard so we can reach the chicken coop and the refuse pit. He has spent countless hours tossing huge shovelfuls of snow into the middle of the yard so he can maintain his daily walks. Whether he intended it or not, that pile has grown into a small mountain that Alexey now claims as his own. It doesn't take my brother long to realize that if he climbs to the top and sits on top of a trash lid he can slide to the bottom with frightening speed.

And so it is that on February 14, 1918, the day the Russian calendar changes to the Gregorian calendar, I sit with Alexey on the snow pile and watch a company of Red Guards march across the frozen river and approach the house. They advance upon us like a horde of spiders, long-limbed and purposeful. I find myself struggling to breathe, as though there's a hand at my throat. When I turn to Alexey he too is stricken with terror, his mouth open, his eyes wide. We scramble down the snow heap at once and bolt toward the house, without exchanging a word.

Father bursts through the kitchen door just as we enter. "To the study," he demands, "all of you." And then he tells us in rushed, breathless sentences what Alexey and I have already seen. We hear shouting and stomping at the front door. We hear boots in the hall.

"But how?" I ask. "You said the boats wouldn't be able to pass for months. You said we were safe."

"I was wrong," he says, pained. "They must have come by wagon and walked across."

"What happens now?"

"We stay close together at all times. And trust none of them."

And then the door to Father's study swings open.

The man who stands there looks as though he has been swallowed by his own clothing. He is all wire and tendon, cinched in the middle by a thick leather belt. His skin is olive, his hair is black, his eyes are small, dark, and deep-set. When he steps into the room I think he looks like a vulture, like he could happily pick us to shreds. What I do not expect is his voice, a deep boom that fills the air and demands immediate attention.

"My name is Yakov Yurovsky," he says. "And I have come to take command of this garrison." He looks around the small study, at the bookshelves and rug, at the chairs and writing desk—all small comforts we've brought with us from Tsarskoe Selo. He holds his hands out to the cheerfully popping fire, standing there for several minutes, letting his fingers warm until he finally says, "It is time you were brought to justice."

Anna

THE ROOT OF ALL EVIL

1928

Kenwood Estate, Oyster Bay, New York
July 1928

It takes six months for Anna to convince Xenia Leeds that she is Grand Duchess Anastasia Romanov.

Her host is kind but naturally suspicious. Instead of pressing Anna with questions, Xenia waits patiently for any signs of fraud. She cares little for the grandiose stories her other guests ask Anna to tell. Sergei Rachmaninoff, the famous composer, wants to hear escapades of the Russian court and exploits of the tsar. He has come to visit Anna several times during her stay, is always magnanimous, showing deference to the point of worship. Xenia tolerates this behavior, but from a distance and with misgiving. She is always watching. Always waiting. The tests she gives Anna are more subtle and harder to pass. Xenia observes how she folds her napkin in her lap, mounts a horse, crosses her ankles, and cuts her filet. Xenia listens to the inflection of her voice when she says certain words, notes Anna's diction and accent. The way she carries herself, her posture and gait when walking through a room, the way she holds a teacup. How a full curtsy means one thing and a partial curtsy means something else entirely. Unlike the other skeptics Anna has met through the years, Xenia Leeds is intimately acquainted with the small manners of the Russian court—she is, after all, a Romanov cousin and princess in her own right. Anna feels those dark, noble eyes on her constantly, searching for the truth. Some days Anna cannot bear the weight of them, and she retreats to her suite, leaving Xenia to her husband, William, and young daughter, Nancy, in their opulent surroundings. William is laughably American in his looks: sandy hair, bright blue eyes, broad white smile, and, to add insult to injury, is tall, tan, well built, and so handsome as to be distracting. He looks like he might have come directly from California or perhaps from the loins of Zeus.

Anna is only a breath past thirty, but she feels ancient, exhausted beneath the weight of the Leedses' scrutiny, strained from trying to live up to their expectations.

"Why don't you speak Russian?" Xenia asks one afternoon in early July. She has entered Anna's suite wearing her tennis whites, and watches curiously as Anna feeds two green parrots from the end of her fork. Their little hooked beaks pick delicately at pieces of cut apple, and they squawk happily, perched on her forearm.

"I do speak Russian. You heard me, just now, as you stood in the door."

Xenia blushes. "Forgive me. I wasn't trying to snoop. I was curious, that's all. You don't speak it often. Just a few words and only to the birds. Whispers really."

Anna still has her head bent toward the parrots. "They don't speak at all, so I hardly think a full soliloquy necessary."

"Touché," Xenia says, but the corners of her pretty mouth draw in tighter. She isn't ready to give up. Anna's refusal to speak her native language is one of the main arguments flaunted by her detractors. "But you won't *converse* in it. Or at least not with any of us. Why?"

Anna is tired of debating this issue with Xenia. "Russian was the last language I heard spoken in that house," she says, eager to bring the questioning to an end. Even with her face turned she can see Xenia flinch.

"Ekaterinburg?"

"Yes."

"I'm sorry." Xenia is abashed. "I wasn't thinking . . . I mean that never occurred to me."

Anna carefully deposits the birds back in their cage and forgives her host with a smile. "People are curious. It's understandable."

Xenia stares over Anna's shoulder, out the window, to the tennis courts beyond. Her cool facade of disinterest is complete except for one small detail. She is wringing her hands. "Will you be staying in your rooms today?" she asks. "Or would you like to join me for a round of tennis?"

They have played several times since her arrival in February, but Anna lacks Xenia's height and long years of practice. Losing occasionally is fine. Losing constantly is demoralizing. "No thank you," she says. "I might go for a walk along the beach later."

A tiny flash of relief crosses Xenia's face, and therefore a thread of suspicion begins to hum at the back of Anna's mind, like an exposed wire.

"Come find me when you're ready," Xenia says. "It's been weeks since I walked the harbor."

"I would very much enjoy the company," Anna lies, then watches her host leave in much the way a cat would watch the parrots in her cage.

Xenia is the most competitive woman she has ever known. A ruthless tennis player. A veritable card shark. A chess prodigy. A formidable equestrian—she competes in local show-jumping competitions. She is a strong swimmer. A princess of European birth, thus making her the highest-ranking member of her social circle. Wife to an aristocrat. Mother of a beautiful daughter. Owner of the largest estate in Oyster Bay. Driver of new cars. Wearer of designer clothes. Friend to few. Admired by all. Moneyed. Titled. Winner at everything she sets her mind to and there is no reason why Xenia would relinquish an easy victory on the courts today, or any day, unless she doesn't actually want Anna to play.

"Interesting," Anna mutters as she crosses the room to look at the tennis courts. They are currently empty, but Anna opens the window and settles into a large chair beside it to wait. She thumbs through her mail, deciding which letters to answer and which to toss—there are always so many. She has three from Gleb, one with the words "Urgent! Please respond!" scrawled on the back of the envelope.

"Always so dramatic," she mutters, slicing it open with her paper knife.

Since his dismissal from Kenwood in February, Gleb has been on a mission to learn everything he can about the inheritance mentioned by the Romanov family in their statement to *The New York Times*. It was the first time they confirmed that the tsar's rumored fortune actually exists. Such an inheritance would change Anna's life entirely. No more relying on friends and strangers and relatives. No more being passed around like a charity case. From the moment it came to his attention, Gleb has set his sights on recovering this fortune for her as if it was her salvation. And perhaps it is. Anna looks around the opulent suite where she lives by the good grace of Xenia Leeds—the damask curtains, the cherry wood floors, the gilded mirrors, Persian rugs, four-poster bed—and daydreams about what it would feel like to have a home of her own.

Dearest Anastasia, Gleb begins his letter, *I have learned for a fact that the late emperor did have considerable sums of money in the Bank of England . . .*

Her breath catches in her throat and she begins to read faster, her eyes landing on one stunning sentence and then another.

. . . The Tsar deposited five million rubles in the Bank of England for each of his children before the Great War in 1914 . . .

. . . I have taken the liberty to secure you an attorney by the name of Edward Fallows. It is time you had an expert on hand to protect your financial interests. Mr. Fallows has written to say that there are reliable indications that said money will be paid to the tsar's last known legal heirs at the end of July, the ten-year anniversary of his death, if your claim to the fortune is not officially presented to the court. Please, you must contact me the moment you receive this. I've tried ringing you on the telephone, but Xenia has given instructions to her butler that I am not to speak with you. She claims it upsets you, but I suspect she is stalling, trying to ensure that we run out of time . . .

He goes on like this for three pages, laying out in detail what he knows, and also his aggravation that solicitors for the Bank of England refuse to respond to his inquiry.

. . . They say information regarding those balances can only be granted to the account holder, he writes, *and thus it is more impera-tive than ever that we prove your identity . . .*

Anna is pondering the significance of this news when Xenia Leeds passes beneath her open window. She is in the company of a man who is not her husband, and Anna pulls back from the window in case Xenia looks up.

"But how can you be so sure?" Xenia's companion asks casually, and in Russian. His voice echoes clearly through the courtyard.

Anna knows that voice.

"She has lived with me for six months. I've had ample oppor-tunity to observe her," Xenia replies in Russian.

"Our family history is widely published. Anyone could fake it."

"No. Not anyone. She knows things. Things only a Romanov could know."

He stretches his arm by swinging his racket in a wide circle. "Like what?"

"She knows about the *otkritie navigatie*."

"That doesn't mean anything. She could have looked it up in a book."

"Not if she doesn't speak or read Russian like they claim. Besides, a detail like that means quite a bit to a Romanov. The Opening of Navigation is tradition. Don't you remember?" she asks.

"Of course I do."

"Then you cannot discount a detail like that. Any daughter of the tsar would remember the Commandant of St. Petersburg bringing that glass of water after the final thaw. It was the beginning of trade each year. I drank from that cup twice myself as a child. I know you did too, Dmitri."

"It is only one thing, Xenia. And it does not convince me. It won't convince our aunts either."

Dmitri Leuchtenberg. No. It can't be. Not that hateful, conniving bastard. So Xenia has broken her promise not to involve the family. Anna can feel her rage begin to boil. She glares at the two figures below.

"It's not just that," Xenia continues. "There are dozens of other things. Small things only Anastasia would remember. But please, it can wait. William needs to be part of this discussion. He's in the study working but will be ready in an hour. For now let's play. You promised to let me win at least one game."

They walk away, their voices swallowed by distance. The farther they get from the house the more relaxed Xenia appears, and then they step through the gate and onto the courts.

Anna does not leave her chair for that entire hour. She stays seated, back straight, feet crossed at the ankles, Gleb's letter resting on her lap. Occasionally she can hear the deep whack of the racket as it connects with the ball, and every once in a while a bit of laughter or a word in Russian reaches her ears, but the conversation itself is entirely lost.

Xenia and Dmitri emerge sometime later, red-faced and laughing. Whatever tension was present before is gone now, and Anna can tell by the look on Xenia's face that she prevailed on the courts. The look on Dmitri's face suggests that she did so by her own skill and not because of any gentlemanly gesture on his part.

The moment they pass beneath her window again, Anna leaves her suite and makes her way to the study on the first floor.

———

It is easy to get lost in the house at Oyster Bay. Even after six months, Anna finds herself turned around in the hallways and often mistakes one room for another. Four sets of stairs. At least a dozen different hallways. Endless doors. So, although she hurries, it takes her several minutes to find the study, and by then the door is already closed, its occupants safely tucked inside.

"Damn it all," Anna hisses and retreats several feet down the hall to stand behind an enormous potted fern that is nearly as tall as she is. She needs a moment to think. She needs to know what they're saying. If the windows to the study were open she could risk going outside and sitting beneath them, but she would likely be discovered. If not by William himself—she's seen him sitting on the window ledge more than once smoking his pipe—then certainly by the gardener, a man who tends the bushes by the house with nothing short of religious zeal.

She is lamenting her lost opportunity when the maid approaches from the other direction, balancing a silver tray laden with lemonade. Anna has seen the girl on multiple occasions. She's neither pretty nor smart, but she is dutiful and efficient and never gets in the way. But her hands are full at the moment and she cannot open the study door. So she taps at it quietly with one foot, and it is opened from within. She emerges a few minutes later carrying the same tray, now loaded down with an empty coffee service.

Even from this distance Anna can see the consternation on the girl's face. Unable to shut the door with her hands full, she pulls it toward her with the toe of one shoe, then walks away, leaving a crack some three inches wide. The moment she's gone, Anna creeps back down the hallway and stands outside the study door. A lucky break.

"What game are you playing, Xenia?" William's voice is neither a whisper nor a growl, but some other menacing sound that stops Anna short.

Xenia's answer, when it comes, sounds more bored than defensive. "Tennis, darling. Isn't it obvious?"

"That's not what I mean and you know it." She hears the thump of something heavy being set on wood and guesses that William Leeds is done with his lemonade. "First you bring that strange woman into our home—"

"How else was I supposed to determine her true identity?"

"And have you?"

"I believe so, yes."

"And now this man," William finishes.

Dmitri speaks in English, with a heavy Russian accent. "I invited myself. Multiple times, in fact. Your wife was reluctant to see me."

William's voice is dry. "I can't imagine why."

"He has brought an offer," Xenia says. "From the family."

William curses loudly and without apology to their guest. "*The family*. Of course. I should have known. Of all the families on God's green earth to marry into, I go and choose the Romanovs. I ought to be damned for my stupidity." He sighs. "What do they want?"

"To make your guest an offer," Dmitri answers.

"What sort?"

"The sort that will make everyone happy."

"Why do I have the feeling it is designed to keep her quiet and to shut her out?" William asks.

Dmitri clears his throat and speaks to Xenia. "I fear you have been duped, cousin. Unforgivable, considering how much is at stake. A motivated impostor could learn many things about our family."

"I do not believe she is an impostor."

"What of Ekaterinburg? Does she speak of that? Does she have an explanation?"

"She will not talk of the murders, and I cannot blame her."

Dmitri snorts. "Have you pressed her?"

"Of course not!"

"You should. It would be very telling," he says. "What of her escape?"

"Only that it was a 'long, long journey' and that she remained unconscious for most of it."

"Convenient. It prevents her from giving geographical details. It also prevents us from finding witnesses."

"You are a terrible cynic."

"This woman poses a great threat to us. It is my duty to be cynical. I'm surprised you haven't embraced your own duties."

"It would be nice if she started with her own immediate family," William says, "and cared less for the one abroad."

"You knew what you were getting when you married me. As I recall, you liked it at the time," Xenia snaps, and then, to Dmitri, "I embrace the truth. Nothing less."

Anna wishes she could see their faces and read their body language. Words are important, but they only tell part of the story. It's impossible to know their full meaning without seeing how they glance at one another, pull at their sleeves, or hold the glass in their hands. A thousand truths are written across the body during any given conversation, and they often say more than the words spoken aloud.

"You exaggerate your nobility, Xenia," Dmitri says. "This is a game to you and you want to win. Though I don't agree with the others that it's the money you're after. You seem to have enough of that."

Anna can hear the dangerous note in Xenia's voice. "They think I'm after the *money*?"

"Not all of them. Just our aunts. It's a considerable amount after all."

"There is no proof the funds even exist."

"I am told the accounts are not in the tsar's name but in his children's. And only the account holder can request a receipt. Or," he pauses for effect, "a recognized claimant."

William Leeds sounds truly interested for the first time. Money is a language he understands very well. "Recognized, meaning—"

"The courts would have to officially declare her to be Anastasia Romanov before she could even request a balance much less have access to any funds."

"But the family—"

"Receives everything in the absence of a more direct next of kin."

"Bloody ruthless bastards," William says with a note of appreciation.

Anna takes a step back and leans against the wall, her ear near the hinges, still listening, but now pondering her situation as well. So Gleb was right about everything. No wonder he's been so frantic to get in touch with her.

Dmitri sips loudly from his glass. "So you can see why the family is loathe to declare her, why any action must be taken with the utmost care and only in the face of undeniable evidence. It is unthinkable that such a fortune be placed in the hands of a fraud."

"And they think I am being swayed in her favor?" Xenia pauses briefly and then her voice goes flat in disbelief. "You are here to ask that I expel her from my home."

Dmitri doesn't deny it. "They fear she has a strong hold on you. That you are beginning to take her part. They sent me simply to express their concern."

"They sent you to get rid of her."

"No," he says vehemently. "They sent me to *interrogate* her. To help them make a case should this end up in court."

"I will not allow it. Not in my home." Xenia shakes her head. "And I cannot believe this is coming up again. I know what they're getting at. But I am certain she is not that Polish peasant our aunts claim that she is."

"Be careful with that assertion, Xenia. And for God's sake don't let that get into the papers. The family is getting ready to make a public statement about the Schanzkowskas. We must keep a united front."

It is at these words that Anna stiffens. She had hoped that the name Schanzkowska would never be uttered in her hearing again. She thought the matter was taken care of, but apparently this is one issue she cannot put to rest. The Romanov descendants have an unshakable grip on that name. And now the accusations are surfacing again. But she will not be caught off guard this time.

There is a single telephone in the house. It's on the first floor, in the main entrance, and is zealously guarded by the Leedses' butler—a man so ill-humored and dour-faced he could put any imperial servant to shame. Anna breezes past him in the foyer and raises one hand as if warding off an evil spirit. She lifts the receiver without asking permission and dials Gleb's home number.

When he finally answers he's out of breath and sounds as though he has just run up a flight of stairs. "Botkin residence, Gleb speaking," he gasps.

"I need you to come get me," Anna says without so much as a hello.

"Thank God! You got my letter. I've been trying desperately to reach—"

"Xenia has broken her promise," Anna interrupts. "She's let Dmitri onto the property to interview me."

He curses loudly and then says, "I thought we were rid of him."

"Oh no. He's back and has already brought up the Schanz-kowska affair. He says the family is preparing to make a statement."

"Go pack your bags," Gleb says without a pause. "Immediately. I will be there before nightfall."

———————

The shouting match is extraordinary. Gleb and Xenia have been at it for nearly half an hour. Anna has remained silent the entire time. She is perched at the edge of a divan, hands folded in her lap, face expressionless. William Leeds sits on the window ledge behind his wife, ready to step in the moment things get out of control. Gleb and Xenia stand toe-to-toe in the middle of the study, like two boxers getting ready to tap gloves. All of this is witnessed by a third man who looks uncomfortable at best and, at moments, stricken by terror. His name is Edward Fallows and he is, apparently, Anna's attorney. But they've not even had the chance to shake hands or greet each other properly because the screaming began the moment Gleb marched up the front steps and into the foyer. The butler at least had the good sense to herd them into the study and away from the eager ears of the staff. If Dmitri is still on the grounds he has long since made himself scarce. It's the only intelligent thing the man has done all day.

"I cannot believe you brought a lawyer onto my property," Xenia growls between clenched teeth.

"I cannot believe you broke your promise. You swore not to trap her the way they did at Wasserburg."

"Dmitri is my cousin. I have the right to visit with him if I choose."

"You should have done it elsewhere."

It would appear that William Leeds is actually enjoying the altercation. He smiles and draws on the lit pipe in his hand. He's been puffing at the thing for the last thirty minutes, from the moment his wife called Gleb a disgrace to all Russians.

"I believe this estate is ours," William says. "And we're rather entitled to entertain whoever we like."

Gleb glares at him but doesn't respond. His fight is with Xenia alone. "Why was Dmitri here? The truth."

"He was sent by the family."

"For what purpose?"

"To interview her. Something," Xenia raises one long, elegant finger and points it at Gleb's nose, "I obviously didn't allow."

"Only because Anna got wind of it first. Tell me about his offer."

"It is an olive branch."

"How so?"

"This is a very complex matter for my family," Xenia says. "One with many moving parts. But they are aware of Anna's suffering and do not want to inflict more upon her. They are not as indifferent as they appear."

"They appear cruel," Gleb interjects.

"Let me finish. Please. You barged in here and forced my hand. At least have the courtesy to hear me out."

Gleb snorts. "Hear *you*? I get the distinct impression that I am, in fact, listening to the tsar's sisters right now."

"You are listening to us. The family as a whole. We have a proposition—a compromise if you will."

"Oh, so now it's the royal we? This ought to be good."

"It is better than good. It is generous. Gracious, even." Xenia turns from Gleb and crosses the room to sit beside Anna on the divan. She takes both of her hands and squeezes them reassuringly. "I am sorry about today. I never meant to betray your trust. I am your friend. You have to believe that."

Anna says nothing, allowing Xenia to feel the full weight of her embarrassment.

"Your offer?" Gleb prompts.

"The tsar's sisters are prepared to support you financially for the rest of your life."

"In exchange for what?" Anna asks. They're the first words she has uttered directly to Xenia since this afternoon.

"They will find you a secluded spot in Europe," Xenia says, avoiding the question. "A place of your choosing. Perhaps Crimea. I know how much you love it there. Or the South of France. Tuscany, if you like. Bavaria. Switzerland. Maybe a lovely chalet in the mountains. You'll have enough to buy a home, keep a handful of servants. Live comfortably and in peace for the rest of your days. A home of your own. I know that's what you desire."

It sounds too good to be true. There must be strings attached, Anna is sure of it. "And what exactly must I give in exchange for such a *privilege*?"

The sound that Xenia makes is not so much a sigh or a groan but a sort of gasp. The kind of noise you make when you know you're about to be struck across the face. A pre-emptive admission of guilt. To Anna's credit, she keeps her hands limp inside Xenia's firm grasp. Anna does not flinch much less strike her when the answer finally comes.

"All that the family asks in return is that you renounce all claim to the name and title of Anastasia Romanov."

"Oh!" Gleb screams with such ferocity that William Leeds finally takes a step forward in concern. "Is that *all*? How fucking *generous* of them!"

The profanity falls like a glass bowl, shattering the room into silence. Xenia is aghast, her royal sensibilities more offended by the word than by the degrading offer she's just made. Gleb, for his part, is choking on his anger and cannot summon another word. William Leeds is giddy with the entertainment of it all. Anna half expects him to roll up his shirtsleeves and exclaim that he hasn't had this much fun in months. Edward Fallows, however, has the look of a wolf sniffing blood. He's leaning forward in his chair, fingers steepled, brow furrowed, bouncing on the balls of his feet.

Anna's voice is dry and quiet when she finally responds. "They want to buy me off? To sweep me away like a bit of unwanted rubbish?"

"No." Xenia shakes her head. "On the contrary. They want to protect you. And themselves. This is the easiest way."

"The easiest way for them," Gleb says, finally mastering his power of speech.

"Don't you start," Xenia hisses. "You're the one who brought a lawyer into this."

"And they're the ones who went to the papers with word of the inheritance. How were we supposed to respond? Ignore the fact that her father left her a fortune? Let it be taken by someone else? They meant to smear her name with that announcement, to say she's only claiming to be Anastasia to collect a fortune, and now they mean to strip her of her title as well."

"They are prepared to take financial responsibility for her!" And now Xenia pulls out her trump card and plays it with aplomb. She turns those eager, hopeful eyes on Anna and swallows her in their dark depths. "If you accept I will take you to Copenhagen to see the dowager empress."

Even Gleb is surprised to hear this. The dowager empress has refused to meet with Anna at every turn, never so much as responding to a single letter or public plea. Her acknowledgment is the one thing Anna needs to end her quest, a thing so far beyond her grasp that she can only hope for it. It would only take a word from the tsar's mother and she would once again have the right to her own name.

"She asked to see me?" Anna cringes at the undisguised hope in her voice, trembling and desperate.

A long pause. "No, but—"

"She has agreed to it at least?"

"I am certain she will if only—"

Anna jerks her hands away from Xenia. "She doesn't even know!"

"I can get a meeting with her. I promise."

"Like you promised to keep the other Romanovs away? Like you promised not to ambush me?"

Edward Fallows speaks for the first time. His voice is deep and rich and calm, not the voice Anna expects from such a timid-looking man. "I am loath to interrupt here given the fact that my presence is not exactly welcome. But as Anna's legal representative I am obligated to ask if any part of this offer has been put in writing. Is there a document my client can study or amend?"

"Not yet." Xenia stiffens at this interruption. "Dmitri only brought word of the offer today. But I am certain papers can be drawn up immediately."

"Again we are asked to rely on your word alone," Gleb says.

Here William Leeds claps one giant hand onto Gleb's shoulder. "Take all the shots you like at her family—hell, it's no secret they're all a bunch of spoiled tyrants—but I'll not have you insult my wife."

Gleb shakes the hand away. "Your wife is a *Romanov*."

Xenia Leeds finally snaps at the intended insult. "And you will very much regret meddling in the affairs of the House of Romanov!"

"I regret only that I have allowed a tawdry bribe to be dangled in front of the tsar's rightful heir. And for what? A pittance."

"Do not make this about money! It should be about her welfare."

Gleb growls. "Easy for you to say. You have all the money you'll ever need. She, on the other hand, lives in constant fear of being cast into the streets."

"She will have all the money she needs if she simply accepts the offer!"

"But not as much as your aunts. What they are offering her is a fraction of the interest that fortune earns each year. They will send her quietly away and then fill their own coffers to the point of overflowing. And yours as well no doubt. That's the real reason you've kept her locked away all summer. You needed the statute of limitations to expire—ten years to the day since the tsar's death, I believe. The time is up this month." He spits out the next words as though they are a mouthful of poison. "How close you came to stealing a fortune, Xenia."

Only Gleb can say too much and ruin everything. He has always been like this. Loyal to a fault. Protective. Zealous in his devotion to Anna. And she loves him for it, she really does. Even when he goes too far. Even when he knocks down the whole damn house of cards. Because there is no one else who cares this much about her.

Xenia jumps to her feet in outrage, and William sets his pipe on the desk, his eyes locked on Gleb as he begins to roll up his shirtsleeves. Anna is certain things will dissolve into madness, that punches will be thrown and lines crossed if she does not intervene. So she rises to her feet and asks a question.

It goes unanswered in the cacophony.

Edward Fallows, good man that he is, comes to her aid by letting loose a deafening whistle. The sort one would need if hailing a cab in the middle of Armageddon. "The lady just asked a question!" he roars when all eyes turn to him.

The room falls silent and Anna clears her throat.

"And what will happen if I do not agree to this offer?"

"Then I am afraid I will have to ask you to leave Oyster Bay within forty-eight hours. I have been told, in no uncertain terms, that if I am to remain in the good graces of my family I can no longer be your host."

Anna has loved her time at Kenwood. Her walks through the woods collecting mushrooms and pine cones. Her time on the beach with her feet in the cold, clear water. She keeps a jar of smooth stones she found on the shore, all pink and gray and cream. They look like the Jordan almonds she used to eat as a child. Anna loves the horseback riding and solitude and her little suite of rooms. This place has been a good home for her. But she will not beggar herself in order to keep it.

"I am very sorry to hear that," Anna says, finally, and rises to her feet. She offers Xenia, and then her husband, a noble nod. "And now if you'll excuse me, I need to go pack my things."

Anastasia

A CHANGING OF THE GUARD

1918

Tobolsk, Russia
February 1918

The first thing Yakov Yurovsky does upon taking command of the Governor's House is send most of our guards away and replace them with members of the Red Guard—the Bolsheviks' hastily formed military. In the end, two hundred of the three hundred and fifty soldiers who came with us from Tsarskoe Selo are dismissed to fronts and futures unknown. We watch them go, more and more every day, our unease growing as every wagonful of men departs.

Each day I wait for Tomas to be among those dispatched from the Governor's House, wondering if he'll be allowed to say good-bye or if he will simply disappear from my life altogether. Yakov gave the order to replace our guards, but Leshy is required to carry it out. He spends the first few days at the barracks nearby, giving soldiers their notice one by one, and comes back to the house each night smelling of cigar smoke and looking guilt-ridden, as though he has murdered a puppy.

Tomas grew distant the moment Yakov arrived. He no longer speaks to me or acknowledges me when we pass in the hallways or in the yard. There is no more flirting. The glancing touches and warm comments cease. I do find him staring at me sometimes when he thinks Yakov won't notice, but he looks away or leaves the room whenever I make eye contact. At one time Tomas's presence could be guaranteed the moment I stepped into the yard, but now strangers accompany me as I do my chores, barking at me that I should not get too close to the wall and that I must work faster. Sometimes I find Tomas watching me from one of the upstairs windows, but I dare not wave or smile. He looks sad, as though he's lost something important, and I always turn away before the strict new guards notice my gaze.

The second thing Yakov does is increase the number of guards stationed inside the house. Prior to his arrival there were twenty men living upstairs. They watched and protected us but never interfered with our daily lives. Yakov adds thirty to that number, and we feel the strain immediately. The house grows crowded and loud, and there are eyes on us constantly. Our world shrinks again, like a belt being tightened two notches. We can still breathe, but our movements become constricted and uncomfortable.

It is alarming how quickly Semyon finds favor with Yakov. He is promoted, again, and placed in charge of the Governor's House. He hovers near us, taking every opportunity to criticize and humiliate us. He kicks the dogs and spits indoors. Our only defense is to ignore him, to rise above his vile insults.

At the end of the first week Leshy calls us into Father's study. He taps his thigh with the edge of a folded telegram while we take our seats. All that dark hair is wild, as though he's been tugging at it all day.

"Vladimir Lenin," he says without preamble, "is no longer willing to pay for your living expenses—"

"That is unacceptable!" Father jumps to his feet. "You cannot keep us in exile and then leave us to starve!"

"He is no longer willing," Leshy says again slowly, "to pay for your living expenses beyond six hundred rubles a month, per person. That includes your family *only*."

"What of our staff? We can't support them on . . ." Mother counts off the total on her fingers, "just over four thousand rubles a month."

"Yakov suggested all of your staff be lined up outside and shot dead. But I convinced him that it would be better to let them live."

"He wouldn't," Mother whispers, aghast.

I think of Botkin and Dova, Gilliard, Trupp, and Cook lying dead in the yard, and I begin to understand the reality of our situation. I want to throw up. I want to cry and run from the room. But I force myself to focus on what Leshy is saying.

"He would. He *wants* to, in fact. You may have noticed that since Yakov's arrival I hold little power in this garrison. But I have persuaded him that five slaughtered servants will create a problem he is not equipped to deal with. Take the opportunity while you have it. Make do with your new allowance."

Mother's voice trembles. "We cannot make this work. It is cruel."

"Not so cruel as a firing squad. You must make do. For their sake."

———

"I am afraid that you have run up considerable credit with many of the merchants in Tobolsk," Pierre Gilliard says later that evening. He spreads the accounts on the table, pointing at one sum and then another. "They must be paid. And quickly lest you make even more enemies."

"How?" Mother's voice is constricted with emotion. She pauses, clearing her throat. "There is no room in our allowance."

"You must find a way. Pull something from what you've set aside. You cannot afford to make enemies in town. There may come a point when you need their help."

Poor Gilliard. I have underestimated the man terribly. I

have mistaken commitment for cruelty. I want to tell him that I am sorry, that I am ashamed, but all his attention is turned toward Mother.

In the end she does as he suggests, sending Gilliard off with a purse full of money to pay the accounts. The fact that twelve people remain in the house while only seven of us are granted a stipend is a problem we're expected to solve without complaint. Whatever my parents suspect might lie in store for us is a thing they do not share. But I notice that Father and Gilliard continue to pore over maps at night. They continue to whisper among themselves.

———

"This is a ration card," Yakov Yurovsky says the next morning. He drops it into Father's lap. I flinch, startled, as always, at the cannon-like sound of his voice. "Like all other *citizens* in this country, you are entitled to a basic food allowance."

Leshy stands at the door to the study, his face expressionless and his hands folded before him. That red kerchief hangs from his pocket like a warning flag. This is the posture he assumes whenever Yakov is near. Detachment. It's the same attitude shown by Tomas and Ivan in Yakov's presence, and I hope it's only a facade, a way of feigning disinterest in order to protect us.

Father lifts the small rectangular green piece of cardboard from his lap. His voice is terse as he recites the specifics printed before him. "Nicholas Romanov, 'ex-emperor' of Freedom Street." He glares at this description but continues. "Six dependents. Ration card number 54, good for flour, butter, and sugar."

Mother peers at the card. "What of coffee? We ran out last week."

"That," Yakov says, "is a luxury unavailable to the general populace."

Mother rubs her temples. She has, for as long as I've been

aware, relied on coffee for comfort and sanity the way Father relies on physical exercise. In the days since our supply dwindled and then disappeared entirely, she has suffered from one long, unending headache. Mother insists that it is concentrated entirely in her right temple, and as a result, that eye has watered for three days straight.

"I will manage," she whispers, brushing the pad of one thumb across her wet eyelashes.

It is the first time I pity my mother, the first time I see her as completely human. A woman who can be broken by something as simple as a headache. It is an unsettling realization, and I wonder, if she, with all her age and experience, can be broken in such a way, what will become of me?

THREE WEEKS LATER

Tobolsk, Russia
March 15, 1918

Gleb and Tanya Botkin are sent away at first thaw. They stand on the boardwalk outside the house, suitcases in hand, staring at the schoolroom as though watching a funeral procession. We do our best to cheer them, waving and smiling, but they turn away, despondent.

"This is twice now that Botkin has dismissed them," Maria says over my shoulder. "Gleb is tired of being treated like a child."

"He is a child."

She jabs me in the ribs with her elbow and I yelp. "Takes one to know one."

I'm about to argue but she interrupts me.

"Has your menses started?" Maria correctly interprets my silence. She grins in triumph. "Like I said. A child."

"You don't have to be such a donkey about it," I hiss.

"Ass. The word is *ass*. If you're going to insult me, do it properly."

"I might not be bleeding like a stuck pig every month the way you are, but at least my *ass* is not the size of a donkey's."

I'm out the door before she can think of a suitable retort, but I notice how she slides her hands along the back of her skirt. It's a subconscious movement, a show of insecurity, and it proves to me that the insult hit home. I know it's cruel and I should apologize, but I don't have time to stroke my sister's vanity today. Dr. Botkin will be leaving any minute to escort Gleb and Tanya to the steamship waiting at the dock, and there's something I have to find before they leave.

The photo album is at the bottom of a small wooden chest that rests at the foot of my camp bed. It is small and square with a brown leather cover, but they will recognize its significance. The little album is filled with pictures of my family, our trips, and images of daily life at the Alexander Palace. And sprinkled throughout the pages are pictures of our friends and servants, Gleb and Tanya among them. I brought it on a whim and haven't opened it once since our arrival. But I know my friends, so glum and disappointed, will love the memento.

I catch Botkin as he's walking out the door. "Wait for me!" I shout.

"You can't come with me, Schwibsik."

"I know. I just . . . I want to say good-bye."

Semyon and Tomas straddle the door and Botkin looks to them for approval. "Let her go to the gate. It won't hurt anything."

"What is that?" Semyon asks, looking at my hands.

"Only a photo album." I flip it open to show him there's nothing hidden inside. "A farewell gift."

He stares at it for a moment, thinking, then shakes his head. "No. Outside contact is forbidden."

"That's not fair—"

"Argue again and I'll confiscate it."

Botkin grips my shoulder with his huge, warm hand and squeezes just enough to make his warning clear. He kneels before me and pries the album from my hands. "None of this is fair, Schwibsik. None of it. But I will give this to the children for you and they will treasure it always."

In the seven months they've been in Tobolsk I've been allowed to visit with Gleb and Tanya only once—during our trip to church on Christmas Eve. Yet their dismissal hits me harder than I expect. It seems an arbitrary cruelty.

"Tell them I'm sorry that I couldn't see them more often. I wanted to."

"They know. And they would do anything for you, Anastasia. Gleb in particular. I fear my boy is besotted with you."

Botkin brushes a tear from my cheek with one knuckle, and I look up in time to see a curious expression sweep across Tomas's face. Pity? Jealousy? Maybe anger. I can't identify it. He remains still, keeping his post without argument or emotion.

"Tell them good-bye," I say, swallowing the lump in my throat. "Tell them not to forget me."

He pulls me tight against his chest. "Fear not, Schwibsik, you are not the sort of girl one forgets."

ONE WEEK LATER

Tobolsk, Russia
March 21, 1918

We are surprised by an early spring. Winter sweeps out in the same sudden rush in which it arrived. Within three days the only snow left in the entire town is Alexey's mountain in the yard, now a pitiful, dirty pile of slush. He takes the loss of his favorite plaything like a personal insult. I find him one after-noon trying to mount the hill with his garbage-lid sled only to end up knee-deep in melting snow, his trousers and shoes soaked, his mood foul.

"Where are you going?" I shout after him as he turns and trudges toward the house, gripping that sled as though he is off to battle.

My brother has always been a docile, quiet boy so I am star-tled to see the look of pure rage and determination on his face.

"Sledding!" he shouts, pushing through the back door of the house. "They can't take everything away from me. They *can't*."

"No one took anything from you, Alexey! The snow melted!" I yell, picking up the hem of my skirt and trudging after him through the mud.

But he goes through the kitchen door as if he hasn't heard me. Curious and a little alarmed I follow him into the house, making it just in time to hear Mother shout, "Don't you do that, Alexey. No! Stop it right now!"

And then there is a thunderous clatter of metal on wood, and I step around the corner in time to see my brother hur-tling down the stairs. For one moment there is a look of pro-found joy on his face. The look he used to get when we pulled him in the wagon as a toddler. Or the look he got while sitting atop the elephant's back at Alexander Palace. It is an expression of wild abandonment, of little boyhood, and adventure. It is euphoric. But it turns to terror in the time it takes me to blink because the edge of his stupid, ridiculous, murderous garbage lid catches the lip of the next step, and flips so quickly he's flung into the air, arms and legs flailing wildly.

It happens the way all terrible accidents happen, in slow motion. Time suspended. Your body frozen. Your mind racing. Alexey lands, legs split at an unnatural angle, near the bottom of the stairs. And then he slides the last few steps, thumping to a stop near Mother's feet. I can see the scream building in his chest as he gasps silently, searching for breath. And then the sound breaks free, shattering the air. Surprise and pain and fear. In the time it takes me to cross those last few steps to where he lies, Alexey thrashes on the floor, shrieking and clutching his groin as though he's been cleaved in half.

Mother is frozen, horrified and silent. Reaching him first, I scoop Alexey up and drop onto the bottom step. I draw him onto my lap and can feel him shudder. My ears ring with his wailing. He writhes in my arms, but I clamp him tighter against my body, knowing that he has to calm himself and be still. I can feel the warmth of his blood pooling where he sits on my lap. I can feel it but I refuse to look.

I won't look.

I can't look.

Because when Alexey starts to bleed he doesn't stop.

Anna

The Pier at East Thirteenth Street, New York City
February 9

Gleb allows the driver to make one stop as they leave Manhattan: a newsstand on the corner of Nineteenth Street and Eighth Avenue. He quickly buys a copy of every newspaper available, then rushes back to the car.

"Look!" He lifts a copy of the *Herald Tribune* and points to the headline. "Lost Daughter of the Tsar Hides on Ship in Bay."

Another reads "Legendary 'Duchess' Lands."

The New York Times, The New York Post, The New York World, The Wall Street Journal, The New York Herald Tribune, the *Gotham Gazette,* and half a dozen other papers all cover the story, each of them taking a different angle on her arrival and identity. Gleb is positively giddy.

"Don't you see, Anna, we're winning!"

"I didn't realize we were competing."

"Of course we are! Good grief, woman, did you just get here?" He laughs at his own joke because yes, she did, in fact, arrive only hours ago.

"You aren't making any sense. Competing with whom?"

"The family. The Romanov cousins. And those two wicked aunts of yours."

She hasn't made the connection between today's headlines and her ongoing feud with the dowager empress and the tsar's sisters. There are other battles raging of course, small fires that keep erupting all over Europe every time a distant relation learns of her claim, but none burn so bright as those involving the immediate family.

Anna shakes her head. "I don't see victory. I see chaos."

"No. No. It's the perception. *Everything* is about perception right now. People are truly beginning to believe that you are Anastasia," he says, lifting the *Herald Tribune* and reading part of an editorial aloud: "'She comes surrounded like the exploits of Colonel T. E. Lawrence—with the full publicity of a complete reticence . . .'" He runs a finger along the page until he finds the line he's looking for. "Yes. Here it is. 'She granted no interviews, but locked herself in her cabin, preserving an impenetrable manner that divided between regal hauteur and utter indifference to openly expressed skepticism.'"

"That makes me sound impossible."

"It makes you sound imperious." He grins. "A good thing."

It took one week for Anna to make the journey from Castle Seeon to New York. Her passage was paid for in equal parts by Xenia Leeds, the tsar's niece several times removed, and Sergei Rachmaninoff, the famed Russian composer. Exactly how he'd gotten involved she doesn't know, but she's grateful for the escape regardless. Anna wasted no time leaving Germany and had, ceremonially, wiped the dust from her feet. She boarded the steamship *Berengaria* with a passport and visa under the assumed last name of Anderson—a necessary concession since the passport office would not issue one to her as Anastasia Romanov. So she is now Anna Anderson. It will take some getting used to.

Seven days at sea proved that she has no stomach for traveling by boat. Anna spent the majority of her time in the stateroom, practicing her English and praying to the porcelain throne in her private lavatory.

"*Ich habe Angst, ich habe Angst,*" she muttered over and over in her worst moments, lying cradled on the floor with her arms wrapped around her stomach like a child.

I am afraid, I am afraid. Afraid the sea sickness would kill her, and, sometimes in the throes of a wild bout of nausea, wishing that it would. Afraid this journey would be in vain.

But she survived the trip, and when they finally reached New York Harbor they could not dock and were forced to wait in the bay until the heavy, soup-like fog lifted. And then, this morning, they were met with an entire press corps that had camped out all night on the dock. They shouted questions and shoved cameras in her face and pressed against her as Gleb guided her to the car.

"Show us your face!" they shouted.

"Who are you really?" they asked.

"Have you come to break into the film business?"

"Are you here for an arranged marriage?"

"Will you stay?"

"Will you live in Manhattan?"

"Tell them," Anna whispered into Gleb's ear as he shoved her into the backseat of the waiting car, "that I will give no interviews. Not today. Not tomorrow. Not ever."

Dutiful as ever, Gleb obeyed, and finally her heart has stilled its frantic pace as they maneuver their way out of Manhattan and on to her next great adventure.

———

Oyster Bay is a community of summer homes and tennis whites. Manicured lawns and garden parties. Yachts and country clubs. The closer they get to the home of Xenia Leeds, the lower Anna sinks into her seat.

"What's the matter with you?"

"What if she doesn't acknowledge me? What if this is a waste of time?"

"She invited you. She wants you here."

"She is one of them."

"She is your only option at the moment."

The drive from Manhattan to Oyster Bay takes an hour and a half, and, despite her nerves, Anna finally does relax. The Long Island Sound stays in view for much of the drive, and she keeps her gaze on the choppy steel-colored water and the vessels that traverse back and forth: ferries, yachts, tugboats, and great, long trawlers piled high with garbage and steel beams. They pass over bridges and through tree-covered lanes. Soon she has lost interest in the Sound and has turned her gaze to the sprawling brick homes that line the road. It doesn't take long to figure out that the more elaborate the mailbox, the more stately the home. After a while the estates are set so far back from the road that she can see nothing but rock walls, hedges, and wrought-iron fences.

After a while they slow to take a bend in the road, and a long white fence, anchored by brick columns, comes into view. But unlike the other fences she's seen so far, this one stretches for nearly a quarter of a mile. And then they slow even more and turn into a driveway of crushed gravel. Anna has to crane her neck to see the top of the gate as they pass through.

"This is it?" she asks, stunned.

"Not what you expected?"

"I didn't realize it would be so . . . large."

Gleb laughs. "The first thing you need to know about William Leeds is that he does not do things on a small scale. He's the son and heir of a tin magnate. They say that God owns the cattle on a thousand hills, but William Leeds leases him the farmland. Think about it"—he rolls down the window so she

can smell the sharp, clean scent of freshly raked pine needles—
"the man went and found himself a bonafide Russian princess
for a wife."

When they pull into the circular driveway there is a full
entourage waiting for them, both William and Xenia Leeds,
along with much of the household staff. It is nothing short of
a royal reception, complete with curtsies, bows, and a bouquet
of bright, fragrant winter jasmine.

Gleb helps Anna from the car and they present themselves
before the family.

If there is a prettier, more fashionable woman anywhere in
the world, Anna has never met her. And she suddenly regrets
her juvenile choice of an entirely white wardrobe in Paris the
day before they set sail, because Xenia Leeds, in less than thirty
seconds, has shown her how to make dove gray look transcen-
dent in the dead of winter.

"I am so delighted you agreed to come," Xenia says, in English, but her Russian accent is strong. "It is a pleasure to see
you again."

Anna dips her head, just enough to acknowledge a peer, but
not so much as to show deference. "The pleasure is all mine.
Thank you for having me."

"Please," Xenia says, "meet my husband, William."

It should be a crime for any two people to be so attractive.
Anna is a bit unnerved to see that William Leeds is almost pret-
tier than his wife. Anna feels suddenly shabby and laughable.
She drops her eyes. Pulls at the cuffs of her simple wool dress.

"Call me Billy," he says. "William is such a stuffy name."

"One that I insist on using despite his arguments," Xenia
says with just the slightest hint of disapproval. It's there in the
twitch of her nose, something akin to a sniff.

Anna guesses that Xenia prefers the stuffy name, so she says,
"Then I shall do the same." She motions Gleb to step forward,

and it is only then that she realizes Xenia is stubbornly refusing to acknowledge his presence. William, for his part, looks at Gleb with pity. "And of course you know Gleb Botkin."

"Of course, but I am afraid he is not welcome at Kenwood. Not today or any other day." She says this in the dryest, most disinterested tone, as if Anna had suggested they take in a stray cat.

Gleb stands there, mouth opening and closing like a dying fish as he tries to find an acceptable reply.

Anna speaks instead. "I don't understand—"

Xenia turns her dark, obsidian eyes on Gleb. "We agreed that there would be no press." She nods to the butler, who dutifully unfolds a copy of *The New York Times* with a bold headline proclaiming Anna's arrival.

"Yes . . . but we needed—"

"I'm afraid you have complicated things for me immensely."

"I meant no harm. I only wanted—"

Xenia sighs and the sound is filled with three hundred years' worth of exasperated monarchs. "What you wanted is irrelevant given the circus that is about to descend upon my doorstep."

"No," he insists. "I told the press we were going elsewhere. No reporters will show up here."

"It's not the press I'm worried about," Xenia says.

Anna has gone from feeling elation to the confusion that happens immediately prior to a betrayal. She does not realize that she is backing up until she bumps into the car.

"Please," Xenia says, "we mean you no harm. Our invitation stands. Your room is ready. And we are delighted to have you as a guest, but if he wishes to remain in Oyster Bay, he must find other accommodations. He cannot stay here. Not now."

"I don't understand why the news of her arrival is so upsetting."

Xenia lifts the newspaper from between the butler's gloved,

pinched fingers and hands it to Gleb. She points at a paragraph below the fold. "It's not the arrival; it's the accusation."

He reads for several seconds, eyes growing larger with each word. "But I didn't give this statement. I know nothing about it."

"Of course you didn't. It was wired to the *Times* by a spokesman for my family, my cousin Dmitri."

"Dmitri Leuchtenberg?" Anna asks.

Xenia frowns. "Yes, but how—"

"I was staying with his family prior to leaving Germany. What," Anna asks, desperately trying to keep the anger from her voice, "does that article say?"

Gleb pokes the newspaper with a single finger. "This article accuses us of masterminding a conspiracy to wrest control of funds that the tsar's sisters are trying to claim."

Anna's irritation is growing by the second. "*What* funds are they talking about?"

Gleb looks at her, almost apologetically. "Your father's. The long-rumored missing fortune of Tsar Nicholas the Second. Untold millions. Held in trust, at the Bank of England, for his heirs." He turns on Xenia. "So it's true then! The money does exist. Your family has denied it for years."

"My family is . . . complicated. And that is why you cannot disrupt the situation further with your presence. They will hear of it, and whatever progress has been made with your cause will be lost."

Anna pulls the newspaper from Gleb's hands and reads the article for herself. "Why didn't you say anything about this in the car? You bought all the papers."

Two bright circles appear on his cheeks. "I admit that I only skimmed the articles. I did not read below the fold on most."

She would smack him across the head with this paper if she thought it would help. But Gleb's mouth pulls in at the corners and his eyes close to slits. It's the face he gets when he's thinking furiously, and she knows that he is formulating some new plan, something that will help them adapt to this turn of events. "I understand your concerns," he says at last, to Xenia. "And I agree with you."

"I am glad to hear it," she says.

"I will leave her with you and I won't interfere with your visit. All I ask is that I may contact her on occasion."

Xenia gives a curt nod. "I have no problem with that."

He turns to Anna. "You will be safe here. And I will check on you regularly." The trust that Anna places in Gleb is similar to the trust she places in a chair. She believes that he will be there to support her because he has been there for so long doing that very thing. If the legs are wobbly, she tries not to think about it much because it's the only chair she has.

Anna hasn't taken into account that Gleb will not be in Oyster Bay to help deflect any difficult questions. They cannot discuss the situation openly here in the driveway, before the Leedses and the household staff. She thinks, quickly, desperately, as she tries to read all the unspoken messages that flash across Gleb's face. There are so many ways for this to go wrong.

Finally, she asks, "May I make a request?"

Xenia has not moved from her position at the bottom step. Her hands, now freed of the newspaper, are folded primly before her again. "Of course."

"Can you promise me that no member of the Romanov family will be brought to see me without my permission? Can you assure me that I will not be ambushed in your home?"

A pause as Xenia tries to divine what is behind the request and then she says, "Yes. Of course. I promise."

"Then I am delighted to stay." From the corner of her eye she sees Gleb relax.

William Leeds seems content to watch the exchange without

contributing, but Anna does not, for a moment, believe that he is disinterested. He has an expression—something around his eyes and the laziness of his smile—that gives him the look of a speculator, the sort of man who would gamble on a horse race or a cockfight. Anna is certain that he is taking notes, trying to ascertain who in this group has the most to lose. William Leeds seems like the sort of man who is accustomed to being on the winning side.

Gleb does not prolong his good-bye. He gives Anna a quick hug, a kiss on the cheek, and one final assurance that she will be safe and well cared for at Kenwood. Once her trunk has been removed from the car he gives her a nod and then slips into the backseat.

"You must forgive me," Xenia says a few moments later when he is gone. "Every word I say in your defense puts me at odds with my family. I'm simply trying to do the right thing for everyone involved. Please do not think me cruel for sending him away."

Anna smiles kindly but does not answer because the truth is that she does not know Xenia Leeds well enough to think anything of her at all.

———

Kenwood is a sprawling, three-story house on a fifty-six-acre estate set into a cove in Cold Spring Harbor. Every window offers panoramic views that could inspire even the most cold-hearted landscape artist. It is painted white brick with green shutters and leaded glass windows. The house has a swimming pool, six-car garage, a dock, horse stables, and its own private beach. They put Anna on the top floor in a suite of private rooms overlooking the tennis courts at the back of the property.

By time Xenia is done giving her a tour of the house, the staff has already unpacked her belongings and hung them in a cedar closet. There are fires burning merrily in all three fireplaces in the suite—one each in her bedroom, bathroom, and parlor—and lunch is set out in the small dining area.

"I thought you might want to eat in your rooms today. I imagine you're still exhausted from your trip."

Normally the smell of roast beef, baked potatoes, fresh bread, and strong coffee would be impossible for Anna to ignore. But her attention has been arrested by something in the middle of the room.

"Oh! Those are for you. A gift. Something I bought for you on our trip to the West Indies last month. You're welcome to name them. I haven't gotten around to that yet. They're both female."

In a cage on a round table in the middle of the room sit two gorgeous green parrots.

Xenia laughs at the look of stunned delight on Anna's face. "Neither one of them can talk, I'm afraid. But I remember how much you love animals, and I thought you might like to have some company in this corner of the house."

"Thank you," Anna says, a bit overwhelmed. "I love them." She gently lifts the bar that secures the door and slides her hand into the cage. Anna pets the soft feathered head of one bird, and then the other. They are identical in size and color. Twins perhaps. Or at least sisters. Finally, Anna looks at her host, inspiration written on her face. "They will share a name. I will call them both Janus."

20

Anastasia

TOGETHER NO MORE

1918

Tobolsk, Russia
April 23

I'm the last one to enter Father's study. There's static in the air, an almost palpable electric charge as my parents sit, tense and furious, before Yakov. He paces the room, fingers laced behind his back, looking at each of us in turn. My sisters are on the verge of tears. Leshy is in attendance as well. Those odd, feral eyes of his are slightly pinched. Anger perhaps. Or alarm. I can't decide what, exactly, he's feeling. So I take a seat in the corner of the room on a hard wooden bench beneath the window and wait for Yakov to deliver whatever bad news awaits us.

I wonder how thin he really is beneath that baggy uniform. The way his jacket hangs from his shoulders and flaps at his thighs makes me think that his arms are rails and his legs spindles. I wonder whether I'm strong enough to smother him in his sleep. Probably not, I decide; little men are quick and ruthless and they often fight dirty. That's what Father says. They fight like mercenaries. Yakov would likely stab me in the eye before I could get the pillow over his face. Such thoughts! Only a year ago I was planting cabbages and now I'm plotting murder.

Yakov finally comes to a stop before Father. His smile is eager, his eyes shadowed by that pronounced, heavy brow.

"Citizen Romanov," he says, "I have been assigned to remove you from Tobolsk."

Father blinks at him as though trying to make sense of what he has just heard. "What do you mean?"

"I *mean* that you are to be put on trial and I am to take you to another location so preparations can be made."

Father grinds out his next question between clenched teeth. "What. Location?"

"I am afraid I cannot reveal that."

"No," he says. "I will not leave my family."

"I never said you had to leave your family. They will accompany you."

It is here that Leshy steps forward, dwarfing Yakov with every inch of his impressive height, and his impassive face finally turns to granite. "Alexey is too sick. He won't be well enough to travel for many weeks yet."

My brother's tumble down the stairs nearly killed him. There was nothing Botkin could do to stop the bleeding. We have taken turns sitting by his bedside, terrified he would die at any moment. Though the worst has passed, Alexey is still bedridden, bruised, and unable to eat or even roll over without assistance.

While Yakov considers the situation his eyes tighten and release several times as he weighs the benefits and disadvantages of a dead thirteen-year-old heir. "We do not have weeks," he says finally. "Nicholas and Alexandra will leave first thing in the morning. They will bring one daughter and half the servants. The others can stay to care for the boy until he is recovered."

———

My parents spend the rest of the day with Alexey, hugging him, kissing him, and saying good-bye. My brother sleeps through most of it, still too weak to raise his head or speak. Meanwhile, they leave the decision of who will go with them up to us. While they weep in the next room, we sit on our beds and settle the issue the way we have settled all other disputes since we were children. We draw straws. Maria argues, in vain, that my straw is shorter than hers, that I should go and she should stay. But Olga orders us to lay them down side by side on the floor and it is clear that I will remain in Tobolsk. I would like to think that Maria's devotion to Alexey is what drives her to tears, but I suspect it is Ivan she does not want to leave.

My parents' trunks are packed quickly and thoroughly with the basic necessities while Cook hustles to make a last meal of borscht and hens stuffed with rice and hazelnuts. I wish, morbidly, that he had cooked D'Yavol, but I don't say it aloud. My parents are not in the mood for jokes tonight. So we eat our dinner quietly, without fanfare. None of us have much of an appetite.

"What will we do while you're gone?" I ask, finally, unable to bear the silence around the table any longer.

"Exactly what you're doing now, Schwibsik," Father says. "You will do your lessons and run the house and care for your brother."

"But—"

"Alexey will be well soon," Mother interrupts. "Then you will join us."

I hear the note of obstinate belief in her voice and I don't argue. There's no point upsetting her more. I've been afraid since Yurovsky's announcement but now I am angry as well because I want my mother to comfort me and she doesn't. She is drowning in her own fear and cannot be bothered to assuage mine. This, I suppose, is what it means to be grown. I add this feeling to the list of things I hate.

The day soon evaporates, and then there is nothing left to

do but whisper good night and go to bed. My sisters and I toss and turn in our beds that night, listening to one another fret while the dogs snore at our feet.

Yakov comes to collect our parents, Maria, Dova, and Trupp in the morning, but he doesn't allow us to accompany them to the dock. As we have every other time, we are forced to say our good-byes at the house. They are quick, stoic, and tearless. We all stand in a dismal circle on the front porch as my parents and sister are wrapped in lambskin coats and driven away without comment. Behind them rattle two carts, loaded with trunks carrying the last of Mother's hidden treasure, all the large pieces that were too cumbersome and heavy to sew into our clothes.

———

Yakov is gone, at least, but he leaves Semyon in command. The first thing that odious man does, once the *Rus* steams away from Tobolsk, is to dismiss Leshy from his service.

"I have performed my duties faithfully!" Leshy argues as they stand in the hallway between Father's study and the schoolroom.

Semyon shrugs. He cannot match Leshy's physical presence so he relies on his rank instead. "Your services are no longer required. You and your men are to pack your things and report to the garrison commander in Petrograd immediately."

Leshy dares not look to where I am standing, just inside the study, listening. "You cannot send us all away. You will be grossly understaffed."

"I'm not. You will leave the twenty men stationed in this house. And you will remind them that all forms of insubordination will result in a visit to the firing squad."

"It is a pity," Leshy says, his voice heavy with contempt, "that Bolshevik diplomacy always equips one man with a rifle and the other with a blindfold."

Semyon laughs at him. "Do you know why Lenin was able to wrest control from the provisional government? Because he understands that a revolution is *useless* without a firing squad."

"So you are Bolshevik now? Pity I did not know your loyalties sooner."

Again, Semyon laughs and I cringe at the sound. "If you had been paying attention you would have realized that I have no loyalties."

———

We don't see Semyon again until after dinner when he barges into the study—now rather bare since being stripped of several pieces of furniture and Father's personal effects.

While he speaks to all of us his eyes are on Olga. Her face burns and she stares at her lap as he says, "Things will be different under my command. It's time the three of you learned to respect authority. You will report all household expenses to me directly for approval. Your tutor will also be required to submit his lesson plans on a weekly basis so I can determine whether your education has become subversive."

It is so hard not to lose control, to scream or throw something at this cruel, arrogant bastard. But that's what Semyon wants. He is looking for an excuse to punish us. Looking for a way to make our lives even more miserable, to shrink them further, to crush every last scrap of joy—and I will not give him the satisfaction.

Olga remains still, avoiding him altogether, but Tatiana's hands tremble as she holds needle and thread in her pinched white fingers. Thankfully we have long since finished our work with the corsets. Tonight we are simply mending skirts and blouses that have grown threadbare from too much wear and washing.

"Well?" he demands, eager for an argument.

Imperiousness is our only weapon and we use it to good

effect, refusing to acknowledge his pronouncement. Tatiana and I regard him with every bit of disinterest we can muster. There are ways to make a man like Semyon feel small. You look at him with pity—it's far more effective than disdain. You cooperate with his demands but in a way that makes him feel you're only doing so because he is weak and must be cosseted. The goal is to make him hate himself for being a man unworthy of respect. We learned all these techniques in the years we spent in the imperial court, and we unleash them on Semyon as he stands before us in the study.

He does not take it well.

The remaining staff is busy—Botkin with Alexey, Gilliard in his rented rooms, Cook in the kitchen—so we are left alone to hear Semyon's final threat.

"And you will no longer be allowed to lock your bedroom doors at night." He reaches for the doorknob and strokes it obscenely. He flicks his tongue between the gap in his teeth. "The locks have already been removed. On my orders."

I wake sometime in the middle hours of the night to the deep warning sound of Jimmy's growl. As usual he sleeps at the foot of my bed, and I feel the rumble in my legs like a train picking up speed. I blink heavily and peer into the darkness. It takes a moment for me to see the shadow, charcoal against the blackness of the room. My heart begins ticking faster when the shadow moves and my breath catches in my throat as the figure takes a step toward Olga's bed.

Slowly, quietly, I slide my hand beneath my pillow and feel the cold metal of the paper knife I smuggled out of Father's study at the Alexander Palace. I have slept with it beneath my pillow every night since Yakov came.

There in the darkness I can see Semyon's profile outlined against the window. I can see him lean over Olga and tug at the front of his trousers. I can hear his breath, heavy and filled with lust.

"You cannot be in here," I say, gripping the handle of my paper knife a little tighter. Jimmy leaps to the floor with a thump, his growl deeper and more menacing now. "Go. Or I will turn him loose."

Semyon takes a step back from Olga's bed, hands up in surrender. "If that dog ever touches me, I'll kill him." His words are slurred but I think there is a note of fear there as well because he continues to move backward toward the door.

I lie there, smelling the scents of angry canine and drunk soldier long after Semyon is gone.

21

Anna

ENTRAPMENT

1927, 1926, 1925

Wasserburg am Inn, Germany
May 11, 1927

The town of Wasserburg sits in the bulb at the top of a hairpin curve in the river Inn. It's a teardrop-shaped peninsula surrounded by a natural moat and connected to the picturesque countryside by a narrow sliver of land. Like many cities in Bavaria it is filled with colorful buildings, old-world charm, and a sense of history that cannot be re-created in larger, more modern cities. Bicycles lean against walls, their small baskets filled with bread loaves and bouquets. The occasional horse-drawn cart clatters down the cobblestone streets. Flower boxes crowd the windows and clotheslines stretch across the alleys. There are statues and arched doorways and fountains around every bend. Anna thinks it is the most beautiful and delightful place she's ever seen.

The Wasserburg Inn looks like something from a Bavarian postcard with its white plaster walls, dark timber accents, red roof, and climbing vines. The street smells of yeast, of bread and beer. She half expects to see a man in lederhosen when she and Gleb pass through the heavy double doors. What they find instead is far more troubling.

Dmitri Leuchtenberg, oldest son of her current sponsor,

Romanov cousin, and a man who has been, for the last year, a continual thorn in her side.

Anna stops short and turns to Gleb. "Why is he here? He's supposed to be in Copenhagen."

"I don't know," Gleb mutters, but his eyes are on the other two men seated at the large round table. One of them Anna has met before, the other she hasn't.

"Let me guess," she growls, "that's your private investigator?"

She takes his silence as an affirmation. Gleb talked her into this meeting by saying he'd met a detective who could help them gather irrefutable proof that she is Anastasia. Gleb has been corresponding with the man for months, trading letters back and forth, discussing their plan for bringing this business to a conclusion once and for all. But the way this man chats and laughs with Dmitri makes it obvious they have been betrayed. Anna knows this because she knows the face of the third man seated with them. She knows why he wandered into a mental institution near Berlin seven years ago.

"We should go," Gleb says, placing a hand at the small of her back. It's a protective gesture, an intimate gesture. He has taken to touching her like this since his arrival back in Germany, trying to make his intentions clear. He has grown familiar with her, and she is unsure how to feel about it. Anna does not know how to surrender to his affections. Nor is she certain that she wants to. But it's too late to leave the inn now. They have been spotted.

Gleb's private investigator approaches where they stand in the doorway. He extends a hand to Anna. "Martin Knopf," he says. When she doesn't accept the hand he motions them toward the table. "Please. We have much to discuss."

They could run. Or refuse. Or make a scene. But that would only complicate the situation. Anna allows herself to be led by the elbow to the table. Martin Knopf pulls out her chair. Gleb slides into the one beside her with a curse.

The Private Investigator nods at each of them in turn. "Good to see you again, Mr. Botkin. I assume by now that you have realized my duplicity in getting you here. For that I would apologize—"

"It would be in vain," he says.

"I cannot fault your animosity. Which is why I'll get directly to the point." The Private Investigator grins, not out of triumph, but because he is, strangely, a man of impeccable manners. He turns to Anna. "I assume you know these gentlemen? Dmitri Leuchtenberg and Felix Schanzkowska."

There are half-empty frosted mugs on the table in front of each of them. Anna fears she has wandered into a celebration. "I am well acquainted with Dmitri," she says. "But I do not know this other man."

Felix is going to speak but Anna glares at him. He looks to the Private Investigator instead.

"There appears to be a difference of opinion regarding that detail," the Private Investigator says. "Mr. Schanzkowska has assured me, in great detail, that he does know you. That he has known you for some time, in fact."

"Then Mr. Schanzkowska is lying."

Unfazed, the Private Investigator continues. "I feel we're getting ahead of ourselves. Please, let me explain my presence here—"

Anna snorts. "I believe they call it entrapment. Or are you unfamiliar with the term?"

"Are you currently in the act of committing a crime?" His voice is suddenly firm. Sharp. "Because if not, I'd say that's the wrong word. I prefer to think of my work here today as *unmasking*."

"I wear no masks."

"Another point of contention, I'm afraid."

"Speak plainly, Mr. Knopf. My patience is wearing thin."

"Very well. Before I met your friend Mr. Botkin, my services were engaged by Dmitri, on behalf of his family, certain members of the Romanov family, to determine your true identity."

"I have made my identity plain."

"It is the belief of the Romanov family—"

"My family is dead—"

"Your *family* has nothing to do with the Romanovs. A point that Mr. Schanzkowska can attest to." He gives Felix a pointed look. "The *recognized*, legal, and surviving family of Tsar Nicholas the Second believe that you are a fraud."

Anna glances at Gleb and then back at the Private Investigator. "And they hired you."

"Correct."

"And you hid this fact from Gleb?"

"Yes."

Gleb offers a miserable groan and waves the barmaid over. He orders a pint of Schwarzbier and pinches the bridge of his nose. "Shit. How could I be so stupid?" and then, "Anna, what would you like?"

"I hate beer." And she does. All her years of drinking have not changed this absolute reality. Beer tastes like horse piss marinated in despair.

"Pear cider, then? I know how you love pears."

"Sure," she says, dryly.

The Private Investigator waits politely for them to receive their order before continuing. Gleb's lager, which comes a few moments later, is so thick and rich it's almost black. It looks like tar to Anna. She takes a tentative sip of her cider. It is surprisingly sweet and refreshing, and she takes another pull at the frosted glass, summoning a bit of courage for whatever comes next.

"Mr. Botkin believed I was working on his behalf," the Private Investigator says. "This artifice, though unfortunate, was necessary to ascertain the truth."

"Because you knew I would refuse to attend this meeting otherwise? Especially considering that I am without recourse or legal representation."

He shrugs. "I am afraid that is your concern, not mine."

"How very churlish of you."

Dmitri Leuchtenberg sets his elbows on the table and leans toward Anna. "You might have my father convinced, but not me. Or my mother. Or anyone else in my family. I knew you weren't who you claimed to be the moment I saw you, and now I can prove it."

Dmitri has been like sand in her underwear from the moment she arrived at Castle Seeon. Abrasive. Constantly grinding on her nerves. He is arrogant and contentious. He protests every mark spent on her care. He resents his father's devotion and the staff's enchantment. Dmitri's mother alone shares his disdain, and they nurse their grievances by pen and telephone with "the family" at every possible opportunity. It was her understanding that Dmitri and his mother would be in Copenhagen this week, arguing their case directly before the dowager empress.

Dmitri leans back in his chair and motions for Felix to speak. "Tell them who you are."

"Felix Schanzkowska."

"And who is this woman?"

He hesitates only a moment before turning to Anna, his eyes dark and pleading. Desperate. "This woman is my sister, Franziska, a Polish factory worker, missing these seven years."

"You are lying!" Gleb says, slamming his stein down on the table. He flings lager from his fingers and Anna dodges the spray.

"I ought to know my own sister."

"Then you are mistaken. Or in the pay of Dmitri."

"That is uncalled for!" Dmitri shouts, slamming his own mug down on the table.

"What's in it for you?" Gleb asks. "Has the dowager empress promised you a title? Or a trust fund? Why are you working so hard to discredit Anna?"

"Because the memory of my cousin shouldn't be dishonored by a charlatan!"

Anna hates the barbaric nature of men. The way they long to fight and draw blood. The way they need to prove their point with brute force. So when both Gleb and Dmitri push back from the table she also rises.

"Enough," Anna says. "I have had enough of all of you."

She does not say good-bye to any of them, offers no formalities or polite excuses. She simply leaves the inn and lets them think what they will. It will be used against her at some point, no doubt, another bit of circumstantial evidence that she is not courtly enough to be a grand duchess.

Anna is halfway down the street before Gleb catches up with her.

"We'll go to America," he declares. "We'll prove your case there."

"You don't ever give up, do you?"

He grabs her arm and stops abruptly before a flower shop. Directly across the street is the little antique shop she visited with Tanya yesterday. "Is that what you want?" Gleb asks, his hand softening on her arm. "Do you want me to give up? Like everyone else?"

"No."

"Then let me help you. Let me make up for this damned fiasco. Let me find other sympathizers. Other means of support. You need to get out of Europe for a while. You need to find a fresh audience. The Russian loyalists here are too jaded. Too political."

"I don't know anyone in America."

"You know me."

Anna's head swims a bit. Too much has happened in too short a time. She drank her cider on an empty stomach and her eyes feel heavy, like they might roll out of her face at any moment. She needs a nap. Or food. Or both. Something, anything but this incessant scheming.

"Nothing will come of this, Gleb," she says, shifting away from his touch.

"But if it does? If I can raise support will you come?" He is pleading, desperate to fix his mistake. "Please?"

"If you are able to arrange the details I will come to America."

ONE DAY EARLIER

Wasserburg am Inn, Germany
May 10, 1927

"Here," Tanya Botkin says, pulling Anna toward a small shop whose sign reads simply ANTIQUES. "This is the place I was telling you about."

From the outside it hardly looks like a black market emporium for imperial Russian goods. Nor does it on the inside. As they enter a little bell rings above the door, announcing their arrival, and bits of dust whirl through a patch of sunlight on the worn wooden floor. The shop is long and narrow with a tall ceiling that makes Anna feel as if she has just stepped into a tunnel. The space is filled with old rugs and heavy pieces of ornate furniture; the walls are covered with gilded mirrors while half the flat surfaces showcase Tiffany lamps in primary colors.

"May I help you?" a pretty young shop girl asks. Anna would guess she's not a day over twenty. Too young to be dealing in stuffy antiques and expensive home accessories.

"Is Albert in today?" Tanya asks. Gleb's sister is the sort of woman who is pretty, but only when she smiles, and she turns on the charm for this young shopkeeper, showcasing a row of straight bright teeth.

The girl runs her hand through her ponytail, letting the strands fall between long, thin fingers. "Perhaps. May I give him your name?"

Tanya hands the girl a card, folded in half with her initials embossed on the outside. The girl turns elegantly, her hair and the hem of her skirt swirling out behind her, and retreats through a door at the back of the shop without another word.

A dancer, Anna thinks. *She has to be a dancer. Most likely a ballerina. Normal women can't move like that.* The girl returns minutes later and motions them to follow. They pass through a heavy wooden door, down a hallway, around a corner, and into what appears to be a broom closet.

Anna stops short, confused, but the girl tugs on a sconce attached to the back wall and a panel slides aside.

"Watch your step," the Shop Girl says. "The stairs are quite steep."

And rickety.

And poorly lit.

They go down, single file, holding on to the wall for balance. Anna has an innate fear of cellars. She would turn and bolt back toward the daylight if Tanya were not blocking her escape.

"Go on," her friend whispers. "I promise you it's safe."

"We shouldn't have come without Gleb."

"He's meeting with the Private Investigator. Don't worry. We'll be fine."

"I hate it when people tell me that. It never turns out to be true."

And then they step into an opulent, well-lit basement. The room is filled with lamps and cabinets. There are ample places to sit—couches and chairs and divans, all of them padded and covered with rich brocade. Anna has never seen so many knick-knacks and paintings and chests. There are at least a dozen swords mounted to the walls, jewelry cases, shelves upon shelves of books. An entire case of knives. One Fabergé egg on a marble column in the middle of the room. And any number of wooden boxes, baskets, and bins.

"Welcome!" announces a voice filled with age and gravitas, in Russian.

Anna suspects that the man who offers them a stiff, formal bow is older than anything in this room. He is as thin as a table leg and as wiry as a billy goat. He has a long white beard but not a single hair atop his head. His teeth remain—all of them straight—but he is in possession of only one milky eye. Or so she assumes, for the other is covered with an embroidered patch. And clearly the man has a sense of humor because the image stitched on the patch in gold thread is an evil eye.

"Albert." Tanya steps forward to clasp his hand. "Thank you so much for seeing us. I have heard that this place is astonishing, but the rumors do not do it justice."

He receives this compliment silently. Waits a beat and says, "Tatiana Botkin. Daughter of Eugene Botkin, physician to the imperial family of Russia. How may Albert assist you today?" He asks this, bizarrely, in the third person.

Tanya elbows Anna in the ribs and shakes her head slightly, indicating it's best not to ask. "I would like you to meet my friend . . . *Anastasia*," she says.

Albert peers at Anna with that single eye for a great length of time. She feels as if her skin will peel away under the examination. And then, suddenly, the old man drops into another stiff bow. "Tsarevna," he whispers. "I am at your service."

She is at a total loss, but Tanya eases between them to tell Albert the reason for their visit. "I have been told that you trade in certain . . . items. Small things of sentimental value to those loyal to the old regime. My friend would like a memento to take with her. Something to remind her of happier days."

"What you have heard is true. But I deal not only in small things. I can acquire almost anything, large or small, if time and resources are not limited."

Anna laughs and Tanya clears her throat. Clarifies. "Unfortunately we are only here for a couple days and funds are . . . ah . . . *finite*."

Albert nods, unruffled by their predicament. "This is not a problem. I have many things that might be of interest to you." He offers Anna his arm as though helping her into a carriage. "May I?"

Tanya gives her an assuring nod, and Anna places her hand on the fine silk of his sleeve. He leads her, like a military escort, through the cavernous basement. Albert says nothing, points out nothing in particular. He simply watches Anna's face for any signs of interest and when she slows or looks at something for more than a second or two he elaborates on the provenance of an item or, in some cases, gives an explanation of the item itself.

When Anna lifts an ornate ivory pawn from a chess set Albert sighs. "Yes. You have good taste. Do you play?"

"Not in many years."

"This was carved by hand from the tusks of an African bull elephant. At one time the animal was a pet of Tsarevitch Alexey. The elephant was killed at the beginning of the revolution, under orders of Alexander Kerensky. The traitor took the tusks for himself and commissioned this set."

Anna holds the pawn in her hand, running her thumb over its edges and curves lovingly. There is no emotion in her voice. "A beastly thing to do."

"War is beastly, Tsarevna. But do not fret, the chess set was confiscated from Kerensky's office when the Bolsheviks took power."

"The Bolsheviks were worse."

"True. But at least Kerensky did not have the satisfaction of keeping his prize."

"And how did you come by this?"

He moves on, taking her with him. "Albert never reveals how he comes by his treasures."

They drift through the room, Tanya at their heels, until they come to a crowded shelf at the back. It is filled with smaller, tattered items. An ink drawing ripped from a sketch book. A broken fountain pen. A chipped hand mirror. Anna lifts an old, worn icon from the shelf. She raises it to her mouth and blows away a thin layer of dust.

"Saint Anna of Kashin," Albert says. "The holy protector of women. This icon once belonged to Viktor Zborovsky, captain of the Imperial Guard, and held a message, written by Empress Alexandra, begging the British monarchy for help during the revolution. I am told that Zborovsky was stopped on his way to Petrograd shortly after being dismissed from the palace. The icon was taken from him and the message destroyed. As you know, help never arrived for the imperial family."

"Yes," Anna says, her voice a whisper. "I know."

Albert pats her hand and moves forward again, but Anna stops him. "How much for the chess set and the icon?"

He looks at her, his eye clouded and watery. "For you, Tsar-evna, nothing."

ONE DAY EARLIER

Castle Seeon, Germany
May 9, 1927

Castle Seeon was once a Benedictine monastery but is now a sprawling lakeside castle occupied by a family that cannot decide whether Anna is friend or foe. The father champions her cause while the mother and son thwart it at every opportunity. They are a house divided. For her part, Anna tries to avoid the lot of them whenever possible. This is easy enough, given the size of the estate, and she spends most of her time reading in her room or exploring the grounds.

Built over a thousand years earlier, Castle Seeon has been a medicinal spa populated by bohemians, a barracks used to house any number of Russia's armies during any number of her wars. It has seen countless lives and been witness to countless stories. It has spied on chaste monks and wanton artists. These walls have been built and burned and razed and built again times without number. They have housed Haydn and Mozart. Priests and soldiers. Scholars and lunatics. At the moment, however, the duke of Leuchtenberg and his acrimonious family claim ownership.

Anna loves to wander the spacious confines of these ancient walls, visiting the crypt and then the oratory. The chapel and the ballrooms. The library and the now-vacant infirmary. But the towers, with their onion-shaped copper roofs, are her favorite place, and she climbs them on clear days to look across the lake. Occasionally she wanders through the cemetery and counts the gravestones of the long-dead abbots who gave their lives in service to God, and now their bodies in service to the flowering bushes that line the castle walls. The walls are white and the roof is red and the lake reflects this image in perfect, upside-down symmetry. If it were not for its occupants, the castle would be nothing short of magical. It sits on an island in the middle of Lake Seeoner Seen and is connected to the mainland by a narrow causeway. The water is deep and blue, peppered with lily pads and cattails along the shore. There is a small dock beside the boathouse and sometimes, when the weather is warm, Anna sits on the edge and dangles her feet in the water.

When Anna first arrived at Castle Seeon she had a steady stream of visitors: either skeptical aristocrats maneuvering themselves into position for some future advantage, or extended members of the Romanov family peering at her with suspicion, looking for reasons to reject her out of hand. These days she entertains few people who are not friends. Mostly she sees Gleb and Tanya Botkin.

Today she sits with Tanya in the tidy kitchen garden on a carved stone bench between fragrant bushes of rosemary and lavender. Anna doesn't cook—can't in fact remember the last time she stood in front of a stove—but she does enjoy being in this place. Watching things grow. Nibbling on the herbs.

Tanya plucks a sprig of rosemary from the bush and rolls it between her thumb and forefinger. She inhales the scent and then flicks the twig away. "Have things gotten any better with Dmitri?"

Anna cranes her head to look at the terrace three floors above them. Dmitri Leuchtenberg's suite overlooks the garden, and sometimes, when she knows that he is in residence, she sits here to torment him.

"What do you think?"

Tanya laughs. "Still being an odious prick, is he?"

"And recruiting others to his cause."

"Meaning?"

"He left for Copenhagen two weeks ago."

Tanya groans. "Spiteful bastard."

"With his *mother*," Anna adds.

"To make their case with the dowager empress in person? What could you have possibly done to light that sort of fire under him? Expose his sexual proclivities to the press?" When Tanya smiles, her face is transformed from unremarkable to the sort of pretty that makes a man trip over his own feet. She knows this, of course, and has developed a wicked sense of humor that gives her ample opportunity for laughter. It's a pity she doesn't have her brother's cheekbones, Anna thinks; they would match her smile perfectly.

"I know nothing of his *proclivities*," Anna says, "nor do I want to."

"Well, you must have done something. He's usually content to fester in private."

"We got into an altercation the day before he left."

"About?"

"The *otkritie navigatie*."

Tanya shakes her head, confused. "That's a new low for him. Why on earth would he want to argue about the Opening of Navigation?"

"Because I knew what it was and what it meant. Because I got it right, and every time I explain something correctly it infuriates him. He doesn't like being proven wrong. He hates the fact that his father believes me, so he is determined to see me proven a fraud."

"Such a pity the man has the disposition of a hemorrhoid; he's devilishly handsome."

"Well, the devil can take him as far as I'm concerned."

The garden gate swings open and Gleb steps onto the gravel path. "The devil can take who?" he asks.

"Dmitri."

"Fair enough. But I'd like to get my fists on him first."

"Then you'll have to go to Copenhagen," Anna says. "He's currently maligning my character almost a thousand kilometers away."

"Excellent! He won't be able to meddle in our plans."

Tanya looks at her brother with suspicion. He's nearly bursting at the seams with enthusiasm. "You're here early," she says.

"I thought we'd get a head start." He turns to Anna. "Are you ready?"

"Do I have to go?"

He does that thing with his lip that Anna finds charming,

where he pulls the bottom left corner between his teeth and chews lightly in an awkward half smile. "You said you would."

She grunts, entirely unladylike. "Remind me why I agreed?"

"Because I want you to?"

"Unlikely."

"Because I asked?"

"Blackmailed."

"Cajoled. Really, it was more like a gentle prompt if we're being honest. Besides"—he grins, widely—"this will help our cause. It's just a few days in Wasserburg. This man can help us establish your identity. With any luck we'll have it wrapped up before Dmitri returns."

"What's his name?" Anna asks. "The one you're bringing me to meet? You've been very secretive about him."

"Martin Knopf."

"And what does he do?"

"He's a private investigator. And he will, I am certain, help us prove your identity once and for all."

"And how exactly did you meet him?"

"We have been corresponding for some time. He has been looking into your claims at my request."

"And you trust him?"

"Why wouldn't I?"

SIXTEEN MONTHS EARLIER

Mommsen Clinic, Berlin
January 1926

Gleb sets the folded newspaper down carefully on the table beside Anna's bed. She's been in the clinic for months, unable to fully heal from a tubercular infection in her lungs. But even with the fever and the infernal ringing in her ears she can hear him sigh. It's a sound that has grown familiar in the last few years: he's gotten some news that he doesn't want to tell her.

"What?" she asks and her voice is raspy, her throat swollen and raw from coughing.

Fingers lightly brush the hair away from her forehead. "I didn't mean to wake you. I'm sorry."

"You didn't. Now tell me, what are you reading?"

"The *Nationaltidende*."

"I'm not familiar with that paper."

"It's out of Copenhagen."

"Ah. The City of Liars."

"Don't you mean spires?" Gleb asks.

She curls her lip in response. "No, I do not." Anna lets her body go limp into the pillows again. After weeks of fever and coughing, with her lungs heavy with fluid, even the smallest things, like sitting up, feel overwhelming. "So what's the bad news?"

"The tsar's older sister has been quoted in an article."

"Saying?"

"Very unflattering things."

Anna reaches for a rose-colored silk shawl beside her pillow and runs the fabric through her fingers. "That doesn't make any sense. She sent me this for Christmas. A month ago."

"Let's just say I doubt you'll be getting any more gifts from her."

Anna studies the shawl dispassionately. She runs her thumb over the tiny stitches along the seam. It's handmade. Expensive. Luxurious. Four weeks ago she considered it a sign that the tsar's sister had made up her mind about her identity. "Read it," she says.

"I don't think—"

"Then just read the worst part. That's all that matters anyway."

Gleb clears his throat and begins to read, " 'Frau Anderson

leaves the impression of a poor, highly strung invalid who believes in her story and is confirmed in the belief by the people around her. We hope that she can be freed of this idée fixe in the Berlin clinic where she is now being treated.'"

"How did they know I was here?"

"Pierre Gilliard, I believe."

"And how does *he* know I'm here?"

"You don't remember?"

Anna coughs again and she can taste blood in her mouth. The spasm lasts for nearly a minute, and she is thoroughly winded afterward. "Remember what"—she takes a shaky breath—"exactly?"

"That he came to interrogate you in October."

Anna stares at the ceiling. There is a vague memory that presses against her mind. A man in dark clothing. Endless questions. A sharp, raging headache. But nothing concrete. She shakes her head. "No."

"Of course you don't. You were bedridden with fever. Delirious, in fact. Not that he cared. But he made his judgment about you in that condition and will not be moved from it now. I could kill the staff for letting him in to see you."

"He says I am a fraud?"

"Oh, he says worse than that." Gleb shakes the newspaper and then stabs it with the end of one finger. "He says you are a vulgar adventuress and a first-rate actress. Pierre Gilliard has become the lead witness in their case against you."

THREE MONTHS EARLIER

Mommsen Clinic, Berlin
October 1925

It feels as though someone is standing on Anna's chest, as though she has to fight for every breath. She can hear the swamp beneath her ribs, the air moving and bubbling inside her damp lungs. Anna can't lift her head from the pillow or her hands from where they lie at her sides. Her temples throb and her eyes water. She wants to sleep but there is someone talking loudly beside her bed.

"Do you know who I am?" a man demands.

Anna turns her head. Tries to focus. His head is there. Dark hair. Pale skin. His voice seems familiar, but she can't make out the features of his face. She tries to tell him this, but the words won't form properly, and he takes the shaking of her head as a no.

Anna is freezing despite the three heavy blankets that cover her. Wave after wave of chills wash over her body, raising goose bumps on her skin and making her muscles seize. She wants to curl into a ball and sleep. She wants this man to go away. But still he interrogates her, one question after another, a relentless stream.

"Tobolsk," he says. "Tell me what you remember of Tobolsk."

"Tell me about our last conversation."

"Do you remember why you were punished in the schoolroom that day?"

"Tell me what you remember of your Latin."

"The Anastasia I knew was fluent in French. Tell me something in that language."

"What was the last thing I said to you on the train platform in Ekaterinburg?"

On and on and on he goes, the hard notes of each syllable matching the fractious pounding in her skull.

"Why are you here?" Anna whispers.

He leans close to her ear and she can feel the warmth of his breath against her skin. "I want proof."

"Look . . . at . . . me." Anna heaves each word from her burdened chest. "That . . . is . . . all . . . the proof . . . I have."

She sees his head turn as he takes in her small, emaciated form. Her jutting collarbone. Her spindled arms. Sunken cheekbones. Unable to eat, unable to sleep, she has lost weight in recent weeks.

"The Anastasia I knew was round and pretty. You are something else entirely."

There is a whoosh and a clang as the infirmary door swings open and slams shut, and a nurse is standing at her bedside. "You have to go now, Monsieur Gilliard. Your time is up."

22

Anastasia

THE BAGGAGE

1918

Tobolsk, Russia
May 3

"Your parents were not taken to Moscow," Pierre Gilliard says as soon as we enter the schoolroom. "Yakov has them imprisoned in Ekaterinburg, about five hundred and sixty kilometers southeast of here."

Tatiana shakes her head. "No. That can't be right. Ekaterinburg is in the heart of . . ."

"The penal colonies," Gilliard finishes for her. "I know. I find this alarming as well."

"So you've heard from him?" Tatiana asks, hope and desperation lighting her eyes.

Gilliard pulls a letter from his coat pocket. He stares at it for a moment but does not open it, deciding, I think, to summarize it instead. He has the look of a man who is trying to withhold something, to soften a blow. "They arrived safely four days ago. Word had gotten out, of course, and there was an angry horde of protestors waiting for them at the station, demanding they be hung on the spot. To his credit, Yakov refused to hand them over. After a three-hour impasse they were taken to the Ipatiev House by military escort."

I don't realize I'm holding my breath until it comes out in a rush. "They are safe, then?"

"Yes. But all of their trunks were thoroughly searched upon arrival." Gilliard says this carefully, gauging our reaction.

So there it is. The jewels. I dare a glance at Olga, but her face has gone pale, drained entirely of color. "And what of the . . . *contents*?" I ask.

Gilliard knows precisely what I mean. "Confiscated," he says. "Along with a set of maps, a significant amount of cash, and a series of coded letters your father kept hidden in an extra pair of boots. It would seem they were planning to escape. Whatever the plan, it was meant to be executed from Tobolsk, and Yakov has put an end to it."

His mouth is pinched as he says this, and I know Gilliard is anguished at the news. He spent many hours poring over those same maps with Father, and I suspect he was at the heart of this plan.

"Who was planning to escape?"

None of us noticed Alexey enter the schoolroom. He is barefoot and wears nothing but a frayed tunic and a confused expression. He stands there, eyes large and curious, hair sticking out in all directions. His voice, unused for weeks, is deep and hoarse and altogether unfamiliar. It's the voice of a man who has woken from a deep sleep.

But he is awake! And standing on his own! I reach him first, but the others pile on within seconds. It's a wonder we don't crush him in our delight. However, as with all blessings these days, this one is mixed. Alexey is well enough to stand, which means that soon he will be well enough to travel. And that means the rest of us are headed for the penal colonies in Ekaterinburg as well.

THREE WEEKS LATER

Tyumen Train Station
May 23, 1918

We travel on the *Rus*, once again, from Tobolsk to Tyumen. Another three days aboard that dank, smelly ship, locked in the hold, under constant watch by Semyon and his soldiers. Thirty Red Guards sent from Ekaterinburg arrived the day before with the single purpose of escorting us to join our parents in the red Ural Mountains. These soldiers are different, even from the ones Yakov brought from Moscow. They are Latvian workers and Hungarian prisoners of war conscripted into service by the Bolsheviks. Men angry at their lot in life, and angrier at us for representing a job they do not want to do. They are frightful looking, with their lewd stares and dirty, ragged uniforms. They smell of sweat and coal mines and look as though they would cut our throats sooner than speak to us.

We carry our most precious items out of Tobolsk in a small trunk. The corsets and camisoles, the belts and hats that we have so carefully stuffed and sewn back together. We keep them near at all times, not daring to let them out of our sight for a moment.

The entire contingent of the Red Guard piles onto the *Rus*, along with the twenty men stationed in the house. The hold feels every bit as claustrophobic as it did a year earlier. The heat is oppressive, the noise of chattering guards enough to make our heads pound. Semyon instructs us there will be no wandering around the ship this time, no loitering on deck or chatting with the crew. We are to stay below, out of sight, and bide our time in a way that will not cause him trouble. Our small retinue once again takes the far corner of the hold. I commandeer a lower bunk and laugh when Jimmy leaps up beside me and licks my face. He lingers at my side constantly, ready to growl and bare his teeth anytime soldiers drift near.

Yet Jimmy remains oddly silent when one of the guards steps into the aisle and claims the bunk directly opposite mine. Such an intrusion would typically be enough to at least raise the hackles along his spine. But he stays, curled up next to me, chin on his paws, and watches the soldier, tail thumping happily against my leg.

Tomas.

I lie back on my pillow, arms crossed behind my head, and stare at the underside of Tatiana's bunk. Her legs dangle over the edge and I see that she's worn a hole straight through the sole of one boot.

"I'm surprised Yakov hasn't sent you away already," I say, barely loud enough for him to hear.

"He assumes that we all hate you the way he does." Tomas sits on the edge of the bed, chin propped on his elbows, looking for all the world like a bored soldier settling in for a long voyage.

"And do you?"

"I think you know better than that. Or at least I hope you do."

The hold is lit only with bare lightbulbs screwed into fixtures in the ceiling and set at fifteen-foot intervals. There are no portholes or other means of letting in natural light. The space is dim and murky, but Tomas sees my smile anyway. The one he returns is enough to make my stomach flip.

His presence makes the journey to Tyumen bearable. And when I emerge into the fresh, early evening air three days later he isn't far behind.

The train is waiting, but Semyon refuses to let us board until our belongings are loaded into one of the freight cars. It is dark, and we are hungry by the time we follow him down the platform to a dirty third-class carriage near the rear of the train.

Gilliard, Botkin, and Cook move to follow us up the stairs, but Semyon stops them.

"No," he says, barring the way. "You're at the back, in the goods wagon."

Gilliard steps forward. His voice is drenched with offense. "You cannot mean to separate us from the children. It's not appropriate."

As usual Semyon's indecent stare falls on Olga. I think he looks her up and down purposefully just to make Gilliard furious. "Oh, they're hardly children. But you have no say in the matter regardless. You can take your place at the back of the train or you can stay behind. It matters little to me what you decide." Gilliard steps away from the train, hands raised slightly in defeat.

Semyon turns to Tomas and says, "Go to the office and have the station master wire Ekaterinburg. Tell him to say 'the baggage' is loaded and will be delivered tomorrow."

On the way to Tobolsk we were given an entire car, but now we are confined to a single compartment. The other compartments in this car are occupied by Semyon and a handful of guards. The rest of the Red Guard files onto the remaining cars.

There are four bunks in our compartment, and I notice immediately that the mechanism allowing us to lock the door has been broken off. All vestige of daylight is gone and there is no mention of dinner, so Alexey scrambles into one of the upper bunks without comment and reaches for Joy. I hand the little spaniel to him and they curl up beneath the threadbare blanket and are asleep in moments.

It takes much longer for my sisters and I to settle in. It is nearly midnight by the time the train whistle blows and those rusty old wheels begin to clatter down the tracks. The movement is jarring at first, so different from the steamship, and I rock back and forth in my berth, trying to adjust. I know my sisters are awake, but we don't speak. They are stacked in the bunks across from me, Tatiana on the bottom with Ortimo beside her, and Olga on top. I can barely see my sisters in the darkness over Jimmy's huge, snoring body.

After an hour we start to drift off but are startled awake by raucous bursts of laughter from the other compartments.

"Do you think they're drinking?" Tatiana asks finally.

"Yes," I say.

"Do you think they're dangerous?"

"Yes," I say again.

We force ourselves back to sleep, but I wake when Jimmy's snoring becomes a dangerous rumble. It is matched within seconds by growling from Ortimo and Joy. My eyes are wide but my body is still as a brick when the door to our compartment slides open. The light from the hallway reveals three men standing in silhouette.

"We thought you girls might like to play," comes Semyon's deep, oily voice.

The three of us remain completely silent as the growling of our dogs grows more urgent. I shrink back against the wall, claiming every inch of distance I can. In the bunk above me I can hear Alexey moan in that high-pitched, terrified way of his. Be quiet, I will him silently.

Ortimo, bless his brave little heart, is off Tatiana's bunk and on the floor barking madly the moment Semyon sets foot within the compartment. When Semyon takes another step, Ortimo shrinks back, afraid of him once more. But Semyon is drunk and bold and he reaches down and grabs Tatiana's little bulldog by the collar before teeth can meet flesh. He lifts Ortimo in one hand and shakes him.

"I should have shot you months ago," Semyon hisses, rattling him again, harder, and Ortimo yelps, legs flailing as he tries to fight his way free. Semyon laughs. "Not such a fierce guard dog after all, are you?"

"Put him down. Please!" Tatiana begs, crawling to the edge of her bunk, a note of desperation in her voice. It makes me sick to my stomach. I hate to hear her beg that man for anything.

Semyon's grin is malicious. Tatiana pulls back. "I'd be happy to," he says, and then crosses to the window. He opens it with his free hand and, without another word, pitches Ortimo into the darkness. The wind howls at the open window but it isn't enough to drown out the little dog's terrified yelp.

I did not know my sister could make such a noise, but she throws herself at Semyon, scratching and clawing and shrieking. She may as well have been beating a brick wall for all the good it does. He bats her hands away and then grips them tightly, grinding her wrists together. Tatiana cries out in pain and her knees buckle.

"Take her," Semyon says to one of the guards behind him. And just like that, as if she were some discarded piece of luggage, he hands her off and I watch as my sister is dragged down the hall to some compartment out of sight. She thrashes and screams but it does no good. Seconds later a door opens and a group of unseen men cheer her arrival.

Semyon turns to the other guard, face still shrouded in darkness, and points at me. "You can have that one. I want her sister."

He has always wanted Olga. That much has been clear since he painted the graffiti on the garden wall at Alexander Palace. He has wanted her and has waited for his opportunity. Tormented her. Mocked her. Semyon has molested her with his gaze a hundred times, and those eyes burn bright now, as he steps toward her bunk. He's been patient. He's been shrewd. This is why he ingratiated himself with Yakov and why he dismissed Leshy. He has finally manufactured the chance to put his fantasy into action.

I hate myself for staying frozen and terrified as he reaches up and pulls Olga from her bunk. I hate how thin and feeble her arms look as they hit him. How perfectly useless they are. I hate myself for not grabbing my paper knife and slashing at his arrogant, cruel, hideous face. And I hate her screams because I cannot make them stop. They echo those of Tatiana down the hall, growing louder and more frantic by the second. But mostly I hate Semyon. Hate him like I have hated no one before. When Semyon cannot get a decent hold on Olga's arms he hooks an arm around her chest, one hand gripping her breast, and drags her from the compartment while she twists and writhes and screams.

In the chaos I've forgotten Jimmy. Forgotten that bulwark of canine fury between the door and me. He isn't barking. He doesn't need to. Jimmy's entire body quivers with rage as that last guard takes one tentative step, and then another, toward me.

PART THREE

This Too Shall Pass

The great enemy of the truth is very often not the lie—

deliberate, contrived, and dishonest—but the myth—

persistent, persuasive, and unrealistic.

—JOHN F. KENNEDY

23

Anna

Romanisches Café, Berlin
January 1925

"Thank you so much for getting me out of that house," Anna says. "I couldn't take it any longer."

"I don't know how you've managed this long. Three years with Maria von Kleist would drive anyone to distraction. That woman is"—Tanya waves her hand around in a circle, searching for the right word—"*devious*."

"Oh, look at you, being polite this morning. I was going to call her a Harpy." Maria is the wife of Baron von Kleist and together they are her benefactors. Russian émigrés deeply loyal to the old regime. Generous but meddlesome. Anna is grateful for the home, but sometimes it's all a bit much.

"You know, the Harpy is a mythical creature I've never really understood." Tanya takes off her fur-lined cap and shakes the snowflakes from her hair. "Half woman. Half bird. Screechy. Smelly. Bosoms hanging out. Clearly invented by some impotent man hell-bent on subjugating his wife."

And this is why Anna has grown fond of Tanya Botkin. She has opinions. And she speaks them aloud. Frequently. And not only this, but she is funny and sure of herself and has an utter disregard for her own reputation. She is refreshing. Tanya can also be counted on in a pinch to rescue Anna from the confines of the Baron's drawing room and his prim, scheming wife.

It's snowing in Berlin, but everyone knows this is the pre-amble to a ferocious blizzard. Before long the entire city will be locked indoors. But for now, the flakes are coming down like cotton balls, thick and puffy. They stick to the street and the lampposts and the cars parked outside the café. The snow is the only reason they could get a table. The Romanisches Café is known for its eccentric clientele. Artists and musicians and political dissenters, who gather for coffee in the morning, beer in the afternoon, and schnapps at night. It's exactly the sort of place Tanya would like, and it is, with few exceptions, filled to overflowing. Apparently the artsy types don't care for inclement weather. Tanya has secured them a coveted seat by the window without any trouble.

"I wouldn't worry too much about Maria von Kleist if I were you," Tanya says. She takes a sip of her lager and then licks froth from her bottom lip. "She's all bark and no bite."

"That's just it. She doesn't bark. Ever. She watches and lis-tens and then slips off to whisper in her husband's ear. I feel like I'm being kept out of some big secret. It makes me nervous."

Tanya waves this observation away and then peels off her heavy wool coat. "Maria imagines herself the puppet master in that relationship. If she were a smarter woman she would realize that the Baron does what he wants. Besides, you won't be with them much longer regardless. Gleb has found someone sympathetic to your cause. You'll be moving to Bavaria soon."

"Bavaria?"

"Castle Seeon to be exact. It's gorgeous. You'll love it." Tanya looks flushed now, suddenly nervous. She takes a deep breath and pulls two small packages from a deep pocket inside her coat and sets them on the table. "I have something for you."

"What is this?" The packages are wrapped in brown paper and tied with string.

Tanya pushes them across the table. "Go on. Don't be shy."

"What's the occasion?"

"Do I need an occasion to give my friend a gift?"

"I don't have anything for you."

"Oh, good grief. It's not Christmas. Besides, these belong to you anyway. I thought it was time you had them back."

Now Anna is truly curious. "Which should I open first?"

"Doesn't matter."

The larger package is thin and about eight inches square. She pulls one end of the string and it unravels easily. Inside is a photo album with a cracked leather cover. She doesn't look at Tanya as she lifts the lid. There are thirty stiff cardboard pages inside, each page covered front and back with black-and-white photographs. Anna sets her finger lightly on the first picture. Five little faces stare back at her. Four dark-haired, light-eyed girls and one chubby-cheeked baby boy. Slowly, carefully, Anna turns the pages, realization dawning. Each is filled with small moments of a private life. Amateur photographs taken by the Romanov family and their friends. These pages give quiet glimpses of a loving, tight-knit family and their closest friends. Gleb and Tanya are sprinkled across the pages as well, usually in the arms of their father. Beneath each picture is written names, dates, and sparse details in a tiny, precise script.

Anna tries to speak but chokes on her own voice.

"I have kept it ever since you gave it to my father in Tobolsk. Gleb and I would look at it sometimes when we thought you"—she clears her voice—"when everything happened. I wanted you to have it back. I know it hurts to see their faces. But I think it would probably hurt worse to forget them."

"I don't know what to say."

"Don't say anything. Just take it. Please. You gave it to me once and it brought great comfort. I hope it does the same for you." Tanya nudges the long, slender package closer to Anna. "Open this one too."

She obeys because she does not know what else to do. The simple act of pulling string and ripping paper grounds her to this moment and she is able to keep the other, overwhelming emotions at bay. Tanya does not know, cannot know the importance of what she has just given her.

The paper knife is heavy and ornate. It has a silver blade and a mother-of-pearl handle. Anna runs her hand over the embossed emblem of Empress Alexandra. She looks at Tanya again, speechless.

"Gilliard gave it to me . . . afterward," she says. "He told me how he always regretted taking it from you at the train station. He said he used to lie awake at night and wonder if he'd robbed you of your only means of protection. Not that a paper knife is much of a defense." Tanya looks up, apologetic—this is not a thing they openly discuss—and her eyes are wet. She shrugs. "He said he was sorry. For everything. For being so hard on you in the classroom. And for not insisting they let him follow you into Ekaterinburg. He has never forgiven himself."

THREE YEARS EARLIER

Borough of Nettelbeckstraße, Berlin
June 6, 1922

There is a gentle knock at the door and Anna shoves the hand mirror beneath her coverlet. She's sitting up in the massive bed, alternately nibbling at a French roll and inspecting her new hairstyle. The Kleists insist on having their maid serve her breakfast in bed every morning. At first she found this strange and unnecessary, but she's grown quite fond of the ritual in the week that she has lived with them. It gives her a few moments alone before being forced to spend the day with her benefactors. They love nothing more than talking and shopping and sightseeing. Anna finds it exhausting but suspects they've stayed so busy because they don't really know what to do with her. Regardless, she has become familiar with Nettelbeckstraße and the surrounding areas. She now knows where to go if she needs to leave.

If. Funny how she's gone from *must* to *if* in a mere seven days. Anna isn't stupid. She knows this newfound comfort has weakened her resolve. *And why not?* she argues with herself. It's been a very long time since she had any comfort to speak of. Why shouldn't she enjoy a warm bed and then breakfast the next morning? This new haircut, however, is a strange development. Anna has never worn her hair short, can't remember a time that it didn't drape well past her shoulders. Yet the Baron's wife swept into her room the day before and announced that she'd procured an appointment with Monsieur Antoine and that Anna should put on her best dress and come quickly. And so began a surreal visit with a Polish hairdresser who went by a French name and was in Germany for only three more days before returning to America. Anna wasn't sure how Maria von Kleist appropriated one of his three available appointments, but she did know that the haircut cost five hundred marks—a detail she attributed to her newfound penchant for eavesdropping. Maria hadn't been so much complaining when she told her husband the cost, as adding it to Anna's ever-growing tab.

After an hour in Monsieur Antoine's chair, her typically lank dark hair rested in thick waves against her chin. He explained that the style could be worn straight or curly, but he suggested she wear it curly given the natural wave of her hair. It feels strange and in the way, but Anna can't deny that it makes her look older and sophisticated. She hasn't been able to stop looking at the change, examining her face and the angle of her jaw in every mirror or window she passes.

Again, the knock at the door, this time louder and more urgent. Anna realizes that it has been nearly a minute and she hasn't yet answered.

"*Komm herein.*"

The Maid pushes the door open and ducks her head in respect. "You have visitors, Tsarevna."

She looks at the clock. "I didn't think the mahjong party was until much later." The Baron's wife is oddly obsessed with the Chinese game played by removing tiles from a board. She has insisted that Anna join her and her friends in playing it twice this week already. There is another round scheduled for this afternoon. Anna cannot, for the life of her, think of a polite way to excuse herself.

"These guests are not for Frau Kleist. They are for you." She lowers her voice and whispers, "Russian émigrés."

The Maid walks to the wardrobe and opens it. She pulls out a beaded cream dress and lays it at the foot of the bed along with a petal-pink cloche and satin heels. She is so specific with these choices that Anna suspects that Maria von Kleist told her exactly what to choose. Just as well. Anna likes the way she looks in white.

"May I help you dress?"

The Maid asks this every day, and Anna refuses just as often. "No thank you. I can manage." It's bad enough when the girl stares at the scars along her temple and clavicles; she can't tolerate the thought of her seeing the rest. "I'll be out shortly."

As soon as the Maid steps out of the room, Anna rushes to finish the remainder of her breakfast and dress. If nothing else the Baron's wife has good taste; the ensemble makes her look elegant. This new style of dress favors the tall, tubular woman, but Anna wears it well enough even though she is short and busty. There are some things not even a wealthy patron can change.

She follows the Maid to the drawing room where a man and woman wait. It is clear that they are brother and sister, very close in age if not actually twins, and not that much younger than Anna. They gasp in unison when she enters the room. And then they are on their feet, bending at the waist and curtsying. Anna looks to the Kleists in alarm. The Baron is flushed with joy, while his wife is utterly stunned. Stupefied, actually, sitting there on the settee, her jaw completely slack at the response Anna has drawn from their guests.

The way the young man bows reverently and whispers his greeting makes the hairs on Anna's arm stand up. "Tsarevna."

And then his sister speaks. "Anastasia."

"We finally found you," he says in Russian.

And then there is a rush of words and chatter and joy. Anna holds up a hand and the room falls quiet. "In German, please," she says, her voice strangled. "Russian is dead to me now."

A clearing of throats. Flushed cheeks. Apologies.

"Of course," the young man says. "We understand. Forgive us."

Anna is frozen to the spot as they step closer. She extends a hand—partly to stop the approach, partly to appear friendly—and the young man takes it lightly and turns it in his hand so he can kiss the back of her knuckles. He releases it quickly and steps back in deference.

They are all looking to her, but she doesn't know what to do, so Maria motions toward the furniture. "Please, everyone take a seat."

The guests settle back in their places and Anna chooses the chair closest to the open window. Maria von Kleist is smoking again, a Helmar Turkish cigarette tucked into the end of an ivory holder. Anna detests the smell of cigarette smoke. It reminds her of gunpowder and fire and death. Anna *refuses* to smoke, despite much cajoling. It has become one of those things society women do together in an effort to look elegant and prolong inane conversation. She wonders if all the drawing rooms in Berlin are filled with choking clouds of smoke.

The Baron cannot contain himself. He leaps triumphantly from the couch. "You see it too, then? This is Anastasia! We found her. She's alive!"

"Only a fool would mistake her for anyone else," the man says.

"It could be no one else," the girl says. Her hair is the same brown as her brother's. Eyes the same green. But her face isn't as nicely formed as his. She is pretty in a pleasant but forgettable way. Until she smiles at Anna, and then she is transformed. "Of course you don't recognize us. It's been so long. I am Tanya Botkin and this is my brother, Gleb."

Gleb Botkin is the sort of handsome that can make a woman stare. And this is exactly what Anna does, taking in his perfectly angled square jaw, straight nose, and long black lashes. There are observations she would like to make about his mouth as well, but she realizes that she hasn't yet answered Tanya.

"Of course." Anna clears her throat. "Of course I remember you."

ONE WEEK EARLIER

Borough of Nettelbeckstraße, Berlin
May 30, 1922

Anna is not asleep, but the Kleist family doesn't know this. The Baron and his wife sit quietly in the front seat as their vehicle rumbles through the streets of Berlin, but it is their children, two young girls with almond-shaped eyes and a gift for incessant chatter, who make Anna uncomfortable. The girls aren't twins, but they could be, given how close they are in age and appearance. Dark hair, brown eyes, pale skin, bright freckles. Tiny clefts in their tiny chins. They are pretty and strange, and they want to talk to Anna, to pat her hands and offer their eager smiles. They want to please. Anna wants to pull away from their small, cold fingers and their desire to impress. But she can't. They're all crammed together in the backseat of the Baron's car, so Anna has taken to feigning sleep instead.

"Why is she asleep, Mama?" one of the girls asks.

"She's tired, darling."

"But it's daytime."

"She's tired on the inside. She's been through a lot."

"But I want her to wake up," the other girl chimes in. "Can I poke her?"

"No!" Then softer, "No. She'll wake up soon enough. Let her rest for now."

The situation isn't ideal, of course. Anna would like to know where she is—where they are taking her. But she needs to gather her wits and determine how long she must endure their company before she can slip away. A week? Maybe a few days? Any sooner would be suspicious. She does not want people looking for her again. But Anna is without resources. She has only the clothes on her back and a small satchel with a night-gown and basic toiletries. No money. No papers. She doesn't even have a map, much less a sense of direction. If she's going to leave the Kleists she'll need to go about it the right way.

Anna's cheek is pressed to the window and her hair hangs across her face like a drape. But still she persists in this facade. Anna watches bits of the city pass through slit eyes. A long, manicured hedgerow. Sidewalks. Manor houses. And then the street gets narrower and turns to cobblestone; the passing cars become more frequent and expensive on this artery that leads into the heart of the city. They pass a fish market. The build-ings stretch taller. More brick, less stone. Lampposts and street signs and crowded corners filled with bistro tables and pretty women in spring dresses. Paperboys standing on milk crates and peddling the morning headlines. The clatter of a crowded omnibus. The Kleist girls slide into her when the car turns hard to the right into the Nettelbeckstraße—a wealthy district of Berlin filled with Russian émigrés, lesser noblemen, and the independently wealthy. It's quieter here. Still vibrant, but moneyed and restrained.

"Can we be sure that woman is really Anastasia Romanov?" Maria von Kleist's voice is little more than a whisper in the front seat, and Anna has to strain to hear her husband's reply.

"No. We can't," the Baron says.

"So there's no way to really know who we've invited into our home?"

"I'm afraid not."

"We're fools," she hisses. "We'll be the laughingstock of this entire city."

The Baron sighs. "Listen, this is a risk worth taking. If that woman is the Grand Duchess we will be at a great advantage when the old order is restored."

"*If* it's restored."

"It will be. There's no other option. I doubt Lenin will remain in power. The other Romanovs will be found as well." The Baron has one of those calm, reassuring voices. So level and sincere that he makes others feel as though all is right in the world.

"We don't even know if the tsar or his family is still alive. No one has seen any of them in *four years*. The rumors about what happened in Ekaterinburg are ghastly."

"They're rumors."

The gentle tapping of a long fingernail on the window fills the silence. Maria von Kleist is thinking. Anna holds her breath and stays very still, afraid of being caught eavesdropping.

Finally, she asks, "And if that isn't Anastasia? If we've been duped?"

Anna imagines him shrugging, unconcerned, behind the wheel. "Then we find a way to get rid of her. It won't matter in the end. We'll be considered heroes and patriots either way."

"Or fools."

"Maybe you're right. Maybe the others are dead. It's tragic, certainly, but even that works in our favor. If that young woman is the last surviving Romanov it means we've rescued an empress."

A sly change of tone. "And she will be indebted to us."

"Exactly."

At least Anna understands what they're getting at now. She isn't so much worried about their machinations as she is intrigued by them. She's not unfamiliar with politics. Moves and countermoves. If the Kleists plan on using her, Anna is more than happy to return the favor.

A few minutes later they pull to the curb beside a tall, ornate building with wrought-iron flower boxes beneath each window. The car door opens so abruptly that Anna almost spills into the street. She barely catches herself before landing on the feet of a doorman, and then makes a show of stretching and yawning to convince the Kleists that she's just woken up.

"Fräulein," he says, extending a hand and offering to help her out.

Anna hesitates only a moment before taking his hand. The girls slide across the seat, giggling as the doorman lifts them by their little waists and plants them gently on the sidewalk, then moves on to help Maria von Kleist out as well. Baron von Kleist unfolds his long body from the car and stretches while the doorman retrieves Anna's bag from the trunk.

"Welcome to our home," the Baron says, sweeping his arm toward the enormous, grand facade.

The building is eight stories tall and swallows nearly half the block.

Anna gapes. "*This* is your home?"

"Yes."

"All of it?"

He laughs then, genuine and good-humored. "Of course not."

"Only the top floor," his wife adds.

There is barely enough room inside the elevator for Anna, the Kleists, and the doorman. She shrinks into the corner, trying not to panic as the grate slams shut and the cage rises with a clang and a squeal toward the eighth floor. When it stops thirty seconds later she finally exhales. They pile into an elegant foyer with parquet floors and wall sconces that frame a gilded mirror hung above a console table set with a vase of fresh spring flowers.

The Kleists' apartment has vaulted ceilings, polished floors, and arched windows with leaded panes. There are three bedrooms and three bathrooms, all of them flooded with light and draped with expensive fabrics. There is a dining room, a drawing room, a family room, an office for the Baron, and a kitchen somewhere at the back that Anna never sees. But it is the guest room that nearly brings Anna to tears.

"This is where you will stay," Maria von Kleist tells her, swinging the door open to a bright, lovely room with a four-poster bed, a dressing table, and an armoire. It has its own furnished balcony and a bathroom with a claw-foot tub. "Why don't you freshen up? Make yourself at home. Rest for a while. I know this is all very overwhelming."

"Thank you." Anna touches her dry cheeks and cracked lips. Runs her fingers through her knotted hair. Looks around for her satchel.

"I'll have your things washed. But you won't need them right away." Maria opens the armoire and reveals an entire wardrobe of new clothing—complete with tags—hanging inside. There are slippers and undergarments neatly stacked at the bottom.

She looks a little embarrassed. "I guessed your size. We can exchange anything that doesn't fit."

"I don't—"

"It's the least we can do. You were in that horrid place for so long. If we'd only known we would have come sooner."

"But I can't—"

"Let us help you. Please. You don't owe us anything." Her words are kind, but her body is stiff and ill at ease. "Take your time."

And then the great mahogany door to her room closes and Anna is alone—really, truly alone for the first time since that night on the Bendler Bridge.

She can hear the Kleist family chatting in German with some faceless member of the household—a woman with a deep voice—but the sounds are muffled and distant. Anna takes her boots off and sets them against the wall. Her stockings have holes in the toes, so she peels them off as well and tucks them into the toe of one boot. They are not nice enough to go in the armoire with her new things. Perhaps not even worth keeping now that she *has* new things.

Anna hasn't owned anything store-bought since she was seventeen; everything since then has been handmade. She runs her fingers along the fine stitching and gauzy material of the new clothing. She inhales the deep, earthy, coriander fragrance of silk and cotton. Anna strokes the pillows on her bed and the curtains at her window. She walks barefoot across the Oriental carpet. Anna sheds her clothing on the way to the bathroom the way a snake sheds its skin in spring: one long, continuous peel falling to the ground. She doesn't notice the dirt beneath her toenails or the grime at her ankles until she stands naked on the polished white marble. The air is cool and smells of towels dried in the sun. Anna doesn't care that the curtains are open or that anyone in the apartments across the street could see her if they only looked out their own immaculate windows. All she sees or cares about or notices are the deep, curving lines of the bathtub.

Expensive soap and soft towels are at her disposal. The bath mat is plush, and a heavy robe hangs on a hook at the door. The label inside the robe reads LE PAVILLON DE LA REINE. A favorite hotel in Paris, no doubt. A purchase made on one of the Kleists' many Parisian holidays. The robe probably costs more than the average Berlin factory girl makes in a month, but Anna can't quite bring herself to judge them for the excess when she drops it across her narrow shoulders. It's heavy like an expensive blanket, and soft like a kitten's ear. It falls all the way to the floor and pools at her feet. Anna sighs audibly and turns on the tap.

Anna draws one finger along the faint, striated lines that run vertically below her belly button. It's been so long they are almost invisible now. She drops her hand. Takes a deep breath. Refuses to wander down that mental path.

Anna shrugs out of the robe and lowers herself into the soapy water beneath the open window. Below her are the sounds of city life, the early evening commotion of businesses closing for the day. Cars and horns and delivery trucks. Wealthy women chatting in French and German and Russian as they leave the shops below, little affluent cliques of émigrés bent beneath the weight of their shopping bags. Laughter drifts up from the cafés and mixes oddly with the crying of a child in the court-yard across the street. The water in this tub is still warm, and she is clean. It's all a miracle. Anna relaxes finally, ridiculously happy for the first time in years.

24

Anastasia

THE HOUSE OF SPECIAL PURPOSE

1918

Trans-Siberian Railway, Halfway to Ekaterinburg
May 24

Once, before the revolution, my siblings and I studied ancient
Rome. Gilliard led the expedition beginning with the conquest
of the Sabines in the eighth century BC and ending when Rome
burned to the ground in AD 64. He took that opportunity to
foist Latin upon us, insisting it was the foundation of literature
and without it we would be illiterate. I might have taken to the
language if not for a single word learned early in our review of
the Sabines: *raptio*.

Rape.

The Rape of the Sabines. A singular moment in history made
famous by Renaissance painters and sculptors: Romulus's mass
kidnapping of women from villages surrounding Rome. The
poor daughters of Sabine were lured to a festival hosted by the
men of Rome and, once there, were taken away and compelled
to marry their captors. Human plunder. Along with the Latin
and the history, we studied the paintings themselves. Gilliard
argued—supported by the writings of a number of scholars,
Livy among them—that what transpired in Rome was better
translated as conquest than violation. And to prove his point he
took us on a field trip.

It took days to reach Paris on the imperial train, but upon

our arrival, Gilliard wasted no time in shuffling us directly to the Louvre, where he had arranged a private viewing of Nicolas Poussin's *The Abduction of the Sabine Women*. So obsessed was the artist with this subject that he painted it twice in his lifetime. And to Poussin's credit, I respected the fact that he depicted the women fully clothed. Pietro da Cortona, Jacques Stella, Johann Heinrich Schönfeld, and Peter Paul Rubens all rendered the women in various stages of voluptuous nudity. Almost all of them titled their paintings *The Rape of the Sabine Women*.

Raptio.

Rape.

Rapacious.

Rapine.

Raptor.

Ravish.

Only in Latin can one root word be the basis for myriad appalling descriptors. Horrible, vulgar, violent words. Brutish and masculine. I hate them all and the language from which they originated. Latin deserves to be a dead language, and I do not mourn it.

Now, as the train rattles west toward Ekaterinburg, I think it's a pity that Nicolas Poussin and his contemporaries did not open their fields of artistic expression to women. I am certain female painters would have eradicated the themes of masculine valor from those bright, chaotic canvases. They would have illustrated, as legend did in the end, that the Sabines and not the soldiers were the saviors of Rome.

The train is silent now, and the night's terrors are replaced by an eeriness that settles heavily in the air. Beside me the thin cushion shifts and the soldier who lies there slides from the berth. Pretending to be asleep, I listen as he slips quietly from our compartment. Only when he is gone do I roll over and look out the window. The sky is cold, the color of gunmetal, and I can see only broken glimpses of it as we pass through a towering forest. Above me Alexey and Joy snore in soft, whistling harmony. My brother fell asleep in the night, too exhausted and traumatized to stay alert any longer. It was a relief, to be honest. He could offer no protection, and I didn't want him remembering anyway.

I lie awake until Semyon slides the door open and shoves Olga back into the compartment. She flinches when the door slams closed again. Olga seems like a ghost, standing there in the gloom, wringing her hands. When she finally looks at me, her eyes are glassy, bottomless.

"Are you okay?" I whisper, knowing that she's not. I want to embrace her. I want to weep. But she appears so fragile in her rumpled clothing, so temporal that I am afraid she will disintegrate at the slightest touch.

"No," Olga says and crawls into the berth directly across from mine. She draws the thin blanket across her shoulders, pulls her knees into her chest, and closes her eyes. Sleep is her only refuge and she races toward it. Within seconds the rise and fall of her chest is slow and rhythmic.

"Please, God," I whisper. "Do not let her dream."

Tatiana stumbles in on her own a few minutes later. She goes straight to the window, her face slick with tears, her lips swollen. Tatiana adjusts her clothing, checking the buttons on her blouse and then straightening her skirt. She runs her hands through her tangled hair, combing it with her fingers, then spreads them across the fabric of her blouse, over and over, trying to press the wrinkles away. Finally, when her sobs became so hard she cannot catch a breath in between, she lays her forehead against the window. I fear she might shove it aside and throw herself out.

"I am so sorry about Ortimo," I say. My voice is ragged from all the crying I've done myself, but I have to say something, and everything else feels unmentionable.

"I wish I'd drawn the short straw," Tatiana says, her voice

empty of all emotion. "I wish I'd been the one to go with Mother and Father."

I had wished this for myself a hundred times during the night and cannot escape the guilt I feel for having done so. The only comfort I can offer Tatiana is to confess it. "So do I."

When Tatiana finally turns from the window she looks hollowed out. Whereas Olga's eyes were filled with sorrow, hers are altogether empty. My sister stands before me, but she is missing somehow, removed from her body. So I lift my blanket and she climbs in beside me, rigid and straight, as though fearing human contact. We lie there, back to back, unspeaking, as the train slowly rocks her back to sleep.

I think about the daughters of Sabine as I drift away myself. The purpose of art, Gilliard had said as we stood on the polished marble floors of the Louvre, is to tell the truth. He waved an arm at the canvas, at the boldly painted forms of tangled humans crowding that Roman courtyard. Without those women there would be no Rome, he said. The greatest empire on earth would never have existed. That great city would have been left to decay within a generation. Yet I knew now that both Gilliard and Nicolas Poussin were mistaken about the most fundamental aspect of the story: There is nothing artistic about rape. Taking a woman by force makes a man no better than the rooster in Tobolsk. It simply makes him an animal.

———

We arrive in Ekaterinburg at midnight. The soldiers immediately file from the train and crowd onto the platform for instruction. Within moments dim electric lights flicker on and we can see them head to the freight cars and begin to unload our belongings. We watch, faces pressed to the window as they grab boxes and trunks and pieces of furniture and toss them onto the droshkies—open, four-wheeled carriages pulled by enormous draught horses. It begins to rain within the hour, and the temperature drops soon after. Twice I catch a glimpse of Tomas and Ivan, shivering in the cold, their lips forming curse words that I am forbidden to speak aloud.

At some point my siblings and I fall asleep again, huddled together for warmth on one of the lower berths. We are woken intermittently by the stomping and cursing of the soldiers. Every time the door to our car slams open we cringe. Every time we hear footsteps in the hallway we grab one another tighter. But the soldiers leave us alone that night, and when morning dawns, hours later, we get the first real glimpse of our new home.

Despite it being late May, snow is still on the ground in Ekaterinburg. It is piled high against the sides of buildings and shoveled into dirty heaps in the gutters. The streets are filled with mud and the sidewalks lined with spectators. Beyond the train station is a sprawling city of square stone buildings with small windows and sloping roofs. The city is built, not on a grid as one would expect, but on a system of meandering streets and narrow dead-end lanes that remind me of the deer trails outside Tsarskoe Selo. The Iset River runs through the middle of the city, forming a respectable lake at its widest point, and then narrows again as it turns to the south. Around this lake are built the wealthiest homes. But we can see only the barest glimpse of the broad, silver water from where we stand on the platform.

Alexey holds on to Olga and Tatiana, and I think that the three of them look like a tiny, despondent island amid the activity. Heads bent together. Eyes downcast. Shoulders rounded. Exhausted. Weepy. Hungry. Demoralized. My siblings are broken, and the only thing that can help is being delivered safely into the arms of our parents.

Gilliard stands beside me and I turn to ask how much longer we have to wait, but his attention is at my feet, his frown causing that spectacular mustache to droop at the corners. He blinks three times, then bends his mouth to my ear and asks quietly, "What is that? Please, for the love of God, do not say it is a knife."

My laces have come undone, and in the process Father's paper knife has come loose from its hiding spot, the mother-of-pearl handle standing out against the black leather of my boot. "No," I say, shaking my head slowly so as not to draw attention from the guards who swirl around us. "It is a *paper* knife."

"A letter opener? Have you lost your mind? Do you think these men will make a distinction between a paper knife and a regular knife? They will only see a weapon. And they will punish you for having it."

"I don't care."

"You should. Your life is worth more than you think. And angering these men to make a point is unwise."

"You have a high estimation of my life. I do not think these men share it."

"Then that is all the more reason for you to guard it ferociously."

"Now you want me to be ferocious. I wish that freedom extended to the schoolroom."

"I fear your lessons have come to an end, Tsarevna. Now is the time for you to put them into practice."

I nod toward my boot. "Pity sword fighting wasn't part of your curriculum."

"I'd hardly call that a sword. And besides"—he lets go of my wrist and taps my temple soundly with one finger—"this is the weapon I expect you to use going forward."

He is a good man. Sturdy and steadfast, and I haven't given him enough credit. He looks so somber that I feel a rush of affection for him. "Any sharpness therein is a credit to you."

He does smile then, proudly, but looks away when my eyes begin to cloud. "You have a remarkable disposition, Anastasia. Has anyone ever told you that?"

"Oh, it's been remarked upon. Endlessly."

He snorts, but I've apparently enjoyed the last of Gilliard's humor because he returns to his typical, stoic demeanor. "I need you to stand very still," he says.

"Why?"

"Because I'm going to tie the laces of your boot. And you are going to let me."

I want to say that I need the paper knife, that its sharp blade and wicked point are a comfort in the night when every door is unlocked and wicked men roam the halls. But to explain that is to invite questions I am not ready to answer. So I nod and Gilliard goes down on both knees beside me. The sleight of hand is so swift I almost do not see that slim blade slide into his shirtsleeve.

"Is there something wrong with her boot?"

Gilliard ignores the question, his nimble fingers now tightening and looping my laces. I wait until he is done to lift my foot and show Semyon the hole in the end of my boot. He stares at the ripped leather and the stocking-clad toe that peeks out from beneath it.

"Indeed there is," I say, anger pulsing in every word. "I will need new ones."

Semyon knows that we have not told our servants what happened on the train. He knows, I am certain, because his teeth remain intact. They'd be knocked out otherwise. I do not doubt that Semyon considers this a victory, that he thinks we are ashamed. So he smiles, cold and cruel. "I believe that the ones you have will last until the end of your life."

———

A single carriage comes to collect us. Even as we stare at the six available seats we do not immediately understand what this means. I think Gilliard knew all along, however.

"You will go no farther," Semyon says when our tutor moves toward the carriage. "They go on from here alone."

As women we are taught that bravery and valor exist in the grand gestures. We believe that kindness is weakness and arrogance is the same as courage. But it is not so. Sometimes restraint proves the mettle of a man's heart more accurately. Gilliard could argue or throw a punch. He could slip the paper knife from his sleeve and drive it through Semyon's throat. It would be satisfying, I won't lie. But he takes the nobler course instead. He steps back and in so doing not only protects us but also saves his own life.

"Smart man," Semyon hisses, the words whistling between his teeth. "Now leave while you can."

Gilliard is circumspect in his farewells to each of us. A kiss to the cheek. A formal bow without regard to the consequences. And a single word whispered in our ears. "Tsarevna," he says, face turned to stone, emotions squelched.

We watch him board the train and disappear inside the compartment before we climb into our carriage. When we left the Alexander Palace all those months ago we were accompanied by a skeleton crew. Now it is only the four of us, Cook, and Botkin in the carriage, followed by several dozen of Semyon's guards. They jog steadily behind us as we rattle through the streets. Alexey holds Joy firmly in his lap, but Jimmy refuses to climb up with us. So he trots along beside, dodging puddles in the street and keeping clear of the wheels. Occasionally he looks up at me for encouragement, but he never lags behind. Once, when I glance over my shoulder, I see Tomas in the group of soldiers directly behind the carriage. He doesn't look at me. His gaze hovers protectively over Jimmy. And I love him for it.

It is an unnerving thought to have in such a moment.

I love him.

It is a stunning, wonderful, entirely human realization at the worst possible moment. I am headed to prison, and I am in love with a boy. It takes a good five minutes before I am able to take in my surroundings once more. And then reality comes crashing in again. The rickety carriage, the bustling street, the stomp of soldiers' feet behind me.

Whereas Tobolsk was utterly flat and nearly treeless, Ekaterinburg boasts rolling hills and numerous parks. The farther we travel into the city, the prettier it becomes. And the more attention we get. It must be odd, I suppose, to see our carriage clatter by, followed by ranks of armed soldiers. People stand on the streets and point. They stare from open doors and windows. They whisper to one another or dart out of the way when we draw close.

I spot our destination from the bottom of the hill. A giant wooden fence has been built across the front of a house, effectively blocking it from view. The fence is two stories high and made of rough-hewn wood. So new are those planks that they glow golden in the morning light. Once we pull up beside it, the smell of pine is pervasive, and I can see little rivulets of sap running down the boards and pooling in the knots.

Semyon kicks against the gate and it swings open a moment later, revealing a two-story stone building. It is the color of bisque and perfectly rectangular. The roofline is ornamented with corbels, and there is a fountain in the courtyard. But there are bars across the windows and armed guards stand at the front door.

"Welcome," Semyon says, "to the House of Special Purpose."

25

Anna

TWO YEARS AT DALLDORF

1922, 1921

Dalldorf Asylum, Berlin
May 30, 1922

Anna once lived through a night so long and so excruciating she thought it would last an eternity. Each minute seemed to stretch like taffy softened in the sun, pulled to its thinnest, most tender strand. She believed that if she was lucky enough to survive that night, she would live in slow motion forever. The experience became a door in her mind that, when pushed too hard, swings toward madness. In the years since, as her episodes have become less frequent, Anna still distrusts time itself. She suspects that it is in league with the enemy and the wretched memories embedded in her mind. She fears that time will forever be slower for her, that each injustice and hardship and cruelty will have to be lived through at half speed. So it comes as a surprise to her how quickly her days at Dalldorf slip away. First a handful. Then dozens at a time with her barely noticing them. Weeks. A month. A year, then two. Each day falling into a predictable rhythm.

———

In the years that Anna has been housed within these walls there have been very few surprises. She wakes and dresses and goes to eat in a small communal area with the other residents of her ward. She is often allowed to work on the grounds or in the sewing room. The staff is careful not to give her scissors or anything else that could be transformed into a weapon. Anna finds it infuriating to sit and wait for a length of cloth to be cut for her, or to have the needle in her sewing machine replaced. But she likes the work. There is a therapeutic rhythm to the rocking of the treadle beneath her feet and a satisfying burn along her calves after she has been working the machine for several hours. She likes taking scraps and remnants and turning them into something useful, whether a table runner or a shirtsleeve. Anna isn't stupid. She knows that the staff at Dalldorf take the best work and sell it to vendors. She knows that they are profiting from her labor. She also knows that if she protested they would say that no one is funding her stay at the asylum and this is how she earns her keep. Worse, she knows that if she makes trouble they will move her to another ward with less freedom. On still, quiet nights Anna can hear the screaming from across the courtyard. She knows what happens in other parts of the asylum. If not having scissors is the price she pays for this relative freedom, then so be it.

Anna suspects that the gauzy pieces of fabric she's sewing today are meant to be women's undergarments. Most likely slips. The material is a gray, raw silk and it bunches beneath the needle if she works the treadle too fast. So she is bent over her machine, very carefully rocking the paddle with her foot and feeding her fabric through the needle half an inch at a time. She doesn't see the nurse, the one she has nicknamed the Duck, enter the workroom or stand beside her. Anna is so focused on the clatter of the machine that she doesn't hear her name spoken the first time.

"Fräulein Unbekannt!"

Anna jerks in surprise and the pad of one finger is pulled

beneath the pounding needle. When the needle is raised a second later, there is a smear of blood on the silk and another bright red bead dripping down her thumb. Anna puts her thumb in her mouth and sucks, trying to numb the sting.

"Why did you yell at me?" she asks.

"You didn't answer me."

"I didn't hear you."

"Come with me. You have visitors. Again."

It's been a week since the Baron left and the bright thread of hope Anna felt after his visit has begun to fade. It flares to life again now, a white-hot undercurrent to her pulse. But she won't let the Duck know, won't give her that advantage.

Anna wraps the cuff of her shirt around her wounded thumb and carefully drops her hands to her lap. She lies. "I don't want to see any more visitors."

The Duck gives her an exaggerated bow and sweeps her arm toward the door. "And yet you must."

Anna knows she's being mocked, but there is uncertainty in the nurse's voice. Nothing came of the events last week other than a general sense of unease sweeping across the ward. The staff stares at her now. So do the other patients. Anna doubts the Duck or Dr. Arschloch believe her, but they aren't about to abuse her in any way either. Not with émigrés sniffing about.

Anna tidies her workstation slowly, forcing the Duck to wait, enjoying the subtle noises of impatience behind her. Finally she allows the Duck to lead her out of the workroom and through the maze of narrow halls and into the tidy reception room.

Baron von Kleist and Dr. Arschloch are waiting for them. The Baron is brimming with euphoria. Dr. Arschloch looks as though he's being asphyxiated. The Baron bows slightly and says, "Tsarevna."

The two men continue whatever heated argument was interrupted by her entrance, and it takes Anna a moment to realize that her discharge papers are being discussed.

"You will get them ready immediately," the Baron says. "I am not leaving here without Anastasia."

"I'm afraid it's not that simple—"

"Of course it is. You said yourself that she is neither a criminal nor insane—"

"I'm afraid there's some disagreement on that point—"

"And that the only thing required for her immediate release was a statement declaring her identity and a written notice of my willingness to care for her upon discharge—"

"Yes, however—"

"You will see that I have provided both in writing"—the Baron pulls two folded sheets of paper from a pocket inside his suit coat—"and that they have been notarized by the local magistrate."

Dr. Arschloch's face is torn between competing expressions of fury and fear. He looks to Anna, trying to gauge her reaction, desperate to see if she will officially confirm this claim. Terrified that she will.

Anna smiles at the doctor, her face lighting up with every ounce of vindication she feels. She takes a step closer to the Baron, and this is all the consent he needs.

"Collect your things," the Baron says. "You're coming with me."

ONE WEEK EARLIER

Dalldorf Asylum, Berlin
May 21, 1922

A woman has come to visit her but she isn't alone. She's been escorted by a man so wealthy and so striking that Anna cannot help but stare. The woman is pretty in the way all wealthy women are pretty—because of great care and attention to detail. She drips with the scent of expensive perfume, but the man smells of cedar and leather and fresh air. He's older than all the women in the room. Late forties, most likely, and the very sight of Anna brings a look of triumph to his face.

"See! I told you. The likeness is unmistakable. It's just as Clara said."

Anna says nothing and this seems to unnerve him.

He tilts slightly at the waist—a near bow—and says, "My apologies. Of course you wouldn't recognize us. It's been so long." He extends his hand and Anna takes it cautiously. "Baron Arthur von Kleist." He tilts his head to the left. "And this is my wife, Maria. We got here as quickly as we could."

This strange, well-heeled woman glares at the Baron. She does not reach for Anna's hand. She offers no greeting but radiates uncertainty instead. If the Duck had been interested in Anna's visitors before, she is dumbfounded now.

"I'm very glad to see you again," Anna says, and watches with great pleasure as the Duck lifts one eyebrow in a high, curious arch.

Baron von Kleist offers such a bright grin that Anna cannot help but give him one of her own.

"No," Maria says suddenly, loudly. "It cannot be her. I do not believe it."

"But it's obvious. Just *look* at her."

"I have." Maria shakes her head. "She is too short to be Tatiana."

The woman gathers her purse and walks to the door without another word. The Baron, confused, moves to follow her.

"Wait!" Anna says, taking a step toward him. He reaches for his wife and pulls her to a stop. "How do you know Clara Peuthert?"

"She is the daughter of a friend," the Baron says. "And she tells me you are the daughter of the tsar."

"And you believe her?"

"I do now," he says, and then the two visitors are gone.

———

They have been alone for less than a minute, and Dalldorf's head nurse is staggered. "Who *are* you," the Duck asks, "to get such a reaction from a man like *that*?" The questions come quickly. "Am I right in assuming those people believe you to be Tatiana"—she clears her throat—"Tatiana *Romanov*?"

"Clearly not. You heard them."

"I heard *her*. The Baron believes something else entirely." The Duck is furious, in a pure, holy rage as she rises from her chair and takes three cautious steps toward Anna. Her words are careful and measured, spiked with indignation when she asks her next question. "Why did Clara Peuthert tell them you were Tatiana? *Why?*"

"I did not say I was Tatiana. Not one time. Not to Clara and not to them."

"Who are you then? What is your name? That"—she points to the door—"can never happen again. Do you understand?"

Anna has held on for so long. She has kept the truth of her identity wrapped tight against all prodding, pleading, and threats. It has been the one thing that no one could take from her. But sitting here before the window, bathed in a perfect rectangle of light, she is transfixed by a single name. The one name that can free her from this prison. All because of Crazy Clara's aggressive reverence. Thanks to Clara, and to the Baron, there is the possibility of freedom now. All she has to do is speak. So she does.

"My name," she says, "is Anastasia Nikolaevna Romanov."

ONE WEEK EARLIER

Dalldorf Asylum, Berlin
May 14, 1922

"Don't be a fool," Anna says. She wants to shake Clara, to rattle her teeth, but she doesn't. Physical contact is prohibited between patients, and the scolding isn't worth spending her day in the small, dank room in the basement used for punishing rule breakers. "You're the only person in this whole godforsaken place who doesn't want to leave."

"But you are here."

"Oh, good grief. Not this again—"

"You need me."

"No. I don't. I've gotten along just fine without you for many, many years. Go home, Clara. Your family misses you."

Clara's eyes are big and glassy on a good day, when she's happy, but at the moment they are huge gray pools that threaten to overflow. Anna hates it when Clara blubbers. Hates it for reasons she doesn't even understand. The poor girl can't help it. She's fragile and emotive, but Anna only sees weakness. Someone who is easily manipulated. Clara is the sort of woman who doesn't know *how* to think, only *what* to think.

"What about *your* family?" Clara whispers.

Anna looks away, whispers, "My family is gone."

And then Clara is weeping into her shoulder, unconcerned about rules and policy or any threat of punishment. They've been allowed into the courtyard for a few glorious minutes, and Anna doesn't want the time to be cut short by Clara's hysterics. It rained earlier in the morning, but the sky is clear now and the air smells of warm grass and damp soil. Anna was enjoying herself immensely before Clara plopped down next to her on the bench and complained about being released. Anna shakes her off, afraid that the staff will see the outburst and blame it on her.

"Hush. Enough. You'll get me in trouble."

"No." Clara shakes her head, determined. "I'm going to tell them who you are. That will fix everything."

Anna laughs. "You've been telling them for months."

"Not them." She points to the Duck and two orderlies who keep watch over the courtyard. "Important people. On the outside."

Anna sighs. The chances of Clara knowing anyone important are as good as Anna waking up with brown eyes in the morning. But it won't hurt to let her try. "That would be great. Very helpful."

She squeezes Anna's hand and drops her voice to a whisper. "I promise. You'll see. I'll get you out of here." The simple, foolish girl laughs, like they've shared some confidence. She pats Anna on the shoulder. "It's okay. You don't have to pretend anymore. Good-bye, *Tsarevna*."

SEVEN MONTHS EARLIER

Dalldorf Asylum, Berlin
October 3, 1921

One day Anna is consumed by silence and boredom and then the next she is summoned twice by the Duck to be inspected by strangers. From then on the visitors come in streams, one or two a day. Sometimes three. Men and women who have misplaced a loved one and have seen Anna's photo in the paper. They hope against all reason that their daughter, sister, wife, or mother has been found. Every day Anna is ordered to dress and go sit in a small waiting room. Every day Anna sees hopeful, desperate, broken families, and every day she breaks them a little bit more. This is the worst of it for her, being an unwilling participant in their personal tragedies.

The waiting room is deceptively warm, furnished with plush couches and framed by a large window overlooking the manicured lawn facing the entrance. It feels comfortable and calm, nothing like the stark, cold reality within the wards themselves. The Room puts families at ease when they come to visit their loved ones, but like everything else at Dalldorf, it makes Anna angry.

Most of the visitors turn away immediately upon seeing her. They shake their heads, wipe their eyes and leave, muttering their apologies to the Duck. Only one man has tried to claim her, and it was clear to everyone that he was crazier than any of the patients housed within these walls. The orderlies dragged him from the room after he lunged at Anna and tried to tear off her blouse. "My wife!" he screamed as they promptly removed him from the premises. "I want my wife back!"

The Duck had the decency to apologize for that one at least. "They told me he seemed normal enough at the gate," she said afterward.

"Pity you weren't at the gate yourself," Anna said. "Since you're so good at making judgments based on appearance."

Even after that, others come, only to be devastated to learn Anna is not the daughter who slipped out of an open window to meet her lover and never returned. Or the wandering prodigal or the straying wife or the feebleminded cousin. Day after day she remains unclaimed.

Fräulein Unbekannt. Miss Unknown.

She sits, yet again, in a chintz wingback chair beside the window, waiting for today's visitor. The fog has descended, shrouding the lawn and the long drive so she doesn't see the black truck until it pulls up in front of the building. The man who emerges looks determined even from this distance. But when he lifts his face to take in the enormity of the square brick building she sees something else beneath the brim of his worn hat. A hardness along the jaw line. An impatient gait as he slams the truck door and disappears beneath the awning. It's not long before she learns that he has come looking for his sister, some woman who wandered away from a boarding-house in Berlin. The Duck says that this man saw her picture in the paper and read how she had jumped from the bridge. This is the first Anna has heard of the newspapers publishing that detail. That's all she's told. But it's enough to put her on edge, and the Duck notices the way she fidgets nervously with the hem of her dress while they wait.

"Do we have to keep doing this?" Anna asks.

"Has it occurred to you that I don't enjoy playing babysit-ter? That I have to stop what I'm doing every time someone shows up at that gate to speak with you? That I'm required to record the details of your time together? If you want to stop this, tell us your name. But if you're not willing to do that, shut up and quit complaining."

This is the harshest the Duck has ever been with her, and Anna is taken aback. "I'm sorry to be such a burden." A sarcas-tic tone punctuates each syllable.

"Then stop being one."

Not that sorry, apparently, because she is sullen and unco-operative when the guards escort the man, slightly older than Anna, into the waiting room. He is considerably taller than she is but they are similar in appearance—dark hair and blue eyes. The Duck sits up a bit straighter to make a note of this in Anna's file.

"Felix Schanzkowska," the guard says by way of introduc-tion.

When it comes to poker faces, his is every bit as good as Anna's. He stares at her, head tipped slightly to the side, and gives no indication at all of what he's thinking. Anna doesn't break eye contact, but she does pick at her cuticles—one small show of nerves that she can't disguise.

"Why don't you introduce yourself to this young man?" the Duck says. It's a test and Anna won't fall for it.

She studies this Felix instead and finds a very sad face regarding her in return. Unlike the others he doesn't ask questions or try to touch her. He simply looks at her. At her clothes. At her face. At her hands, her fingers, and raw cuticles. And, for quite some time, at the ragged scar that deforms her right temple. He seems to be reading her mood. Her thoughts. The temperature in the room. She stares at him, defiant and quiet, willing him to leave.

This exchange is so different from the others that the Duck glances at them—back and forth repeatedly—scribbling notes on the page without looking down.

Finally, he curls his lip. Then clenches his jaw. Sighs. "I do not recognize this woman."

And he's gone that quickly. Anna feels both triumphant and oddly bereft. She belongs to no one. "Can we stop this game now? Please?" she asks.

The Duck closes her folder and tucks the pencil into the pocket of her shirt. "Last I checked, Fräulein Unbekannt, you were the only one playing a game."

26

Anastasia

BORROWED TIME

1918

Ipatiev House, Ekaterinburg, Russia
May 25

"How was your trip?" Father asks. "We were quite worried about you."

We sit in a small room off the first-floor kitchen eating our usual dinner of chicken, roasted potatoes, and fresh bread from a linen-clad table awash in candlelight. Even here in this miserable outpost we keep up the illusion of grandeur.

Father drags a bit of bread around his plate, soaking up the chicken juices, and looks at me expectantly. I watch him pop it in his mouth and chew slowly while I struggle to find a suitable answer.

"Absolutely horrible," I say, finally, and Olga goes completely still beside me. Her fork is suspended halfway between her plate and her mouth. Her hand begins to tremble and a piece of chicken wobbles off the tines and falls to the floor where Joy swoops it up greedily. Mother eyes Olga with suspicion. I can see my sister retreat into herself and shutter her eyes. So I shrug. I try to seem disinterested. "The journey was cold and long and we missed you terribly."

Everyone relaxes then. Father nods compassionately and my sisters each take another bite. Mother peers at me intently, however, not eating. I can feel that probing intuition stretch toward me. Observing. Measuring each of my words to get at the truth. She always knows when I am lying. It's an innate sense that I do not understand but learned to fear at an early age.

"And the guards," Mother asks. "Did they treat you well?"

Olga and Tatiana push food around their plates, not looking up, hardly breathing. Maria, oblivious, slices a piece of chicken from the bone and eats it with the finely tuned manners of a princess. My brother gazes at a greasy spot on the floor where Joy licks gristle from the wooden planks. But my parents study me, and I know that my words will determine much of what happens next. So I roll my eyes and shake my head.

"Of course not. They were *odious*. As always. I don't know why they have to be so vulgar and uncivilized. So cruel. Sometimes I think that frightening us is their greatest entertainment. They wouldn't let us lock the door to our compartment, and they stood in the hallway all night, drinking and cursing and making those awful bawdy jokes, but we did our best to ignore them." I know that I'm rambling nervously so I nod, as though to convince them of the veracity of my story. It is a gesture meant to convey our bravery and composure. I tear off a piece of the warm, crusty roll beside my plate and set it in my mouth, pretending that I don't have a care in the world. I chew the bread slowly, gathering myself to tell them what they want to hear. "We didn't feel comfortable undressing for bed, so we slept in our clothes. I can't wait to have a bath and a good night's sleep."

I didn't realize how tight Father's shoulders were until they drop in relief.

"I'm sorry the trip was awful," he says. "But I'm glad we're together again."

Mother takes a sip of water and smiles at me. There is something about the way her lips struggle to curl upward that makes me think she doesn't believe a word of what I've just said. "Where is Ortimo?" she asks.

Tatiana shudders at the question, her body folding in on itself. Her lips tremble. Her eyes flood. And then she is gasping for air, wracked by sobs.

So I tell them how Semyon barged into the cabin, drunk, and threw Ortimo from the window. But I tell them nothing else. I cannot. Olga reaches for my hand beneath the table and squeezes it in gratitude. Father is enraged, but this news mollifies Mother somehow. She sits there, searching our faces, wanting to believe we suffered no other harm on the journey.

"I am sorry," Mother says, pulling Tatiana against her side. "I am so sorry about Ortimo. We will speak with Semyon. We will address this."

"No!" Tatiana says, and then, lower, "No. It won't change anything. Just keep him away from us. Keep all of them away from us."

"He will not go near you again," Father growls.

Something occurs to me then. "Where is Yakov? I haven't seen him since we arrived."

"Gone to Moscow," Father says. "He does that occasionally."

"Why?"

"He doesn't say."

"Have you asked?"

Father sets his fork down on the edge of his plate. There is an angry slant to his mouth. "Yakov Yurovsky does not answer to me."

It is not like Father to be evasive, but I don't see much point in pushing him any harder in the middle of dinner. Father refills his glass from a crystal decanter on the table and drains it in four long gulps of water. It makes me sad to think that same decanter once held wine. Part of a serving set we used daily, it is now one of the few luxurious things we still have in our possession.

When we arrived in Ekaterinburg hours earlier we found that our living quarters were greatly diminished even from what we'd had in Tobolsk. The room where we now eat, once a formal dining room for the previous owners, is expected to be dining room, parlor, and study combined. The table is crammed in one corner with the chairs crowded together, and two couches are arranged along the other wall in an L shape. Some of Father's books are stacked in piles against the walls. The rest are stacked in crates in a back room, unopened since his arrival a month earlier. During the day he uses the table as a desk. Dova has tried, with little success, to make the room comfortable by arranging rugs and hanging curtains, but the overall look is tattered and haphazard.

Beyond that we are granted use of the kitchen, a single bathroom, and three bedrooms to be split between us and our few remaining servants. My parents and Alexey share one. Botkin, Trupp, Cook, and Dova are in another. And my sisters and I have been given the last.

Our bedroom, as it turns out, hasn't been prepared for our arrival. So we make do, piling cushions and cloaks and spare blankets in the middle of the room. We peel off our clothing and throw it in the corner, relishing the feel of clean nightgowns and good hairbrushes. The baths will have to wait. We are too exhausted.

Tomas and Ivan are somewhere on the grounds—I didn't miss the look of delight on Maria's face when she saw Ivan. But the bitter surge of jealousy took me by surprise. Maria is oblivious. She has no idea what happened on the train. Luck of the draw spared her from our fate, and there is now a distance between us that I do not know how to bridge. I doubt Olga and Tatiana will even try.

We're in a strange city in a borrowed home and are still surrounded by countless soldiers. But our parents are here. We are as safe as we can be at the moment. It is true there are no locks on the doors, but Semyon will not dare touch us with our protectors nearby. He is a coward at heart, a greedy, loathsome opportunist. And we are utterly spent. So my sisters and I curl into that makeshift pallet in the middle of the room and give ourselves up to the great and merciful gift of sleep.

Maria is the first to begin snoring, and when she does I feel a hand reach out and brush my cheek. Then Tatiana's voice. "Thank you, Schwibsik," she says. "I couldn't bear it if they knew."

TWO DAYS LATER

Ekaterinburg, Russia
May 27

We enter the storeroom to find everything we own in shambles. Boxes emptied onto the floor. Crates overturned. Furniture broken. Clothing is strung about and books lay open, their spines cracked and pages mangled. All of our silver, crystal, and fine china has been stolen. Sold, no doubt, to some secondhand store in the city. The trunk containing our corsets was taken to our room immediately upon arrival; otherwise, it would have certainly been pillaged as well.

Dr. Botkin and I have come to retrieve our camp beds so we won't have to sleep on the floor again. Many of the items that traveled with our parents and almost everything we brought from Tobolsk is stored in this large, empty room at the back of the house. In hindsight it's obvious that the soldiers have unrestricted access to this room, but we had no way of knowing that our belongings were being pilfered.

It is one thing to have everything you own picked through

and winnowed down. It is something else to see it trampled on and torn to pieces. Pillaged. Violated. Ravaged. I have never been one to hold my anger, but I lose all pretense of control upon finding this mess.

"Anastasia," Botkin warns, "don't."

But it's too late. I'm already picking up my skirts and running. Because the truth is, my anger has nothing to do with our belongings and everything to do with the rage I have held, bottled and corked, since that night on the train.

I find Semyon outside, beside the fence, surrounded by a group of men. Their heads are thrown back and their throats filled with the coarse sort of laughter that makes my stomach churn. I know what they're talking about, why they're laughing, and I am driven forward in fury. There's a momentary flash of uncertainty on Semyon's face when he sees me storming across the grass, arms pumping and face red. For a second it looks like fear. He hides it quickly, however, and by the time I reach him, his true emotions are masked with that ever-present sneer.

"You," I say, breathless, as Botkin trots up behind me.

Semyon rests one foot against the fence and crosses his arms over his chest. "Yes?"

"You let your men go through our things. You let them steal from us."

"I didn't let them do any such thing," he says. "I *ordered* them to."

Soldiers draw closer from all across the yard, curious about the commotion. In my peripheral vision I see Tomas and Ivan shift from their posts at the front door, rifles slung over their shoulders, and wander close enough to hear.

"You have no right!"

Botkin's hand settles heavily on my shoulder. Challenging Semyon like this is foolhardy, stupid even. I've seen firsthand how merciless he can be. Yet the dam has burst, and all that pent-up rage comes spilling out.

"I have every right. You are not royalty. You are not even citizens. You are prisoners, and your belongings are property of the state. Be thankful we left anything at all. Yakov ordered me to sell the valuables. I could have burned the rest." Semyon pushes off the wall and eyes me curiously, as though he has only now noticed my existence. He looks me over slowly, the way he does with Olga, and I force myself not to shrink back when he reaches out and fingers the collar of my blouse. "I could have sold your clothing, you know. I could have left you all naked."

My spit is dripping from his eyelashes before I realize what I've done. The hand that was playing with my collar a moment earlier grips me tighter. He yanks me forward, inches from his face, while he wipes the spit from his eye with his other hand. He is a good bit taller than I am, but I roll up onto the balls of my feet, unwilling to back down. I can feel Botkin's long fingers digging into my shoulders as he tries to pull me back. And I can see Tomas in the edge of my vision slide the rifle from his shoulder. He holds it loosely before him, ready to aim.

Semyon shakes me once, hard enough that my head snaps backward and pain shoots through the base of my skull.

"You should be more careful with the things you value. Or they will be taken from you." He raises his hand and brushes it along my cheek, tucking my hair behind my ear. Then he plucks the diamond stud from my earlobe and holds it up to the light. It looks enormous there, pinched between his fingertips, like a button. Semyon tucks it in his shirt pocket and yanks the stud from my other ear as well. "Don't bother me again, you stupid little girl. You have no rights."

Botkin steadies me when Semyon pushes me backward. I can do nothing but retreat, and I hate myself for it. My only consolation is the look of pure hatred on Tomas's face as he glares at Semyon. He has returned to his post at the door by the time we pass through, but he has not repositioned his rifle. It still hangs loosely in his hand, finger hovering over the trigger. Tomas catches my eye just as I shake my head. I hope he understands my meaning. Don't do it. Not yet.

ONE WEEK LATER

Ekaterinburg, Russia
June 5

No one ever tells you that time grinds to a halt when you are in captivity, that each day becomes a year and each week becomes a lifetime. That you will live a dozen slow lifetimes over the course of a single month. I thought that life was hard when we were put under house arrest at the Alexander Palace. We couldn't travel or visit with friends. We had only the palace and the grounds at our disposal. And then we went to Tobolsk and our lives narrowed even further. A house, much smaller, and a meager yard defined our existence. But we had many of our things and a good rapport with the guards. We did not understand how lucky we were in either place until the reality of Ekaterinburg began to settle in. Now we have only a handful of rooms and a small, weedy garden that we are allowed to visit for thirty minutes twice a day. Our lives shrink to a pinprick of what they were before.

With June comes the heat and, since Semyon will not let us open the windows, oppression soon follows. We make fans out of ruined books. I chose *War and Peace* because, masterpiece though it is, I've never gotten through it without skimming entire sections. I console myself that I am finally able to appreciate Tolstoy's penchant for philosophy. How can I not? It is waved in front of my face for hours every day.

"We can only know that we know nothing. And that is the highest degree of human wisdom." Those words are burned upon my

gray matter. I dream of them, pouring from the heavily mustachioed mouth of Pierre Gilliard. Mr. Philosophy himself.

"Nothing is so necessary for a young man as the society of clever women." Tomas whispers these words to me in my dreams, and I curl into them, begging him to say them over and over.

"If everyone fought for their own convictions there would be no war." Father.

"We are asleep until we fall in love!" Maria, cooing this into Ivan's ear as he dangles upside down from a tree while eating one of my pears. This part, I admit, is odd, but dreams are not meant to be rational.

"Everything depends on upbringing." Mother, sternly shaking her finger at me as I pick willow sap from my hair.

"One must be cunning and wicked in this world." Semyon, congratulating himself as he straightens the front of his trousers. Even in my dreams I am nauseous and enraged.

On and on these dreams go, tumbling over one another, voices and messages mingling together until I wake one morning, shaken, my hairline damp and my breath ragged. It is that early, nebulous hour before dawn when the sky can't make up its mind what color it wants to be and you don't know whether it is today, tomorrow, or perhaps yesterday.

As the last vestiges of sleep drain away, I roll over, looking for my sisters—a new, alarming habit I've developed, a head count of sorts—but find only two. Maria is gone, and I am gripped by a flash of panic. I dress quickly and shut the door quietly behind me, hoping that I haven't woken Olga and Tatiana. They sleep uneasily these days, tossing and turning, crying out in the darkness, and I don't want to rob them of precious slumber.

I find Maria in an alcove beneath the stairs wrapped in the arms of Ivan Skorokhodov. I've never seen such kissing. Certainly not from my parents nor in the paintings we've studied.

This is something else. Primal and hungry. Frantic. Ivan has one hand in her hair and the other on her bodice, his thumb caressing the rounded underside of her breast. I stare at the motion he makes with that one finger, circular and tender, and it takes a moment to realize that Maria is still in her night-gown. Only a thin layer of fabric separates her skin from his hand.

I gasp and they pull apart as though they've been touched with a branding iron. Ivan takes one look at me and flees. Maria on the other hand cannot decide on an emotion.

Anger, fear, embarrassment, stubbornness, euphoria. All of these things flash across her face before she says, "Please don't tell Mother and Father. They'll be furious."

I want to threaten her, to say that I will tell our parents everything, but it would be a lie. "You're going to get caught."

"Not if you don't tell."

"It will happen eventually," I say. "And what then? Aren't things bad enough for us already?"

"He loves me." Maria's voice turns tremulous and weepy. "He's the only good thing I have right now. And he's going to help us get out of here. I *need* him. *We* need him."

"Don't be a fool. That boy can't help us."

"He's not a boy, and you don't know that."

"Go back to bed," I tell her, "before someone finds you here."

Maria pushes out her jaw, stubbornness winning the battle of emotions. "You've already found me."

"And you should be thankful that it was me and not Semyon."

"So you won't tell?"

It is stupid not to. Maria needs to have some sense shaken into her. But what does it matter anyway? Why rob her of the one thing that gives her hope? I would want her to keep the secret for me if the situation were reversed. If Tomas . . . "No. I suppose not," I say, banishing the thought altogether. "But this is the second time I've found the two of you together. You're being sloppy."

"Thank you," she whispers and plants a kiss on my cheek before tiptoeing back to our bedroom.

TWO WEEKS LATER

Ekaterinburg, Russia
June 18

My seventeenth birthday comes and goes without celebration. Cook bakes a pastry and my family toasts me at dinner, but it is nothing like the vacations and parties we used to enjoy. I wasn't expecting much. Yet I am still sad.

I lay awake feeling sorry for myself long after my sisters begin to snore. I listen to the sounds of this strange new house, the creaks and groanings. The footsteps upstairs as the soldiers walk back and forth. Water in the pipes. The occasional burst of laughter in the yard. The protest of the stairs as someone steps on the loose board halfway up. The gentle, feminine breathing of my sisters, now deep in the recesses of sleep.

I press my face into my pillow and chide myself for wanting more than I can have and missing what I cannot get back. I've worked myself into a good, frothing cry when the door handle to our room rattles gently and then turns. The lights are off across the house, so when the door creaks open all I see is more darkness. I reach instinctively for the boot beside my bed and remember that it is empty. The paper knife is gone. I am defenseless. Jimmy stirs at my feet. The sound draws the intruder's attention and those careful, quiet steps turn toward me.

The scream is building in my chest, furious and unhinged, when I hear my name.

"Anastasia?" A whisper. And then, even quieter, "Hush, Jimmy."

I let my breath out in a huff and sit up slowly. Jimmy thumps his tail against my feet. "Tomas?"

"Where are you? I can't see anything in here."

"Over here." He shuffles slowly in my direction and stops when his shins hit the edge of my bed.

"What are you doing?"

"I came to give you your birthday present." He sits down beside me and his thigh is warm against my own.

I swallow, fearing my voice will waver. "How did you know?"

"I heard them toasting you at dinner. But I would have come to find you anyway."

"Why?"

"To return these." He reaches for my hand and presses something small and hard into them. "Your earrings."

"How—"

"Semyon gambled them away the night he took them from you. We all play cards. It passes the time. But he has no skill for the game, and the man who won them can't hold his liquor." He pauses and takes a deep breath, then curls his hand around mine. He keeps it there as he explains, "So I made sure he had plenty of vodka and when he passed out I took them from his pocket."

The words come out strangled and pathetic as I start to cry again. "Thank you."

"Oh, hey," Tomas says, releasing my hand and then gripping my face gently in both of his. "There's no need for that."

He runs his thumbs over my cheeks, pushing the tears aside. I don't know which of us leans in but it doesn't matter because we find each other. First the tips of our noses—which brings a nervous giggle—and then our lips—which brings total silence.

And awe.

And heat.

And amazement.

And suddenly I understand what would drive my sister out of bed in the early hours of the morning to kiss a man beneath the stairs. Because I would do this with Tomas anywhere, at any time of day.

His lips are soft and gentle and he kisses me until he has to pull away for breath. "Happy birthday," he whispers.

"Do you know," I say, opening my hand so the studs lie in my palm, "that this is the second year in a row that I've gotten these earrings for my birthday?"

Tomas rests his cheek against mine and his answer is a gentle whisper in my ear. "I wouldn't go around wearing them. It's best if everyone thinks they were lost or stolen."

I lean away and drop the studs into my boot. "I promise I'll keep them safe."

Tomas slides his thumb across my lips but he does not kiss me again. Because kisses are dangerous and we have been foolish enough for one night.

27

Anna

MISS UNKNOWN

1920

Dalldorf Asylum, Berlin
June 1920

Anna has not seen the Clerk since being admitted to the asylum, but he is waiting for her when she and the Duck enter his office. He has brought two of the larger orderlies with him and they stand quietly, hands folded at their waists, on either side of the file cabinet. They watch cautiously as she enters, then stops abruptly just inside the door.

"What is this about?" Anna asks. "I've done nothing wrong. I've done nothing at all, actually. They barely let me out of my room."

"Dr. Reiche sent for the police. It's time we learn your name," the Clerk says. He sits behind the desk and runs a hand across the top of Anna's closed file.

The police don't know it either, you fool. Anna doesn't speak the words aloud but wishes she could.

The doctor comes in a few minutes later, followed by the Sergeant who arrested Anna in February. If anything he looks more incensed than he did at their first meeting. "I see she hasn't changed much," he says.

Anna decides to address him directly. "I don't get out much. There's little chance to get sun on my face, if that's what you mean."

"I *mean*," he says, placing two boxes—one large and one small—on the Clerk's desk, "that you still look defiant and ungrateful."

"You seem to have the misguided notion that the natural response to imprisonment is gratitude."

"And you continue in *your* misguided notion that I care how you feel." He opens the smaller of the two boxes and takes out a rectangular inkpad and notebook. "I am here because the good doctor wants answers once and for all about your identity. I assured him that the moment you become too great a burden, I'd be happy to take you off his hands and place you in custody. You are lucky to have found such sympathetic doctors." The Sergeant looks her up and down slowly, intentionally, as though suspicious that she has offered carnal incentive to be kept from arrest. "Let's begin with your fingerprints, shall we?"

Anna doesn't move, and when the Duck sets a hand on her elbow to usher her forward, she jerks it away. "No."

The Sergeant doesn't bother to argue or cajole. He simply waves a hand at the orderlies and says, "Take her arms."

And then Anna is dragged to the desk, elbows locked and arms extended. The Sergeant is quick and adept. He folds out her clenched fingers one at a time to press them against the ink and then the paper. Anna remains stiff and uncooperative through this ordeal, but she doesn't struggle until she sees him begin to unload a camera from the large wooden box on the table.

"No photos! I don't want my photo taken. You can't. I do not give my consent."

"I can. I will. And your consent is not required. Once this photo has been developed, it will be sent to police stations and newspapers in Stuttgart, Brunswick, Hamburg, Munich, and Dresden. I'm going to make sure your face is published in every newspaper in every corner of the Weimar Republic. We'll see if we don't learn your name then, won't we?"

Anna can feel all the little threads that tether her together begin to grow taut and fray at the ends. She can feel the rebellion boil and begin to spill over into rage. What right does he have to violate her privacy like this? She has hurt no one. She has done nothing but keep her own council and guard her secrets closely. Her only crime was trying to end her life in a broken, desperate moment. Had she succeeded, no one would have even cared. They would have buried her in a cemetery for indigents outside the city without a tombstone or marker. Yet as punishment for surviving, her secrets will spill out, one after another, like buttons from a jar.

When the orderlies lift her from the desk and press her back against the wall, Anna wishes for an episode to come crashing in. She would love to lose control and thrash herself into oblivion. There's no way he could get a photo then. But her mind is oddly, infuriatingly clear. She is angry but not afraid. There is no darkness, only searing, righteous indignation, so the best she can do is scrunch up her face and twist her head to the side, to obscure her face with her hair. But the officer is more cunning than she gives him credit for. The flashbulb goes off with a blinding snap and Anna knows that whatever picture he's taken will do him no good with her face lowered and partly in shadow. But when she lifts her face to him triumphantly, he snaps another photo, this one clear, her expression almost joyful.

"That will do," the officer says. "I have what I need."

THREE MONTHS EARLIER

Dalldorf Asylum, Berlin
March 30, 1920

Later Dr. Arschloch describes what happened to her in the exam room as *an episode*. Whatever he may call it, Anna thinks of it only as darkness and nightmare and memory. She thinks of it as tangible despair. It feels like cotton in her lungs and snakes on her skin. When she wakes again fully, she is alone, strapped to a bed by her wrists and ankles, in a large, dim room. There are windows high on the wall but they are only eight inches tall and barred on the outside. It takes her a moment to remember who she is and even longer to remember where she is, but she comforts herself with the fact that until today, she hasn't had one of these *episodes* in three months. This is progress. They came daily at first. And she's never known what to call them until now.

Anna can lift her head only a few inches, but she sees that the room is filled with empty beds, each of them covered with worn quilts in different colors and patterns. She counts seven from where she lies but guesses there are more out of sight. When she turns her head to look, she sees that she isn't alone after all. A young woman stands to her left, staring at her.

Anna flinches. "Who are you?"

The girl blinks at her, curious.

"Why are you here?"

"I'm so sorry," she stutters in a soft, lilting voice. "I didn't mean to startle you."

The girl is older than Anna, but not by much, and appears to be unbearably nervous. She sits on the bed, then stands again. Smooths her skirt. Wrings her hands.

Anna says nothing. She simply watches, but the silence seems to rattle this strange young woman even more. She begins to chatter like a squirrel.

"I am Clara. I live here." She sits down on the bed beside Anna's. Pats the mattress. "Right here. I live right here." She is pretty in the way that dolls are pretty, with pale skin, a small red mouth, and eyes so large they're almost disturbing. "Welcome. I mean . . . *Scheiße* . . . I'm sorry you're here. No one *wants* to be here. But they put you in the best place. It's quiet in this ward. For the most part. The others are awful. Those poor women are *crazy*. The ones here just have a nervous disposition. Like me. I'm nervous. Do I make you nervous? I'm really sorry if I do. Dr. Reiche says I make people nervous. You're lucky to be in this ward."

Anna tries to sit up but can't. Her heart begins to tick a little faster. "Will you unbind these restraints? I'd like to sit up."

"Oh!" Clara presses a hand to her mouth. "They don't know you're awake! I'll go tell them."

"No! No." She clears her throat. It's an effort not to shriek. She can't move. She feels trapped. "Don't bring them back. Just unbuckle my wrists." Clara *is*, in fact, making her nervous. Anna doesn't want anyone else to come and prod her again with questions or needles. She wants to be left alone, to plan her escape. Anna takes a shaky breath and lifts her hands, palms up, as far as she can from where they lie at her side. "Help me. Please?"

Guileless. Absolutely guileless. Clara probably wouldn't survive five minutes outside this institution. She smiles at Anna as though they have been friends for years.

"Of course." Her fingers hover just above the restraint binding Anna's wrist. Clara's large, gray eyes are bright with interest. "You look *very* familiar," she says.

ONE DAY EARLIER

Dalldorf Asylum, Berlin
March 29, 1920

Anna refuses to give her name when asked by the admittance clerk at Dalldorf Asylum. He sits behind a metal desk that is bolted to the floor, as is his chair and the file cabinet behind him. The Clerk is not amused with Anna, despite the fact that he has been warned—Dr. Winicke told him not two minutes ago that she consistently balks at this—but he still takes it as a personal offense.

"I cannot admit you without a name." He taps the folder in front of him with his pen, but Anna only crosses her arms and presses her lips together. There is a single painting on the wall behind him—a murky green abstract that matches his eyes—and she looks at it instead of at him. The painting is supposed to be a landscape but it's mottled and juvenile. She wonders if he painted it himself. He seems like the sort of man who would celebrate feeble attempts. The Clerk turns to Dr. Winicke, who is seated beside her. "I can't admit her without a name."

"You'll just have to figure something out then, won't you?"

"It's against policy."

"Hospitals do it all the time. She's been in my care for weeks and I still don't know her name."

"What did you call her, then?"

"A pain in the *Arsch*."

"Funny."

"If you're looking for sympathy you won't find it here. I've done what I can. Now it's your turn." Dr. Winicke lifts his fedora from where it rests on his knee and places it back on his head. He is ready to be gone from this stark institution.

Anna watches Dr. Winicke prepare to leave and feels a

twinge of sadness. His kindness has been purely professional in all things except one: rather than handing her over to the Berlin police he has sent her here in the hopes that she will get better. He wants her to have a chance. Even though he doesn't understand what drove her to jump from that bridge, he doesn't want her to attempt it again. That is what he said on the drive to Dalldorf this morning, his hands gripping the steering wheel and his eyes locked on the winding road ahead. Anna did not answer; she simply stared out the window and tried to loosen the restraints at her wrists without success.

The Clerk looks at the file again and sighs. "What kind of diagnosis is 'melancholia'?"

Dr. Winicke offers an exasperated sigh. "It is a mental illness of a depressive character. Like I've written in the chart. As you can plainly see."

"But what of her sanity? This is an asylum for the mentally insane."

Dr. Winicke appraises Anna with his keen, dark eyes—she has seen him change his mind about whether or not she is mad at least a dozen times in the last few weeks—but if he has come to a conclusion he does not share it with the Clerk. "As you will note, in the chart, I have offered no opinion about her sanity. That is for your doctors to determine." He rises from his chair and lays his coat across his arm. "But do let me know if you ever learn her name. I'd be lying if I said I wasn't curious."

"If she won't declare her name then I will give her one." The Clerk scratches two words on the front of Anna's file: *Fräulein Unbekannt.*

Miss Unknown.

————

"I don't need another examination." Anna stops abruptly in front of a door labeled INFIRMARY. After Dr. Winicke left, Anna thought she was being taken to her room. But as the Clerk lifts a key ring from the loop at his waist and unlocks the door, Anna realizes she was mistaken. He holds it open and motions for her to walk through. "All new patients are required to undergo a physical examination. It's *policy*, Fräulein Unbekannt."

"Do I have a choice in this?"

"Of course you do. If you *choose* not to cooperate I will call the orderlies and you will be placed in restraints. The examination will happen regardless."

Anna has a sneaking suspicion that the Clerk would like nothing more than to call the orderlies. And to observe her exam. For administrative purposes no doubt. He seems like the sort of man who likes to watch.

She is then turned over to another physician and his attending nurse to be subjected to another invasive exam. She can feel the muscles in her arms and legs begin to coil in defiance. The nurse is short and squat and stands beside the exam table, her hands folded behind her back. She looks strong and capable, but Anna can't tell from the expression on her face whether or not she is compassionate as well. Her nametag reads THEA MALINOVSKY and her demeanor reads indifferent.

"Please," Anna begs, turning to the nurse, "look at my chart. Tell him I don't need another exam." The nurses at Elisabeth Hospital were efficient and kind and there is a chance this woman might sympathize with her as well. Anna offers her most hopeful, pleading expression. "Dr. Winicke took thorough records. Nothing new has happened to me in the last two hours. Look at his notes. Tell this doctor what you think."

"I think you should do exactly what Dr. Reiche tells you," she says.

Duckmäuser, Anna thinks. Coward.

"It would be best if you cooperated with this exam, Fräulein"— the doctor looks at the chart—"Unbekannt? Don't you have a name?"

Anna is so tired of that stupid question.

Dr. Reiche lifts the stethoscope from where it hangs around his neck. "I assure you the exam will go quickly and will be painless if you cooperate."

"I don't need an exam," she says.

His lip curls in irritation. "Very well. If that's how you want to proceed."

She decides then and there that the man is an utter *Arschloch*. Asshole.

He has not threatened her with the orderlies, but she knows they linger nearby. They always do in places like this. Anna doesn't fight him, not at first, but she does record the details of this new indignity with clinical precision, listing them in her mind as though writing in a chart of her own. She labels it: Dr. *Arschloch* and Nurse *Duckmäuser*. The Duck, for short. There, she has nicknames for them now. Easy enough to remember.

Dr. Arschloch's hands are freezing. His voice is too high for a man of such advanced age. It rises at the end of each sentence as though he's asking a question. He is immediately curious about the scar at her temple.

"How did you get this?" He looks to her file for details.

Anna says nothing.

He rattles off her physical details like she is a specimen in some lab that must be catalogued. He hands her file to the Duck to record his findings. "Weight one hundred and ten pounds. Height, exactly five foot one . . ." he looks at his tape measure, ". . . and one half inches.

"The patient is reticent and refuses to give a name or any details about her age, occupation, and family history. The patient is impossibly stubborn." He pauses to make sure the Duck has gotten all of this information. When she concurs he looks to Anna and asks, "Do you hear voices or have hallucinations?"

Anna shakes her head. "Of course not."

"You know, I wasn't sure that you could speak when Dr.

Winicke called yesterday to warn us about you. Did you know he called?" he asks.

"How would I possibly know that?"

"He told me, off the record, that he does not think you are insane. He believes you are unspeakably frightened, though he does not know of what. Are you frightened, Fräulein Unbekannt?"

"Not of you."

"Who then?"

Anna says nothing.

"Dr. Winicke also said that when you feel threatened you use the silent treatment. Do you feel threatened now, Fräulein Unbekannt?"

"I feel angry."

"At what?"

"At being asked stupid questions."

Dr. Arschloch looks to her file again. "It says here that you are not a virgin. How did you lose your virginity?"

Anna hates that she cannot hide the feral note to her voice or the rage that rolls across her face like a wave. "That is none of your business."

"It is, actually."

Anna says nothing.

"Dr. Winicke believes you are a prostitute and that the shame you carry over this drove you off that bridge. But I don't agree with him. I see a lot of prostitutes in this facility. They're often here because they've been beaten or abused to the point of insanity. You, however, are too clean and well spoken and demure for that profession. You have all your teeth—nice, pretty, straight ones at that. Your skin is unwrinkled, and that leads me to believe that you neither smoke nor drink in excess. Your German is perfect but you have a Russian accent. There's crispness to your speech that I can't quite identify. Your diction is strong. No, I believe you are something else."

"And what is that?"

If the corner of his mouth wasn't twitching in a victorious grin he would seem disinterested as he answers, "Jilted."

"You know nothing about me."

"I'm an educated man. I make educated guesses." He pushes his glasses a little farther up his nose. "If I had to *guess*, I'd say that you are—or at least you *were*—engaged to be married. Perhaps your fiancé called off the wedding? Perhaps he found another woman? One who is not prone to manic episodes? How close is that to the truth, Fräulein Unbekannt? Should we call your fiancé? Or should we simply continue your physical examination and you can tell us where these appalling scars came from?"

The shaking starts in Anna's hands. She isn't sure whether its source is rage or terror, but it spreads across her body regardless, and in a matter of seconds she has to clench her jaw to stop her teeth from rattling.

Dr. Arschloch lifts a thin cotton hospital gown from the shelf at her side and holds it out to her. "You can change into this," he says. "You can remove your clothing or I can have the orderlies remove it for you."

Anna feels the panic clawing up her throat and she grips the edge of the exam table. Her fingertips begin to throb. "You already know what you will find. It's all written there in Dr. Winicke's file."

"I must confirm it for myself."

"You *want* to confirm it!"

He laughs at this. "You foolish young women always think that I enjoy looking at the ways you've damaged yourselves. Let me assure you, Fräulein Unbekannt, I am not attracted to suicidal madwomen who mutilate their own bodies."

"I will tell you *nothing*. I will show you *nothing*. You can go to hell!" Anna spits the words at him and scrambles backward on the table. The edges of her vision begin to darken, and Anna can feel that old, hated memory pressing in on her, demanding her attention, demanding to be replayed for the thousandth time.

"Have it your way," he says. And then he turns to the nurse. "Call the orderlies."

28

Anastasia

LOSING COHESION

1918

Ipatiev House, Ekaterinburg, Russia
July 10

"Your daughter is a whore," Yakov says, his hand knotted in Maria's hair, turning her from side to side, making sure we can properly see her shame. Her hair is mussed, blouse unbuttoned, corset loose, and breasts exposed. Semyon stands behind them, grinning, as he holds a pistol to Ivan's head. The boy is stricken with terror as he stares at Maria and the consequences of their tryst.

The sight of Maria, sobbing and half naked, startles my family into silence. But Jimmy bounds to his feet, hackles stiff along his spine, teeth bared, and a rumble building in his chest.

I grip his collar carefully. "*Nyet,*" I whisper. "Stay." The growl dissolves but Jimmy remains tense, ready to leap at the intruders.

Yakov shoves my sister so hard she lurches into the room and stumbles to her knees. "Cover yourself," he says.

Maria collapses into a heap, too ashamed and terrified to meet our eyes. She fumbles with the buttons of her blouse, unable to push them through the holes. The harder she tries, the more her hands shake. When she can no longer catch a breath between sobs I go to her.

"Let me do it," I say, gently pushing her hands away. I make quick work of the buttons, then wrap my arms around her, pulling her close.

Not once has Ivan taken his eyes from my sister, and only when she is fully clothed does he relax. Semyon's pistol is still pressed into the pale skin of Ivan's temple, but he lets out a long, shaky breath. That is when I realize Ivan Skorokhodov truly loves my sister.

"What is the meaning of this?" Father asks, finally gaining enough composure to rise from the table where he was playing a game of dominoes with Alexey. He steps forward, barely containing his rage.

"It's obvious enough, don't you think? I found her in the cellar playing the harlot with this fool. Shall I tell you the exact position they were in? Or would you rather young Ivan give you the details? He experienced them firsthand."

Mother and Olga sit together on the couch, knitting needles limp in their hands, expressions of pure disgust on their faces. They glare, not at Yakov but at Maria. Tatiana and Olga have grown more and more distant from Maria since we arrived in Ekaterinburg. It is hard for them to accept that she was spared even though they would never wish such violation on her. I see this in the way they look at her sometimes, jealousy and then guilt written in the line of their brows, or how their lips pinch at the sight of her. This is how the human heart beats, a twisted staccato of love and envy, of anger and relief. I doubt that Maria can define this loss of affection with our sisters, but I am certain the estrangement has driven her further into Ivan's arms.

Mother, of course, knows nothing of the silent bitterness among her girls. "How could you do this?" she hisses at Maria.

"It was my fault," Ivan says. "Please don't be angry with her." The words tumble out distraught and desperate.

Father steps closer, his finger shaking in Ivan's face. "How dare you touch my daughter?"

Yakov laughs at this, and the sound of utter disdain makes my stomach hurt. I hate him for enjoying this. "She is not innocent."

"Of course she is! She's only a girl. She has no idea what she's doing."

"You didn't see her in the cellar. You daughter is not a little girl. Nor is she virtuous. How long has this been going on right under your nose?"

Maria stiffens beneath my arm and I shush her, patting her hair, trying to quietly assure her that I will not reveal what I know.

While Mother sits cold and pitiless across the room, Father's rage grows hotter by the second. He turns his fury from Ivan to Yakov. "This is your fault! You should be able to control your soldiers. A good leader would never have allowed this to happen."

"Are *you* going to lecture *me* about leadership, Citizen Romanov? Your *leadership* turned your own people against you. It inspired a revolution. They would tear you limb from limb if I handed you over today. And I for one would enjoy watching them do it." He nods at Maria, still wrapped in my arms. "You deal with your daughter. I will deal with my soldier."

"Your soldier deserves to be shot," Father spits.

"No!" Maria pulls away from me and reaches toward Ivan, but I grab her arm and yank it back.

"Quiet," I hiss in her ear. "You will only make this worse."

"Look how she tries to protect him. Do you still think she is innocent?" Yakov grins, victorious, then adds, "The punishment I have in mind is far more effective than a bullet in his skull."

———

Yakov makes us watch as Ivan is stripped to the waist and tied to a stone column in the courtyard; his feet are lashed together and his hands tied behind his back. It is an exquisite punishment, designed to torture everyone equally. Chairs are brought from the dining room and placed before the column at Yakov's command. And then one by one, the soldiers are required to step forward and deliver their worst blow. If they fail to satisfy Yakov, he orders them to hit Ivan again. And again, if necessary, until the punch carries sufficient weight. Until the damage is visible. I am close enough to Ivan that I can smell the sweat and fear and blood. The soldiers have the worst of it, however. They are Ivan's friends, his brothers-in-arms. Men who guarded him in the trenches. Reloaded his rifle. Shared a tent.

"A lesson," Yakov says after Semyon gleefully takes his turn. "To teach all of you how dangerous it can be to forget your place. If it happens again we will use bayonets."

Father's rage is subdued thirty seconds into the ordeal when Ivan begins to moan. The thud of fist on flesh is nauseating. Unbearable. He is just a boy, barely older than Maria, and his only crime is falling in love with a pretty girl. Yet here he is, blood running down his chin, trying not to sob.

Maria is not allowed to leave her chair or Ivan will be shot. If she looks away Ivan will be shot.

"Stop," Maria begs, after another blow splits open his bottom lip. She lifts a trembling arm, her voice raspy. "Please."

"Hit him again. Harder," Yakov says to the soldier at the front of the line. There is an audible crunch and when Ivan spits a tooth onto the ground, Yakov looks at Maria, his head tilted to the side. "Interrupt me again and your father gets to shoot him in the head. Isn't that what he wants? To defend your *honor*."

Maria sits by me since Mother and Olga will not speak to her. They are furious and disgusted. Mother is ashamed, but Olga, I fear, is drunk with outrage, appalled that my sister would freely offer something that was so brutally taken from her. But I don't know how to explain this to Maria. She wasn't on the train that night. She couldn't understand. And the secret is not mine to tell. She collapses against my shoulder, gripping my hand so hard her fingernails cut into the tender skin of my palm.

I suspect Tomas hoped to spare himself by standing at the back of the line. Perhaps he thought the beating couldn't possibly go on for so long. But he has only made things worse for himself. Tomas watches every blow with rising dread, and by the time he steps into position, Ivan is unrecognizable, his face is something *other*, inhuman and ghastly. He is a gasping, bloody mess. Both eyes swollen shut. Lips split open. Two teeth knocked out. Nose broken. He can no longer lift his head from his chest. Thin rivulets of blood run from his nostrils and splash onto the cobblestones at his feet.

"Do it!" Yakov screams at Tomas, spittle flying in a wide arc.

Tomas does the only merciful thing he can. Another blow to the head will likely kill Ivan, so he jabs him in the ribs instead, quick and hard. We all hear the sound of cracking bone. Ivan can't see. He isn't expecting a punch to his torso, isn't able to brace for it, so he groans and coughs and spits blood on Tomas's boot.

"Good!" Yakov shouts. "Now, all of you, back to your posts."

Tomas trembles, hatred and fear etched across his face, but he obeys the order. I am too afraid to watch him go, afraid my feelings will betray me.

Yakov nods toward Ivan's broken and bloody form. "Arrest him."

Semyon unties the bonds around Ivan's wrists so that he falls forward onto the stones, arms twitching, blood pooling beneath his nose. Because Ivan cannot walk he is dragged across the courtyard, through a heavy wooden door, and into the cellar. A final twist of the knife for Maria. Yakov's idea of poetic justice given that he found them in that very cellar less than an hour ago.

Satisfied with the results of his ghastly demonstration, Yakov kneels before Maria. He squeezes her jaw between his long, bony fingers, forcing her to look at him. "Was your little tryst worth it, Tsarevna? That handsome face is ruined. Your honor is tarnished. You will be forever known as the Romanov who spread her legs for a common soldier. Congratulations."

Maria doesn't respond, but she doesn't look away either. Snot runs down her chin. Those huge, beautiful blue eyes are bloodshot and swollen. Her entire body shudders with defiance, but she does not buckle beneath his triumphant sneer.

"Oh, you hate me, do you?" Yakov squeezes her chin tighter until she grinds her teeth in pain. "Good. Now we understand each other."

"Get your hands off my daughter." For the first time that afternoon Father's voice is deadly calm. His lip is curled and his fist is raised. But the blow never lands. It's a token protest. Impotent.

Yakov laughs and pushes Maria away. "All of you, get out of my sight."

29

Anna

THE ELISABETH HOSPITAL

1920

The Elisabeth Hospital, Berlin
February 18, 1920

Anna's eyes fly open when someone slaps her left cheek. Shouting. Questions. There's a roar in her ears so she can't make out the words. She rolls to her side and coughs until her throat burns. Anna can feel her ribs, probably not broken but certainly bruised from impact, protesting each violent spasm. There is canal water in her mouth and her nose. It tastes like pond scum and old fish. Her entire body bends and clenches trying to force the last drops of liquid from her lungs. She lies there for a moment gasping, feeling as though her chest is simultaneously waterlogged and on fire.

A man kneels beside her, but she can't make out details of his face in the darkness, only the policeman's cap and the hard, guttural sounds of his voice.

"Who are you?" he demands. "What is your name?" The questions are short and harsh, like gunshots, and she flinches as the sharp edge of a gruesome memory presses against her mind. Anna shakes her head, pushing it away, and tries to sit up.

The man is in uniform. Older and angry. Anna peers at the emblem sewn onto his shirt. A police sergeant. She scoots away from him and looks around her to find a crowd. Pointing. Gaping. Whispering. All of those preoccupied lovers she'd passed on the embankment are now hovering nearby, watching the spectacle.

"She needs a doctor!" someone shouts.

"No," the Sergeant says. He sets a large, meaty hand on each of her shoulders and shakes just enough to make her teeth rattle. "She goes to the police station. Unless she tells me her name and why she jumped from that bridge."

Anna looks at him and sees only a caricature of authority. Cruel and selfish and brutal. It's easy enough to make her decision in the light of his cool indifference. She shakes her head. No. She will not give him answers.

"Have it your way," he says.

———

The police station is nearly two miles from the canal, a slow drive down narrow, uneven streets. They shackle her in the back of the police wagon without a blanket or any other basic comfort. Her fingers are numb and her entire body convulses with cold and shock. She is only semiconscious by the time they reach the station. When the Sergeant helps her through the heavy wooden doors and into the holding room, Anna slumps to the bench and pulls her knees against her chest for warmth. She watches the hem of her skirt drip water onto the concrete floor. She struggles to keep her eyes open.

"What is this?"

Another officer. Another question.

"Some rat we dragged from the river."

"She jumped?"

"That's what they say. And she sure as hell hasn't shown us any gratitude for saving her life."

Anna stares at the floor. Counts the drops. Watches the small puddle grow larger and spread across the tile. It darkens a grout line. Her eyes grow heavy.

"Suicide is illegal," the second officer says.

If Anna had any desire to speak, and if the muscles in her jaw would unclench long enough for her to do so, she would explain the irony of this. She presses her tongue against the roof of her mouth instead, because she knows anything she might say will come out slurred and incomprehensible, and she doesn't want to be charged with public drunkenness as well.

The Sergeant kneels in front of her, determined to make eye contact. "But the thing is, you didn't die, did you?"

She blinks hard, trying to stay present.

"So that means we can prosecute you."

She hadn't taken the possibility of prison into account. But then again, the future was a useless consideration when she went over that rail. Anna simply threw herself toward the darkness, hoping to be consumed.

"You will receive no help until you tell us what happened on that bridge."

A glimmer of defiance returns. Anna lifts her chin and several seconds pass before she can pry her tongue from the roof of her mouth and control the shaking enough to form words. "I have not asked for help."

And then she falls from the bench, unconscious.

———

Anna wakes again, this time to the sensation of warm towels and soft hands on her extremities. She can feel her fingers and toes, and her nose and earlobes are no longer cubes of ice. She can smell the canal water in the damp strands of hair that hang across her face. Someone rubs her hands, drawing the blood back to her fingers, and then they move on to her feet. This gentle massaging is repeated on all of her limbs, and she feels the muscles across her body slowly relax. It takes several minutes for her to realize that she is completely naked beneath the towels.

Anna sits up with a start only to feel someone press against her forehead and lightly push her back down. The hand is warm and gently calloused. "Lie still," a woman says. "We aren't done yet."

A nurse.

So the police brought her to the hospital. This surprises her. Leaving her to die would have made things easier on the city of Berlin. One less indigent to provide for. Yet here she lies, behind a curtain in the open ward of the women's wing. She has little privacy—only this curtain—and she listens to the other patients with growing dismay. Some of them are sick. She hears coughing and vomiting. Some are wounded. Pathetic whimpering comes from a bed nearby. Others are clearly insane—screaming, babbling, chattering. And above this din Anna can hear police officers shouting in the hallway, demanding answers, demanding to be let in to interrogate her.

"Ignore them," the nurse says when she notices Anna's panicked glances toward that end of the ward. "They can't come in here. Dr. Winicke won't allow it."

Anna relaxes back onto the pillows, and the two nurses exchange a glance.

"I am Agatha," one says, "and this is Hedy. What is your name?"

Anna should warm to the kindness; she should be grateful for it. But she suspects that is exactly the point, so she says nothing at all.

Agatha continues, as if they are having a pleasant, normal conversation. As if they have known each other for years. She is plain and small, her dark hair tucked beneath a white cap. She picks up Anna's damp skirt. "Let's see what we have here." And she begins to list Anna's possessions while Hedy writes them down on a clipboard. "Black wool skirt. Black stockings. Linen blouse, soiled and torn at the cuffs. Underwear and brassiere.

Black boots. Tall. They lace to the knee." She pauses, allowing Hedy enough time to note all of these details on the chart. "And a shawl. No papers. No identification."

Anna watches with morbid interest as they rifle through her clothing, looking for initials, laundry marks, and labels. They find nothing and, in the end, Hedy pronounces the clothing homemade. This is also written on the chart in quick little marks. Hedy should be beautiful. She has all the right features: large eyes, high cheekbones, full lips. Yet everything about her looks wrong, as though her face has been drawn with a thick pencil by the clumsy hands of a child.

Once Anna's personal items have been catalogued, they move on to her body.

"We need to remove the towels now," Agatha says. "But you will be fine. No one can see you." She looks at Anna and there is a genuine plea in her eyes. "Please don't fight us. If you do we'll have to call the orderlies and they will be far less gentle."

She's giving Anna the option of being protected from male view. It's a small mercy, so Anna nods and rests her arms lightly at her sides, allowing the nurses to remove the towels. As each piece of terry cloth is stripped away, their eyes grow wider and the worried glances they give each other increase.

"So it's true then," Hedy whispers, aghast.

Anna knows what they see, what it looks like, but there is no explanation she can give that will not make this situation worse. Anna turns her face to the cinder-block wall. She tries to count the scratches left by other patients, but there are too many and her eyes blur with tears anyway.

"What have you done to yourself?" Agatha asks.

Nothing. Anna has done nothing. But they won't believe her—not after what happened tonight.

Hedy holds the clipboard while Agatha takes inventory. She places the pad of one finger at various places along Anna's body. Her left shoulder. Beneath her right collarbone. The side of her neck. Her temple. One foot. Her right calf. They turn her over and look for exit wounds.

"How many?" Hedy asks.

"Six."

"Bullets?"

"I think so."

Hedy waves her free hand across Anna's naked body indicating the web of thin silver lines. They cover her torso and abdomen and are sprinkled across the tops of her thighs. Long, thin puckered scars. "And these?"

Agatha looks at Anna with horror. When she speaks the words, it's a request for confirmation. "Stab wounds?"

There are other marks as well, between her hips, along the soft skin of her lower belly. Faint red stripes a few inches long.

Anna stares at the ceiling, inspecting a tiny crack that weaves and splits above her. She focuses on this fissure, pushing all other thoughts aside. The nurses' questions are resurrecting memories that she wants to leave buried.

"Look at me please," Agatha says.

Anna does, noting the black rings around Agatha's blue irises. They make her eyes look darker than they really are.

"Did you do this to yourself?"

No. She shakes her head, but she can see the pity in their eyes and knows they don't believe her.

"Can you speak?" Hedy asks.

A nod.

"Then it's time you do so. Help us understand what happened to you. Otherwise you'll go to jail. Suicide is a moral crime. They prosecute it in Berlin. You know that, right?"

Anna nods.

"What is your name?"

Silence.

Their pity is tinged with frustration now. "Tell us who you are."

"No."

They leap at this single word in triumph. "Where are you from?"

"Nowhere."

"Do you have family?"

Anna swallows hard, as though there is a stone in her throat. "No."

Agatha is the first to realize they will get nowhere with these questions. "Okay then," she finally says, throwing her hands up. "I'll get you a gown. Hedy, go fetch Dr. Winicke."

The hospital gown is thin, faded cotton but it covers her entire body and she feels protected again, safe from their condemning glances. Agatha brings her a blanket as well, and Anna lies back against her pillow, warm for the first time since she left the bus station yesterday.

A few minutes later, Dr. Winicke pulls back the curtain and she thinks that he looks very much like a physician: old and gray with astute eyes and more patience than personality.

"You've caused quite a stir tonight, young lady."

She doesn't answer.

"She can speak," Hedy says. "She just doesn't want to."

Dr. Winicke isn't so much kind as curious. And it's clear that Anna isn't wounded or dangerously ill. She's frightened, though, so he doesn't touch her.

He removes the clipboard from Hedy's hand and flips through the pages, looking at her notes, and then those written in different handwriting. "The officers who brought you in tonight want to see you in jail."

Her stubbornness isn't helping, but she can't think of how to answer their questions in a way that won't make matters worse. "Why?" Anna asks in a small effort to cooperate.

"You jumped from the Bendler Bridge."

Anna lies. "I fell."

Dr. Winicke writes this on the chart. "The problem," he says, "isn't just your attempted suicide. Prostitution is also illegal."

"I am not a prostitute."

"What are you then?"

Silence.

"Do you work?"

A long pause and then she nods.

"So you're a *working* girl." He writes this on the chart.

Damn him. He's using her words against her. "That's not what I meant. I told you I'm not a prostitute."

"Where do you work, then? Who can vouch for you?"

She presses her lips together. Again, silence.

Whatever patience Dr. Winicke is willing to extend runs out. He sighs and lays the clipboard on the bed. "Your situation is far worse than you realize. Over a dozen witnesses claim that you threw yourself off that bridge tonight. Your body is covered in alarming scars." He glances at the chart. "Six of which appear to be from bullets. And eighteen"—he looks at Agatha in disbelief, needing confirmation—"*eighteen* seem to be stab wounds. Just how many times have you tried to kill yourself?"

"You don't understand."

"Yes I do. The life of a prostitute is very difficult."

"I am not a whore!" she screams and her throat is immediately raw. She can taste blood at the back of her mouth. All that coughing has left her with a raspy voice and a ragged esophagus.

"I'm afraid my exam suggests differently."

"What exam?" This is the first time she's ever seen Dr. Winicke, and he hasn't set a finger on her.

The nurses have the good grace to look ashamed, but Dr. Winicke matter-of-factly says, "You were unconscious for some time when you first arrived."

"You—"

"Performed a medical exam, yes. That is my job. I assessed your condition and learned a number of things."

Anna doesn't ask him for details but he continues anyway.

"For starters, you are significantly underweight and malnourished. You appear to be about twenty years old. Your body has endured significant trauma in the recent past, and you currently have some rather alarming bruises on your rib cage and tailbone." He waits for her to refute any of this. When she doesn't, he continues. "The thing that is most damning, however, is the other scar tissue. It's consistent with many of the *working girls* I see."

"I don't know what you're talking about."

He leans a little closer, not unkindly, simply pressing his advantage, trying to coax a confession. "I think you do. It is quite obvious that you have engaged in sexual congress."

30

Anastasia

THE WARNING

1918

Ipatiev House, Ekaterinburg, Russia
July 17, 1:00 a.m.

I can hear the cannons booming in my dreams. The White
Army coming to rescue us. That is what Cook told me earlier in the day when I helped him knead dough in the kitchen.
Our guards were nervous, muttering in the courtyard as Cook
went out to smoke a pilfered cigarette. He heard them talking
about the Whites and their rebel forces. "They are coming to
rescue us," Cook said, "and Yakov is growing more uneasy the
closer they get." The big guns fired all afternoon and into the
evening, the sound ricocheting off the hills surrounding Ekaterinburg. It reminded me of the morning the revolution spread
to the grounds of Alexander Palace.

The longer the White Army's cannons fired, the more restless our own guards became. They whispered in the hallways
and stood in the door, peering at that great wooden fence across
the yard as though they could see beyond it. Yakov and Semyon
disappeared after dinner. It was a welcome absence, and our
meal was almost lighthearted as a result. Later we went to bed,
feeling real hope for the first time in many months. I fell asleep
to the sound of those cannons, and it may as well have been
church bells ringing out our liberation.

Sometime later a hand slips over my mouth in the dark.

I wake instantly, trying to gasp for air, but the fingers press harder, pushing me back into my pillow. I can see nothing in the darkness. I have no idea what time it is, and a sudden, ferocious panic seizes my limbs.

"Ssshhh. Please. It's Tomas. You have to be quiet." Even at a whisper his voice is pitched high in fear. I still beneath his hand, but he doesn't pull it away. "You have to come with me."

I shake my head. Ivan's battered face is still fresh in my memory.

"You will die if you don't." Slowly, carefully, Tomas draws his hand away.

I can't see him so I reach for him instead, finding first his chest and then his shoulder with my hand. I cup his cheek in my palm and can feel the soft bristles of a young beard brush against my skin. "What are you talking about?"

"Please. I can't explain here. You have to trust me. We have to leave. Right now."

"Tomas. You're scaring me."

"Good!"

"No. Stop. This doesn't make any sense. Why are you here?"

"Ssshhh. You'll wake the others. I'll explain. I promise. Just meet me in that spot beneath the stairs. The one right outside the kitchen. Two minutes."

"I need to get dressed."

"There's no time for that!"

"All right." I sit up, trying to sweep the cobwebs from my mind. The sound of cannons is clearer now that I am awake. "Two minutes."

Tomas squeezes my hand and slips away without a noise. I don't even hear the door creak on its hinges. I sit on the edge of my bed counting slowly to one hundred and twenty and then pad barefoot to the door. It's open. So I slip into the hallway and wait, listening for the usual sounds of Ipatiev House in the night. Restless soldiers upstairs. Rusted pipes. Footsteps.

Snoring. But all is eerily quiet. I make my way to that alcove beneath the stairs, fingers lightly brushing the wall. Down the hall. Second right. Up three steps and around a sharp corner. When I reach the stairs Tomas grabs me and pulls me against him, heedless of the consequences.

"You're all right," he whispers against my throat. "I thought I was too late."

I try to resist, but he hugs me tighter, his entire body trembling, and that's when I realize he's crying. Tears dampen my neck and pool in the hollow of my throat. I do not know what to do with this boy weeping into my neck, so I let him hold me until the tears subside.

"What's wrong?" I run my fingers through Tomas's hair.

"Yakov called eleven soldiers into his office while your family was eating dinner. He said you will all be shot tonight."

He may as well have said we were all going to sprout feathers and fly away. "I don't understand."

"Don't you get it? Eleven victims. You. Your family. Your servants. One soldier for each captive."

I am still so tired and disoriented his words make no sense to me. I press the heels of my hands into my eyes. Shake my head.

Another round of cannon fire sounds in the distant hills. "Do you hear that?" Tomas asks.

I nod.

"That's the White Army. Yakov thinks they are coming to liberate your family."

"Are they?" Hope, sudden and bright, springs into my voice.

"I don't know. But it doesn't matter. They'll never get here in time. They are still five miles away. Yakov is determined to see you and your family dead long before they reach the front gate."

Slowly my mind catches up with his words. "How do you know this?"

"I have learned to pay attention and to listen very carefully."

"You overheard them?"

"It wasn't hard. They were bragging about it afterward."

I wish I could see his expression. I would like to know how he looks at me. But I can only run my fingers over his face. It is my turn to wipe the tears from his cheeks. He kisses the pads of my fingers when I brush them against his lips. Once again his arms loop around me, but gentle this time, at my waist. My response is swallowed by his kiss.

Tomas has to bend down several inches to press his forehead against mine. He rocks it back and forth, agitated. "You have to come with me. If we can get to the White Army you'll be safe."

"Right now? I'm not . . . I'm not even wearing shoes. My family. I . . ." The reality of what he's asking is impossible. "I'm in my nightgown."

"There is no time. None. Yakov is only waiting for the truck."

"What truck?"

Tomas moves his hands to my shoulders and squeezes urgently. I think he wants to shake me. To rattle my teeth and make me understand. His words come out strangled. "For the *bodies*. He intends to remove your bodies before dawn so no one will know what he's done."

Panic. Pure, unbridled terror. Fear like I had never known takes hold of me then. I want to take his hand and run. Every instinct in my body urges me to flee. I am ready to go right now, this second—I *want* to go running with him into the night—and then a thought comes so suddenly I am nauseous. "I can't leave my family. I have to warn them." A moan, deep in my throat. "My brother. He's still so sick."

Tomas is crying again. "We can't help them. The two of us can slip away. But eight people? It's impossible."

This is too much. I drop my face to my hands. Shake my head. "How will we even get out of here? The house is guarded. So are the grounds."

"Not tonight. They're preparing for . . . Yakov has most of the guards busy elsewhere." Tomas pulls me close and cradles my head against his chest. "If we go *right now* we can get away."

"You can't be certain of that."

"I *am* certain. That's where I've been tonight, finding a way out. The yard leads to the woods and that leads to the river and that leads to freedom."

"Why are you doing this? You saw what they did to Ivan. They'll do worse to you if we fail."

"Because I love you. Don't you know that already?"

I do. He has shown it a thousand different ways since we were thrown together. I should respond in kind. I want to. But he is asking me to abandon my family. How can I run for safety and leave everyone else behind? He is asking me to walk away without warning them. How can I doom them to such a fate? How can I choose between Tomas and my family? It is like choosing which side of my body to keep, the right or the left.

"How am I supposed to leave them, Tomas? How am I supposed to do that?"

"Let me take you. Let this be my fault. I will carry that decision for you. My entire life if I have to."

I hate crying. Utterly loathe it. And never more so than in the moments I need to cry the most. My eyes burn with tears and I cannot hold them back. "I *can't*."

I think Tomas might throw me over his shoulder and forcibly carry me from the house, if not for a sudden commotion in the courtyard. Shouting. The gate clattering open. The revving of an engine. And then voices by the front door, low but insistent.

Tomas's voice drains of all emotion. "The truck is here."

31

Anna

THE BENDLER BRIDGE

1920

The Netherlands Palace, Berlin
February 17, 1920

Frost is on the gate and Anna wraps her fingers around the iron bars, grateful she can still feel the cold, grateful that her hands aren't yet frozen solid. Her shawl has done little to keep her warm since she left the bus station, and she has long since misplaced her gloves. Perhaps on that ferry crossing the Rhine? She can't remember. Anna has no mental energy to spare for trivial details such as where she lost her gloves or how she got the tear in her stocking.

"What are you doing?" A man steps from the guardhouse beside her and approaches with the stiff, formal stride of a long-time soldier. His uniform is new but he looks old and phlegmy; the capillaries are broken in a delicate web along the end of his bulbous nose. Irritated, asthmatic puffs of breath trail behind him, and when he reaches her side he swats her hands away from the gate. "You can't be here."

"Please," she says, pulling a rumpled newspaper article from her pocket. "I must speak with Princess Irene."

If the Guard is curious, he doesn't let on. "Why?"

"I have news of her family."

The Guard yanks the newspaper from her hand and scans it. He looks from Anna, to the elaborate gate, then down the gravel drive toward the palace. All the windows on the first floor are lit with a soft electric glow, and, even from this distance, she can see thin curls of smoke drifting from the fireplaces. Anna can count five chimney stacks, but she wouldn't be surprised to find that there are more at the back of the palace away from view. Everything about the building speaks of warmth and comfort and opulence, and Anna cannot help but lean closer to inhale the faint smell of burning cedar. Again she reaches out for the gate and again the Guard knocks her hand away, this time rapping her knuckles in the process. She winces and shoves her hands into the folds of her shawl.

He turns his full attention to her, taking in the tattered black skirt and stockings. Her linen blouse is stained and torn at the cuffs, and there is a hole in the toe of her right boot. The borrowed shawl is the nicest of her garments, but even that is working-class, heavy and shapeless, knit with coarse wool. Anna is certain he has formed an opinion of her when his scowl turns to a leer.

But she is not proud, and this man doesn't scare her. "You have to let me in."

"I have to do no such thing. Now go away before I have you arrested. They don't let whores in the palace."

"I'm not—"

The Guard reaches out and grabs the folds of her shawl. He jerks her forward and she swats at his forearms. He has to bend low to growl in her face. "You are a fool if you think a little begging will get you through this gate. Princess Irene will feed me to the pigs if I let in trash like you. Now go away while I still have a mind to let you."

He sets his hand flat against her collarbone and shoves hard. The force sends Anna stumbling backward and she falls to the gravel driveway. Sharp pieces of stone dig through her skirt and into the skin covering her tailbone. She gasps and cries and then scrambles backward before he can reach out for her again.

"Go," he says, the command cruel and final.

And what other choice does she have? Anna sits on the ground for a moment longer, her pride and tailbone smarting, until finally, there on the frigid ground, her last, fragile thread of hope disintegrates. She has been running for so long. She has begged and stolen and lied. Trespassed. Crossed borders in the middle of the night and eaten things she cannot identify. Anna has slept in barns and under bridges. Every choice leading her here. To see the woman who lives beyond these walls, the one person, she believes, who can actually help her.

The Guard has already turned his back and retreated to the small rectangular guardhouse by the time Anna picks herself up and brushes the frost from her clothing. He watches her from his little perch, hands folded over a small lantern for warmth, eager to see her leave. She considers the gate for a moment. There was a time when she could have climbed it easily, but even then the twenty-foot drop to the ground on the other side would have likely given her a broken ankle. There's no point considering it now, so she throws a last, longing glance at the palace, then limps back the way she came. But instead of turning right, toward the bus station, she goes left toward the park. Raw pangs of hunger gnaw at her belly, and her fingertips tingle with cold. As she wanders deeper into the trees she counts her other afflictions: empty pockets, a bruised backside, a toothache. The sun set over an hour ago and Berlin is slowly going to sleep. The only signs of life come from ahead, along the Landwehr Canal, where lovers stroll beneath the gaslights, hands entwined, heads bent toward one another. So Anna continues in that direction because she has no other options, and she watches with a jealous, despairing ache as these couples laugh and nuzzle each other. They all have somewhere to go. They all have someone to go there with.

Both sides of the canal are bordered by neatly manicured footpaths. The smell of frost and pine needles is heavy in the air, and she stumbles along, pushing past the couples, startling them out of amorous embraces. It isn't until she reaches the bridge that Anna realizes she's crying—hard, guttural sobs that come from deep inside her. It's the sort of crying that makes her throat hurt and her nose run. Someone calls out behind her, asking if she needs help, but she ignores him. Anna goes to the middle of the bridge and looks at her shaky reflection in the water below. Pale and gaunt and fragile, it seems to mock her. She barely recognizes herself in the glassy black surface.

How could it come to this?

Anna is small and scared, and she has no stomach for blood. She's seen enough of that to last a lifetime. Too timid for other methods, she pursues the only option she has left. Anna leans over the rail and tumbles headfirst into the canal below. It is not gentle or elegant. It is a graceless plummet marked by flailing arms and flapping clothes. Anna lands hard, on her back, and the splash is spectacular. It feels as though she has fallen onto a slab of granite. The impact forces the air from her lungs in a rasping whoosh. It is only the ferocious cold and shocking pain that brings her back to her senses. Her heavy, sodden shawl pulls her beneath the surface. Her lungs burn and her eyes fix on the light of a single lantern from the path above. Her boots fill with water. She struggles in vain against the weight of her clothing. She resists pulling in a lungful of murky water. What a stupid thing she has done. What an idiotic, foolish, asinine thing. But it doesn't matter now because Anna is sinking fast.

32

Anastasia

THE CELLAR

1918

Ipatiev House, Ekaterinburg, Russia
July 17, 1:30 a.m.

"I love you too," I say, kissing Tomas hard. "Please take care of Jimmy."

I shove Tomas deeper into the shadows and step from the alcove just as the hallway lights come on. Yakov Yurovsky stands ten feet away.

The light is bright and harsh and I throw my hand across my eyes.

"What are you doing out of bed?" he demands.

Words. I can't find them. Cannot for the life of me summon a thought after what Tomas has just revealed. I gape at him stupidly and then, after a moment, point in the general direction of the bathroom. "Toilet," I say, but my voice is shaky and high so I swallow and try again. "I needed the toilet."

I am still in my nightgown, barefoot, and clearly disoriented. Nothing about me looks like a girl preparing to flee. So he says, "Go back to your room."

What else is there to do? I take one tentative step forward and then another, skirting around him and then rushing back to where my sisters are still sleeping. Jimmy lies sprawled across the foot of my bed right where I left him. A moment later he presses his cold nose into my thigh, welcoming me back. He is so accustomed to the sound and smell of Tomas that he didn't complain when he entered or when I wandered away after him. I scratch Jimmy's ears, trying to push aside the panicked cacophony in my mind.

Think. I have to think.

The hallway light remains on. It casts a yellow beam beneath the bedroom door, and I can faintly see the room now. Olga is turned to the wall. Tatiana is curled into the fetal position like a small, frightened child. Maria is sprawled on her back, one arm hanging off the bed, the other draped across her forehead. I want to wake them. To warn them that a monster is coming for us.

Jimmy is raised up on his forelegs, watching me intently, sniffing at the air. Searching for the source of my fear. The front doors bang open and there are more footsteps in the hall. A growl begins to build at the back of his throat, and it blooms into a full-throated bark when a heavy fist bangs on our bedroom door. Two more impatient knocks and then it swings open. Yakov hovers in the door, a dark silhouette, before he steps in and turns on the overhead light.

"Get up. And get dressed. There is trouble in the city and we have to take you to a safer place." The way he says this is so convincing that I wonder if Tomas is wrong. "Did you hear me?" Yakov asks.

I nod weakly. "Yes."

"Wake your sisters. Do as I said."

"What about everyone else?"

"I'm going to tell them now," he says and pulls the door shut behind him.

My sisters are roused but not fully awake. I have to shake them and repeat myself numerous times before I can get them into a sitting position. They rub their eyes. Yawn. Complain about the hour. Ask questions I can't answer.

"Where are we going?"

"What does this mean?

"Does Father know?"

I don't know. I don't know. I don't know. It becomes my mantra, repeated every few seconds as I tug on their arms and yank the pillows out from under their heads when they attempt to lie down again.

The only thing I know for sure is that we need to be prepared. So I throw open the enormous, heavy trunk and toss out the frivolous pillows and shawls that hide our jewel-studded undergarments.

"Put these on," I say. "As many as you can. We can't take anything else with us."

We help each other dress. Tightening corsets. Buttoning collars. Fastening belts. We all wear simple black skirts and white blouses. Nothing elaborate, nothing that would differentiate us from any other woman on the street if we are lucky enough to escape. We have to escape. That is the only option. The only acceptable outcome. Tomas is wrong. Tomas is wrong. Tomas *has to be* wrong. I repeat this to myself over and over as I help button and lace and belt my sisters.

I cannot wear my earrings, I cannot risk letting Semyon know I've gotten them back, so I tuck them into the pocket of my blouse praying desperately that I will see Tomas again. The four of us are huddled together when Yakov returns.

"Leave the dog," he says, "and follow me."

"Stay," I say to Jimmy when he leaps off the bed and tries to follow. I get down on my knees and pull that great black head against my neck. I hug him and stroke his ears. I run my hand down his back and he licks a tear from my cheek as my shoulders begin to tremble. "Stay," I whisper again. "Wait for Tomas. I love you, big dog. You have been a good friend to me. I am so sorry." I tell my loyal defender good-bye, then shut him inside the bedroom so he can't follow.

Father leads us into the courtyard carrying Alexey. My brother looks like a toddler, arms wrapped around Father's neck, face buried in his chest. Legs hanging limp. Utterly exhausted. Absolutely trusting. I can feel a fracture beginning deep within my chest. A growing ache that threatens to consume me.

Mother is a step behind Father, then my sisters and me, followed by the servants. No one speaks. No one questions Yakov's instructions. We wait quietly on the cobblestones, standing close to one another.

Father bends his mouth to Mother's ear and whispers, "We're finally going to get out of this place."

The fissure in my chest widens.

I want to tell them what is about to happen. I have to. But when I open my mouth to speak I hear the agonized braying of a dog. It comes from the clearing directly behind the house. I have never heard Jimmy make such a noise in all the years I've owned him. It is an unfamiliar, brokenhearted sound yet unmistakably his. I listen as he whines and cries and moves farther away into the woods that lead toward the river. The sound grows fainter and then the night is silent once more. I wait, certain Yakov will send someone after Tomas and Jimmy, terrified they will be caught.

"This way," Yakov says, concerned only with those of us who are in the courtyard. He leads us across the cobblestone, away from the waiting truck, and through another door. On the other side is a narrow hallway and then a steep staircase. I count each rickety wooden step on the way down. Twenty-three. At the bottom is another long hallway and then a set of double doors at the end. Yakov marches us toward those doors, passing two smaller, closed rooms on the way. Inside those rooms the thump and whisper of men.

"You will wait in there," he says, pointing to the double

doors at the end of the hall. "Until the other vehicles arrive. We must all leave together."

Maybe the lie is so egregious to me because I know. Perhaps I would believe him too if I hadn't been warned. I can do the same for them. I can warn them of Yakov's intent. But we have no weapons. No means of escape. There are ten soldiers on the grounds for every one of us. So I walk into the room with my family knowing that the only mercy I can extend is the gift of ignorance. And I know it's not enough.

The cellar is built into the hillside beneath Ipatiev House. Rectangular and damp, lit by a single bulb in the middle of the low ceiling, it is completely empty. I wonder briefly if this is the room where Yakov discovered Maria and Ivan. She's not crying, so I decide it must be one of the other rooms down the hall.

We were told that Ivan survived his punishment and is serving a prison sentence for treason two hundred kilometers away. But this information came directly from Yakov, and I doubt that even a word of it is true. I doubt that Ivan survived the day. Yakov Yurovsky is not a man who likes leaving witnesses to his cruelty.

"Why are there no chairs in here? Are we no longer allowed to sit?" Mother's voice drips with anger and arrogance, and of all the things she could say in that moment, it is the least helpful.

Yakov's dark eyes are filled with disdain and I see his true opinion of us then. Spoiled, entitled, separated from all reality. He despises everything we are and everything we represent. He believes that he is doing the world a great service in eliminating us. He hates us entirely. These thoughts are plainly written on his face when he gives Mother an exaggerated bow and says, "I will bring two. One for you and one for the boy."

When the chairs come Mother drops into the first with the air of a martyr. She presses the back of her hand to her forehead and closes her eyes. It is warm and damp in the cellar and she fans herself. Father settles Alexey into the second, crouching beside him to make sure he is comfortable. My poor brother. So small and ill and feeble. After a moment he pulls his knees up and lays his head against them, eyes drooping in exhaustion.

"I will go check on the vehicles," Yakov says. He closes the doors behind him, and I hear the lock slide into place. There is no other way out of the room.

Mother sighs. "I hope this doesn't take long. I hate waiting around."

There is a unique sort of misery that comes with standing around in the middle of the night after you have been woken from a dead sleep. My mind ticks along two speeds too fast while my body lags behind, swaying and struggling to stay upright. My sisters lean against the wall while my parents huddle near Alexey. I see Cook reach for Dova's hand and she weaves her fingers through his. No one speaks. And the only person who even appears nervous is Botkin. He keeps looking at the door with squinted eyes as though deliberating and finally moves to stand in front of my brother. I can almost hear the physician's mind making a diagnosis and then desperately trying to think of a solution. He knows.

We wait only ten minutes before the sound of revving engines fills the courtyard outside. I hear the rattle of the lock, then the doors are pushed open and Yakov steps inside followed by eleven soldiers.

Each of them holds a weapon. Rifles with bayonets attached. Pistols. Several have knives in sheaths at their waists. All of them, except Yakov, are drunk. Semyon is a man who will violate a woman on a train in the middle of the night but cannot kill her unless he has spent the evening with a bottle of vodka. His eyes, fixed on Olga, are hazed by liquor and drooping at the corners, but still they are filled with regret.

"All of you stand," Yakov says.

My parents and Alexey rise from their chairs, confused.

Yakov lifts a piece of paper and reads aloud, "The Praesidium of the Ural Regional Soviet has declared you all to be sentenced to death."

33

Anna

Schreiber Boardinghouse, Berlin
February 17, 1920

Anna wakes to the fading light of early evening. She has slept through the day again. Dammit, dammit, dammit, she thinks as she throws back the covers and crosses the narrow room to look out the window. The sun hovers above the Rhine, turning the serpentine river gold. It will be dark in an hour.

She meant to rise and dress this morning. She had every intention of going about her day as usual. But the nightmares are back, and once again they left her trembling and nauseous for much of the night. Anna remembers laying her head on the pillow as dawn pushed against the sky. She remembers how relieved she was to close her eyes and not see the gory images that have flooded her nightmares for the last two years. She remembers how good it felt to drift away into the oblivion of dreamless sleep.

But there are consequences to losing another day, and Anna is only now beginning to realize them. Her job, for starters, is certainly forfeited. As is this week's paycheck. She's had the position less than a month, and it was a good fit too. Needle-work at the Mueller Shirtwaist Factory. Anna got the job fifteen minutes into her interview when she showed the supervisor her finish work. She and her sisters learned to sew at the insistence of their mother, and it is one of the only marketable skills she has. Anna never meant to keep the job for long; it was simply a means to secure lodgings and buy some time before figuring out what to do next.

"*Scheiße*," Anna hisses, stumbling through the pile of clothes on the floor, looking for her skirt and blouse. Without that job she has no money.

There is a loud, aggressive pounding on her bedroom door and then, "Fräulein! Are you well?" The high, clipped voice of her landlady.

"Yes. I'm fine."

"You did not leave your room today."

She scrambles for an excuse. "I'm feeling poorly."

An impatient sigh. "Do not forget that rent is due in the morning."

And then the woman is gone without another sound. Anna marvels at how quiet the woman is, how she seems to hover above the floor when she walks, with nary a footfall or squeaking floorboard. It's disconcerting.

Anna does not have rent money. Or money for anything else. Dinner has long since been served and put away—her landlady is something of a fanatic about mealtimes—but that is little comfort to the rumbling of her stomach. She bought three *Brötchen* last night when she ventured out, but there is only one roll left now, stale and wrapped in yesterday's newspaper. It will have to do.

Anna chews and swallows the dry bread, chasing it down with tepid water from the jug on her nightstand. She's about to wad the paper up and throw it away when a headline on the front page catches her attention: *Princess Irene Uses Considerable Resources to Find Imperial Family*.

She drops to the edge of her disheveled bed and smooths the paper over her legs. Anna reads how the sister of Empress Alexandra has appealed to the courts for help investigating the disappearance of the imperial family. She refuses to believe the rumors that they are dead. She will not believe it, the article says, until she has solid evidence. She will not believe it until she is able to bury her sister. Anna reads the article again. Her eyes drift back to the headline and a paragraph detailing how Irene is offering a reward for information that leads to the tsar's family. Irene has resources. She is motivated. Anna wonders if she would believe the impossible if it came knocking on her door.

———

An hour later, Anna gathers her clothes and stands before the chipped mirror. She pulls the tattered nightgown over her head and drops it to the floor. She studies her body, the reality of what she is about to present to Princess Irene of Hesse and by Rhine. Hideous scars, many of them still red and puckered. She is fairly certain those will elicit pity. It's the other marks she's worried about: ten striated lines running vertically beneath her belly button. It's only been a year. The stretch marks have not yet faded to silver. Their meaning is clear.

Anna decides that telling her story to Irene is a chance worth taking. Her only other option is being turned into the street first thing in the morning. She dresses quickly, then counts the coins in her skirt pocket. She has enough for the ferry and a bus ticket that will take her through the city. It's only five miles; she could walk but that would take hours. The streets of Berlin are not kind to women who walk alone at night. Decision made, Anna puts the newspaper article in her pocket and leaves the boardinghouse to find Princess Irene.

Antonescu Refugee Camp, Bucharest, Romania
January 1919

Anna is not a screamer. She knows that thrashing and shriek-ing won't stop the pain, nor will it stop the baby from com-ing. It will only anger the Midwife and upset her neighbors in this sprawling, rank tent city. So she sits cross-legged on her thin mattress and rocks back and forth, letting each con-traction roll across her body. They're only minutes apart now and they begin in her lower back, as though someone is shoving a branding iron into the base of her spine. They wrap around her abdomen, tightening, squeezing until she is conscious of nothing but pain, until her eyes water and her breath comes in heaving little gasps.

And then nothing. The vise releases and for a few brief, wonderful seconds there is no pain, only exhaustion and a lingering terror that she cannot push aside. But this has been going on since late yesterday, and Anna knows the respite is short. The contractions have slowly increased, coming closer together, giving her less rest in between. She has been riding this wave for fifteen hours.

"You need to lie down," the Midwife says when the pool of moisture beneath Anna spreads across the mattress. "Your water has broken. It will be soon now."

Not soon enough, though. Because what she had taken for pain earlier is nothing compared to what is wringing her body now. And she is lost. Scared. Her face sweats, but her hands and feet are cold. She is shaking and overwhelmed. She is hungry and thirsty and nauseous all at once. Anna is angry with the women who huddle in the doorway of her tent, drawn by the communal instinct of childbirth. They whisper and shake their heads. She feels their condemnation from five feet away. But they know nothing about her and have no right to judge. She wants to scream and order them to leave but she doesn't have the breath.

Anna leans back on her elbows, knees apart, as the Midwife scoots her dress up around her swollen belly. She had no idea a part of her could grow so large. It is obscene. It is fascinating. She hates it and she is protective of it at once.

Anna bears down and it feels as though her entire body is being turned inside out.

"Don't hold your breath," the Midwife says. "Try to relax."

Anna releases a guttural, furious growl and a string of profanities that makes the Midwife laugh. "Much better."

There is no break between contractions now. They come, one after another, wave upon wave, each more intense and painful than the last. She drops her head to the mattress. Two of the women move forward to hold her legs. They mutter calming, maternal things as she weeps and tries to catch her breath. Above her the tent is translucent, letting a watery brown light in through the dirty canvas. She counts the stitches in the seams.

The Midwife goes quiet, working quickly now to mop up the growing mess between Anna's legs.

"What's wrong?" one of the attendants asks.

"Too much blood," the Midwife mutters. "She's very small. She needs to get this baby out quickly."

They urge her to push harder. And she does. Anna pushes until the edges of her vision blur and her lips grow numb.

"Better," the Midwife says. "Now do it again."

She does this a dozen times. After a while she can no longer keep her eyes open. She cannot lift her arms. Again and again and again Anna pushes until her entire body convulses with one last spasm, and then she feels a *whoosh* and release. Her legs are set gently on the mattress, and the women who have tended her now move to help the Midwife. Their voices blend together in a jumble of words that she disregards entirely when she hears a tiny helpless squall. It is so timid and weak, and her entire being is pulled toward the sound.

She feels tugging and wiping and pushing as this little stranger who has taken her body hostage is separated from her completely.

"It is a boy," the Midwife says, but not to Anna. "Wrap him. Take him to the nurse. The social worker will be here soon."

Anna tries to protest but can only get out a single word. "No." They have not discussed this. She has not given consent. Anna has not even seen the child and he is already gone, the tent flaps falling back into place, a cold breath of wind on her bare skin.

She is dizzy. Exhausted. But still Anna tries to struggle into a sitting position. The Midwife sets a firm hand against her breastbone and pushes her back to the mattress. "Stay still. I have to sew you up. You've lost a lot of blood."

Another word, all that she can manage. "Baby."

There is genuine pity in the Midwife's voice when she answers. "You didn't really think you could keep him, did you? An unmarried woman? Abandoned. Penniless. It is better this way. He will be given to a family that will care for him. Don't worry. He will never remember where he came from."

But I will remember, Anna thinks as her eyes grow heavy and her limbs become weak. I will always remember.

34

Anastasia

THE FIRING SQUAD

1918

Ipatiev House, Ekaterinburg, Russia
July 17, 2:45 a.m.

Knowing doesn't stop the hysteria. I feel the panic hit my bloodstream in a hard, cold rush, first freezing my body, then turning it to liquid. My knees buckle and I reach for the wall.

The cellar fills with a chorus of "No!" as everyone shakes their heads and wails. Father steps forward and demands, "What do you mean?"

"This," Yakov says without further explanation. He simply draws the pistol from the holster at his side, aims it at Father's chest, and fires.

The gunshot in the small room is like the sound of a cannon being fired within my skull. And then the world erupts in violence.

It is a direct hit to the heart, and Father drops to his knees. I am glad that I stand off to the side and cannot see his face. I don't want to know what passes across it in his final moment. Yakov's shot wakes the soldiers from their stupor and they too turn their guns on Father, firing madly. Botkin, Trupp, and Cook are caught in the volley of bullets, and I see each of them fall, torn open by gunfire.

They fire and they fire. The room fills with smoke and the acrid scent of gunpowder. Chunks of plaster and splinters of wood explode from the wall behind us and I crouch, screaming in my corner, with Olga and Tatiana beside me. We are unable to move. Unable to look away.

There is no end to the bloodshed. Yakov turns and fires, point-blank, at Mother. Her head snaps back and she drops into her chair, then folds sideways onto the floor in a heap. The back of her head is gone entirely, and the jeweled hair clip she always wears rests on the floor beside her, covered in bits of things I don't want to name.

When Yakov and Semyon turn their pistols on Alexey, the fissure in my chest rips apart completely. I want to close my eyes, to press my hands over my ears, but my body will not respond. I cannot turn away, nor can I hear the sound of my own screaming above the gunfire. I watch my brother fall, and I die one hundred deaths in the time it takes him to hit the floor.

Maria is gone. A single dark hole in her forehead. Her round blue eyes are open, staring blankly at Mother as though pleading for forgiveness. Eyelashes still wet with tears.

Two of the soldiers stand there gaping at the carnage and then fall to their knees, vomiting.

Tatiana and Olga tremble violently as Yakov leads Semyon toward us. We scramble backward until we reach the wall, and then we watch them draw closer through the smoke. There is moaning and crying on the other side of the room. A man, Botkin, maybe. His misery is dispatched with a single gunshot.

Dova wakes at the sound and pushes herself onto her hands and knees. She is bleeding everywhere. One of her ears is gone. Three fingers on her right hand are missing. But she stands anyway. A soldier fires, but his gun is empty, so he goes after her with his bayonet, stabbing her repeatedly as she runs along the wall. Yakov stops to watch the horrific scene, head tilted to the side, curious about how she could still be alive. By the time

Dova falls, the soldier is sweating, and then he too bends over and retches onto the bloody, gore-covered floor.

"Please," Olga says, reaching a hand toward Semyon. She sounds like a tiny, frightened bird. "I will do anything. Just don't kill me."

"Shoot her," Yakov says.

Semyon looks ill. His eyes are wet and glassy and he's sweating. Semyon gags twice but presses the back of his hand against his mouth, then lifts his rifle and sets it against his shoulder. He takes a deep breath. His eyes are focused, not on her face, but on the wall behind her.

"No." Olga shakes her head. Begins to sob. "Don't."

I do not beg as Yakov raises his pistol. But neither do I watch. I close my eyes and wait, hoping for instant darkness. They fire.

It sounds like tiny bombs going off beside my ears, and it feels like a punch in the ribs. One after another after another, each knocking the breath from my lungs. I feel others tear through my upper arms and my thigh. The side of my neck. My collarbone. But nothing pierces the corsets. Mother's ridiculous jewels form a diamond-hard barrier that protects my heart and lungs.

Tatiana gurgles beside me. Her eyes are desperate as she presses her hands to the wound in her neck. Blood pours through her fingers and down her blouse, unstoppable, unrelenting. And I see her life drain away with each frantic pump of her heart. Seconds later she is gone, without a word, collapsed to the floor beside me.

My eyes sting. My lungs hurt and I can't get a full breath. My ribs are broken. I taste smoke and dirt and blood. I hear the dying, last breaths of those I love. When I reach for Olga's hand she does not squeeze it back. It lays limp in mine, slick with blood.

Yakov stares at me, disbelieving, then points his pistol at my head and pulls the trigger again. A vacant click as the hammer strikes air. The gun is empty, but he tries again and again, furious. On the fourth attempt he throws the pistol against the wall and yanks a bayonet from the hand of a stupefied soldier who stands looking at the remains of my tiny, helpless brother.

"Why won't you die?" Yakov screams, then rushes me with a feral howl.

I do not think it is mercy that causes him to lift the butt of that rifle and bring it down hard against my temple. I think he does not want me to fight back while he stabs me. The man is exhausted from slaughter, overwhelmed by the sheer work required to kill eleven people.

Darkness swallows me immediately. And I am glad because it blunts the rise and fall of that bayonet, sparing me every brutal slash of Yakov's blade. But I am not dead. Not yet. And I do not stay unconscious for long.

35

Anna

PRAYING TO DIE

1918

There is blood everywhere. On her face. Her hands. Her clothes. It covers the floor and the wall behind her. She can taste it in her mouth and smell it in her hair. Like rust and salt and liquid warmth. She can feel it streaming from her body. There is also pain. Pain beyond reckoning or explanation. It feels as though someone has pulled white-hot coals from the bowels of hell and placed them at dozens of points along her body. Her temple. Her collarbone. In the dip beneath her right shoulder. Ribbons of fire on her abdomen and across her thighs. Flames scar her calf and her left ankle. The blaze wipes the breath from her lungs and every coherent thought from her mind.

"Stop moving," a male voice hisses in her ear. The words are distorted, as though they come from a great distance. "Stop screaming."

Anna doesn't realize she is screaming. She feels the burn in her lungs, the panting, but she can hear nothing except the bizarre, undulating sound of his voice and a faint ringing. It is as though her ears have been stuffed with cotton.

"I can't help you if you're screaming. You have to be quiet. Please." Again that voice, desperate, begging now. He grips her under the arms and pulls backward, dragging her across the floor. Taking her somewhere away from this carnage. Away from this blood.

———

Anna is naked. Laid out flat on a table in a cold room beneath a single, flickering lightbulb. Someone is touching her, running a wet cloth across her wounds. Dabbing gently. Hesitantly. Trying to soak up the blood.

"There's so much." It's that same male voice she heard earlier. Moments ago? Hours? A lifetime? Time has lost all meaning. The voice is clearer now. Panicked. "It won't stop."

Anna tries to open her eyes, but her lashes are glued together with clumps of something thick and sticky. She sees only a ribbon of light and figures moving within it. Male and female. Older and younger. Steady and unsure.

"We have to stitch the wounds."

"I don't—"

"You don't have a choice," the Woman admonishes. Her voice has the gravelly sound of someone who is capable of doing what needs to be done. "But first we have to remove the debris."

A finger presses against the wound in her thigh, and Anna can feel the little shard of metal slice farther into the muscle. "We'll start with this one. Hand me the tweezers."

The sound that comes rattling up Anna's throat is inhuman and involuntary. Animalistic. There are so many places on her body that hurt. A hundred fires burning on her skin. But this one suddenly flares to life, bigger than all the others. She can feel the wet, warm trickle of blood slip down her thigh as the tweezers plunge into her flesh and pull the ragged chunk of metal from her body. And then the small *clink* as it's dropped into a glass.

"You have to pick," the Woman says. "Extraction or stitches. I can't do both."

His voice is tremulous when he answers. "Extraction."

"Try to keep your hands steady. It will hurt her less that way."

"Isn't there anything we can give her?"

A snort. "Does this look like a hospital to you?"

"She's in pain."

"She's lucky to be alive. But she won't be for much longer if we don't work quickly."

A warm hand presses against the tiny mound in her belly. "Is this what I think it is?"

"Yes," the Woman says, and then they go to work, prodding her body, inch by inch, plucking chunks of metal from muscle and bone. Once each wound is cleared, a needle is pushed through her skin. Perforations and sutures. Over and over. At some point Anna passes out completely, her body goes limp, her last thought a prayer for death.

36

Anastasia

Tomas was the third soldier who entered our compartment that night on the train as we rattled toward Ekaterinburg. Tomas who slid the door shut behind him and promised no one would hurt me. Tomas who risked extending his hand to a ferocious and protective Jimmy.

"You can put that paper knife away," he whispered. "I know you keep it in your boot. I've seen it. I have a gun and no one can get past that."

"Tomas." I had no voice at all. Nothing but a wretched, terrified squeak.

I saw him shift forward but he stopped. Tomas very slowly slid the rifle from his shoulder and leaned it against the wall beside my berth. He folded his hands behind his back. "Are you all right, Alexey?" he asked.

A muffled sob from the upper bunk. "I think so."

"What about Joy?"

"She's scared."

"Are you scared too?"

"Yes."

"There's nothing wrong with being scared. But you're safe now, I promise. Do you believe me?"

Alexey didn't answer right away but finally he said, "I think so."

"Are you tired?"

"Yes."

"You can go to sleep. I won't let anyone in this cabin. I promise."

Tomas stood by the door waiting to hear Alexey's breath settle, waiting while my sisters' screams turned to muffled cries, and then defeated silence. He stood there waiting for almost an hour watching me, and only when my brother began to snore did he speak again.

"Will you let me hold you?" he asked. "I hear your teeth chattering. I know you're terrified and I cannot bear it."

"I don't know what to do."

"There is nothing you can do, Anastasia. Let me hold you. Please."

I nodded.

Tomas moved slowly toward the berth. He offered his hand to Jimmy again, asking his permission as well, then scratched him between the ears. Only when Jimmy began to wag his tail did Tomas sit beside me. He pushed the hair away from my face and the tears away from my cheeks.

"I'm so sorry," he said, gently stretching out beside me. "I couldn't stop this."

"It isn't your fault."

"It's wrong," he whispered in my ear. "And I am sorry."

"You've already said that."

"I will say it all night long."

That's when the tears came. Hard, guttural, chest-heaving sobs. The kind of crying that leaves your throat raw and your eyes stinging. Tomas let me come unhinged. He let me wail and beat my fists against his chest. And when I was spent, he wrapped his arms around me and whispered in my ear. He stroked my hair. And he apologized a thousand times as the night stretched long.

Neither of us slept. And we did not talk. Every time I flinched at some noise he pulled me tighter. Every time one of my sisters cried out in pain he set his palm over my ear. Every time a soldier laughed in the corridor he damned them to hell. And twice when the door to our cabin opened he flew from my berth and grabbed the drunken soldier by the throat and growled that I was his and he didn't share. We were not bothered again after the second attempt.

Tomas waited until the car grew quiet and then he waited longer, making certain the threat had passed, before he slipped away. He did not say good-bye and I did not thank him because such words were useless. He could only spare one, so he spared me. He saved me that night on the train to Ekaterinburg.

But Tomas could not save me tonight in the cellar. I had my chance. I could have gone with him. It was insanity to stay. I know that. But we would have been discovered sooner or later. Yakov would have stopped at nothing to find me. And the price would have been Tomas's life as well. But he is still alive. And he has Jimmy. That will have to be enough.

I am roused again when Yakov and his men begin unloading the bodies from the back of the truck. But I cannot open my eyes. I cannot move. Nor do I know where we are. Dawn will be here soon, and the men are nervous, rushing through their work. Greedy hands rip off my corset in the dark, searching for jewels. Once every bit of treasure has been plundered from our bodies they drag us, wrapped in sheets, toward the entrance of an old, collapsed mineshaft. It is not ideal. But they are running out of time.

"Just put them in," Yakov says. "We'll come back later and bury them."

My ribs explode in agony when they toss me onto the cold, hard ground. I want to scream but I can't. Beneath those shattered ribs one of my lungs has ceased to work entirely, and the other is slowly filling with liquid. Gurgling. Every breath shallow, strained, and heavy.

The soldiers shuffle away, the truck roars to life, and then I am alone, each breath hard-won and coming more slowly than the last. My family is gone. Botkin. Dova. Cook and Trupp. Every one of them dead. And I would think this a great mercy but for the sound of the cannons in the distance and the barking of a dog nearby.

Anna

THE MUNITIONS FACTORY

1918

Anna doesn't mean to drop the grenade. It is cupped in her palm one moment and the next it is falling in a strange, slow arc, tumbling end over end like some sort of dislodged pineapple. She knows that she should reach out and grab it, that she should stop it from smashing to the scuffed concrete floor. But her body is frozen and her thoughts sluggish, stuck on the telegram she received this morning and the two dozen words that irrevocably altered her life:

> The Secretary of War desires me to express his deep regret that your fiancé, Hans Nowak, was killed in action in Amiens, France, on August 9.

Anna cannot command her limbs to obey the order that her mind is shouting. So she watches the grenade fall, then bounce and skitter, the slim silver pin flying from the arming mechanism. The grenade comes to a stop where her supervisor stands ten feet away, his back turned, shouting instructions into the busy, clamoring factory. Anna knows that there are seven seconds from when the pin is dislodged to when the grenade explodes, yet she does not move. Does not speak.

It is as though her mind was cleaved upon reading that telegram: one half eerily calm and the other disintegrating into myriad pieces that ricocheted inside her skull. But between these two halves a curtain was drawn, and Anna's conscious mind was trapped on the still, quiet side, unable to process the horrific reality that Hans is dead.

Six seconds. Anna pushes against that dense barrier in her mind but she cannot access the necessary panic or the words to warn her supervisor. She cannot step away or run.

Anna walked the two miles to the factory today. She donned her cap and apron like she has every day for the last year. Stuffed wool in her ears to muffle the incessant rattle and clang of the machinery. She went to her place at the end of the assembly line and for two hours she did her job, unable to think or cry or feel. All emotion muffled, all reality blurred. There was only the work in front of her, the ability to do the next thing.

Five seconds. She may as well hear the tick of a clock in her mind, counting down until the people in front of her are obliterated.

Hans was so alive, so warm, so intimate just a few months ago, pressed against her in the dark, whispering and laughing in her ear, hands exploring all the swells and hollows of her body. He cannot be gone from her. She did not feel his passing. August 9 came and went without so much as a shudder in her soul. Without any sense that he had slipped away. How could she not have known? It shouldn't be possible. And yet, somehow, it is. Hans is dead, and he will never know that she carries his child, that a piece of him has taken root inside of her.

Four seconds. She tries to speak but still the words do not come.

So Anna did her job all morning. And then she lifted the grenade from its place within the assembly wheel and checked the safety mechanisms. Striker, lever, and pin. She rolled it over in her hand, examining the compact metal ball. It was identical to the others except for the fact that the triggering pin was loose, pulled an inch out from the shell.

Three seconds. She lifts her hand. Tries to wave. Tries to get her supervisor's attention.

When Anna first noticed the loose pin, she looked around the room for her supervisor. That is protocol. He is the only person on the floor who is allowed to reset the pin. In all the time that Anna has worked here he has had to do it only three times, and never for her. But just as her supervisor's name formed on her tongue there was a nudge deep within her. A gentle, prodding poke. An acknowledgment of existence. Not so much a kick, but a greeting. Hans's child saying hello. She gasped. The grenade fell from her hand.

Two seconds. The curtain in her mind shudders and splits apart at the realization that she too is about to die. Hans's child is about to die. There is no time to run or scream or hide. No time to pray. The only thing she can do before her entire field of vision detonates into blinding white light is fold in upon herself and press her hands against the small, firm swell of her belly.

Hellfire.

Thunder.

Shrapnel.

A cloud of red as her supervisor is eviscerated before her eyes.

Franziska Annalie Schanzkowska is blown backward into the wall, jagged bits of metal ripping into her temple, torso, and thighs.

I Told You So

Oh, don't look at me like that. I *never* promised you a happy ending. I have lived long enough to know that such things do not exist. In the end there is only the truth, and it isn't my fault that you don't like it very much. I warned you about this at the beginning. I said you might not forgive me. But you insisted on hearing this story anyway. Everyone does. You're all so enamored with the legend. Yet here is what you, and all the others, fail to understand: there would be no legend without me. *I* am the one who stopped her from being a tragic little footnote in history. *I* kept Anastasia Romanov alive for decades.

She *needed* me.

You don't like to hear that, of course. But I did what I did, and I am not sorry for it. Don't you understand what it is to suddenly know that everything is lost and that you are left entirely alone? Can you see, then, why I persisted down this path? My fiancé dead. My body ruined. My child taken from me. You would have done the same thing in my position.

And, like me, you would have enjoyed it for a while because it was fun. Luxurious. People giving you things. Throwing money at you. *Bowing*. This new life so different from anything you've ever known that you become addicted to it. What little guilt you feel is assuaged when you see how desperately they want this fiction to be true. How badly they want their princess to be alive. So you let them take up your cause, to begin fighting your battles. Then, many years later, you wake up and realize it's too late. You can't back out now. Your only choice is to embrace the lie, to *become* it.

You're angry now. I can see it there, written on your face. *Good*. Now is when you can truly understand what I've been getting at all this time. You have proven my point. I might have told the lie, but you perpetuated it with your irrational hope and your willing suspension of disbelief. Don't you see? You are angry with me—not because I was desperate and broken and wanted more from my life, but because it was just so *easy* leading you to water.

You *wanted* to believe that I was Anastasia.

Author's Note

A word of caution to the overeager reader:

In high school I went through what I like to call my "Stephen King phase," meaning that I read everything he'd written over the span of my sophomore and junior years. I loved his books (still do), but I had a certain order in which I read them. I began with the Author's Note. There are few things more enjoyable to me than a good Author's Note, and King's are spectacular. Which brings me to my point. If you also like to flip to the end and read these missives first, I must ask you to make an exception here. Spoilers abound below, and you will be displeased to get your answers before you have asked the questions. In this instance you would be well advised not to peek behind the curtain. Turn back now. You will thank me in the end.

That said, I never meant to write this book. I am not that girl who has been fascinated with Anastasia Romanov since childhood. Princesses were never my thing. I was turned off by them, entirely, upon reading "The Princess and the Pea" in kindergarten. Any girl who complains about a lump in her mattress would not be my first pick for a sleepover. And what else, really, is a novel but a 350-page sleepover? Every book I've ever loved has gone to bed with me at some point in the reading process. Decades later, my aversion to royalty remains intact. For the most part, I have little interest in reading about the aristocracy or the privileged rich. I grew up with dirt floors, kerosene lanterns, and no indoor plumbing. I bathed in rainwater heated on a woodstove. But I'm grown now and I've made a different life for myself. I live in a normal house in a normal neighborhood, and my children roll their eyes when I tell them I had to shovel snow in the winter just to reach the outhouse. They are not impressed. My husband, however, has seen where I come from, and he understands why my sympathies still lie with the lost, the downtrodden, and the disadvantaged. He would be the first to explain why I am drawn more toward Anna Anderson than to the young grand duchess. And that's why I wrote this novel in the end. Because there are two sides to this story: one shimmering with privilege and affluence and nobility, the other blunted by sorrow and privation and neglect. What we forget as a culture is that *both* stories are worthy of our attention.

But I digress. I had another novel in mind when the idea for this book crashed into my life. It was another moment in history. A different mystery in a different part of the world, and I plan to get back to that story at some point. Hopefully soon. But this one showed up uninvited and pre-empted all of my plans. I'm still a bit peeved about it, to be honest. I've never liked being told what to do, and this novel did exactly that.

Write me, it demanded.

Nope, I replied, not gonna do it.

It dug in its heels.

I cussed vociferously (a thing I excel at though I try not to do so in public).

It was unyielding.

So I went to my literary agent, the wise and lovely Elisabeth Weed, for backup. I don't have time for this, I said. You don't have time for this, I said. Tell me to get back to work on the other thing that we all agreed that I would write next.

We need to talk to your editor, she said.

It was over at that point, but I still thrashed around a bit for good measure. A token protest. I *knew*. I knew this would be my next novel the moment I read about the German authorities pulling Anna Anderson from that canal in Berlin. She brought me to this story because she was a nobody. Fräulein Unbekannt. Miss Unknown. And, God help me, I have a soft spot for nobodies. Little did I know at the time how much trouble she would be and how her name would become my own personal curse word (I invented several in her honor), and how I would wish, a thousand times over, that I'd chosen to write about the history of barbed wire instead. Anything but this tangled, sentient, malevolent novel. Because of her I spent the better part of a year up to my armpits in Bolsheviks—not a thing any decent woman would sign up for.

Anna Anderson has been called "a cunning psychopath," a "vulgar adventuress," and a "first-rate actress." In other words, she is perfect fodder for a novel. She has been assigned the role of villain for decades. But I like to think she is misunderstood. I believe there was so much more to her life and her motives than her detractors care to admit. Her supporters are equally blinded by their own opinions, however, and it was nearly impossible to find a resource that did not blatantly try to tell me what to think about her from the outset. So my goal with this book was to let you make up your own mind. I wanted you to see the evidence both sides had to offer, and I wanted you to be unsure all the way through, because that is how Anna's contemporaries felt. They did not have the benefit of history or DNA or proof. They only had what sat before them: a scarred, maligned woman with a striking resemblance to Anastasia Romanov.

It will come as no surprise to anyone even vaguely familiar with Romanov history that I had to take liberties with this story. I did so primarily because the historical record contains a cast of hundreds, and that is simply untenable for a novel of any sort, much less one that is already complex and nonlinear. I've no time to list all the changes I made, or the reasons for them, but here are a handful, all of them necessary for the sake of clarity and narrative drive. I combined the two Romanov tutors—Charles Sydney Gibbes and Pierre Gilliard—into one man and let him go by the name of Gilliard. I combined the figures of Yakov Sverdlov (the man who gave orders to assassinate the Romanov family), Vasily Yakolev (the man who took control of the Romanov family in Tobolsk), and Yakov Yurovsky (the man who ultimately carried out the orders to slaughter them in Ekaterinburg) into one man—Yakov Yurovsky— simply because I had no easy way of differentiating between so many Yakovs, and only room for one besides. This compilation is meant to be a living symbol of the Romanov demise. I gave Evgeny Koblinsky the nickname "Leshy" so his character would not get muddled with that of Alexander Kerensky. Koblinsky. Kerensky. I find these Russian names all sound the same. It's damnably confusing to me so I thought to spare the reader as best I could. The man I call Semyon never existed in real life, though many others like him did. He was simply a means of bridging the three different men who held the family captive during the novel. I am afraid that Anastasia's dog—the sweet, loyal, protective Jimmy—did not survive that night in Ekaterinburg. There are differing accounts of what happened to him, but they all end with his passing. I have a big, black dog myself, and I very badly wanted him to live. So I allowed it to happen in print. It's a small deviation from the truth, and I am not sorry for it. You will, however, be delighted to know that Alexey's dog, Joy, did make it out of Ipatiev House alive. She went on to live for many years.

A few biographies I turned to again and again while writing *I Was Anastasia* were *The Romanov Sisters* by Helen Rappaport; *The Romanovs* by Simon Sebag Montefiore; *The Riddle of Anna Anderson* by Peter Kurth; *The Last Days of the Romanovs* by Helen Rappaport; *The Resurrection of the Romanovs* by Greg King and Penny Wilson; *The Jewels of the Romanovs* by Stefano Papi; *Anastasia: The Lost Princess* by James Blair Lovell; and *The Romanovs: The Final Chapter* by Robert K. Massie.

Many of the events and conversations portrayed in this book actually happened, and some of the details used therein were drawn from the books listed above. Among many, many things I learned from them is how the Romanovs lived under house arrest, what jewels they sewed into their clothes—"every corset, coat, camisole, belt, and hat," as Montefiore describes in *The Romanovs;* how they interacted with servants, how they squandered one of the greatest dynasties on earth, the devastating reality of Alexey's hemophilia, how the family became friends with some of their captors, and, most regrettably, what happened on the train to Ekaterinburg and also in that cellar on the last night of their lives. I learned about the weather in Ekaterinburg and the garden at Alexander Palace. I learned about Anna Anderson's wedding and her visits with Maria Rasputin. At times, when appropriate, I used actual bits of dialogue drawn from these biographies, usually as recorded in letters. This was particularly true with the Anna Anderson biographies. Her friends and supporters kept meticulous records and were more than willing to speak to the press. Sometimes I included newspaper clippings, excerpts from letters, or court verdicts. Sometimes I drew details from the correspondence of the Romanov servants and used it to add color and authenticity to the narrative. One such example is a line in chapter 16 where Anastasia says their days "took on a pattern of frost, thaw, sunshine, and darkness." This is something Anna Demidova (the character I call Dova—because another Anna would have been too confusing) wrote in a letter to a friend in November of 1917. I took the liberty of using it and attributing it to Anastasia. I wanted to present their situation as authentically as possible. Anastasia's nickname. The pets' names. The small rivalries within the family. It's all accurate and drawn from these resources.

The Romanovs themselves were all prolific letter writers. Their lives, clothes, personalities, habits, health issues, and opinions are all well documented. However, I used only that which suited my story, and any proper historian will note that I've left out far more than I've included. I was interested only in the last eighteen months of their lives as seen through the eyes of one teenage girl who had lived a privileged, sheltered life. A narrow focus to be sure. But necessary to get to the heart of this particular story. Any mischaracterizations, mistakes, or omissions are my fault entirely. I am an enthusiast, not an expert. And I am sorry for all the things I've no doubt gotten wrong. Writing about the Romanovs is a bit like playing with a bag of feral cats.

It is worth noting that I read all the Anna Anderson biographies backward, from last chapter to first, so I would remain a little off balance while writing the book. It is, admittedly, a strange way to research a novel, but in this case it helped me keep the mental framework needed to maintain the structure of this book. A structure that—for the record—felt a bit like juggling chainsaws. Only the chainsaws are on fire and you're blindfolded.

And speaking of the structure: thank you for sticking with me. I know it's all very *Memento*-esque (a movie I happen to love), but it is a risky thing to render on paper. I enjoy nonlinear timelines, and I knew the only way to bring this novel to a proper close was to tell Anna's half backward. I knew from the beginning that she was not Anastasia—the DNA research is crystal clear in that regard—but I *wanted* her to be. Wanted it so badly, in fact, that I spent several weeks orchestrating a number of cockamamie ways to have Anastasia survive. And then, finally, I realized that was the point of the entire novel. I *wanted* her to be Anastasia. Wanted it to the point where I was willing to believe almost anything.

Several things led to the success of Anna Anderson's claims. She lived and died in a different time. There was no Internet. There were no genetic testing nor facial recognition programs. There was no way to definitively prove or disprove her claims. Anna Anderson died on February 12, 1984, of pneumonia. The mass grave holding the remains of the Romanov family was not discovered until 1991. However, even then, two bodies were missing: Alexey and one of the daughters. There is some debate as to whether Anastasia or Maria was the missing daughter. Regardless, this discovery once again made the news and convinced thousands that Anastasia did in fact escape the carnage in Ekaterinburg. As a result, Anna's claims took on greater credence. It did not matter that hair and tissue samples retrieved from Anna Anderson during a surgery prior to her death did not match the DNA of the remains found in that grave. Genetic testing did confirm, however, that those remains match that of surviving Romanov relations. The issue was laid to rest only sixteen years later when, in 2007, the final two bodies were discovered in a separate grave near the first gravesite. All seven of the Romanovs have since been identified. They are all accounted for. None of them survived that night in Ekaterinburg. Russian, British, and American genetic testing all confirm this.

It is awful, and I think this is why Anastasia Romanov's legend has lingered for so long and with such power. We *want* the story to have a happy ending. But I gave us the ending we need, instead. And I think it is far more satisfying this way.

Acknowledgments

The difference between the almost right word and the right word is really a large matter — 'tis the difference between the lightning-bug and the lightning.

— MARK TWAIN

This part of the writing process always leaves me stumped. Not because I don't know *whom* to thank but because I don't know *how* to thank them. I want to find the right words. I want to appropriately honor the people who have helped this book come to be. I will do my best. Please bear with me.

My agent, Elisabeth Weed, has been a friend and champion for many years. She is the perfect blend of ferocious advocate, astute businesswoman, and patient listener. She also has a preternatural ability to send encouraging e-mails at exactly the right moment. I would have long since gone batty without her. Everyone at the Book Group is a delight to know and work with, Hallie Shaeffer, in particular, because she has an uncanny ability to always sound as though she's in a great mood. And I would be remiss if I didn't acknowledge Jenny Meyer, who handles foreign rights and endless questions with aplomb.

My editors on this book—Melissa Danaczko and Margo Shickmanter—are clever, encouraging, and thoughtful. They were the perfect bookends to a project that threatened to break me daily. Also, for the record, they were right about *everything*.

Blake Leyers was, as always, the guardrails to my careering vehicle.

Marybeth Whalen has been a true friend for more than a decade. I am grateful for our many adventures and endless laughter. I am grateful that she has seen me at my worst but hasn't kicked me to the curb. She can read my mind, finish my sentences, and divvy up a bottle of wine like no one else. As iron sharpens iron, so one friend sharpens another.

JT Ellison and Paige Crutcher are the sort of women who know how to drink Scotch and do yoga. Likely at the same time, though I've not yet tested that theory. They make me laugh and they keep me sane. I'm honored to call them friends.

My publishing team at Doubleday is an impressive group of geniuses. I am endlessly thankful for my publicist Todd Doughty (a man who is equal parts Merlin and Superman), Judy Jacoby (marketing maestro), Bill Thomas (publisher and faithful champion), John Fontana (jacket designer), Nora Reichard (the most patient production editor in all the land), Lorraine Hyland (production manager), Pei Koay (text designer), and Maggie Carr (copy editor). The Penguin Random House sales team is superb. Special thanks goes to Cathy Calvert, Ann Kingman, Stacey Carlini, Emily Bates, Lynn Kovach, Beth Koehler, Beth Meister, James Kimball, Janet Cooke, Ruth Liebmann, David Weller, Jason Gobble, and Jen Trzaska.

Additional thanks to the many friends, family members, mentors, and leaders whose presence in my life is an endless blessing: Abby Belbeck, Josh Belbeck, Emily Allison, Tayler Storrs, Dian Belbeck, Jerry and Kay Lawhon, Blake and Tracy Lawhon, Andy and Nicole Kreiling, Jannell Barefoot, Kristee Mays, Michael Easley, Kaylee Storrs, and Christine Flott. To the teachers and baseball coaches who mentor my boys: you are saints, each and every one. Thank you for pouring into my children.

Karen, from Apple Tech Support, quite literally saved this novel. I'm a bit sad that I never asked her last name (in my defense, I *was* rather panicked). But she knows who she is.

For my friends in publishing and in real life, I am thankful for you every day: Helen Ellis, Anne Bogel, Lisa Patton, Laura Benedict, Joy Jordan-Lake, Patti Callahan Henry, River Jordan, Niki Coffman, Deanna Raybourn, Karen Abbott, Amy Kerr, Denise Kiernan, and Angry Joe.

Helen Simonson, Patti Callahan Henry, Jacquelyn Mitchard, Karen Abbott, Jillian Cantor, JT Ellison, and Laura Benedict all offered kind and gracious words of endorsement for this novel. Thank you for reading those early copies and for lending your voice to this project.

My husband, Ashley, makes me laugh every day. I am so grateful for that gift and the irreparable crow's-feet that come along with it. He is my best friend, my coffee maker, my wine buyer, my laundry folder, my morning person, my joyful singer, and my project finisher. I've known him for exactly half my life—it is the better half by far. Twenty years in and he's still the best thing that has ever happened to me.

I've said it before but it is still true: the Wild Rumpus (London, Parker, Marshall, and Riggs) is the part of my heart that walks around outside my body. They are loud and boisterous and unnerving in their intellect and honesty. But they are also soft and tender and some of the kindest young men I know. Being their mother is one of the greatest joys of my life.

Someone once told me that to sign the word *help* you make a fist with your right hand (thumb pointing up) and hit it once against the palm of your left. Help. Help. Help. Jesus, please help me. That is my daily prayer while writing. I speak it aloud and I speak it in sign. And He does, this Jesus of mine. He helps. For that, I am, and will always be, grateful beyond words—spoken or otherwise.

FLIGHT OF DREAMS

On the evening of May 3, 1937, ninety-seven people board the Hindenburg for its final, doomed flight. Among them are a frightened stewardess who is not what she seems, the steadfast navigator determined to win her heart, a naive cabin boy eager to earn a permanent position, an impetuous journalist who has been blacklisted in her native Germany, and an enigmatic American businessman with a score to settle. Over the course of three champagne-soaked days, their lies, fears, agendas, and hopes for the future will be revealed—and one in their party will set a plot in motion that will have devastating consequences for them all.

Fiction

THE WIFE, THE MAID, AND THE MISTRESS

One summer night in 1930, Judge Joseph Crater steps into a New York City cab and is never heard from again. Behind this great man are three women, each with her own tale to tell: Stella, his fashionable wife, the picture of propriety; Maria, their steadfast maid, indebted to the judge; and Ritzi, his showgirl mistress, willing to seize any chance to break out of the chorus line. As the twisted truth emerges, Ariel Lawhon's wickedly entertaining debut mystery transports us into the smoky jazz clubs, the seedy backstage dressing rooms, and the shadowy streets beneath the Art Deco skyline.

Fiction